## "I wouldn't be charming

She knew that voice. Stepping away from the window, she drew closer to the gentleman, until she could see him in the low lamplight.

As he turned to watch her approach, she could see that he was tall and broad-shouldered with glints of gold in his short, thick hair. Other than that, he was a shadow, backlit by the lamp. But he could see her.

"Christ Jesus," he rasped.

She froze, heart pressed hard against her ribs. They were both beneath the light now, but she was afraid to look. Still, her chin lifted with a will that was not her own, forcing her to gaze up into eyes she already knew would be golden green and as beautiful as they had been on the day she'd looked into them and promised to be a good wife.

"Jack."

*Romances by* **Kathryn Smith**

# When Marrying A
# SCOUNDREL

## Kathryn Smith

**AVON**

*An Imprint of HarperCollinsPublishers*

This is a work of fiction. Names, characters, places, and incidents are products of the author's imagination or are used fictitiously and are not to be construed as real. Any resemblance to actual events, locales, organizations, or persons, living or dead, is entirely coincidental.

AVON BOOKS
*An Imprint of* HarperCollins*Publishers*
10 East 53rd Street
New York, New York 10022-5299

Copyright © 2010 by Kathryn Smith
ISBN 978-0-06-192300-5
www.avonromance.com

First Avon Books paperback printing: June 2010

*This book is dedicated to all the wonderful people at Rose Hope Animal Shelter in Waterbury, Connecticut. Your huge hearts, and commitment to advocacy and caring for so many homeless animals, are an inspiration. Thank you for Sasha, who brightened our lives for the brief year we were lucky to have her, and for Spike and Faye, who have filled our house with all the love and mischief two kittens can!*

*Also to Steve, because you have the kindest heart of anyone I know. And you let me sing when we play Rock Band.*

*"I don't know what a scoundrel is like, but I know what a respectable man is like, and it's enough to make one's flesh creep."*

JOSEPH DE MAISTRE

# When Marrying A
# SCOUNDREL

# Chapter 1

*London, July 1877*

It was bad luck to tell your own fortune. Sadie Moon had known this from a very young age, ever since Granny O'Rourke first set her on her knee and showed her the images made from the tiny brown leaves on the bottom of a teacup. When Granny had asked her how the images made her feel, Sadie hadn't hesitated to peer inside the rim and take a good look.

And then she promptly burst into tears.

Sadie had seen a casket—her mother's. Less than six months later her mother was dead, leaving Sadie and her two older brothers to Granny's care.

Nothing good ever came from trying to read the leaves at the bottom of your own cup. A fact Sadie would have done well to remember before absently turning over her cup on its saucer, and spinning it three times widdershins before righting it and peering inside.

In fact, once she took the first peek, she immediately flipped the delicate china upside down again and set it clattering on the saucer. She pushed it as far across the violet tablecloth as she could.

There was nothing astounding about a clump of tea leaves in the shape of a heart with a crack through it. That in itself normally wouldn't set her own heart pounding so painfully, but it was the feeling the image invoked that made her vaguely nauseous.

*Jack.*

His image had filled her mind so clearly and brightly that she could have sworn he was right there in the tent with her. She'd almost been disappointed to discover she was alone.

*Almost.*

Had something happened to him? Had he finally succumbed to his reckless ways? Such an overwhelming feeling could only mean one thing. But the idea of anything having the power to actually hurt Jack—*kill* Jack—was unfathomable. No, it simply had to be the time of year that made her mind turn to him, and not the leaves. Nothing good came from looking at your own leaves, and being reminded of Jack was punishment for her transgression, that was all. Better to believe in superstition at times like this than her own talent.

The sounds of the party came into range once more. For a moment she had forgotten that nothing but a few well-draped lengths of fabric separated her from several hundred of England's social elite. The brightly colored Gypsy-inspired tent allowed her to be part of the festivities, and to retain some degree of privacy for appointments. It made her feel less on display and gave those who sat opposite her the illusion of intimacy.

People talked more in intimate surroundings, revealed more. Those little disclosures often aided Sadie in deciphering the story the leaves struggled to tell. It was only tea after all, not a crystal ball. Plain, simple, and oh-so honest tea.

She had to brew more; two more sittings and she'd be out. Then there'd be hell to pay if she had to make them wait. Charge these aristocrats a small fortune and they'd wait like faithful lap dogs for you to deliver. Offer them something for free, and they had all the patience of a wee one in the middle of a tantrum.

As if on cue, Sadie's assistant and good friend Indara slipped into the tent, parting the swaths of fabric with one slender, bejeweled arm. "Are you ready?" she asked in a low, melodic voice that clung faintly to the cadence of her childhood in India.

Many English had a prejudice against the Indian culture and wondered how Sadie could befriend an obviously loose and heathen woman. But the English were also prejudiced against the Irish, so Sadie had no time for such nonsense. Indara had answered the advertisement for an assistant that Sadie had run in the paper two years ago. She couldn't afford to pay much, but Indara hadn't needed the money. In fact, Sadie wasn't exactly certain why the woman had answered the ad at all, but they'd got on smashingly and became fast friends, eventually becoming housemates.

"Yes." Rising to her feet, Sadie took one of the delicate china pots in her hands and carried it to her friend. "I need more hot water."

Indara nodded, the jewels at her ears and in her hair twinkling in the lamplight. "It is hot in here. You will take a break soon?"

"I just took one."

Reproach and concern shone in those exotic aqua eyes. "You will take another."

It was pointless to argue, so Sadie smiled. "In thirty-five minutes I will take another break, I promise. Send the next person in, please."

Indara only nodded, teapot cradled in her ringed fingers. Somehow she managed to combine an exquisitely tailored English gown with accessories made by the finest craftsmen in India. The look should have jarred and clashed, but Indara made it work, right down to the tinkling bracelet of bells around her left ankle, hidden beneath the voluminous layers of her burnt orange silk evening gown. Sadie felt quite drab next to her even though her own gown was a most violent shade of violet trimmed with crimson. She also sported a broad-brimmed hat in the same shade of red adorned with violet plumes. If one wanted to be considered spectacular, one had to dress the part.

As her friend and assistant parted the fabric once more, a woman pushed passed her, rudely shoving Indara aside as though she was a stray dog rather than human. Indara said nothing, but the look on her face said clearly that she would love to push back. Instead, she shot Sadie a wry glance and slipped out to fetch more water.

"Well," Lady Gosling chuffed as she straightened. She had her hand up by her hair lest the flimsy door of Sadie's tent somehow injure the mass of jewels and combs that adorned her head. "It's about time. I've been waiting for almost an hour!"

Sadie inclined her head to the side. The weight of her hat pulled slightly at her scalp, threatening to fall and take her carefully crafted hairstyle with it. "It was very good of you to wait so long. You surely did not have to." She had learned the best way to deal with these overgrown spoiled children was to chide them politely. Thank them for their condescension and then convivially remind them that she didn't want or need it. It wasn't really an insult so Lady Gosling couldn't sputter and make a fuss, and it was almost as satisfying as inviting her to kiss Sadie's chair-sore arse.

Lady Gosling sniffed, and had the grace to look slightly—very *slightly*—contrite as she slid into the chair on the opposite side of the table.

As she did every time she saw the lady, Sadie allowed her gaze to drift over the woman's face. She would be beautiful if she didn't always look so angry. There was something familiar about her perfect complexion, sable hair, and dark green eyes. And it wasn't the simple fact that she came to Sadie for a reading every time she worked at Saint's Row. No, there was something that made the back of her skull tingle whenever she looked at Lady Gosling—like she should know her from *somewhere*.

"Are you going to pour, or do you plan to stare at me

all evening?" the lady demanded, brusquely stripping off the delicate silk of her gloves.

Was that proper behavior? Sadie didn't think so, but she'd long ago stopped wondering at the actions of rich women.

"Forgive me," Sadie murmured as she reached for her remaining pot of tea. Gently, she swirled it, stirring the leaves up from the bottom so that they'd follow the hot, fragrant liquid into the waiting cup. "Cream and sugar, correct?"

Another sniff. "I don't think you are the least bit sorry at all."

Lifting her head just enough, Sadie peered at her companion from beneath the wide brim of her hat. She met Lady Gosling's challenging gaze with a level one of her own. The lady, it seemed, was in an ill temper and spoiling for a fight. "You are mistaken, ma'am. Cream and sugar?"

Clearly miffed to have not raised Sadie's temper as well, Lady Gosling gave a stiff nod. "Please." And then, to Sadie's surprise, "It was wrong of me to snap at you. My apologies."

Sadie started. Hopefully Lady Gosling wouldn't notice that her hand hesitated over her cup for a fraction of a second before dropping a lump of sugar into the tea.

When had one of *them* ever apologized to *her*?

She set the cup and saucer in front of Lady Gosling. "Do not trouble yourself, my lady."

That was the extent of the conversation between them until Lady Gosling quickly finished her tea. Many ladies chose not to speak to her any more than they had to, and that was fine by Sadie. She wouldn't know what to say. With Vienne and people of her own sphere she was fine, but the upper classes made her uneasy—too much double entendre and thinly veiled remarks wrapped in a veneer of distorted propriety. The only time she was comfortable speaking to them was when looking into their cups, when she had a glimpse of their secrets.

Only Jack had made her feel otherwise, and look where that had gotten her.

Lady Gosling inverted her now-empty cup on the saucer and went through the proper motions without being instructed. At least she remembered. Most ladies needed to be told, no matter how many times in the past Sadie had read for them. It was as though anything she'd say to them before looking in their cups didn't stick. Clearly, Lady Gosling wasn't as much like those ladies as Sadie first thought.

The bruises across the knuckles on the lady's right hand took that theory one step further. Sadie noticed them as she took the offered cup.

"Do hurry," Lady Gosling urged. "Madame La Rieux has the most delicious companion with her this evening and I wish to make his acquaintance."

Ah yes, the business associate Vienne had mentioned to Sadie. Mr. Friday, or something. Sadie almost smiled, as she peered into the gilt-edged china, tempted to warn Lady Gosling that she would be no competition for Vienne should her friend's *appetite* be whetted by the gentleman.

*Jack.*

She almost dropped the cup, so violent was the emotion that seized her. She had to grip the table to keep from sliding off her chair.

"Are you all right?" Lady Gosling demanded, more affronted than concerned.

Sadie gave her head a gentle shake—as much as her hat would allow. "I'm fine. Forgive me, Lady Gosling." Why the devil had she seen Jack in this woman's cup?

"I hope you do not faint in the middle of my reading," Lady Gosling said, a touch of anxiety lacing her tone.

Sadie arched a brow, trying very hard to hide her amusement. How else could she react to such selfishness? "I'll do my best."

The lady appraised her with a blunt gaze and obviously found her lacking. "You should eat something. And for goodness sake, do something about this ungodly tent! It's positively suffocating in here."

Lady Gosling had a point, because when Sadie looked in the cup again, she saw nothing that made her think of Jack. Nothing at all. Obviously the heat of the evening was beginning to wear on her.

"Your wish is very close to the edge of the cup," she remarked, still not quite herself. Fortunately the leaves made their intentions so clear to her she didn't have to be. "You will get what it is you desire."

Lady Gosling looked so relieved Sadie wondered just what it was she'd wished for. "Wonderful."

Sadie glanced at the leaves once more. "It won't come easy, however. In fact, the course you set in motion will take you in many different directions, force you to make many choices before you achieve your goal." Indeed, the path she saw in the leaves was a veritable maze, twisting and turning in a jumbled mess before righting itself.

"That matters not, so long as I achieve it." The lady's tone was determined.

Sadie frowned, then looked up, once again peering around the brim of her hat. "Have a care, Lady Gosling, that you do not act rashly. Your path is not without dangers."

Darkly fringed eyes narrowed. "What do you mean? What do you see?"

Sadie shook her head. "I cannot say. It's more of an intuition. There's a darkness around your wish that forces me to believe it will come at a cost. Perhaps a great one."

The lady lost her hopeful expression to a more cynical one. "My dear, all costs are great." She tugged on her glove. "What we have to decide is whether or not they are worth paying."

Unsure of how to respond, Sadie said nothing as Lady Gosling pushed back her chair and rose to her feet. She took several pound notes from her reticule and set them on the table. "Thank you for your insight. Good evening."

That was it? She didn't want to hear what else Sadie saw? She didn't have any questions or remarks? It had to be the shortest and most confounding reading Sadie had ever given. After Lady Gosling departed, Sadie took a leather-bound book from her satchel and opened it to a page marked with a letter *G*. She thumbed through the pages until she found Lady Gosling's entry and made notes on the reading. It was something she often did so she could refer to previous readings if necessary.

And, if she was honest, it was a way of keeping track of things her clients revealed to her. In her position, one never knew when knowing a secret or two might prevent unpleasantness. Unfortunately, she'd had to learn that the hard way.

The next few readings were uneventful and blessedly light. After advising Miss Olivia Clark as to which gentleman's proposal of marriage she should accept—apparently her heart and her head could not be trusted with such an important decision—it was time for Sadie to take her break.

A break that was much needed, she realized as she left the close confines of her exotic tent. Two reminders of Jack in one evening had her mind in a state of confusion and agitation that refused to quiet, no matter what she told herself.

After so many years—all right, months—of not thinking of him, why twice in one night? And why in tea? What were the leaves trying to tell her? It was most irritating—and upsetting.

She filled a small plate for herself from the buffet table Vienne's staff kept beautifully arranged and well stocked. It was a sure indication of her nerves that she loaded up on bread, cheeses, and cold meats. All were foods from her youth, foods that reminded her of what it was to be safe and secure. She poured herself a very deep glass of wine to go with her repast.

She didn't mingle with the other guests. She wasn't one of them, and she would feel that all too keenly tonight. Besides, it was no cooler in the thick of the throng than it was in her tent. Instead, she slipped into one of the chambers off the main ballroom, where the lighting was dim and the large floor-to-ceiling windows were open to the pleasure garden below. A cool night breeze washed over her, bathed in the scent of flowers and darkness.

Sadie sat at one of the windows, on a thickly padded bench with plenty of room to set her hat once she'd removed it. *Ahh*. She rolled her neck, sighing in pleasure as the tension eased.

She gazed out the window into the garden. The paths were well—but not too brightly—lit, allowing patrons to see their way while also providing concealing shadows. According to Vienne, there were all sorts of little grottos and hiding spots for lovers tucked along those pristine gravel paths. There were even buildings, concealed within the flora, with beds, which guests could rent for a romantic liaison. And it all looked no different than any other elaborate garden attached to a London mansion or great country house—not that Sadie had seen many of those. Only a few—those homes to which she'd gone, hired to read for a party of ladies.

But that was Vienne's magic, the secret to her success. This entire club—won at a poker game no less!—gave every appearance of elegance and propriety, fashion and society, but Vienne could make anything her patrons wanted a reality. In fact, her friend took credit—not publicly, of course—for the marriage of Ruined Ryeton and his duchess, a sensation that rivaled news that the Prince of Wales might have found his next mistress. Apparently Ryeton and his lady had begun a torrid affair under this very roof at one of Vienne's masque balls.

Sadie envied Vienne La Rieux. Next to the queen, Vienne was the most powerful woman Sadie knew of, coming from humble and rarely spoken-of beginnings. She wanted to be like Vienne and have her own business to grow and cultivate however she wanted. And she would. Her investments had paid off, and tomorrow she was meeting with a man who represented her new landlord. They were to discuss her plans to open a tearoom. She was finally on the verge of seeing her dream realized.

Sadie sipped at her wine, luxuriating in the pleasant thought of having to answer to no one, and stared blankly out the window. So lost in thought, she did not hear anyone come into the room—until he spoke.

"Apologies. I thought this room was empty."

Sadie sat up. "No apologies are necessary, sir. I was just leaving." Time had gotten away from her. Surely she was due to return to work. She snatched up her hat and resecured it to her hair.

"That's too bad," came a low purr of a voice. "I wouldn't be averse to such charming company."

Sadie tilted her head. She knew that voice. Stepping away from the window, she drew closer to the gentleman, until she could see him in the low lamplight. As he turned to watch her approach, she could see that he was tall and broad shouldered with glints of gold in his short, thick hair. Other than that, he was a shadow, backlit by the lamp. But he could see her.

"Christ Jesus," he rasped.

She froze, heart pressed hard against her ribs. They were both beneath the light now, but she was afraid to look. Still, her chin lifted with a will that was not her own, forcing her to gaze up into eyes she already knew would be golden green and as beautiful as they had been on the day she'd looked into them and promised to be a good wife.

"Jack."

# Chapter 2

Jack Friday's heart was trying to eat him alive. It was the only explanation for the sudden and terrible explosion of pain in his chest. It felt just like the time he'd gotten kicked by a horse as a lad. The doctor said he'd been lucky he hadn't been killed. Jack hadn't felt lucky, spending the next three weeks stiff, afraid to draw a deep breath, and purple as a plum from the ribs up.

He felt even less lucky now, and twice as battered.

He gazed into eyes that never seemed to be just one color, and were far too huge in a pale face. Her eyes and mouth always had been too big, her nose a little too long and tilted at the end. She looked older, even more oddly beautiful than the girl he'd fallen in love with. But less innocent than the treacherous bitch who'd left him without so much as a good-bye.

And what the hell was she wearing on her head?

"Do I know you, madam?" What a good liar he was, he thought as his fingers clenched into fists behind his back.

Her eyes dimmed and narrowed slightly. He'd hurt

her. Unfortunately, it gave him no pleasure. Still, hurting her should have given him some satisfaction after all these years of imagining just how this moment would play out.

In all his imaginings, never had she affected him so viciously.

"My mistake," she murmured all cool politeness, but the faint lilt of her voice soothed him even as it cut. She hadn't lost as much of her Irish as he had, and the cadence of her words reminded him of home and happier times. "I thought you were someone I used to know."

He met her gaze—shades of cold blue, green, and gold. Faerie eyes, he used to call them. Witch eyes, others said. "I can honestly say, madam, that you and I do not know each other at all." He said it without flinching because he had to, and because he wanted to see if he could hurt her again—just a little.

His wife—the frigging harpy—nodded stiffly. "Obviously. Excuse me, sir." Then she brushed passed him with a rustle of skirts, so close that he had to lean back to avoid being hit in the face by her foolish hat. He should knock the ridiculous thing right off her head, but a gentleman wouldn't do that to a lady, particularly one he supposedly didn't know.

Then again, no *lady* would try to take a man's eye out with her headwear, or manage to jab him in the ribs with a spitefully sharp elbow without so much as an apology. But then, he'd known Sadie O'Rourke wasn't a lady when he fell in love with her, and he'd paid the price ever since.

Still, she smelled damn good. Jack breathed a lungful of her before cursing silently. He didn't turn when he heard her pause in the door, but stood there—still and not breathing, choking on his wife's sweet vanilla scent.

No, she wasn't his wife. She was Jack Farrington's wife, and that useless bastard was years dead. He'd died the day he came home to find his wife gone without having left so much as a forwarding address. Oh yes, and that the money he'd sent to her had been put into a bank account with his name on it. She hadn't touched a penny of it.

So, technically, he supposed, the woman who had just tried to decapitate him with her hat was his widow. If he really wanted to split hairs, she wasn't *his* anything. That boy didn't exist anymore and neither did that girl. And if that were the case, then there was absolutely nothing wrong with him taking advantage of all Vienne La Rieux offered, including a private suite should he find a lady who captured his interest.

Sadie had walked out on him, after all.

With that mission in mind, Jack left the cozy room. He couldn't remember why he'd gone in there in the first place.

Back in the ballroom, the party was as hot and as loud as it had been a quarter hour earlier, only now he had purpose burning in his belly and nothing else mattered.

He snatched a glass of champagne from the tray of a passing footman. It was a far cry from scotch, but it would do for now. He downed it in one cheek-bulging gulp, grimaced, and then stole another glass from the same footman. The man smiled slightly when Jack raised the new glass in salute and then dispatched it in the same manner.

"Would you care for another, sir?"

Jack glanced down. He already had an empty glass in either hand, but then the footman offered him a full glass in his white-gloved hand, while offering his now empty tray with the other. "I can take those for you, sir."

"Good man," Jack replied with much more sincerity than the situation warranted as he took advantage of the man's willingness to oblige. "I thank you."

The footman bowed smartly. "My pleasure, sir."

Jack nursed his drink as he moved on through the crowd. As much as he wanted to get completely smashed, it wouldn't do to fall down drunk at Vienne La Rieux's establishment the night of their first meeting—Trystan would have his head if he did. So, he sipped the tart, fizzy stuff and waited for a little numbness to kick in.

He hadn't returned to London to confront his past, though it seemed his past had been waiting for him. The only thing that would make this evening worse would be if his grandfather walked through the door.

"You look like you would prefer something stronger," came a coy voice from his left.

Jack lazily turned his head, his lips readily curved into a flirtatious smile. Beside him stood a woman, a few years younger than he, with dark hair, rich green eyes, and a body she knew how to display to its best advantage. This was a woman with no expectations other than her own pleasure, and no promises other than his. His favorite kind of woman, then.

"That obvious, am I?"

Full lips pulled into an easy grin. "Only to someone paying attention." As she spoke, she brushed the tips of her fingers across her throat and upper chest, drawing his attention to the creamy swells of two marvelous breasts. It was meant to tantalize and it did. It was like offering a dog a bone, of course he was going to be interested, but whether or not he wrapped his jaws around it was another story.

"Were you paying attention to me?" His tone teased as he shifted his body closer to hers. "I'm flattered."

She grinned—good teeth—and offered her hand. "And I'm Lady Gosling."

A bit of wit as well. Normally she'd be exactly what he was looking for—exactly what he needed. But tonight . . . tonight he wasn't all that hungry.

Still, there was no harm in trying to work up an appetite, he allowed, and he took her slender hand in his own and lifted it. His lips brushed the knuckles beneath her glove, and her fingers tightened around his just enough to give encouragement. The lady wasn't shy, that was for certain.

"Jack Friday," he replied with a slightly arched brow. "At your service."

Lady Gosling chuckled, a husky, seductive sound. "Have a care, Mr. Friday, at the promises you make a lady." Her eyes gleamed as she gazed up at him. "Someone just might take you at your word."

He ran his thumb over the tops of her fingers. These little appetizers of flirtation were doing their job. "I am readily taken, my lady."

She moved closer—a small, gliding step that brought her close enough for him to smell the subtle expense of her perfume, floral with a hint of spice. "Are you?" she murmured, gazing at him through the thick fringe of her lashes. "How readily?"

At that moment? Getting cheap horn from her words and blatant availability. Then Jack realized that Sadie might very well still be in attendance. In fact, she might be watching him at this very moment. The notion didn't deflate his libido as it ought to have. Instead, he was filled with a perverse need to shag Lady Gosling sense-less—preferably in front of witnesses, who might then take out a page in the *Times* devoted to his prowess so that all of London would know that he, Jack Friday, and his magnificent cock could satisfy any woman.

And then all of London would know that there would have to be something wrong with a woman who walked away from a man such as he. A deficiency of some kind, perhaps.

"Lady Gosling," he began lowly, roughly, and beyond all pretense of polite flirtation, "I find myself wondering what it would feel like to slide my—"

"Monsieur Friday! There you are."

Being doused by a bucket of iced fish heads couldn't have ruined the moment any better. Neither Jack nor Lady Gosling pulled back from one another—but he did release the lady's hand. Mutual frustration was evident in one last shared glance before their hostess joined them.

Vienne La Rieux was a cool but elegantly lovely French woman with ivory skin and shimmering red hair. She was shrewd and didn't suffer fools. Jack liked her—or he had before she ruined his plans for the evening.

"I've been looking everywhere *pour vous*," Vienne chastised in an accent so much stronger than the one she'd exhibited in their meeting earlier that day that he wondered if it was forced. "My dear Lady Gosling, you will excuse us, *non*?"

For a moment, he thought the lady might protest, that the promise of screwing him would give her the courage to spit in the eye of decorum. He was wrong. Lady Gosling nodded in tight-lipped defeat, cast him a rueful glance and glided away, hips swaying ever so gently like the proverbial ship that has sailed.

Jack sighed and turned to face his tall, willowy hostess. "Did you have need of me, Madame La Rieux?"

She tossed her hand into the air. "Of course not! I simply could not stand by and watch you fall prey to that wolf of a woman."

Jack arched a brow. "Not even if I offered my throat willingly?"

Vienne's eyes were pale blue, sharp and clear as glass. "It was not your throat you offered, and fangs are fangs, *monsieur*."

Jack winced. "You've made your point, and I'll thank you not to say another word about fangs or where they might go."

Her long neck tilted, inclining her head to the side as

she smiled slightly—smugly, Jack thought. "As you wish. May I introduce you to someone far more interesting than Lady Gosling?"

Both his eyebrows rose. *More* interesting? Was Madame La Rieux trying to find him a lover for the night? Or was she playing at matchmaker? It hardly mattered, it wouldn't be good business to refuse, and he was still frustrated enough to look for satisfaction elsewhere.

"Lead on," he said, and offered her his arm.

Vienne led him across the ballroom. They stopped twice so that she might introduce him to someone of importance before continuing on to a brightly swathed tent with a line of people in front of it. It looked like something a sultan's harem might reside in, and Jack couldn't help but imagine a plethora of half-naked nubile young things at his disposal. That would put a tick in Sadie's eye, wouldn't it?

A beautiful woman, obviously of Indian blood, looked up as they approached. She smiled at Vienne. "You have perfect timing. I haven't let another guest in just yet. Go on in." And then she smiled at Jack as well—not the least bit flirtatious, but open and friendly. Jack returned the smile, letting her goodwill knock him off balance.

That was his first mistake. His second was following Vienne into that damned tent. Because the moment he stepped into the jewel-toned cave, he smelled tea and vanilla and his heart stopped.

There was Sadie, in that ridiculous hat, standing beside a small table draped in fabric. He didn't have to look to know that there was a teapot on the table, or a small bucket half full of discarded leaves softened by milky tea.

She was reading leaves. Goddamn leaves—in this place where he was expected to conduct legitimate business. And she had the nerve to look as though there was nothing wrong with it! She just stood there and stared at him with a serene expression on her cursed face. She didn't even look ashamed. At least ten years ago she'd had the grace to be embarrassed, but not now.

And all Jack could think about was that day a decade ago, in a setup not nearly as posh as this, with Sadie looking so shame-faced as a man talked about fraud and threatened to summon the authorities . . .

She'd learned nothing, apparently.

Vienne was oblivious to the tension in the room as Jack and Sadie stared at each other. "Jack Friday, I would like to introduce my good friend Sadie Moon. Sadie has a brilliant gift for turning tea leaves into pound notes." Beneath the wide brim of her hat, Sadie flinched. Jack tried hard not to sneer in satisfaction. "Would you like your fortune told, Monsieur Friday?"

Vienne looked so pleased to offer him this treat that Jack found it difficult to refuse her. But a glance at Sadie's impassive face cured him of that. "No, thank you, madam. I do not believe in divination." He looked the girl he once loved in the eye, and saw nothing of her there. The pain gave him the strength to add, "I believe we make our own fate."

Sadie smiled—seemingly unaffected by his words. "You certainly seemed to have made yours, Mr. . . . Friday, was it?"

His jaw tightened. "Indeed, Miss, or is it Mrs. Moon?"

"Mrs.," she replied. Her jaw was clenched.

"Interesting name." He was all mock interest. "Is your husband here tonight?"

Vienne was paying attention to them now, evident by the crease between her brows. Her head turned toward Sadie, who said frostily, "My husband is dead."

To which Jack tilted his head and asked, "Is he? How unfortunate for you."

Sadie stiffened, but she met his gaze directly. "On the contrary, sir. I do not consider it a misfortune at all."

"Neither, do I suspect, would your husband," he retorted with a bitter grin. And then, before he could say anything else that might add to the horror on Vienne's face, or the pallor on Sadie's, he turned and stomped from the tent.

Somehow Sadie made it through another two hours, but when midnight struck, she told Indara to send the rest of the crowd away. She had a splitting headache and was in a foul enough mood that she didn't much care if her patrons made a fuss or walked away angry. Nothing could make her look in another bloody cup.

She started to gather her wares but Indara stopped her. "I will see to this. You should go home. You do not look well."

Sadie would have laughed had she not feared a slight chuckle might turn into the cackle of a lunatic. No, she probably did not look well. Lord knew she didn't feel well.

She gave her friend a gentle pat on the shoulder. "Thank you. I believe I will go home." The two of them shared a pretty little stucco terrace in somewhat fashionable, yet affordable, Pimlico. It was quiet and Sadie had the most luxurious bathroom there. She wanted to submerge into a tub of hot water and not come out until she was every inch a prune.

Her friend gave her a sympathetic look. "Vienne won't let you slip away so easily. She will have questions."

Of course Vienne would have questions. It was obvious Indara had them as well. How could they not? Both had been there to witness her awful exchange with Jack. The man did a terrible job of pretending he didn't know her, even though he'd been the one to attempt the lie. She hadn't said her husband was dead to hurt him. Well, perhaps she had, just a little, but she'd mostly said it to give him a way out, and instead he said . . . what he'd said. And damn him, he still had the power to hurt her more efficiently than any other.

She should have chosen a different last name. Leave it to him to read something into it.

"I will answer her questions," Sadie allowed after a brief pause. "And yours as well, but not tonight." Let Vienne try to wheedle it out of her, she would meet only failure. Vienne might be tough, but she was no match for Sadie when it came to digging in her heels, and Sadie needed to be alone. She needed a little time to think and accept. And perhaps, she needed a drink and a little time to cry.

"Go then," Indara commanded, giving her a swift,

fierce hug. "I will see to this, and I will bring home food. You need to eat."

Sadie opened her mouth to tell her friend that she wasn't hungry, but closed it when her stomach rumbled and Indara shot her a sharp glance. "Food would be good. Thank you."

She gathered up the paisley pashmina Indara had given her for her birthday and draped it over her shoulders. Then, she exited the tent through a flap in the back that usually allowed her to make her escape without notice. She'd learned a long time ago that people always wanted more from her, even after she'd given them all she could. There would always be at least one waiting outside wanting clarification on something she'd seen, wanting to know what it meant—answers she couldn't give. How was she supposed to know the path of their lives when she didn't even know her own?

There was a door camouflaged in the wall of the club behind the tent, and it was through there that she exited the ballroom. It led into a small chamber used as a kind of green room for the musicians and other performers provided by Saint's Row. Sadie didn't like thinking of herself as "entertainment," though she certainly provided that as well. It brought back too many memories, and an unpleasant creeping sensation on her skin. She wasn't some smoke-and-mirrors charlatan playing at being a medium. She was genuine in her talent, and other than a penchant for color and prodigious head gear, she made no attempts at showmanship.

Not anymore.

She crossed to her left, heels of her slippers muffled by thick carpet, and opened another door. This one led into a corridor that joined the main vestibule of the club with the ballroom—what used to be a theater years ago. People milled about in the open area, moving across the polished marble floor, their voices echoing slightly. It was cooler here, a little less noisy. Perhaps a few waited for their carriages to take them to another engagement, or deliver them to their homes, but most were content to stay until the end of the evening when Vienne hosted such galas. She was a very good hostess, and her refreshments and repasts rivaled the best in London, to the point where many society matrons were loath to host their own gatherings on nights when Saint's Row had a special function.

There were people here every night and Vienne knew everything that went on. Sadie didn't know how she did it, and she shouldn't have been surprised to hear her friend's voice just as she made her way toward one of the footmen stationed at the door.

"Where are you going?"

Sadie halted in midstep. She should have known she would not be able to escape so easily. She turned and watched wearily as Vienne swept toward her, mouth set, eyes bright.

"I am going home. I have a headache."

Immediately Vienne's expression turned to one of concern. "Is there anything I can do?"

Sadie shook her head. "I'm sorry to leave so early, but I . . . I need to go home."

Vienne nodded. Unlike Indara, she didn't try to touch her or offer comfort. It was as though Vienne knew what it was to barely hold oneself together and how easily intimacy of any kind could destroy that façade. "Come for tea tomorrow. We will talk."

"I have a meeting with the landlord of my shop after luncheon, but I will come directly from there."

"Yes." Vienne's eyes brightened. "I will want to hear all about your plans."

For a moment Sadie's mood lifted, thinking about the prospect of having her own business. Her own purpose. "And you have a meeting of your own, do you not?" With the question, a heaviness descended upon her once more.

Mouth thin, Vienne scowled. "Yes." Obviously her opinion of Jack had soured somewhat. "One word from you, and I will tell him to go bugger himself."

The offer almost brought tears to Sadie's eyes, base and coarse as it was. Vienne was a business woman and prided herself on it. That she would give up an important alliance—one she'd spoken of for weeks—because Sadie asked it was humbling, and so very touching. "No," she whispered hoarsely, then cleared her throat. "Do not do that."

A gaze like the edge of a knife locked with hers. There was compassion there, yes; concern and love, but there was also determination. "Tomorrow, you will tell me who he is, *non*?"

Vienne was not stupid. Sadie only had to look at her to know her friend already guessed who Jack truly was, but she nodded. "Yes. Tomorrow. Good night, my dear friend." She said it a little too sincerely, for she saw something flicker in the French woman's eyes—a combination of surprise and emotion competing for the chance to change her impassive features. Vienne La Rieux was the kind of woman who avoided close friendships, for reasons only she knew. For some reason Sadie was an exception, though even she would allow there were things about Vienne to which she would never be privy.

The redhead snapped her attention to one of the footmen. "Bring my carriage around for Madame Moon." The man nodded and rushed off to do her bidding. Vienne then briefly turned back to Sadie. "Good night, Sadie." Her accent, a little thicker than usual, drew out the syllables of her name and softened them, *"Saah-dee."*

Sadie watched as Vienne walked away, heels clicking sharply on the marble. How foolish she was to ever think herself alone in this world when she had such friends as Vienne and Indara.

She waited on the steps for Vienne's carriage. The night was cooler now, carrying the promise of rain on the breeze. She lifted her face to it and breathed its dampness into her lungs. With it came the scents of horse, trees and flowers, coal and dirt. Some of the best and worst smells she'd ever experienced had been in this city. Despite modern sanitation marvels, there were still those who tossed slop buckets into the streets. And while one might revel in the sweet scent of flowers and fresh fruit at market stands, there were also those selling pungent fish—often next to a baker's cart. There was nothing quite so disturbing as the mixing of odors between mackerel and cake.

The shiny carriage pulled up in front of the steps, it's rich, wine-colored lacquer gleaming under the lamps that lined the drive. Four perfectly matched blacks pulled the conveyance, and in the driver's perch sat a smartly dressed man with a velvet top hat and a red cravat.

The footman who'd gone to fetch the carriage hopped down from the small ledge on the back and opened the door for her, flipping down the steps as well. "Mrs. Moon?"

Sadie thanked him and allowed him to assist her inside. Once she was safely ensconced, he thumped the side of the carriage and it began to roll out of the drive. Finally, she was free. She sagged into the corner of the plush cushions and closed her eyes.

It wasn't a long journey to Pimlico, but this was the Season and traffic was always heavier this time of year, so Sadie tried to relax and allowed the gentle swaying of the carriage, coupled with the gentle clip-clopping of the team, to ease the tension that had gripped her from head to toe. When finally she was delivered to her front door, her headache had abated somewhat, but she felt almost completely drained of energy. Reading leaves always took a lot out of her, and seeing her husband after a decade apart, well, that had taken its toll as well.

The housekeeper, Mrs. Charles, met her at the door and took her wrap. Sadie told her she was going to take a bath, and to make certain that when Indara came home she give Mrs. Charles one of the petit fours she liked so much. The pastry chef at Saint's Row was a master. The housekeeper's sweet face brightened even further at the prospect, and then she gave Sadie a vase of roses that had arrived earlier that day, along with a note from Mason Blayne, Sadie's friend who could be more than a friend, and who was to escort her to a display of magic the next evening. Sadie took both the flowers and the note with her, grateful for the small surge of pleasure they wrought. If anyone could make her feel better it was Mason.

Upstairs, Sadie went into her private bath and turned the taps in the tub. She removed the stopper from a bottle and emptied some of the fragrant oil into the rising water, closing her eyes as the smell of vanilla and orange rose to greet her. Then she went into her room and removed her gloves, hat, and shoes. She and Indara shared a maid, Petra, who helped her out of her gown. Finally, in nothing but her chemise, Sadie entered the bath and closed the door.

She was totally alone.

The chemise dropped to the floor and she lifted one leg into the porcelain tub. The water was hot, but not overly so—just perfect. She turned the taps to stop the flow and lowered herself with a sigh. Leaning back, she allowed the edge of the tub to cradle her neck, pressing against the knotted muscles there. She groaned and began plucking the pins from her hair, letting them fall to the floor. Her hair tumbled down. Now she was comfortable.

Only then did she allow her thoughts to turn to the

man who had turned her entire world upside down. He had a habit of that, but shouldn't she have better defenses against him now? After all she was seven and twenty, not fifteen as she'd been when she first met—and married—him. Back then he'd been a pretty boy of eighteen, tall and strapping, with twinkling green-gold eyes and a grin that could charm the devil himself. She'd never seen anything finer in all her young life, and she was ashamed to say she still hadn't.

The years had been kind to Jack Farrington—Friday he called himself now. Not just kind, but munificent. His hair was darker, touched by gold rather than made of it, and shorter, but just as thick. The face that had been pretty was now heart-wrenchingly beautiful, so tanned and chiseled. Mary and Joseph, he even had a smattering of freckles across the bridge of that perfect nose! His tanned cheekbones were sharper, his jaw firmer, but his mouth was exactly as she remembered. Oh, perhaps his lips had a slightly harsher set to them, but they were still full and exquisitely formed—more so than any man should ever be allowed to own.

It was his eyes that had truly pained her, though. Those eyes that she always remembered as laughing and bright—and sometimes dark with desire when they'd looked at her—had lines fanning out from the corners, and they hadn't been laughing when she gazed into them tonight. They'd been surprised and angry and . . . disappointed. He'd looked at her across the stifling confines of her little tent and she'd felt the weight of his disapproval like an anvil on her shoulders.

Disapproval of her livelihood. Disappointment that she was still reading leaves. What right had he to judge her when he had been the one to walk out and leave her to her own devices?

Once, they'd been terribly and passionately in love, as only the young could be. He lived in the "big house" on the outskirts of her little village. And he'd seemed equally fascinated by her as she was by him. They met at a village fair, and though his grandfather didn't often allow him to consort with those beneath him, Jack often found a way to sneak out to see her, and she to him. He'd introduced her to books and helped her better her reading. He taught her about the stars and told her about London and other grand places he'd been. She showed him how to make butter, and how to ride a horse without a saddle. He treated her like a queen and she thought him a prince. They became friends on their way to becoming lovers, but Sadie had never expected him to propose to her. She'd known his world would never accept her, and the romantic notion of it befuddled her mind. If she'd had any sense she would have refused him instead of eloping.

But they'd had such a lovely life those first two years, despite being relatively poor. It had been easier for her, she supposed, than for Jack. He'd never been poor in his life. He seemed to think she was worth wearing mended socks and faded trousers. That was until Trystan Kane came round with his promises of fortune.

She folded her hands over her bare belly and closed her eyes, remembering the emptiness that had consumed her in those dark months shortly after Jack had left. Tears leaked down her cheeks and she didn't bother to brush them away.

It had been around this time of year when melancholy gripped her in a suffocating embrace. She'd lost something of herself then, a part of him and what they'd had together. Ripped away from her like a toy snatched from a child's hands. And she hadn't cared what happened after that. Hadn't cared at all. Jack wasn't there.

And then help had arrived from the least likely source, and she'd returned to Ireland for a brief time to heal and grow strong again. She liked to think she'd helped her benefactor do the same.

She would have to send *him* a note in the morning, let him know that Jack was in London. Let him do with that information what he would. Sadie would make this small effort and then she would wipe her hands of it. It was obvious Jack wanted nothing to do with her—and of course she wanted nothing to do with him. Each of them had a new identity and a new life. And if adultery didn't render their vows invalid, the fact that all record of it had been destroyed certainly did. There was no reason for either of them to fear the other. No reason for them to have any interaction whatsoever.

The resolution strengthened her, and she told herself that this wasn't disappointment but acceptance. She had seen Jack again and she hadn't fallen apart. She was stronger than she ever could have thought, and now she was free to get on with her future, and get on with it she would.

But it wasn't her future that claimed her thoughts as she sank further into the warm caress of the bath, it was her past. And as she reluctantly remembered falling *in* love with Jack Friday, she began to fear that she'd never actually fallen *out*.

# Chapter 3

Chez Cherie's might have sounded like a burlesque house, but it was one of, if not *the*, most exclusive brothel in all of London. It was also one of the most discreet, its location practically a national secret. It was known to stand somewhere between St. James's and Covent Garden, in a pretty stone townhouse more fitting a respectable widow than a house of ill repute. The only indication of anything licentious happening there was apparently the suggestive knocker on the red door. No one ever revealed the details; to do so would result in being blacklisted, and no gentleman—at least not one who counted his prick as his best mate and wanted to keep said organ clean, healthy, and happy—wanted to be banned from Chez Cherie's.

The ladies of the house were beautiful, exotic, and from all over the globe. They were trained in every manner of sensual art, kept their bodies limber and strong. They came in all shapes and sizes, hues and temperaments, and they chose their clients, not the other way around. That was part of the appeal of the club—a gentleman could pursue his fantasy if he so wished, but there was something to be said for being the pursued. It was the height of self-satisfaction to know a beautiful, talented, and educated woman with a healthy sexual appetite had chosen you, not because of the size of your purse (every gentleman who walked through the door had to prove he could afford the privilege), but because she believed you would be the most satisfying.

Jack only managed to make it inside because he had a letter of introduction from Trystan. Being the younger brother of the Duke of Ryeton had its advantages, and being the friend of a brother of a duke obviously had its share as well.

He was there to meet a client. He'd had meetings in less posh places, and he certainly wasn't a stranger to associates trying to buy their way into his good graces with women—whether she be a charming wife whose cook made a delicious pie or a skilled lady for hire meant to cater to his other appetites.

Jack would behave no differently than he had in all those other situations: he'd eat the pie, but sex had no place in business, no matter how delicious the lady in question might appear.

He was told to wait in the foyer, so he did. The space was small, but welcoming—the cream-colored walls decorated with tasteful paintings, the wooden planks of the floor gleamed with fresh polish, the main walking area protected by a richly hued Morris carpet.

The man who had opened the door, and taken his letter of reference, returned from whence he had gone and bestowed upon Jack a benevolent smile. "This way, Mr. Friday. May I take your coat and hat?"

Jack removed both and handed them to the man before following him through a set of French doors into the main body of the house. Damn, but he'd seen upscale residences that had nothing on this place.

Dark paneling, pale embossed wallpaper, plaster ceilings and carpets of the finest quality in shades of crimson, sage, cream, and gold. The space was divided by smooth oak pillars that matched the rest of the buffed woodwork. On one side there was a small smoking area where gentlemen could enjoy a cigar with their scotch or brandy while relaxing in large, wing-backed chairs or plush sofas. The other side had small round tables with chairs set up for dining or playing cards or chess. A good idea, keeping the horny bastards occupied while they waited for some nubile young thing to come sit on their lap.

"Please wait here." The majordomo gestured to the smoking side. There were several available, comfortable looking chairs. Jack nodded his thanks and slipped the man a pound note.

Jack didn't smoke himself, but he liked the smell of it, especially a good pipe tobacco. His grandfather had smoked a pipe and the scent always reminded him of the old bastard—and of a time when Jack thought of him with more kindness than he did now.

There was a decent-sized bookcase built into the wall with a selection of novels and more "intellectual" reading, also a table with copies of the day's newspapers neatly folded on its glossy top. There were a few knickknacks on the shelves and tables, but not a one had a feminine edge to it. There weren't even flowers. Jack had never been to a female establishment were there wasn't at least a picture of flowers if not an entire bouquet. Chez Cherie's might be a house of women, but it had been designed with men in mind. Perhaps that was the secret to its success. It was basically a gentleman's club that offered sexual fulfillment while others could only offer beefsteak.

Jack seated himself in one of the wing-backs, the soft leather accepting his form with a sigh before curving around him. Very comfortable, and he'd had just enough to drink that he could easily fall asleep—all that was missing was a small fire in the hearth.

He consulted his watch. He still had a quarter hour before his client was due to arrive. He had to do something to keep himself awake.

He moved to pick up one of the papers when the man sitting to his left spoke. "Haven't seen you here before."

Jack turned toward the low voice. Staring at him disinterestedly was a man with dark hair, piercing blue eyes, and a blade of a nose. Very English, he thought. And very much in a foul temper. That alone would either make them fast friends or faster foes.

"First time," Jack replied.

His companion nodded and raised a glass of what appeared to be scotch. "Thought so. You have that expectant look about you."

He did? Jack wasn't sure how to take that, so he dismissed it. There was something familiar about this bloke that made it difficult for him to take offense. He may as well play along. At least it would keep him awake. "That obvious, eh?"

A shrug. "Probably not, but I've nothing better to do than stare at other men until the ladies come out to play." He frowned. "I'm not sure that sounded quite the way I intended."

He looked so bemused that Jack couldn't help but grin. A waiter came by and asked if he would like a drink. He gestured at his companion. "What he's having." Then, turning his attention back to the stranger, he asked, "Will the girls come out soon?"

"Any moment. They're very prompt for females." His head rested against the edge of the chair back as he studied Jack. "I think you're here for the same reason I am."

Jack's smile twisted with a hint of wry. "Aren't we all here for the same reason?" Regardless of the terms, it was all business, right?

The man gave his head a shake. "We're all here to get our cocks wet to be sure, but that's not the real reason I'm here, and it's not the reason you're here."

Amused, Jack looked up long enough to thank the waiter who brought his drink—it was indeed scotch—before saying, "Enlighten me."

His companion shot him a sharp look—one smart-arse recognizing another and not impressed. "You're here because some bird dealt your pride a blow and now you need a fancy piece to make you feel like a man again."

Jack's mouth opened, poised to argue, but the bloke was right to an extent. Seeing Sadie had left him unsettled, and if this wasn't a business meeting he might very well look to reaffirm his manhood. After all, he'd missed out on the charms of Lady Gosling. "That's why you're here as well?"

"Yes, sir," his companion admitted without an ounce of shame. "Thought I'd found the woman of m'dreams, but she just wants to get her stepdaughter married off and then run away to see the world." He stared glumly into his almost empty glass. "Told me she *cared* for me, but not enough to give up her dream." He sniffed in derision. "Have you ever heard such rot?"

Jack said, "Huh." But inside a chill chased along his ribs. What had he said to Sadie before he left? That he loved her but this business venture with Tryst was something he *had* to do. He had meant that it was something he had to do for the two of them, so he could give Sadie the life she deserved. She'd understood. She told him to go.

The dark-haired man laughed bitterly. "It gets worse. I begged her to stay—I even proposed. You know what she did?"

Jack shook his head, unable to speak, unable to look away from the naked emotion in the man's face.

"She looked at me like she pitied me and told me she *had* to go. Bollocks. I'm not about to let some pretty little widow make an arse of me, so here I am. If a night at Chez Cherie's doesn't restore my manhood, I might as well put on a frock and join a nunnery."

co...

His ...
in the rest...

As if his wo...
of the room sudden...
a colorful parade of s... ...s.
Jack's eyes widened as o... ...tiful
and exotic women he'd ever se... —some
heading to the tabled section whi... ...ed toward
the section where he sat. It was a good ... g the women
chose who they wanted, because he didn't think he'd ever
be able to make the choice himself.

It didn't take long for one to approach him. He'd
been watching as she glided down the stairs in a moss
green satin gown that bared her arms, a delicious expanse of bosom, and part of one leg. He'd seen more
risqué costumes on dance hall girls, but obviously the
madame of Chez Cherie's knew that the secret to a
man's interest lie in what remained hidden rather than
what was revealed.

The courtesan had rich auburn hair and brows that
were a shade darker, with skin the color of fresh cream
and eyes the same shade as her gown. She wore little
cosmetics, but what she did wear accentuated her Irish
beauty.

"Hello," she said to him in an accent that squeezed his
heart. Oh, he'd heard it plenty of times in New York and
Boston. He'd heard it a little in Sadie's voice earlier this

_ed him so deeply _ood to hear.

_mething in response, to which the _ _Would you happen to be Jack Friday?" _tartled, Jack stared at her. "I am."

The woman offered her hand. "I'm Kathleen Ryan. I hope you haven't been waiting on me for too long?"

Ryan. This stunning creature was the client he was supposed to meet. He'd assumed Ryan was a man as Trystan had been the one to be in direct correspondence. No doubt his partner had forgotten to mention these details on purpose.

Smiling wryly, Jack rose to his feet and accepted the offered handshake. "Not long at all." He glanced around at the other ladies finding their employment for the night. "Should I come back at a better time?"

Kathleen smiled, showing off a set of remarkably good teeth. "La, no. You and Mr. Kane have made it possible for me to take a night off if I want. I may not have to work at all soon."

She didn't sound entirely committed to the idea. Jack had always thought prostitutes sad, pathetic creatures. Chez Cherie's gave him fresh perspective.

The redhead gesture to the stairs. "Shall we go up to my quarters? We can talk privately there."

Jack gestured for her to lead the way. "After you."

"There you go!" crowed the man beside him. Jack had forgotten about him. "I knew you wouldn't have to wait long."

Jack saluted the grinning man before turning to follow

his client up that huge staircase. The corridor above was decorated in the same style as the area below, but it was much, much quieter. Kathleen led him to a door not far from the top of the stairs.

He was surprised when he followed her over the threshold into the room. He'd expected it to be posh, but this was beyond any bordello he'd ever seen. The room was large, decorated in more rich colors, and had a huge four-poster bed in the center of it. There was a private bath that he could see through an open door, with a tall, claw-foot tub. Low burning lamps cast a golden glow throughout the interior—very flattering light to be seen naked by. He had once taken Sadie to an inn with rooms this fancy. She'd thought she'd died and gone to heaven. He could still remember making love to her in that soft, soft bed.

"Whiskey?" Kathleen inquired, holding up a bottle as he closed the door behind them.

"Of course," he replied with an easy smile, and crossed the carpet to the small sitting area near the window. He unbuttoned his coat and sat down on the rich crimson sofa.

Kathleen joined him shortly, with the whiskey. They talked business for almost an hour. His and Trystan's business had made several investments for her over the last four years, several of which had paid off in capital amounts. Added to the income she claimed from the brothel, she was well on her way to becoming an impressively wealthy woman.

They drank as they talked, and after the business part

was done, Jack stayed on for another three drinks when the conversation turned to Ireland. Kathleen had grown up in a different part of the country, but it was nice to talk about home and not have to be too careful about what he said. She didn't know his family. Didn't know him. And after running into Sadie, there was something soothing about having an Irishwoman act as though she found him charming. It was an affectation that came easily to him, and part of his success in business.

A charming scoundrel Sadie had often called him.

His head swimming from too much whiskey, Jack checked his watch for the second time that evening.

"I have to go." He tucked the time piece back into his pocket. "It's late."

A soft, white hand settled over his thigh. "You don't have to leave just yet, do you, boy-o?"

He smiled. "I think we've done enough business for one night."

"It doesn't have to be business." Green eyes sparkled, and the fingers on his thigh squeezed ever so invitingly. "It could be a lovely end to a lovely evening."

A flattered chuckle escaped him as Jack closed his hand over hers. "It could be." He was tempted, so very tempted as he met that lovely gaze. "But it won't."

She looked confused for a moment, but the pucker between her brows immediately smoothed again. "Of course. A gent like you must have a wife waiting for him." She made it sound as though he were some kind of rare creature.

"No," he replied, more gruffly than he intended. "She

gave up waiting a long time ago. But I think I'm better off sleeping alone tonight, despite the offer of such beautiful company."

Obviously more curious than offended, she didn't protest. She simply smiled and said, "Some other time, perhaps?"

Jack returned the smile. "Perhaps." But it was a lie. There were too many complications in sharing this woman's bed, no matter if money was exchanged or not. She reminded him of home, of things he'd left behind and things he'd lost.

She stood when he did and escorted him to the door. On his way to the stairs he saw his friend from downstairs sandwiched between two blond beauties, stumbling into an open room as one tried to remove his coat. The man, he noticed, didn't look any happier than Jack felt.

Outside, it had started to rain, and Jack climbed into the carriage he'd secured for his time in London, thankful that he didn't have to go looking for a hack at this time of night, in his current state. He'd be an easy target for any footpad.

Slumping against the squabs, he stared out the window as the carriage rolled away from the curb and the little house of pleasure. Kathleen had told him to come back whenever he wanted, no matter the reason. If he wanted a lover or just someone to talk to, she would make herself available for him. It had been sweet of her to offer.

But there was no way in hell he was ever going to face her again.

* * *

The inside of his mouth tasted like arse.

Daylight battered Jack's eyelids, blessedly muted by sopping clouds, gray sky, and a thick curtain of rain. Unfortunately, the rain seemed to strike the glass of his bedchamber windows with all the force of a room full of petulant children throwing marbles at his head.

Continuing to drink after returning home last evening had not been one of his more inspired ideas, but it had certainly seemed the right course at the time.

He reached for the blankets to pull over his face and regretted it as both brain and stomach rolled in protest. Moving was obviously not a good thing.

He lay there a little while longer, until the pressure in his belly gave him a choice—get up or piss the bed. He seriously considered making water where he lay, but decency and common sense won out and he slowly— painfully—inched out of bed. His head felt as though it had been cracked open like a soft-boiled egg.

He managed to make it to the bath and relieved himself in the commode. He barely managed to flush before everything left in his stomach became too disgusted to stick around any longer and came rushing up his throat. Retching, Jack doubled over the porcelain and heaved until nothing was left.

He felt somewhat better after that, well enough to strip off his befouled evening clothes and turn on the water for the shower. Thank God this hotel had all the modern amenities he had become accustomed to. Of course, it helped that he was half owner of the establishment. He and

Trystan both had private apartments on the upper floors of the Barrington Hotel. The towering brick structure had been completed earlier that year and was located between the Strand and Victoria Embankment, not far from Charing Cross. Trystan had predicted that the area was ripe for this kind of growth and since his instinct had never been wrong before, Jack jumped in with both feet. Vienne La Rieux had been one of their heaviest investors, which was part of the reason Jack had met with her almost immediately upon his arrival in London. The rest of the reason he wasn't quite clear on, but if Trystan wanted to be vague, he'd earned the right.

As for the Barrington, it hadn't been opened for long and already it was doing a smashing business. It was expensive, luxurious, and over the top in comfort and elegance. Rich people, Jack knew, would pay a lot of blunt to be kept in comfort and even more for other people to *see* them being kept in comfort.

After showering, he shaved and dressed, and found to his delight that coffee and breakfast had been delivered while he bathed. Nothing cured a hangover like a big sloppy breakfast and strong coffee, and he dug into his eggs with gusto.

After eating, he brushed his teeth and then set off for Mayfair. He had letters for Trystan's brothers Greyden, the Duke of Ryeton, and Archer, both of whom were investors in several of the ventures Jack and Trystan had financed together, and many others which Trystan had instigated before Jack became his full partner. He had promised Tryst he'd deliver the letters as soon as possible; and this morning was perfect as he had a meeting later in the afternoon, with a new tenant of one of their shop properties.

The rain had let up by the time he exited the carriage in front of a large neoclassical-styled home in the prestigious West End not far from Hyde Park. It was the kind of house that inspired envy, of course, but Jack also had to wonder just what exactly the upper class did with all that extra room when they weren't entertaining. Places such as this were deuced hard to heat in the winter. He would know; he'd grown up in a house almost as opulent as this.

He knocked on the door and was shown into the house by the butler, an unassuming-looking older man who introduced himself as Westford, and took Jack's hat and coat before escorting him to a large withdrawing room in shades of blue and cream. There, he found part of the Kane family waiting for him.

"Mr. Friday," a man older but having about the same build as Jack said as he rose to his feet. "We meet at last. I'm Ryeton."

The duke was an impressive-looking man, handsome save for a wicked scar that ran down the left side of his face. He had dark hair and blue eyes the same as Trystan, and Jack could see a similarity around the nose and mouth as well.

He bowed. "Your Grace."

"May I present my wife, the duchess?"

Another bow as a beautiful woman came forward to greet him. The duchess was a brunette with sparkling dark eyes and cheeks as soft and pink as her name. No wonder Ryeton had courted scandal to have her.

But it was the third occupant of the room that brought Jack up short. Lord Archer Kane flashed him a cheeky grin as he came forward and offered a glass of scotch. He was the chatty stranger from Chez Cherie's. No wonder he'd seemed familiar. He was Trystan's brother. "Nice to see you again, Friday."

Jack's smile came easier than he expected. "And you, Lord Archer."

The taller, leaner man waved his hand and continued to grin. He didn't seem much worse the wear for his debauchery the night before, but Jack knew a man on a downward spiral when he saw one. "Just Archer, you've unfortunately earned that intimacy."

Lady Ryeton was immediately curious and she made no effort to hide it. "The two of you know each other? Really, Archer. How could you not tell us?"

Her brother-in-law looked vaguely apologetic. "I didn't know who he was, my dear. Besides, it was only last evening."

"Where did you meet?" She asked.

Archer winked at Jack. "A club."

Jack took a drink of his scotch to avoid having to comment, but it seemed there was no need. The duchess rolled her eyes at both of them. "I do not want to know."

"No," Archer agreed. "You do not."

"Well, I do," Ryeton spoke, pinning his brother with a pale gaze. "You can tell me all about it later. Meanwhile, why don't we sit?" He gestured for Jack to be seated in a comfortable wing-back of dark blue brocade. Jack did so willingly, hoping His Grace didn't decide to interrogate him as well.

He gave both men the letters from Trystan, and when the duke asked why he had come ahead of the youngest Kane brother, he explained that Trystan had wanted him to take care of several business matters around town in his absence.

The duke laughed—a brash sound that made Jack jump. "Meaning he wanted to send you in to soften up Madame La Rieux."

There didn't seem much point in hiding it, even though Jack wasn't quite sure that was exactly what he'd been sent to do. So, he merely smiled.

"Did you attend the function at Saint's Row last night, Mr. Friday?" Lady Ryeton inquired as she sat on the sofa, sipping her wine.

Jack rolled the glass of scotch between his palms. His stomach rebelled at the thought of taking a drink. How did Archer manage it? "I did, Your Grace."

She rested her temple on her knuckles as she regarded him with interest. "Did you have your fortune told by Madame Moon?"

The mention of Sadie threatened a return of his breakfast. He swallowed. "I did not have that honor, no."

The duke leaned back in his chair and stretched out his long legs, crossing them at the ankle. Dressed all in black as he was, he was an intimidating sight. "Not a big believer in fate, destiny, and all that, Friday?" He asked good-naturedly.

"I believe in making my own."

The duke grinned. "Don't we all—and then something happens to make a man reckon it's all preordained." The look he flashed his wife made Jack uncomfortable. He glanced away. Archer met his gaze and grimaced. Jack stifled a chuckle. He liked Archer. In fact, it seemed as though he was in danger of liking the entire Kane clan. Of course, he had yet to meet the mother and the sister, but if they were as lovely as Trystan claimed, Jack couldn't imagine not liking them too.

"You should sit with Madame Moon if ever you get the chance," Lady Ryeton continued. "She's quite good."

"I've no doubt she is." The little charlatan.

"She saw Grey in my cup plain as day."

If he'd only a penny for every time he'd heard Sadie tell some gullible young woman that she saw love in her leaves. It worked almost every time—except for that one time when Sadie had mistakenly taken a girl for one of the Sapphic sisterhood. The young lady had pitched a fit of monstrous proportions. That one had bothered Sadie for days. She had actually convinced herself that she was right and the girl had lied to her.

"She must be good," he allowed. "Madame La Rieux wouldn't contract her services if they were less than top-notch." He smiled—a little limply, unable to muster a full grin. "Bad for business."

The duchess fixed him with an odd look, and he

couldn't quite tell if she thought he was laughing at her, or if she was actually laughing at him. As much as he detested being the joke, he'd rather that than the alternative. Pissing off Trystan's family was not what he wanted to do, especially when said family—despite being slathered in scandal—was a very old and powerful one.

"So when is that brother of ours due to join us?" It was Archer who asked, and Jack could have hugged the man for saving him from any more of the duchess's questions or gazes.

"His last telegram said he hoped to be in London by month's end." By then Trystan claimed these "mysterious" plans of his would be set in motion, whatever that meant. But it was his business, not Jack's.

"So you are with us for a while longer," the duke commented. "You must come to dine with us one night next week." He glanced at his wife who nodded. "Rose will send an invitation 'round to your hotel."

Jack bowed his head. "You're most generous, Your Grace."

Ryeton made a scoffing sound. "Hardly. You can give Archer and me all the dirt on what our little brother's been up to these past years. And call me Ryeton, I'm not much for ceremony."

That seemed to be a family trait, Jack thought to himself, but he smiled at Ryeton and his wife. They were perfectly likable people, or rather they would be if Lady Ryeton would stop looking at him like that. Dinner with them would be a welcome distraction, provided the Amazing Madame Moon didn't come up in conversation again.

He just had to get through the next few weeks before Trystan returned and took over. Then he could leave England and never return. Surely he could get through the days without seeing Sadie again? It wasn't as though they ran in the same circles. Surely God would smile upon him—just this once?

# Chapter 4

The northern section of Bond Street, which was sometimes referred to as 'New' Bond Street, was one of *the* most prestigious shopping areas in London. Every day the fairer members of London's upper crust entertained themselves by spending vast amounts of their husbands' money there. Money that Sadie wanted a share of, and planned to one day have.

It wasn't arrogance or snobbery that led her to this location for her tea shop, but rather a conversation with Vienne after a long day of their own shopping. Tired and weary, Sadie had remarked upon how much she could use a cup of tea, a scone, and a loo—not necessarily in that order. And Vienne had replied that wouldn't it be nice if someone opened such an establishment, where ladies could relax and refresh themselves at some time during their shopping excursion?

It hadn't taken long for them to start planning. After all, Sadie had made no secret about wanting her own shop, and Vienne's instinct for business said Bond Street was the perfect location. Things were changing in the West End. Women were changing, and they were demanding shops change with them. Smart shopkeepers knew what side of their bread had the thickest butter. Vienne knew shopping, and she knew business, so Sadie decided to trust her own instincts and went looking for property to rent.

And that search had led her here—to a sweet little shop in a creamy stucco building with a large bay window. The rent was high but worth it, and Sadie had no doubt she could pay it and a staff, and still turn a profit. Her regular clientele alone could keep her afloat, and then some.

Thanks to Vienne's business sense, Sadie had invested most of the money given to her by the Earl of Garret, and now had a sizable nest egg. Rather than sitting on it any longer, she was going to use that money—which she no longer felt guilty about keeping—to realize her dreams.

It was a lovely day, the early afternoon sun warm but not uncomfortably so. Gray clouds threatened on the horizon, but for now the rain was held at bay by a sweet breeze and an otherwise perfect summer day. Soon, the Season would wind down and most of the crowd would leave town for the country. Her life would return to some semblance of normalcy.

Perhaps most would find this the wrong time to open a business, when most of her clientele would be elsewhere, but she needed time to set up, to make changes to the interior. She wanted to be settled, work out the kinks, and have a rhythm established before next Season struck. Better prepared than surprised, she believed.

Sadie was early for her meeting—intentionally so. Anxious now that she was so close to seeing her dream a reality, she stood outside the shop and studied every visible inch of storefront, searching for a flaw. There had to be a flaw—something that would ruin this endeavor. Something always happened to add a bitter taste to her happiness.

Vienne often called her a pessimist, but how could she be anything else when life itself had taught her such a lesson?

Peering inside the window at the clean, posh space, Sadie caught sight of her reflection in the glass. She looked tired and pale, hollow around the eyes. She hadn't slept well the night before. Thoughts of Jack kept her awake for hours. So many feelings were tied to her life with—and without—him that she felt as though she'd been put through a gigantic, emotional butter churn. Unfortunately she also looked it. Not even the rich peacock blue of her tailored walking jacket could camouflage her fatigue. She'd paired it with a flounced bronze skirt and matching hat, the wide brim of which was pinned up on one side and decorated with peacock feathers. Usually calling attention to the clothes rather than the face served her well, but not today.

"Damn you, Jack," she whispered at the wan woman staring back at her.

"Christ," came a voice from behind her. "You have *got* to be joking."

Sadie froze as malicious fate seized the heart in her chest. It was beyond cruel that she should feel any joy at the sound of Jack's voice, but that awful flutter was there all the same. She looked up, too cowardly to turn, and met his gaze in the glass. He stood just behind her, looking far too *right* in his gentlemanly clothes. Vertical furrows cut deep between his scowling brows and his lips were pursed just enough to call attention to the thin grooves around them. When had those lines carved themselves in his beautiful face? Had it taken years to etch them, or had they sprung up quickly—after he discovered that she had given up waiting for him?

She hoped it was the latter. She hoped he searched for her and wondered where she'd gone. She hoped finding her missing had ripped the black heart right out of his chest.

She hoped he had missed her half as much as she missed him. That he had wanted her even a quarter as much. What if he were to learn that he could have found her if only he'd looked in the least likely place?

Thoughts of the past—the taste of old bitterness—gave her the courage to turn and face him. He stood before her, tall and broad in a camel frock coat and chocolate trousers with just a hint of rust pinstripe. He'd never been one for a fussy cravat or head gear and that hadn't changed; the knot at his throat was simple and plain, as was the brown coachman hat on his head. Despite all this, he was still a startlingly handsome figure of a man. Bastard.

"What are you doing here, Mr. Friday?" She asked, intentionally using his alias.

"My company owns this building."

"But that would make you—" Sadie's hand went to her throat in horror. "No." Fate wouldn't be so cruel, would it?

He didn't appear any happier about the situation than she was, though slightly less horrified. "I assume that you are our new tenant?"

She nodded, unable to wrap her tongue around the jumble of thoughts in her head. She'd known something would happen to ruin this. Damn him!

Jack glanced around, aware of the people passing by on the busy street. People who didn't bother to hide their curiosity as they walked by. He took a key from his coat pocket. "Let's move this inside."

It was on the tip of her tongue to tell him she'd rather run naked through a nest of vipers than enter the shop with him, but he was her landlord and this shop was something she'd wanted for a long time. Perhaps he would keep their personal history out of the transaction. Surely both of them could do that?

He held the door open for her and she brushed past him to cross the threshold, catching the scent of cloves as she did. The smell brought back such a rush of memories and sensations that she almost stumbled on the threshold. Washing his hair in the bath while birds chirped outside their bedroom window; burying her face in the hollow between his neck and shoulder and breathing deep, their limbs entwining, clutching at each other as they made love. That smell had meant love and security to her once upon a time.

She turned to face him as he closed the door behind them. God only knew the expression on her face, but if it was anything like the one on Jack's, they were well matched. What did he remember of their marriage in that moment?

If only he hadn't left her. What would their lives be like if he had decided that she was more important than proving himself to an old man?

He stared at her from beneath a fringe of thick lashes. Haunted. "You look good, Sadiemoon."

The regret in his tone was almost her undoing. Sadie closed her eyes against the tightness in her chest. He remembered. Of course he remembered. Sadiemoon, one of the pet names he had for her, because he said she was his moon and stars. Of course he'd been eighteen when he first said it, so perhaps she'd been foolish to think he meant it. Even more foolish to take it as her new surname.

"Remember me now, do you?"

Jack's expression turned to wry exasperation. "I tried to forget, trust me."

It was meant as an insult, but Sadie couldn't quite take it as such. It did her poor heart good to know that he hadn't been able to put her entirely behind him—no more than she had been able to erase him from her own memory.

"That's a god-awful hat," he commented when she said nothing. "I don't remember you having rotten taste in head wear."

"Heaven forbid I change in your absence." It came out sharper than she intended.

Whatever humor he had vanished. "I came home and found you gone."

"You left first, Jack. Even you can't have forgotten that."

Those furrows between his eyebrows were back. He practically vibrated with tension. Good. Nice to know she had the same affect on him that he had on her. "I left to make a better life for us."

"Well, you certainly made a better one for yourself. When it became apparent that you didn't want me in that life, I decided to make a better one on my own."

"Without me."

For a second, she fancied she saw real hurt in his gaze, real anguish, and it cut her to the bone. "Yes."

He snorted and looked away, but not before she saw his expression. He looked as though she'd slapped him. What would his reaction be if she told him why she'd left? But there was no reason to tell him except to hurt him, and Sadie couldn't bring herself to be quite so cruel.

Instead, she watched as his gaze moved about the space, settling on the display cases and the kitchen beyond. "What are you going to open here?"

Sadie swallowed. "A tea shop."

He turned to her, eyes narrow. "A tea shop." He made

it sound surreptitious, degenerate somehow. "With a back room for private *readings*?"

He made it sound sordid. There was nothing wrong with her plans. She refused to be made to feel anything different. His opinion didn't matter, not anymore. She lifted her chin. "That's right."

Jack gave his head a little shake, as though he couldn't believe what he'd heard. "I understand doing it for fun, for charity, but you're going to stake a business on the dregs in the bottom of a teacup?"

She tilted her head, a sad smile flirting with her lips. He never had understood. "Yes. I've made a very good living from those dregs."

Those pretty lips of his twisted in disgust. "I bet you have."

"Don't you dare judge me, Jack Farrington." This time she used his legitimate name—a reminder of their history. "You don't have the right."

"Don't I?" He growled the words.

"No." Ire pricked, she took a step forward. "You gave that up a long time ago, as did I. Jack Friday and Sadie Moon are business associates and nothing else. *Nothing.*"

He glared at her, jaw tight. He looked as though he didn't know what to do with her.

*You never did, Jacky Boy.* As much as she'd loved him—as much as she'd known he loved her—he never understood who she was or what she could do. To be fair, she'd never really understood either, not until left on her own.

But once, a long time ago, she'd thought he knew her better than anyone. Inside and out.

"It's your *business* that concerns me." His jaw was still clenched.

"What of it? I make good money. My rent will be paid promptly and in full, you needn't worry about that."

"What I worry about is having the law breathing down my neck. Did being almost arrested teach you nothing?"

She had wondered how long it would take him to bring that up. "Besides that, you weren't above using your grandfather's name when it suited you? Yes, it taught me that people won't believe what's too good to be true."

He ignored her. "They could have put us in jail, Sadie. Put you in jail."

"For a scheme of your making, Jack." She couldn't help but add, "You know, the magistrate's wife is still one of my best customers. First Thursday of the month, just like clockwork. Surely if I were doing anything underhanded, she'd detect it?"

At that moment, Jack looked as though he could cheerfully strangle her. Color bloomed high on his cheeks, but he'd always been one of those men who looked good flushed. His eyes were bright, his mouth set in a manner that reminded her of arguments they'd had a lifetime earlier. Thinking of those arguments also reminded her of making up afterward. She smiled at those memories— just a little, but he saw it. And her amusement—at his expense—angered him.

He whipped his middle finger off his thumb and flicked

the brim of her hat, hard. It jerked on her head, the pin simultaneously digging into her scalp and pulling her hair.

Sadie scowled at him as she reached up to readjust the broad brim. "Stop that!"

He did it again. This time, she retaliated by shoving both hands against his chest, knocking him back a few steps. "Sod off, you great stupid arse!"

This time when Jack came at her he didn't touch her hat. Instead, he seized her by the face, his palms cupping her cheeks as his strong fingers curved around the back of her skull. He pulled her forward, forcing her up onto her toes. Sadie grabbed hold of his lapels to keep from falling into him. She should slap his face, but she couldn't seem to lift her hands once they met the solid wall of his chest.

Jack tilted her head backward, his eyes bright like green-flecked amber. The muscle in his jaw ticked as he stared down at her, and Sadie could do nothing more than stare back. Was he going to kiss her? Was it wrong of her to wish he would? Just once she'd like to feel those lips against hers again, taste the rich sweetness of his mouth, desperate and hot.

For a second, she thought he might actually give her what she both wanted and despised, but he didn't. Instead, a look of great determination took hold of his features, tightening his brow. "I won't let you do this."

"Do what?" she whispered, so confused now she hardly knew what she was about.

"*This*," he replied, releasing her with a little shove. He

pointed a finger at her. "I won't let you harm what I've worked so hard to build, and I'll do whatever it takes to keep you from harming yourself."

"How in the name of God will a tea shop harm me, or you?"

"Jesus, Sadie, you're a fraud!"

She froze, slapped still by his words. He'd never come right out and said it before, though she'd always known how he felt. Still, that word sounded so terrible on his tongue. So low and base. Dirty.

To his credit, Jack looked aghast that he'd actually given voice to his thoughts, but he did not apologize.

"If I am a fraud in your estimation," Sadie said, voice tight with the effort to keep it from breaking, "it is because you made me so. But regardless of your low opinion of me, I signed a lease for this property, a lease that was agreed to and also signed by Trystan Kane. If you plan to stop me from having my shop, you'd best take it up with him." How full of bravado and certainty she sounded! When in reality her knees were knocking together. Jack wouldn't really try to take her dream away from her, would he? Not when he'd already taken more than he could ever know.

"I will," he replied with a stiff nod. "I will take it up with Kane."

*Oh, Jack.* Sadie wouldn't have thought there was anything left of her heart for him to break, but the familiar pain in her chest proved otherwise.

"Then we've nothing left to discuss." Lifting her chin, she leveled him with the haughtiest expression she could muster with tears burning the backs of her eyes. "Good day, Mr. Friday. I hope I never see you again and that you rot in hell."

He had the gall to look saddened. "I'm afraid that's exactly where we'll meet again, Sadiemoon."

She turned on her heel and marched out the door before she humiliated herself by screaming or bursting into tears. She refused to show defeat, even when she climbed into the privacy of her waiting carriage just outside the shop and tapped on the roof.

Years ago she would have been destroyed by Jack calling her a fraud, but now she was merely disappointed—and angry. She was done clinging to girlish hope where he was concerned, and from this point would go forward as if he were nothing more than a blister on her heel. He might succeed in keeping her from having this spot, but he couldn't stop her from finding another. And he couldn't take away what she knew to be truth no matter how much he denied it.

Jack Friday had decimated all her dreams once before. Sadie would be damned if she let him do it again.

The club at Saint's Row took up almost the entirety of the east side of that small lane. Vienne had purchased the lot on the west side as well and turned it into stables for herself and her guests so that the street wasn't constantly congested with carriages.

The coachman delivered Sadie to the front door before crossing the neat cobblestones to care for the horses. Though the club was closed at this time of day, Sadie's friendship with Vienne gave her certain liberties, so she was able to enter the neoclassical mansion without raising any eyebrows.

Sadie had read Vienne's leaves once—when they first met. Since then the Frenchwoman had never once requested a second reading. She didn't take it personally. Vienne was one of her staunchest supporters, and Sadie knew that at least two of the things she'd seen in Vienne's cup had come to pass. She assumed that Vienne believed in her abilities and simply didn't want to know what the future held.

Or perhaps Vienne simply didn't want Sadie to know any more of her secrets.

To be honest, it really didn't matter. Part of what made her hold Vienne and Indara so dear was that neither woman held her responsible for their lives. So many of her regular patrons seemed as though they couldn't get dressed in the morning without consulting her. It was nice to have at least two people who didn't thank or blame her for the major events of their lives.

She walked briskly across the polished marble floor, with strides as long as her narrow skirts would allow; but she was not in so much of a hurry that she forgot her manners. She said hello to several club employees who were busy readying the facilities for the coming evening, and nodded to a few others, but she did not stop to chat as she normally might. Instead, she hurried up the broad staircase to the first floor, rounded the corner, and continued up to the second, where Vienne's private apartments were located.

She knocked on the wide, white-washed double door and waited impatiently to be received. Fortunately, she did not have to wait long. Vienne's maid greeted her with a friendly smile and quickly ushered her inside the main sitting room where Vienne sat at her desk, reading correspondence. She looked up as Sadie approached.

"You look like you could strangle a puppy," her friend remarked dispassionately.

Sadie made a small grunting sound as she pulled free her hat from her head and tossed the damn thing aside. She couldn't bear to have it on her head one moment longer.

Vienne—still in her silk dressing gown, her fiery hair tumbling down her back—had risen and was in the act of pouring them both a cup of hot, fragrant coffee. A fine brow arched at the discarded hat, which had landed upon her sofa. "Did your meeting with your new landlord not go well, *ma petite chouchou*?"

Sadie scowled at her. Vienne rarely spoke French when they were alone, unless it was to poke fun. "Did you just call me your 'little cabbage'?"

Vienne grinned, and came toward her with a cup of coffee on a delicate saucer. "You know, I believe I did. Forgive me. Sit."

Sadie did just that, seating herself on the well-padded, cream brocade sofa where she'd lobbed her hat. It lay beside her, ignored like an unwelcome guest.

Vienne took a seat in the matching chair across from her. Again, she glanced at the hat with sharp blue eyes. "Poor *Monsieur Chapeau* tossed aside like garbage."

That acute gaze shot to Sadie, all teasing gone. "Do not make me wait. What's happened?"

Sighing, Sadie took a sip of her coffee. Her eyes closed in bliss. Strong and sweet with too much cream—just the way she liked it. How much should she tell Vienne? She couldn't lie to her friend, especially not one who had done as much for her as Vienne had, but if she revealed all it could affect Vienne's business with Jack, and she didn't want that on her conscious no matter how Jack deserved to have his plans stomped upon.

Still, Vienne was a business woman. She wouldn't make a decision based on emotion.

That left only one decision—where to begin?

She met Vienne's questioning gaze. "Twelve years ago I married Jack Friday in a pagan ceremony." Vienne knew she'd been married, and that she'd been deserted, but Sadie had never said his name.

Russet brows jumped, but otherwise the smooth porcelain of the Frenchwoman's features remained impassive. It took a lot more than a youthful impulse to startle her. "A pagan ceremony, how very free thinking of you, my friend."

"Free thinking had nothing to do with it. I was fifteen, he was eighteen and his family had cut him off. We couldn't afford a license." Odd how those days brought a smile to Sadie's lips. Jack had stolen some money from his grandfather to set them up in a flat, but the money didn't last long. All they'd had was their few meager belongings and each other. God, that had been enough back then.

"I've never seen you smile like that," her friend mused, a suspicious look in her eye. "Certainly such pleasure cannot be owed to the black-hearted bastard who left you as though you were a two-penny whore who owed him change?"

Vienne had such a way of putting things—not just at their bluntest and basest, but also in a manner that made Sadie feel wrong for remembering Jack with any fondness whatsoever.

"Not every moment of my marriage was unpleasant, Vienne," Sadie informed her somewhat coolly. "And he didn't leave me like a 'two-penny whore' as you so eloquently put it."

"Of course not." The Frenchwoman's tone was placating and not the least bit sincere. Vienne believed the worst of men—all men. She said it kept her from spending much of her life in a state of disillusionment.

"So, Mr. Friday is your erstwhile spouse, eh? Why did you not mention this last night?"

Sadie shrugged—a beastly habit she'd picked up from Vienne—and took another sip of her delicious coffee. "I didn't want to talk about it."

"And now you do?"

"And now I do, because the great arse says he's not going to let me have my shop!" Let her accuse Sadie of having too much fondness for Jack now! She trembled as rage and fear took hold of her with a vengeance. "Can he do that, Vienne?"

Her friend looked positively murderous. "What exactly did he threaten?"

"That he was going to tell Mr. Kane not to rent to me."

Vienne smiled a little then, and Sadie took it as a good sign despite its predatory appearance. "Trystan Kane is many things, but he won't turn his back on a sound investment just because his partner asks him to."

"But I'm sure he's told Mr. Kane horrible things about me."

"Just as you've told me horrible things about your husband, but that's not going to prevent me from doing business with him. It just means I won't share my bed with him."

Sadie's mouth opened, but she couldn't seem to remember how to make words come out. And Vienne, God love her, laughed in response. "Don't look so shocked, my friend. You of all people should know how very attractive he is."

"Well . . . yes. Of course." But how could Vienne give herself to a man she called a "black-hearted bastard?" The idea of the two of them in bed together . . . She wondered how Vienne felt about *eating* that cup she held.

"You needn't look at me as though you'd like to take out my eyes." Her friend laughed again. "I'm not going to bed your husband, Sadie."

She hadn't looked at her in any such manner, had she? "He's not my husband, not anymore. Legally, I don't think he ever was."

Vienne tilted her head to one side. "Then why do you fear him?"

Scowling, she brushed an imaginary speck of lint from her skirts. "I don't fear him."

A blessed moment of silence followed and then Vienne said, in a voice filled with wonderment, "I believe you still love him."

Sadie had heard just about enough. "Would that make him once again shag-worthy in your estimation?"

Vienne blinked, her eyes huge with surprise. But before Sadie could apologize for her rudeness, the Frenchwoman burst out laughing—a reaction that dimmed Sadie's own regret.

"All these years." Vienne shook her head, still chuckling. "I've been your friend for years and I've never known you could be such a delightful bitch."

A small smile curved Sadie's lips. "I was going to apologize, but you can forget about that now."

"My dear friend"—the amusement faded from Vienne's expression, replaced by genuine concern—"I am so very sorry you have to face this painful reminder of your past. I would take it from you if I could."

Were that but possible. Sadie's throat tightened, and her mouth twisted slightly. "He'll be gone soon enough, and if he convinces Mr. Kane to evict me, then I will find another spot."

"That's the spirit," Vienne enthused. "Although, if Trystan Kane is fool enough to break his lease with you because his prick of a partner has his nose out of joint, then he is not the man I believe him to be."

For a moment, Sadie wondered just what kind of man

that was. She knew little of Trystan Kane other than her own dealings, but he and Vienne had a history together. She wasn't certain of all the details, but she wondered if perhaps they'd had an affair.

As curious as she was on the subject, she wouldn't ask. Vienne would tell her if she wanted her to know, and Sadie had other things—more important things—to think about.

"I should go," she said, finishing her coffee. "Mason is taking me to the theater tonight and I have a million things to do before he arrives."

A dreamy smile floated across Vienne's well-shaped lips as her gaze drifted toward the portrait of herself as Delilah above the mantel. "Mmm, Mason. You should do *him*, my friend."

Sadie chuckled, her own gaze drifting to the painting as well. Mason had done an exquisite job as always. Vienne looked both seductive and dangerous draped in lengths of flimsy silk, a dagger in one hand, a thick hank of long black hair in the other. "You didn't sleep with him, did you Vienne?" she asked, as the horrible thought occurred to her.

Her friend's smile turned wicked. "If I had, he would not yet have the strength to chase you!"

They laughed together, and Sadie was relieved. It would be too uncomfortable to spend time with—be courted by—a man who had shared Vienne's bed. Not only would she wonder if she was being compared to the sensual Frenchwoman, but she would wonder if there were feelings there as well. She didn't like being the jealous sort, but she recognized it within herself. Better to avoid such situations altogether.

"I try to avoid entanglements with men my own age," Vienne admitted coyly. "The older man has such subtle confidence, and the younger . . ." She chuckled. "The younger, has such enthusiasm! But a man the same age? He has too much confidence and not enough enthusiasm."

"Too bad you could not combine the two," Sadie remarked with surprising good humor given her day. "A younger man with all the stamina of his age but the confidence of someone older."

Was it her imagination or did Vienne pale just the tiniest bit? "Yes," the other woman agreed, no longer smiling. "It is too bad indeed. Enjoy the theater. You must tell me all about it, and the delightful Mr. Blayne, tomorrow."

She was dismissed, Sadie realized without injury to her feelings. She hugged her friend and left. One of the footmen sent for her carriage and soon she was on her way back to Pimlico, suddenly drained of all energy.

A hot bath was what she needed. And a glass or two of wine. Oh, and a lovely evening with a handsome, attentive gentleman. That would fix her up, right quick like. Maybe Vienne was right. Maybe she *should* take Mason as her lover. He was certainly attractive, and she knew he fancied her as well. He was a delightful dancer and a delicious kisser, so why not take their relationship to the next level? It wasn't as though she was a married woman.

Oh, why did she have to go and think that? And what on earth was she going to do about Jack?

Nothing. That's what she was going to do. Nothing, unless he forced her to do otherwise. The less she had to do with him the better. She would hope that he failed to turn Mr. Kane against her and that he left town as soon as possible. She didn't want to look for another location for her shop, but she would. She would not give up her dream just because an obstacle named Jack Farrington—Friday now—got in her way.

What the devil kind of name was Friday anyway?

# Chapter 5

The telegram Jack sent to Trystan was as succinct and to the point as possible. Basically he told his friend that he had misgivings about "Mrs. Moon's" business and wondered if renting to her was a wise course given the potential for fraud and police involvement.

He felt a little guilty after it was done and sent. Even when they were young Sadie had, on occasion, mentioned how she'd like to have her own shop someday. It didn't really seem to matter what kind of shop, and if she'd told him she planned to open a simple café or perhaps even a restaurant, he wouldn't have reacted nearly as badly as he had.

She saw him as a villain. His letter to Tryst no doubt proved him just that. There was no way he could make her see that he was thinking of her as well. Good lord, what if someone brought fraud charges against her? London was rife with those who claimed to be clairvoyants, mediums, and psychic communicators and who were really nothing more than actors. When their charades were revealed, it was ruination for them, and often they were arrested.

Her and those damn tea leaves. They'd always meant so much to her. Sometimes he believed they meant more to her then he did. In their youth it had been a lark—a way of relieving rich women of a few coin and keeping food on their own table. When he'd seen how much success Sadie had, Jack added to the show with a few "mystical" occurrences. He'd even talked her into doing the odd spiritual connection. Then they'd attracted the wrong attention, and if it hadn't been for Trystan Kane's intervention, they both could have ended up in jail. Instead, Jack ended up with the chance for a new beginning and Sadie . . .

She was still running the same old game, preying on the hopes and fears of others to earn a living. On one hand, he didn't begrudge her the right. If people were foolish enough to believe their fate could be divined from the bottom of a cup, then they deserved to have their purses lightened. On the other hand, he had left England—left her—to make a better life for both of them and she'd turned her back on that. How long had it taken her to fall back on the old scheme? Had his ship even left port before she went back to that life?

He'd left her and their life to run off into the unknown and make a better one for both of them. If she hadn't wanted something better, why hadn't she told him? Had she wanted to be rid of him? If that were true, why act the injured party now?

If the system of punishment wasn't so damned awful

he'd be inclined to think she deserved to be caught.

But she didn't deserve that. The idea of Sadie being put in gaol, possibly transported, turned his stomach. So his telegram to Trystan was as much for her benefit as it was to protect his own business interests. She may have chosen this, but that didn't mean he had to give her the opportunity to hang herself. He still had some feeling for her, after all. Damn her for it.

Upon his return to the Barrington he found Vienne La Rieux waiting for him in the lounge. He had to admit it wasn't just business that made him want to fight Sadie. And obviously from the way La Rieux looked at him, she knew it as well.

"*Bonjour, Monsieur Friday,*" she greeted him with cool cordiality. She was dressed in a blue walking costume that matched her eyes, a tiny stylish hat perched on top her head.

"Madame La Rieux. I hope you haven't been waiting long."

She smiled then, and Jack thought he saw frost on her lips. This change in demeanor could only be owed to Sadie. "My coffee has not yet arrived."

Jack seated himself in the plush wing-backed chair facing hers across a small table. The coffee arrived then and he was surprised to see that there were two cups on the tray, along with the pot, cream, and sugar.

"I thought you might like a cup as well," she said.

Jack thanked the waiter and dismissed the young man before returning his attention to La Rieux. He regarded her warily as she poured for the both of them. The smell of coffee drifted to his nostrils, seducing him with its rich scent. What had the world done before the gods blessed them with this alternative to weak, spineless tea?

"Thank you. Does this mean you have not decided to despise me completely? Or are you simply trying to lull me into a false sense of ease so that castrating me is that much more pleasurable?"

That warmed her expression a bit. "Right to the point. I've not yet decided. Cream and sugar?" When he nodded, she continued: "I want to like you, Mr. Friday. I truly do, and it would make our dealings that much more pleasant. But you threatened my friend—"

"I didn't threaten anyone," he interjected hotly, not bothering to pretend ignorance. He lowered his voice, "If you want to offer such entertainment at your place of business that is your concern, but I would be remiss if I didn't share with my partner my misgivings concerning the possible ramifications of supporting such an enterprise."

"You speak as though you think Sadie is a fraud."

Jack looked away. He didn't want to discuss Sadie with this woman. His marriage had no place in a business relationship. Or rather, his *lack* of a marriage had no place.

There was the gentle click of cup meeting saucer. He could feel La Rieux's gaze upon him. "*Mon Dieu.* That's exactly what you think. How can you think so lowly of your own wife?"

His head whipped around and he met her accusing gaze with a hard one of his own. "I no more claim her as my wife than she would claim me as a husband." And he was certain Sadie had made no claim whatsoever.

La Rieux sat back in her chair, a strange expression on her fair face. "*D'accord.*"

Jack arched a brow when she said nothing else. "That's it?"

She nodded, red hair glinting in the light. "It is none of my business what happened between you and Sadie. I should not try to make it so. I'm sure you had your reasons for abandoning her as you did."

Heat rushed up Jack's neck. "I didn't *abandon* anyone. I came back to England to discover my home empty, and that my wife—the woman I loved—had walked out on me."

La Rieux arched a fine brow in that way only women could, managing to look both haughty and amused. "And who could blame her when you so charmingly consider her a charlatan?"

Who the hell did this woman think she was to comment on his relationship with Sadie when she knew nothing of it? He'd seen Sadie read leaves. He had seen how often she'd been wrong, and how often she'd been right. Sometimes she got so caught up in it she truly believed she could divine the future, but in private she would simply shrug and say that they were only leaves. Only tea.

"Fate does not reside in the bottom of a tea cup," Jack bit out in way of defense—though he knew he shouldn't explain himself. "Do you think she never read my leaves? Nothing she said has come true. It's all a load of bollocks. She knows it, and I know it." She'd said they'd be reunited after a long separation and then ran off when he hadn't even been gone, what, a year? Her letters became strained, as though written by a stranger, and then stopped altogether.

The leaves had said they'd love each other forever. That's what Sadie claimed, and he had believed her then. But the leaves didn't know shit.

"Is that why you left, because you thought she lied?"

He did not want to discuss this, but he couldn't seem to help himself. "I didn't know she'd lied then." That sorry realization came much later—standing in the doorway of their empty flat, smelling the dust and seeing the shrouded furniture. "I was twenty when I left, determined to make a new life for her, the kind of life I should have been able to give her if not—" He stopped, but it was too late. He'd revealed too much. "But that hardly matters now."

"I suppose you are right." La Rieux watched him for a moment before inclining her head slightly to the side. "Are the contracts legally binding when Friday is not your real name?"

"They are and it is," he informed her from between clenched teeth. "But for your information, so long as I don't commit a crime it doesn't matter what I choose to call myself." It was on the tip of his tongue to suggest she tell that to Sadie, but he kept it to himself.

Smiling now, the Frenchwoman regarded him with interest. She didn't like him, but she was obviously intrigued by him. Any other time, any other woman, and he'd be sharing her bed tonight. "So, I suppose you could say that my friend Sadie is married to another man?"

"Given the circumstances I would say your friend Sadie isn't legally married at all," said Friday, and a sharp pain stabbed him in the stomach. He winced and La Rieux saw it. Fabulous, she probably thought he pined for Sadie when really it was his bowels that were the source of his discomfort. "Regardless, you agreed that it was none of your concern, remember?"

"Ah, *oui*. I will keep that promise. From here on, you will not hear another word of it from me." She stood. "And now I believe we are done. I will take my leave of you."

What a frigging relief that was, Jack thought, rising to his feet as well. He just wanted to get the rest of this business over with as quickly as possible. As soon as Trystan was in town to take over, he could leave. And he planned to get as far away from England and Sadie as he could.

"In fact, as a gesture of my goodwill, why don't you come by the club tonight?" Her smile turned warmer, but Jack didn't trust it. "The magician Nathan Xavier is giving a special performance."

"I've heard he's amazing. I would enjoy the chance to witness his art for myself." He spoke the truth, though he knew he had just walked into whatever trap she had baited for him.

Fortunately, she didn't make him wait for long. La Rieux grinned. "Perhaps you will think him a fraud as well, though I challenge you to prove it."

"So long as he doesn't take my money or impinge upon *my* business, I don't care what he is."

"You protect what is yours. A noble quality in a man." Her head tilted again. "Does that extend outside of commerce I wonder?"

Jack didn't have a chance to respond, because she bid him good-day and turned on her heel to make a snappy exit. What the hell?

Hand on his hip, he rested the other on the back of the chair and stood there. He didn't watch her leave, rather he stared at a painting on the opposite wall—some evocative mythological scene these modern painters seemed so fond of. It had been Trystan's idea to buy it. Said the painter was destined for greatness. Jack believed him because Tryst had believed in him when he advised him to get in on this "telephone" contraption invented by Alexander Graham Bell. It was going to revolutionize communications, he was sure of it.

But he wasn't really looking at the painting, it was just something to stare at. He had arranged to meet La Rieux today to talk business, and possible other ventures that she might care to invest in now that Trystan—and Jack, though not as deeply—was involved in her plans to build a universal provider or "department" store in Bayswater. Last year there had been something akin to a riot against William Whiteley and his corruption of feminine morals by offering so many goods in one spot, but Trystan agreed with La Rieux's insistence that such a venture would be a huge moneymaker. Jack only hoped his friend knew what he was getting into. Vienne La Rieux struck him as the kind of woman who could rob a man of his bollocks without him even knowing.

Jack was rather partial to his own bollocks, thank you very much. Still, life would be easier if he and La Rieux could get on all right. If that meant being cordial to, and about, Sadie while he was in town, then he would do it.

After all, it wasn't as though he hated Sadie. Not really. He hated what she'd done, hated that she'd left so easily, but he couldn't hate her. That was part of the problem. He'd be much happier if he could hate her. Hate gave a man purpose. What he felt for Sadie . . . well, there didn't seem to be much purpose to it.

He was thankfully rescued from the direction of his thoughts by a gentle hand upon his arm. "Mr. Friday?"

He looked down into saucy green eyes and pushed thoughts of Sadie as deep into the back of his mind as he could. "Lady Gosling, this is an unexpected pleasure."

The tilt of the lady's soft lips told him she knew all manner of pleasures, unexpected and otherwise. A man would have to be a eunuch not to have his prick harden in response. Thank God, Jack felt a slight stirring of interest below his waist. Sadie hadn't totally robbed him of his manhood.

"Forgive my intrusion, sir, but I was having tea with a friend when I saw you standing here and I couldn't let such an opportunity pass."

"I'm delighted to be intruded upon, though no man would view your company as such."

She knew flirtation when she heard it, and obviously knew when a man was interested. She took a step closer, brushing her breast against his arm. "I was wondering, Mr. Friday, if you had any interest in magic?"

Now, this was unexpected. Had she heard some of his conversation with La Rieux? Or was this entirely coincidence? He could see nothing in her eyes that would indicate otherwise. "I find I do, Lady Gosling."

"Would you care to attend a performance at Saint's Row with me this evening?"

Performance indeed. He could well imagine what kind of performance her ladyship had in mind. "What of Lord Gosling?"

She glanced down, giving a demure appearance, but meanwhile her tit was still mashed against his biceps. "My husband doesn't appreciate such spectacles."

"While you do."

"Yes." Her delicate chin lifted, giving him a lovely view of flawless skin and wide, tempting eyes. "There are a great many things my husband doesn't appreciate."

"A pity. He must miss out on many pleasures."

"He does."

Jack's hand closed over the one on his arm. A few inches to the left and he could cup her with his palm, give her a discreet little squeeze to tease them both, but his fingers didn't move, no matter how much his libido willed them to. His mind was too busy trying to make him think of all the pleasures he'd missed while estranged from Sadie. "Then it would be my pleasure to join you at Saint's Row tonight."

"Yes," she returned, in a low throaty tone. "I believe it will be. I'll meet you there."

And then she was gone, leaving his arm bereft of warmth and the rest of him oddly relieved. The reason for this conflict he could only assume was the shock of seeing his wife. She had been the love of his young life. Christ, he'd given up everything for her. Been disowned, disinherited and still he couldn't fathom life without her. It made him angry—childishly so—that he should be the one to give up everything for her and she couldn't even give up tea leaves for him.

Lady Gosling offered him pleasure and company, the warmth of woman. And he did not doubt that Sadie would be there tonight, that had to be why La Rieux suggested he come. He wanted Sadie to see that he was not yearning for her. Should he remain celibate during his stay in London just because his past had come back to bite him on the arse?

He would do well to remember that he did not have a wife. No doubt Sadie would be all too happy to remind him of that if he forgot.

Sadie dressed for her outing with Mason unable to believe that less than twenty-four hours ago Jack Friday—presently a huge thorn in her side—had been little more than an unpleasant memory that sometimes tugged at her brain.

Why now? She wondered as Petra laced her into a pale pink silk corset. Why did he have to come back into her life now? Or at all?

And why did he have to look so bloody fine? She studied herself in the full-length mirror a few feet away.

He'd told her she looked good, but was that because of the years or despite them? Time wasn't kind as often to women as to men. Little lines around feminine eyes were unwanted, while on men they were considered a mark of good character. Why was that? So far she was fortunate not to have accrued any such lines, but Jack had them. He had them and he looked good with them.

He looked good with that smattering of freckles across the bridge of his perfect nose as well. He'd always burned and freckled if he spent too much time in the sun—and now look at him, so tanned. It would be scandalous for a woman to wear such a countenance.

No, it wasn't fair that he could treat her so shoddily and come back looking so good. He should have a humped back, or at least a wart or two—something more immediately noticeable than the black smudge on his soul.

A fraud. He had called her a fraud. Worse than that, he believed it. All the years he had known her and he didn't believe in her, in what she could do. But she had realized this a long time ago, so it shouldn't hurt so much to hear it now. It wasn't his fault he had no magic in his soul—his grandfather would have beaten that out of him at a very young age. Man made his own way in the world. Only death was fated.

Jack didn't want to believe that some things were beyond his control. So when she misinterpreted the odd image in the early days, he saw that as proof that she didn't have the gift. And when people lied rather than admitted what was truly in their heart, he believed that as well. It was easier for him than accepting that she could see beyond what the eye could understand.

Once, she'd convinced him to let her read his leaves. She couldn't remember most of what she'd said, it had been so long ago, but she remembered seeing a huge distance between them—a separation. She'd felt that there would be a reunion, but of course that hadn't happened.

Until now.

The thought gave her a little shiver. "Almost done, missus," her maid said, mistaking the shiver for cold.

Sadie assured the girl she was fine, grateful for the distraction of her thoughts. There was no possible way she and Jack were going to reunite. Not after all that had happened. Although, she knew that not all reunions were meant to be pleasant. The day he left her she'd been certain the next time they saw each other would be among the happiest moments of her life. It wasn't often that she was so very, very wrong.

Petra finished lacing her up and moved to collect the astonishing gown Sadie intended to wear that evening. It wasn't the style or cut of the garment that was so eye catching, for it was a very simple evening gown with little fuss or flounce. What made it so fantastic was that the silk had been dyed a rich, deep magenta, which Sadie just happened to look very fetching in.

Petra slipped the delicate material over her head. Sadie sighed as it whispered over her skin. She did so adore silk—almost as much as she adored Avery Forrest, her dressmaker. The woman rivaled Worth in sheer talent, and it wouldn't be long before she rivaled him in cost as well, but for now she was foolishly kind—and affordable—to her friends, for which Sadie was eternally grateful.

"If you don't mind me saying, ma'am, you have to be a brave woman to wear a gown this color."

Sadie smiled at Petra, who rarely wore anything more daring than pastels. "It's about making a statement."

"Aye. Loud and clear."

Chuckling, and in no way offended, Sadie smoothed her hands over the silk skirts. Small cap sleeves cupped her shoulders as the unadorned neckline fell into place. With each button Petra fastened, the bodice became snugger, hugging her torso, the vivid hue making the exposed tops of her breasts seem pale as snow. It was gathered in the back to give the illusion of the slight bustle that was the fashion these days. No big poofy bottoms anymore.

She wore no jewelry save for a pair of pearl drops at her ears and the enameled gold comb that secured the knot of hair at her crown. Ivory gloves and matching silk shawl completed the ensemble.

She's always liked bright colors. Her mother had accused her of being a peacock on more than one occasion, but always with a smile. For a wedding gift Jack had given her a pair of satin gloves dyed the exact blue of said bird. They'd been totally impractical given their circumstances, but she loved them all the same. She still had them. Somewhere.

"I have to admit," Petra commented, standing back to assess her handiwork, "you look stunning. Bright, but stunning."

Sadie grinned. "Thank you." Then she heard the door

knocker. She glanced at the clock. "Right on time."

Gathering up her reticule, Sadie left her room and walked leisurely down the stairs to join her escort in the drawing room. Dressed in black, he stood near the red velvet chaise, hands behind his back as he studied a painting of poppies on the wall above.

"Looking for flaws?" she asked.

He turned with a raised brow and lopsided grin. "Am I that critical?"

"Usually."

"Well, you look beautiful."

Sadie's cheeks warmed. "Thank you. And the poppies?"

He shrugged. "Passable."

Mason Blayne was the kind of man who drew attention and held it. He was tall and lean with black hair and eyes that ranged from chocolate to pitch depending on the day. His complexion was fair with a slight olive cast that hinted at exotic ancestors, and he had a true artist's temperament—sometimes flying into a fiery rant if a paint wasn't the exact shade he wanted. He had the enviable ability to laugh at himself, however—a trait that Sadie deeply admired.

In addition to being handsome and brilliant, Mason was also incredibly easy to spend time with, and he had introduced Sadie to a world vastly different than the one she'd become accustomed to. With him she'd made the acquaintance of actresses and writers, musicians and other talented people who had such wonderful ideas and stories. People who didn't judge her because her father hadn't money or a title, and who thought her ability to read tea leaves was a divine gift from whatever god they worshiped.

Nathan Xavier, the magician they were going to see tonight, was one of those friends. Sadie was very much looking forward to the show, as Xavier could make an audience doubt their very eyes—their very beliefs. Lord knew, she needed a distraction.

"Would you like a drink?" she asked.

Mason shook his head, the light from the wall lamps casting a bluish tint to his glossy hair. "No, thank you. A glass of scotch and your company will make me so comfortable I won't want to leave, and I promised Xavier we'd be there."

He had a knack for knowing exactly how to flatter her without piling it on too heavily. She never thought for a moment that he wasn't sincere, though Vienne would argue that all men were sincere until they got what they wanted from a woman.

"Shall we go, then?" Sadie held out her hand to him. "We can always have a glass of wine there."

Mason's dark eyes twinkled as he came forward to wrap his gloved fingers around hers. She could feel the warmth of his skin through the fabric separating them. "Nothing I like better than free wine."

Outside, the moon was a silver eye, peering between indigo clouds. Mason stopped for a second to stare at it. No doubt committing every shade and highlight to memory for use on a future canvas.

They took his carriage—a small but comfortable vehicle that still had a new smell to the interior. His work was garnering more and more interest as of late; he could now afford luxuries denied him for most of his life.

"Will Ava be joining us tonight?" Sadie asked sometime later.

Mason's face was mostly shadows, but a finger of light revealed the tightening of his wide mouth. "If Autley deigns to bring her."

It was no secret that Mason disapproved of his sister being the duke's mistress—not because he held on to the archaic notion that an unmarried woman must remain chaste while men could sleep with whomever they wanted, but because he held no high opinion of Westhaver Blackbourne, Duke of Autley. The duke had first noticed Ava when she became somewhat famous as a Professional Beauty. Photographs and paintings of her were guaranteed high sales and several photographers and artists wanted her to pose exclusively for them.

Sadie had no desire to press a sore subject. "I wonder if the prince will be there with Mrs. Langtry?"

"Doubtful, though, Lillie might well be in attendance. She likes a good show as much as the rest of us."

She'd forgotten that Mason knew the famous Lillie Langtry. He'd painted a portrait of her shortly before Sir Allen Young's dinner party where she allegedly caught the eye of Albert Edward—"Bertie"—the Prince of Wales. Bets were being placed in all the clubs as to when the lady would become the official royal mistress.

"Did you have an affair with her?" The words slipped out of her mouth before she could stop them.

Black eyes shot to hers. "Would you be jealous if I said yes?"

"I think I would." Oddly enough she had no trouble admitting this. Was that so wrong of her? She hadn't told Mason that her "husband" was back in town, yet here she was demanding to know about a lover he might have had before he began showing any interest in her.

"I do love a jealous woman, but your concern is misplaced. I never shared a bed or any other item of furniture with the delightful Mrs. Langtry."

She smiled a little, despite her shame. "Forgive me. I shouldn't have asked."

"I'm glad you did."

Silence fell between them, and not the comfortable kind. The kind that was fraught with tension. Should she kiss him? Would he kiss her? If he was going to sit there in the gloom and smile so smugly, shouldn't he at least have the decency to try to ravish her?

"You met with your new landlord today," he said, ruining all hopes of ravishment. "How did that go?"

"Not well," she replied honestly. "Mr. Friday thinks I'm a fraud." The minute the words were out, she longed to yank them back. She did not want to discuss Jack with Mason, but she couldn't very well lie and say all was well, could she? If Jack succeeded in keeping her from her shop, Mason would know something was wrong when she had to look for another property.

"Did you tell him you don't give a rat's arse what he thinks of you?"

"Not really, no. He doesn't want to rent to me. I think

he's going to try to get out of the agreement."

"If he does then he's obviously stupid. You don't want to do business with a fool."

Words leapt to her lips—a defense of Jack. Sadie wanted to insist that he wasn't stupid, just angry. Vindictive even, but never stupid. But she stopped herself just in time. She would have to explain to Mason why she defended a man she wasn't supposed to know, and she couldn't do that. Wouldn't. He knew she'd been married once, but he thought her husband dead. It was a lie Sadie almost had herself believing until Jack's appearance.

She asked about Mason's new painting instead, and they talked about it and other topics for the remainder of the drive. There was no more thought of kissing. And she promised herself there would be no more thoughts of Jack either. She wouldn't let him ruin this evening or any other spent with Mason.

Shortly, they arrived at Saint's Row, and Mason's carriage was one of many lined up outside the club to deliver attendees to the night's performance. A mix of aristocrats and upper-class ladies and gentlemen climbed the steps alongside those new to fortune and well-known personages such as politicians, artists, writers, and musicians. It was an amazing mixing of the social spheres and Sadie was thrilled to be part of it. She felt a surge of satisfaction on Vienne's behalf as well. Most of the upper crust wouldn't ever invite her to their parties or events, but they vied for the privilege of giving her their money and attending her soirees.

Inside, the cream and brown interior gleamed under

the chandeliers. The air smelled slightly of spices—warm and inviting. Voices echoed under the vaulted ceiling as some of the crowd broke into small groups, standing about to chat, while the rest drifted into the ballroom where the stage and chairs had been set up.

The lights were dimmer in there, casting shadows around the perimeter. The only bright spot was right above the raised dais where Xavier would perform. Carpet had been set down in the marble aisles to muffle the sound of footfalls. The chairs had curved backs and plush red velvet cushions that matched the stage curtains, adding to the opulence.

"Vienne certainly knows how to set a mood," Mason commented as they found the seats at the front that had been reserved for them. "I can almost imagine a phantom watching us from the wings."

Sadie smiled. "I'm sure if Vienne could have arranged such an apparition she would have." She glanced around at the crowd and froze when her gaze alighted on the couple three rows back.

Jack and Lady Gosling sat close enough for their thighs to touch. The lady leaned into him, whispering in his ear with a coy smile. And Jack listened with an expression that was anything but coy.

She wouldn't be surprised if Lady Gosling ended up walking bow-legged tomorrow. Or maybe, given the lady's reputation, it would be Jack who would have difficulty walking. He had no interest in his own wife, but plenty in someone else's.

It didn't matter. Jack could do whatever he wanted, as could she. She hoped he got the pox.

Sadie turned away before Jack noticed her staring, a sick feeling in her stomach. She glanced at Mason sitting beside her, at his strong profile and the hint of shadow along his jaw. She adored him. Was attracted to him. Could she love him? Or had Jack ruined that for her? Sometimes she wondered if she could ever give anyone her heart again—if there was enough of it to give.

Mason's head turned. He caught her watching him and smiled, dark eyes brightening. He didn't say anything, just offered her his hand. Sadie didn't hesitate. She readily slipped her fingers into his. When he squeezed, she squeezed back.

"You should come in," she murmured. "When you take me home after the performance. You should come in."

His expression didn't change, but something in his gaze did. He understood an invitation when he heard one. He nodded. "I would like that."

The lights lowered, so Sadie tore her gaze away from Mason's and directed it toward the stage, her stomach alight with anticipation. Tonight, she would take a lover and she was going to make certain she enjoyed it.

To hell with Jack Friday.

The man's smile might as well have been a fist, it hit Jack so hard in the gut. He looked away, ashamed and embarrassed to have witnessed it. Angry, too, though he wasn't quite sure why. Probably because he had smiled at her that way once himself. Sadie had a way of making a man smile like a dim-witted idiot.

Obviously she could still make an idiot of out of him because he wanted to charge up the aisle and knock the man's teeth out. Let him smile then. Sadie was *his* wife, damn it.

No, she wasn't. They'd both agreed that they were not married. He distinctly remembered agreeing that there was nothing between them, but there was no denying the jealousy rising inside him. Regardless of everything that had happened, regardless of how raw the old wound was, he still thought of her as his. And that was what rubbed the most salt in.

"Who's that with Madame Moon?" he asked Lady Gosling—*Theone*.

She leaned into him with the pretense of getting a better look at Sadie and her companion, but it was obviously a ruse to flaunt her impressive cleavage. Unfortunately, Jack was uninspired by the sight.

"That's Mason Blayne," she whispered, patting his thigh as she sat back in her seat. "He's been escorting her around town as of late."

Were they lovers? He had no right to be jealous. He didn't *want* to be jealous, but the idea of someone else sowing the field he'd ploughed first pissed him off. Did this man know how she liked to be kissed? Did he know how she liked to be touched? Worse, did Sadie know the same things about this man? This swarthy Casanova?

Yes, he could almost feel Mason Blayne's bite on his knuckles.

The lights dimmed and he couldn't see much of anything other than the stage, so Jack forced himself to look at it instead of the outline of Sadie's head. He pushed his anger and jealousy down, deep inside. He didn't want it.

The curtains parted as a few stragglers took their seats. Applause. Vienne La Rieux—stunning in an icy blue gown—took the stage to welcome everyone and introduce Nathan Xavier. More applause. Gradually, Jack relaxed a little.

Xavier was not what Jack expected. And what he'd expected had been someone more effeminate, not a man who looked as though he could go a few rounds with bare-knuckle fighter Jem Mace and come out the victor.

The magician was tall and powerfully built, with close-cropped dark hair and a jaw that looked like it had been carved from granite. But he had a charming grin and a low, melodic voice that filled the room. His hands were quick and performed tasks and illusions the likes of which Jack had never seen before.

In short, the man was bloody brilliant, and soon diverted Jack from any thoughts of Sadie and her lover. In fact, Jack sat back in his chair and watched the performance with great enjoyment, and when Lady Gosling slipped her hand into his lap to fondle him through his trousers, he almost jumped right out of his seat. She flashed him a saucy grin, and thankfully removed her hand. She trailed her fingers across his leg, meaning to tease him. Under different circumstances, it might have worked. As it was, it took a few moments for him to relax enough to enjoy the performance once more. He kept expecting to be groped by his companion.

"And now, I require volunteers from the audience," Xavier announced sometime later, as he wheeled a long box on a waist-high stand out onto the platform. He pointed into the crowd with that rakish smile of his. "Madame Moon, would you be so kind?"

Jack's heart gave a little thump as a tall, slender woman in a fabulously bright gown approached the stage. Her skin looked like buffed alabaster, her hair rich coffee. Sadie always did know how to dress for attention. She knew her best assets and how to compliment them.

God, she had perfect breasts. Such perfect skin. And perfect hair. She was simply perfect in every way—a fairy come to earth, trying to pass as a mere mortal without success. And he was a tosser who hadn't been able to hold on to her.

"I need one more volunteer," Xavier continued after kissing Sadie's gloved hand. He stepped off the edge of the stage and came down into the seating area. "A gentleman, strong and strapping. You, sir."

Jack's eyes widened at the finger so close to his face. "Me?"

Xavier nodded. "You."

Christ Almighty. Fate was truly out to bugger him senseless. He could refuse but that would only make him look a poor sport, and since at least a quarter of the people in this room had money he'd like to help them dispose of, he couldn't present himself as a man afraid to take a risk.

Lady Gosling clapped her hands—no longer in his lap. "Oh, do go! This is so diverting!"

With a grimace, Jack rose to his feet and was met with more polite applause. He followed Xavier up onto the stage, careful to avoid Sadie's gaze. It was impossible to ignore her completely, though, with her in that gown.

"Madame Moon," the magician said, "Would you be so kind as to climb into this box?"

Sadie, to her credit, didn't argue. She didn't look any more comfortable than Jack did, but she wasn't afraid by any means. She accepted Xavier's hand and allowed him to assist her onto the table and into the open box, which looked a little bit like a coffin, Jack realized morbidly as the magician closed the sectioned lid.

"Are you comfortable?" Xavier asked. Sadie nodded. For a split second, her gaze flitted to Jack's and he saw unease there that had nothing to do with being in a box and everything to do with him.

"Excellent." The magician turned to face Jack. "This is for you, my good man."

Jack glanced down. In the man's large hands he held a gleaming saw, the blade of which had huge, jagged teeth.

"What am I to do with that?" Jack asked. He glanced at Sadie. Was it just him or was that amusement he saw in her eyes?

Xavier grinned, and like any good showman, turned to his audience. "Why, you're going to cut her in half!"

# Chapter 6

**E**ven if she lived to be a hundred and lost all there was of her mind along the way, Sadie didn't think she'd ever forget the look on Jack's face when Nathan Xavier handed him the saw.

He stood over her with the serrated blade in his hand and horror all over his face. It was all she could do not to burst out laughing. Of course, having a sense of humor over the whole thing was easy for her—she knew the secret to the trick.

While Xavier distracted Jack—and the audience—with their dialogue, Xavier's lovely assistant, Honora, had helped Sadie into the upper section of the long box. Once inside, she brought her legs up as far as she could while Honora eased a pair of false feet through the holes where Sadie's should have gone. When the lid was closed it would look to Jack, as well as the audience, that Sadie was fully stretched out within the confines of the box.

All that was left now was for Jack to "saw" her in half. Poor Jack looked as though he'd rather strip naked and run through the aisles than complete the task with which he'd been charged. She almost felt a little sympathy for him.

Almost.

Sadie couldn't take her gaze off him. She should be looking at the audience—hamming it up at Jack's expense, but she couldn't look away. He was truly afraid for her. Or for himself should anything go wrong.

Of all the people Xavier could have chosen, why did it have to be Jack?

The magician made a great show of spinning her mobile prison around so the audience could see that it was indeed solid. Sadie turned her head and smiled at Mason, who grinned at her from his seat. She wondered if he knew how the trick worked as well. He and Xavier were good friends, but it wouldn't do for Xavier to reveal his secrets to more people than he had to, would it? After all, he'd chosen her because he knew he could trust her, but normally he planted volunteers in the audience for the more secretive aspects of his illusions.

"Before we begin," Xavier said. "Madame Moon, would you be so good as to wiggle your feet so there can be no doubt in the audience?"

Sadie didn't move, but she knew the feet sticking out of the box were. How did he do that? The audience practically sighed in response. Jack, however, had a uniquely different reaction. He looked at the bottom of the box, then up at Sadie. And when their eyes met, she knew he'd caught on to the trick. How, she wasn't sure, but when he grinned at her in that delightfully evil way, she couldn't help but grin back.

Dear God, he knew those weren't her feet. Somehow, after all these years, he remembered *her feet* and knew the ones wiggling for the crowd were not hers.

Xavier repositioned the box in front of Jack who, now that he was in on the trick, seemed to have been filled with the spirit of the evening. He raised the saw to demonstrate to the audience how very sharp it was by cutting through a stick. Then, at Xavier's command, he set the serrated blade into the groove at the halfway mark on the box.

He paused, casting his gaze toward her. For a second she saw true concern in his eyes. Of course he knew this was all a sham, but he was still going to come very close to her person with a very sharp blade. There was a slight chance that something could go wrong.

Odd. He truly seemed to care if he hurt her—physically, at any rate. Why couldn't he be so solicitous of her feelings as well?

Xavier clapped Jack on the shoulder, a sign that all would be fine. "I would ask now that the audience give Mr. Friday complete silence as he performs this feat," the magician requested in an ominous tone. "One wrong move on his part could mean dire consequences for Madame Moon."

Jack grinned rakishly at the audience and then at Sadie. "I promise, dear Madame, that this will not hurt a bit."

To which Sadie quipped, "I wager you say that to all the girls."

There was a chorus of titters and chuckles from the audience.

Xavier gestured to the box. "Mr. Friday, please begin."

Jack nodded at the magician. Sadie could almost imagine his fingers tightening on the handle of the saw. She couldn't see, but she heard and felt the movement of the blade as it slipped through the concealed slit between compartments.

Xavier must have put something in the space between the two separate halves to provide resistance, because the blade only made it so far before it hit something solid. Always one for putting on a good show: Sadie gasped—and the audience reacted accordingly. Several women cried out.

Even Jack jerked a little. His wide gaze whipped to Sadie's, but his surprise quickly gave way to laughter. She tried so hard not to smile, but a bit of it slipped out, letting him know that she was fine.

Xavier stepped forward. "Madame Moon, are you all right?"

At Sadie's nod, the magician bade Jack to continue. And Jack did.

When her erstwhile husband began to saw through the box with great gusto and showmanship, Sadie wasn't certain if the tightness in her throat was restrained laughter or tears. They used to have such fun together playing tricks and telling jokes. Rarely did either one of them ever get angry at the other for a good laugh at their expense.

Even now, after all that had transpired and grown bitter between them, he still appreciated the joke, and embraced it wholeheartedly, even when the halves of the box were pulled apart and ladies screamed in response. One even cried out, "Murderer!"

Jack turned his back to the audience then, unable to keep from grinning.

"My good people!" Xavier shouted to the distressed crowd. "I assure you that Madame Moon is quite all right!" He gestured to the lower box and, this time, because of how the two halves had been separated, Sadie could see the wiggling feet. They were very realistic, even as close as she was. And though she knew it was folly, her heart warmed a little more knowing that Jack had realized they weren't hers.

As she watched the wriggling appendages, Sadie was quite certain someone in the audience had fainted.

"Madame Moon," Xavier asked, "how do you feel?"

"As though I'm half the woman I used to be," she replied easily, earning a round of laughter from the astounded audience.

The magician grinned at her. "Then let us make you whole again. Mr. Friday, if you will, please?"

Quickly, Xavier took the bottom half and instructed Jack to do the same with the top. As he hovered over her, hands braced to push the half holding her back into place, Jack glanced down at her.

"Well done," he murmured.

Sadie's smile took a wry curve. "It must have given

you some pleasure to cut me in half." It was meant as a joke, but it was obvious that Jack didn't share her amusement.

His eyes darkened as though clouds covered them. "I've never intentionally set out to hurt you, Sadie. I never have and I never will. Think me every sort of villain, but you know I speak the truth."

She did, and yet she could not say it because the earnestness in his gaze undid her.

For that moment there was no one else in the world but the two of them. He was so close she could smell his soap and she breathed that spicy scent deep into her lungs, because she did so love it, and God only knew when she might smell it again.

He pushed, and she felt herself move. There was a soft thud as the lower half of the box butted against the one she was in. Almost over. Thank God, her hips and legs were beginning to cramp from being bent up. And then Jack walked away.

She would have gladly suffered another hour in that box to keep him beside her. How stupid was that? How foolish was she to wish for him beside her when he had run as far away from her as he could all those years ago?

The audience applauded for her when she finally climbed out of the box and was given back her shoes. No one seemed to notice that her stockings weren't the same as the ones on the feet in the box. Of course, those feet were tucked away inside their compartment now, where no one could see them.

Xavier shook Jack's hand and kissed Sadie's cheek,

thanking them both before sending them back to their seats. Sadie watched as Jack returned to where Lady Gosling sat waiting. They made a very handsome couple, she acknowledged with a bit of a low feeling.

She resumed her seat next to Mason. His dark eyes sparkled at her as he took her hand and leaned close to whisper, "You were brilliant. For a moment even I believed he'd cut you."

Regardless of his claim that he would never knowingly hurt her, Jack had done just that. The fact that he hadn't meant to only made it worse, because it meant he simply hadn't stopped to consider his actions.

One little laugh between them on a stage, in front of dozens of people, could not erase the pain.

Sadie squeezed Mason's fingers and determined to enjoy the rest of the performance. As of that moment Jack Friday didn't exist.

Sometime later Xavier took a short intermission so the audience could freshen themselves or their drinks, or both. While Mason slipped backstage to converse with the magician, Sadie snuck away to the private ladies' retiring room, reserved for guest performers, to relieve herself and blot the shine from her nose. When she came out she spied Jack and Lady Gosling slipping through a set of doors that led to the gardens.

It was none of her business.

She followed them. Oh, she knew she shouldn't. Nothing good would come of it, just like reading her own leaves, but she tiptoed into the night regardless.

They hadn't been that far ahead of her, but they were out

of sight by the time she reached the garden entrance. Straining her ears, she caught the low tones of their voices and the swish of skirts. She lifted her own skirts to follow.

She found them behind a hedge, designed for just such a purpose. If she hadn't known every inch of these grounds she might not have found them at all. Everything about Saint's Row had been built with discretion and privacy in mind so that trysting lovers needn't worry about being discovered—unless being discovered was part of the game.

Here, she had only the moonlight to see by and unfortunately it was a clear night with a fat, bright moon hovering above. She could see all too clearly as Lady Gosling reached up and brought Jack's head down to hers, pressing her mouth against his. Sadie remembered the feel and warmth of his lips against hers. Remembered how sweet he tasted.

The memory brought a sharp slash of pain to her chest. She stepped back, not wanting to witness Jack's arms sliding around the other woman's waist. The hedge rustled as she brushed against it.

Lady Gosling didn't appear to hear, but Jack did. And before Sadie could scurry out of sight, his head had lifted and his gaze pinned her where she stood.

The bastard had the gall to look sorry.

"Is someone there?" Lady Gosling asked, opening her eyes and gazing lazily at Jack with a dreamy expression. One slap would fix that, Sadie thought, ducking behind the hedge and hurrying down the path back toward the club.

She was headed toward a small group of people whom she knew when she heard him call her name. "Mrs. Moon? A moment, please?"

Damn him. She could hardly give him the cut with all these potential witnesses. Gritting her teeth, she stopped on the gravel path and turned to face him. A false smile plastered itself to her face. "Mr. Friday. We meet again."

Jack's smile was just as false, but on him it had a much more dangerous edge. "Indeed." He glanced down at Lady Gosling, who was hanging from his arm like a wet wool coat. "Would you mind, my lady?"

Lady Gosling flashed him a seductive smile. "Of course not. I see some friends I must speak to. I shall meet you inside." The look she gave Sadie before she walked away could only be described as proprietary.

*He's all yours*, Sadie thought. *I hope you choke on him.*

As soon as they were alone, Jack's brow furrowed. "Sadie, what just . . ."

She held up a hand. "It's none of my business."

He snorted. "No, it's not. But you made it your business, didn't you? Did you see what you hoped to see?"

"Shut up!" Sadie hissed. She was not the one at fault here! "I didn't spy on you on purpose."

"Of course you did. You couldn't have simply stumbled upon us, not there."

She could slap him. Kick him. Do all manner of violence to him, but she couldn't because they weren't truly alone. It was very difficult to look at him and make her expression a pleasant one when she wanted to disembowel him.

"I think you wanted me to see," she countered. "Admit it."

"There's nothing to admit," he replied, folding his arms over his damned splendid chest. "But you know me—I would have preferred to give you a bit more of a show. It's all about the show, right?"

Hadn't she thought something similar earlier? "Why did you have to do this here?" she demanded, ignoring his goading. "Don't you own a hotel or something? Go shag her there."

His brows lowered. "What was I supposed to say? No, I can't go out there because my wife might see? Did you happen to notice that she kissed me, not the other way 'round?"

"Your mouth was on hers." It was the first thing she could think of as a suitable retort. "And I am *not* your wife."

"Then why are you acting like a jealous one?"

She stiffened. Flattering himself, was he? And she'd walked right into his trap. Fists balled at her sides, she glared at him with all the venom she could muster. "I hate you," she whispered.

Jack's lips thinned—even then they were still perfect. "You know why I'd want you to see me with another woman?"

"Because you're petty and vain?"

His face turned hard and tight, but his gaze was bright with anger and pain—so much, she could barely meet it.

"Because if you're watching I can't pretend the woman I'm with is you. And maybe then I can get a proper shag for the first time in a damned decade."

He started to walk away, leaving her staring after him in stunned disbelief. But then he hesitated, and tossed one last anguished, angry glance over his shoulder. "Sometimes, I hate you too."

Theone Gant, Lady Gosling, woke the next morning foul, her temperament that of a bear with a toothache.

Stiffly, she rose naked from her bed and moved across the floor to the full-length mirror near the vanity. She examined herself in the glass: bite marks on her breasts and bruising on her thighs—nothing she couldn't conceal. Nothing that would leave a lasting mark.

Jack Friday wouldn't feel the need to mark a woman in such a manner—like he was a wild animal and she the prey. She looked down at her knuckles and rubbed them absently, wincing at the soreness of the swollen tissues. At this point she should know better than to fight back. It only excited him more.

She met her own gaze in the mirror. She had come willingly to this life, just as she had every decision in the seven and twenty years she'd been upon this earth. She would not become some weepy female wailing over her regrets now. Not ever.

Six years she'd been married to Baxter Gant, Baron Gosling. He'd found her trodding the boards at Covent Garden—one of the many actresses used as background scenery. Uneducated and poor, she had her looks and a talent for lying that translated well into work on stage. She taught herself different accents, taught herself to speak like an aristo by mimicking those who frequented the theater. If the opportunity arose to take a rich lover, she did so; but she was never indiscriminate. There had to be a good reason to let a man have use of her body—and that reason was whatever benefit he could be to her.

So when Lord Gosling came backstage, she put on her poshest voice, best manners, and a low-cut gown. She'd been barely one and twenty and that night he'd sucked her nipples so hard she cried. But she let him into her bed again. When he offered her a house she refused, but she slept with him again, gritting her teeth through the indignities and hurt. When he offered marriage—provided she left her old life behind and agreed to live a lie—she took it, even though she wondered if she'd survive the wedding night.

Shrugging into a wrapper of the sleekest emerald silk that she knew made her eyes look unnaturally green, Theone moved gingerly to the bellpull for her maid and gave the cord a hard tug. She would take breakfast in the bath. A nice, hot bath to soak the sting out and relax her. She went to her bathroom and turned on the taps herself. Even after all these years, it was difficult to let the maids do everything for her. Being waited on hand and foot wasn't as amusing as she thought it would be. Sometimes it was damned faster to do it herself.

By the time the tub was filled with hot, jasmine-scented water, her maid had arrived with breakfast on a tray, as she did every morning. Theone never ate with her husband; she would be far too tempted to stab him in the eye with a fork.

The only thing that kept her from killing him was the hope that someone else would save her the bother and the mess.

"Will you be needing anything else, mum?" the girl asked, averting her gaze.

Theone looked down. Her wrapper had gaped a little, revealing a red welt in the shape of teeth on the inside of her left breast. She didn't bother to pull the fabric closed. Let the servants know what he did to her. Let them talk. She might be a bitch, but she was fair to them, and if she could incite their sympathy, she would.

"Not now," she responded. "Come back in an hour to help me dress."

The girl bobbed a curtsey, cast another furtive glance at her mistress's abused flesh, and scurried out the door.

Alone again, Theone dropped her robe on the bath-room floor and stepped into the bath. As soon as the hot water lapped against her skin, much of the tension and bad mood left her. She sank down until the water was almost to her chin. Only then did she reach to the tray for the cup of tea and one of the croissants. No, her life wasn't to be cast aside just because her husband was a prick with abnormal appetites.

This was a stepping stone, and a right good one too. From poverty to Mayfair, she'd gone, and she wasn't about to give it up. She just needed an out. She couldn't leave Baxter or he'd cut her off without a farthing. What she needed was a rich man to support her and treat her nicely. Once, she'd thought the Duke of Ryeton would do, but that had been a colossal miscalculation on her part. And now there he was, married to that little priss. No accounting for taste.

And now life had tossed the scrumptious Jack Friday in her lap. He might not have a title, but he was wealthy enough, and he seemed a good man—a lusty one too. He'd leave a woman exhausted—and he would be nice about it.

She could have landed him last night. She had been prepared to return to his hotel with him after the show. If he'd taken her home with him she might have missed Baxter altogether. He would have been passed out in his study by the time she came in and she wouldn't have to bathe for an hour to remove the filthy residue of his conjugal rights.

But Jack Friday, who had seemed so promising earlier in the evening, hadn't offered to take her to bed. In fact, he hadn't said much of anything during the second half of the magic demonstration.

His disinterestedness had started right after his conversation with Sadie Moon.

Theone first met the flamboyant Madame Moon a few years ago—when she became a regular entertainment at Vienne La Rieux's charitable events. She didn't know either Moon or La Rieux all that well, but she recognized a woman who had clawed her way up when she saw one. She didn't make friends easily—in fact she tried to not make them at all—but if she were to pick a woman with whom she might be friendly, it would be

Vienne La Rieux. At least she could be her friend until a man got in the way.

But she wouldn't tolerate Sadie Moon jeopardizing her chances with Jack Friday. She had to get out of this marriage. Soon, or she'd do something she'd regret. Jack was her chance to do just that.

Once in a while she had the niggling thought that Sadie Moon was familiar to her somehow. And last night, seeing the fortune-teller standing next to Jack, she'd had that feeling again. She knew Sadie Moon from somewhere, but where?

And more importantly, did Moon know her? Immediately she would assume no, because the woman had never mentioned it. But that didn't mean anything. In Theone's experience that only meant the other person hadn't found a need for such information. No, she couldn't be complacent about this. She had to find out as much about Sadie Moon as she could, and soon.

And while she was at it, she'd see what she could dig up on Jack Friday as well. Maybe there was some little tidbit in his past she might use to keep his interest from straying. He had to help her.

Because she didn't know what she was going to do if he didn't.

Jack Friday was not a happy man. And he blamed his wife who wasn't his wife for his black mood. Were it not for their brief truce, followed by her impassioned bashing of him the night before, he might have spent the remainder of the evening having a delightful knock with Lady Gosling, but his libido had gone the way of a tree branch laden with too much snow, and no amount of warm thoughts could bring it up again. So he'd taken the sweet missus home and left her without so much as a kiss.

For the millionth time that morning he wished he had never come back to England. He wished Trystan had taken care of this bit of business himself.

Trystan. That was another thorn in his side, wasn't it? The telegram had arrived that morning—a so short and not-very-sweet note—telling Jack that his partner didn't share his misgivings. Saying that Trystan thought the venture sound and that Jack could remove himself from the project if he felt he couldn't "handle" it.

*Handle it.* Meaning if he couldn't find the bollocks to deal with Sadie. Obviously Trystan knew more than Jack first thought. Or maybe he didn't and was just being a git about the whole thing. Regardless, it was out of Jack's hands. The only thing left to do was tell Sadie she could have her damn shop and wipe his hands of it. It would be Trystan's problem if there was trouble. And maybe she could continue to tell the right people what they wanted to hear and trouble would never find her. He'd hope for that.

"Coffee," he barked at the waiter who'd been brave enough to approach him before he even sat down at his private table in the hotel dining room. "A pot of it."

Then he hooked the leg of the chair with his foot, jerked it out from beneath the table, and fell into it with all the humor and grace of an angry bull.

"Rough night?" asked a familiar voice.

Jack glanced—*glared*—up. Archer Kane stood over him, a sympathetic yet wholly amused smile on his face. "Oh, it's you."

"In the flesh," came the jovial reply. "Care for some company or are you the sort who, like my dear brother the duke, prefers to brood in private?"

Jack gestured to the chair across from him. "Have a seat." Perhaps a little company was what he needed to shake off this thundercloud above his head.

Kane was all affability and grace as he slid into the empty chair. Within seconds the waiter had returned with a pot of coffee and set it on the table between them. Archer requested a stupid amount of food for breakfast. Jack asked for crispy fried potatoes and sausage with eggs. He'd eat until he was stuffed and then he'd go to the boxing club and fight until someone knocked him down hard enough that he couldn't get back up.

And then he was going to find Sadie and tell her that she'd won, that she'd managed to totally unman him. After that maybe he'd have someone kick him repeatedly in the bollocks.

Christ, could he leave London soon? He'd rather go back to Ireland and face the old man than stay here any longer.

"You look fairly murderous," Kane commented as he helped himself to the coffee. "Anything I can help with?"

Jack glanced up and managed a small, tight smile. "Murder?"

His companion laughed and added a dollop of cream

to his cup. "Depends on the victim, I suppose. Might be a bit of a diversion."

Even Jack had to smile at that. "Nothing so heinous. I have to swallow my pride and tell Mrs. Moon she can have her little shop despite my protests to your brother."

Archer regarded him over the rim of his cup. "You are against the venture?"

"I'm against having my business attached to anything that might bring trouble down upon my head," Jack responded.

His companion laughed in response. "Not much of a businessman, then, are you?"

He deserved that one, he supposed. "Let me ask you, do you believe that our fate can be divined from the dregs at the bottom of a cup? Might as well base your future on the shape of a cloud, or a turd in the bottom of a chamber pot."

Icy blue eyes sparkled. "How eloquent you are, Mr. Friday."

Jack rolled his eyes. "You understand what I'm saying, right?"

"Of course I do. But there are a great many people in this city who would disagree with you—people who swear by the woman's talents."

"There are people who actually believe that Lot's wife turned to salt too. People who believe in dragons and who think women are inferior simply because of what's between their legs. That doesn't mean they're right."

"I believe you're a bit of a radical." It was said without malice, only Kane's seemingly perpetual amusement.

"I could be," Jack replied with a careless shrug. "But I don't believe Sadie O—" He cleared his throat, "Moon has the power to see the future—mine or anyone else's. The future isn't set in stone."

Archer tilted his head. "This really has you fired up. Hmm, I wonder if you're not protesting too much, old man. What's the real reason for this? An unpleasant encounter with a fortune-teller in your youth, or did Mrs. Moon reject you?"

Both were too close to the truth for Jack's liking. He was given a brief reprieve from answering by the arrival of their breakfasts.

"While I think you might be making Mrs. Moon out to be more of a threat than she actually is," Archer began, clearly not done with the subject, "you must know that the simple fact of being a friend to Vienne La Rieux is enough for my brother to keep her close."

Jack frowned. "I'm beginning to think your brother is obsessed with that woman." Wasn't he a fine one to talk? Then again, he knew all about obsession and having a woman so far under your skin you couldn't dig her out with a scalpel.

"Just beginning?" Archer's lips tilted sardonically. "You remember about, oh, six or seven years ago? When Tryst decided commerce was his life and he started taking risks and learning all he could about economics and such rot?"

Jack nodded, scooping up a forkful of runny yolk with the sausage and potato already speared on his fork.

That was when things really started to take off for the two of them.

"Well, that was Vienne La Rieux's doing. Shagged my baby brother senseless and then dismissed him because he wasn't enough of a 'man.' Tryst took that badly, as you can imagine. Personally I think the tart did him a favor."

"How so?"

"She had a few years on him and he was infatuated—fancied himself in love with her, but I think he was in love with what she did to him, you understand?"

Christ, did he ever. "By tossing him aside she saved him from making a fool of himself over her."

Archer nodded. "Quite. However, Tryst's been proving himself ever since, and if he gets a chance to shove that in La Rieux's face, then he will." He took a drink of coffee. "So, you see, by doing business with Mrs. Moon, he gets to feel as though he's flaunting his success in Frenchie's face. It's worked you know. I see the look on La Rieux's face when Tryst's name is mentioned."

Jack smiled—a little bitterly. "A woman scorned is but a trifle compared to a man rejected."

Archer raised his cup in salute. "Well said, my friend. Well said."

Jack took a drink of his coffee as Archer launched into another subject. A man rejected, that's what he was. Instead of wallowing in the fact that Sadie had left him, perhaps he should follow Trystan's example.

And make her regret that she had.

# Chapter 7

"I really don't reckon that's a penis, Mrs. Carbunkle." Sadie bit the inside of her cheek to keep from laughing.

Her companion obviously wanted her to laugh as well, because the old lady peered up at her with sparkling blue eyes and a be-dentured grin as she lifted her teacup for inspection. "Do you not, dear? Perhaps you do not see it because you are so young—you haven't perceived as many of them as I have."

Sadie allowed herself a smile. There was no getting around it. "What do you suppose it means that you have a penis in your cup?" she asked softly. It was just the two of them at the table, Sadie having been hired for a private party, but there were still people nearby who might overhear.

The old girl squished her face up—all wrinkles and impish humor. "Well, I hope it means that I'll see one or two more before I leave this earth."

She could no longer hold back; Sadie laughed. It felt

good to laugh, even though some of the ladies present would no doubt look down their noses at her, and call her common for having the gall to enjoy herself when she was here to entertain *them*.

She wiped at her eyes as Mrs. Carbunkle looked pleased with herself, holding the delicate china up in both her arthritic hands. Her large round knuckles were so swollen and disfigured they were actually raised above her fingers, each of which turned outward, giving her hands the appearance of tiny wings. They reminded Sadie of her grandmother's hands.

Maybe that was why she liked the old girl so much.

"Look," Sadie said, leaning closer to point at a clump of leaves near the inner rim of the cup. Mrs. Carbunkle smelled of sweet, powdery roses. "There's your wish. That means it's going to come true soon."

"I knew I could bring Thomas Saybrook up to snuff," the older woman replied gleefully. She set her hand on Sadie's forearm. "Thank you, my dear, for taking the time to entertain an old woman."

Sadie placed her fingers over the gnarled ones and gently squeezed. "Thank *you*, Mrs. Carbunkle."

The elderly woman was to be her last session of the day, so Sadie rose from her chair, stiff from having sat so long, and gathered up her gloves and bag. She made her way across the busy Morris carpet, nodding at the odd lady who deigned to acknowledge her, toward her hostess. She thanked the lady for having her and was demurely thanked in return, and told to see the butler on her way out—no doubt he was to pay her. The lady of the house couldn't be bothered with such vulgarity as the exchange of money.

Sadie didn't need to hold court at these small parties, but she did so because she considered it good advertising. Usually she met one or two ladies—or gentlemen—who had never had their leaves read before, at least not by her. If she impressed them, perhaps they'd tell other people about her or, better yet, bring people to her to have their fortunes told.

God, she couldn't wait until she had her own shop. Then she could set defined hours for readings, keep time free for her private life, and she wouldn't do public readings unless she wanted to. She'd continue to assist Vienne, but that would be it.

Oh, it was going to be lovely to answer to no one but herself. Bloody wonderful.

Having sat for so long, with an endless supply of tea, necessitated that she visit the loo before taking her leave. She stopped a maid and asked for directions and smiled her thanks when given the information. She hurried down the corridor, her knees pressed together in urgency.

She burst through the door to the loo and found herself not alone. "Oh, I beg your pardon."

It was Lady Gosling. She stood in front of the mirror with the collar of her blouse open. She quickly closed the garment, but not before Sadie glimpsed what she'd been examining—a bite mark.

Made by *human* teeth. Had Jack done that? The notion startled her. He had never done such a thing to her—oh, the odd love bite was one thing, but this . . .

Whoever did that had to be very passionate or very cruel. Whatever else his faults, Jack Friday was not cruel, not physically.

"No need to apologize, Madame Moon," the lady replied smoothly, buttoning her collar. "I should have bolted the door. Are you leaving?"

"I am, yes."

"Pity. I wanted to have a visit with you."

"I doubt I'd have anything new to tell you since your last reading." It had only been a few days ago, after all. But that was overstating the obvious, so Sadie didn't say it.

The lady shrugged her slender shoulders. "Perhaps my life has changed since then."

She referred to Jack, of course. That was why Sadie had seen him in Lady Gosling's cup. The two of them were destined to become lovers. And why not? They were both pretty, if not slightly tarnished, people. Sadie had no claim on Jack, nor did she want one. She only wished he had less of an effect on her. If not for him she might have done more than kiss Mason last night when he came home with her. He might not have looked at her with a wry smile, touched his fingers to her temple and asked, "Are you somewhere else?" And when she said no, then asked, "Are you with someone else?"

"Don't be silly," she scolded gently. "There's no one else." And to an extent it was true. In her head there was no one else she wanted to be with but him, but in her heart, she couldn't quite bring herself to go to bed with one man when she was so confused over another.

"Anyway," Lady Gosling said, snapping her back to the here and now, "you look as though you're about to dance a jig. I'll leave you to attend to your needs. Good day." She gave Sadie a long, bewildering look—as though seeing her for the first time and trying to place her face. "By the way, your name—Sadie. It's unusual. Is it derived from anything?"

"Bronach," Sadie heard herself confess, surprisingly. "It means 'sad' so my grandfather jokingly used to call me 'Saddie' as a child. It didn't take long for Sadie to come from that. After he died, I decided to keep the name." Why on earth was she telling this woman all of this? Because she'd asked. No one but Jack had ever asked about her name before.

"Hm," the other woman replied—not much of a reply at all. "How very interesting. Good day, Madame Moon." And then she swept from the room as though she were the queen herself.

Sadie shook her head, bolted the door, and then relieved herself of all thoughts of the odd Lady Gosling as she also relieved her aching bladder. Letting go of thoughts of Jack, however, proved more difficult. This time of year she always thought of him, for so many reasons. Having him so close only made it worse.

She wanted to hate him but she didn't—not completely. She wasn't certain how she felt about him, only that seeing him again had awakened a whole host of feelings, some of which were more pleasant than others. Mostly she was overwhelmed by a great sense of loss and regret.

If only he had taken her with him when he left. How different would their lives be, then? What kind of family would they have had? What kind of adventures? She'd be a wealthy woman—much more than she was now—but Jack wouldn't allow her to read leaves. Funny, but she couldn't imagine letting a man boss her at this point in her life. Couldn't imagine letting anyone boss her about, for that matter.

But then, eleven years ago she couldn't imagine not having children, or being alone at seven and twenty. And here she was. She had a little help, but she had forged a life for herself. She'd survived losing her husband—losing everything—and gone on to build a new life. A life she enjoyed and was proud of. She would do well to remember that the next time Jack Friday called her a fraud.

She would do well to remember it the next time she felt inferior next to a wealthy lady who hadn't done a day's work in her entire life. Or gentleman for that matter. When she first met Jack, he'd bordered on useless. He could hunt to be sure, but if anything needed fixing, it was usually Sadie who knew how to fix it.

But he hadn't been useless in bed, she thought with unexpected whimsy. In all their years apart she'd never met one man who could come close to making her feel desire like Jack had. Although, she had high hopes for Mason.

When she finally arrived back at her own house, Mrs. Charles informed her that a gentleman waited on her in the parlor. This was said with such a twinkle in the old girl's eye, that Sadie's first thought was that it must be Mason. But surely the housekeeper would have mentioned him by name?

Sadie smoothed her palms over her skirts and hair, smoothing some of the day's effect on both. She pinched her cheeks to add some color, knowing she looked tired and pale after such a draining afternoon.

She opened the parlor door to find Indara inside, entertaining their guest. Her friend was brightly clad in a paprika-colored day gown with a crimson underskirt. It was a striking clash of color—one Sadie determined to try herself. Indara was smiling, laughing at a joke her companion told. Sadie smiled at the sight of her friend's joy, but that faded when she realized just who their guest was.

Jack Friday. In her house. Her sanctuary. Looking at Indara as though he'd like to shag her right there on the carpet.

"Who the hell let you in?"

Over the course of their courtship and brief condemnation as man and wife, Jack had, on several occasions, the glorious misfortune of seeing Sadie truly angry. Glorious because she was one of those women who looked both fierce and beautiful when in the midst of a tirade. Misfortunate because often that rage had been directed at him.

Just the sight of her flushed cheeks and glittering faerie eyes was enough to make the bounder in his pants raise its eager noggin. What an article he was, getting horn at the sight of a woman who looked as though she could cheerfully separate his head from his shoulders.

What was she so worked up over? Then it hit him. Aside from hating him, she didn't like seeing him with her friend. With another woman.

*I'll be damned.* Grinning, Jack rose to his feet and bowed. "Madame Moon. A pleasure to see you again." Yes, yes it was, especially now that he saw how far under her skin he was.

"What are you doing here?" she demanded.

The lovely Miss Ferrars, looking confusedly between the two of them, rose to her feet. "I let Mr. Friday in, Sadie. He said you had business to discuss."

Sadie glanced at her friend, but saved her glare for Jack. "I can't imagine we have anything to discuss."

He could. He could imagine plenty, but neither of them would want Miss Ferrars to bear witness. "I thought perhaps I should inquire as to your health since I ruthlessly sawed you in half last night."

She didn't crack a smile. "I've survived worse, I assure you, sir."

It was a good dig, he had to admit. Subtle. No one else would know it was aimed so particularly to wound him. "That is good to know." He glanced at the lovely Miss Ferrars and smiled charmingly. "You missed Sadie's performance at Saint's Row last evening. She was very convincing."

Before the exotic beauty could reply, Sophie intervened, "Indara, would you mind leaving Mr. Friday and me, so we can discuss this 'business' of his?" Her gaze was narrow but no less bright as it locked with Jack's.

"Ours," Jack corrected with a grin, just to needle her. And then to Indara, "Thank you for keeping me company, Miss Ferrars. You brightened an otherwise dreary day."

Indara smiled at him. She really was a beautiful woman, but even her beauty was no match for Sadie's too-long nose and wide mouth. She left them with a polite farewell.

Sadie pounced the moment the door was closed. "What do you mean coming to my house?"

As her husband, it was technically his house too, was it not? But then they'd already decided that they weren't really married, so why bring it up?

"I wanted to speak with you. Surely you've had callers before?"

"You're not welcome here," she retorted hotly. "This is *my* house. Mine!"

Her vehemence destroyed his desire to tease her. In fact, it brought a peculiar ache to his chest, as though she had wrapped the words around a brick and struck him with it.

"Forgive me," he muttered. "I should have sent a card, but I thought you might appreciate seeing me admit to being wrong in person." Now he was the one getting angry.

She stilled—froze with her hands on her rounded hips, drawing his attention to her nipped-in waist. She was like an hourglass wrapped in plum cashmere. It was the most subtle costume he'd seen her wear these past few days.

"Wrong?" Her eyes had lost some of their spark when she looked at him. "What do you mean?"

"I mean that you have your shop."

The changes in her expression were startling. She went from elated—"I do?"—to suspicious. "You're not lying, are you?"

Jack made a face, arms across his chest. "If I was going to lie, it wouldn't be to announce that I made an error. Nor would I offer an apology as I do now."

She pondered that one a moment, searching out his face, he could only assume, for any trace of lie. "No, I suppose not. Thank you, Mr. Friday. You've quite made my day."

Yes, he imagined he had. Not only did she get her shop but she got to crow over him for it. Still, it was worth it to see that smile and know that he was the cause of it. "Consider it a gift."

She arched a fine, high brow. "Now, why would you be giving me a gift?"

"It's the sixth of July," he replied, surprised at how easily it rolled off his tongue. "Happy anniversary."

Her smile and all that wonderful heightened color drained from her cheeks. He supposed he should feel some satisfaction in that, but he didn't. But it did warm him when she placed a hand over her heart, as though the shriveled thing had given her a little jolt.

"You remembered."

Jack scowled—hard. "Of course I remember, Sadie.

How could I forget the happiest day of my life?" He hadn't meant to say that, but her surprise pissed him off. Had her opinion of him sunk so low? What had he done to make her despise him so—other than try to make a better life for both of them?

Her expression was dubious, to say the least. "I would have thought the happiest day was the day you left."

"That was the worst."

"And yet you made it look so easy."

Damn her for sounding so nonchalant, so flippant. "Actually, the worst day was when I came home and discovered my wife had left me."

That killed her dismissive act. Her spine stiffened. "You left me first."

"I told you I'd come back, Sadie." It was true. He remembered his exact words as though he'd said them but a day ago. "I came back. You didn't even leave a forwarding address."

"You were gone for two years, Jack!"

"I sent you money. I sent you letters—many of which you didn't even open because the landlord gave them back to me when I came in and found our empty apartment!" That came out louder than he had intended, but it felt good to shout.

Fists clenched, shoulders forward, she came at him like a harpy ready to claw his eyes out. She stopped short, as though the idea of touching him, even to do violence, appalled her. "Those letters were few and far between in the end. You didn't want me to find you, so how could I know you were really going to come back?"

"Because I promised you I would!" he shouted, his face inches from hers.

They stared at each for what seemed like eternity. "Your promise," she said, voice quivering, "isn't worth the breath used to speak it."

His brow lowered. "You made promises too, Sadie. I assume those weren't worth anything either."

"I kept my promises a lot longer than you, Jack." She spoke through clenched teeth. Her face was so close he could count her eyelashes. He'd forgotten how long they were.

"No," he whispered, "you didn't. Because I came home and you were gone." And there they were, back where they started. She believed he had left her and he believed she left him, and neither seemed to have a convincing enough argument to sway the other.

"I needed you." Her eyes glistened wetly. "I needed you and you weren't there."

A hard lump formed in Jack's throat. "I'm sorry for every day we were apart, Sadie. But I left so we could have a better life. You have to know that."

"What I know is that even though you swore to me that I was more important than your family and money, you jumped at the first chance you had to make a fortune and get away from your inferiorly bred wife."

If she had clocked him with her own boot, he wouldn't have been more shocked. "I never thought you inferior."

"No? You certainly regretted marrying me. You couldn't wait to get away."

"I left because I didn't want you pulling flimflam schemes to make money. I'm rich now, Sadie. Rich. I would have given you anything you wanted."

"My own shop?" she challenged.

"You don't need a shop." As soon as he spoke, he knew he shouldn't have said it, no matter how much he truly meant it.

"Because you think what I do is a 'flimflam' scheme, right?"

Straightening, he threw a hand into the air. "Oh, come on! You don't really believe a person's fate lies in the bottom of a frigging teacup, do you?"

Her mouth tightened and her eyes hardened. "I make a good living doing this, Jack. People make appointments months in advance for my insight."

"Don't you feel the least bit guilty for it?"

She shook her head "No. I do not." Something inside Jack slumped in disappointment. Where had his Sadie gone? What had happened to his darling girl? Was it all his fault? Had marrying him destroyed her sweetness?

"What if I said I did believe that a person's fate could lie in the bottom of a teacup?" she challenged.

Jack couldn't hide his regret. "Then I'd call you a fool."

She smiled—a twisted sad thing that made murky jewels out of her eyes. "Of course I am. I married you, didn't I?"

"Yes," he murmured. "You did." And something in that declaration awakened something deep inside him. Whether it was the tone of her voice or the pained glint in her eye, he didn't know. But something made him reach out and cup his hand around the back of her neck and haul her closer.

Sadie's hands braced against his chest, pushing to no avail. Jack stood his ground. "What are you doing?" she demanded. "Let me go."

"No," came his simple reply as he lowered his head. "Not yet." And then his mouth covered hers. The touch of her lips to his was like waking up from a deep and dreamless sleep. Awareness washed over him, filling him. The flavor of her set his heart pounding and he pressed harder, forcing her to open to him so that he could taste her more deeply, fiercely.

She kissed him back, fingers digging into the wall of his chest. There was nothing soft or gentle or remotely loving about their embrace, and yet it was wonderful in an out of control kind of way.

And then she shoved, breaking their bond and stepping away from him to press the back of her hand to her mouth as though she might wipe all traces of him away.

"Do *not*," she began in a quivering, angry voice, "think that you can leave love bites on Lady Gosling and then presume to make love to me."

Jack's eye brows shot up. "You think I bit Lady Gosling?"

"I know it." The accusation in her gaze was terrible—and hurt.

Jack had never bit a woman in his life. Well, perhaps the odd nibble, but he certainly hadn't done so to Lady

Gosling. It seemed his wife thought him the worst kind of scoundrel.

"I didn't." Why he felt the need to explain himself was a mystery. "Lady Gosling and I aren't lovers, but even if we were, don't you have your artist *friend*?"

"Leave Mason out of this. He's a good man."

Meaning they hadn't slept together. He shouldn't care, but he did. He cared very much, even now when he ought to wipe his hands of this creature and get on with his life.

"But I'm not." Why in God's name did he set himself up like this? He already knew her answer.

"We've been apart a long time, Jack. I can only imagine the legions of lovers you've had over the years."

So only bad men had lovers? If she only knew. But what would be the point? She wouldn't believe anything he said. She didn't want to, and that . . . that made him feel oddly pathetic. The only thing he could do now was leave, while he still had a shred of dignity left.

"You're right," he informed her coolly, as he approached the door. He stopped at the threshold and glanced over his shoulder at her expressionless face. "You *are* a fool."

# Chapter 8

The next few days were almost normal for Sadie. She gave a few private readings, ordered paint, wallpaper, and linens for her shop, went shopping with Indara—whom she finally confided in about her past with Jack—and last night she spent a lovely evening at a salon in Chelsea with Mason and some of his artist friends. She'd stayed out until dawn. It was almost noon and she was still abed, enjoying the feel of the cool sheets against her skin and the surprisingly warm sunshine streaming through the window.

She hadn't seen or heard from Jack at all. In fact, she might have succeeded in not thinking about him at all if not for the kiss. It haunted her beyond reason, sneaking into her thoughts at the worst moments, such as when Mason kissed her good-bye that morning.

It wasn't as though she had never kissed Jack before, but none of those had lingered with her like this, none but the first. She supposed she'd taken his kisses for granted after that, so often she experienced them. It made sense in a way that this one should stick with her. With lips as perfect as his, how could it not?

Damn him, for reminding her of what they'd once shared. Damn herself, for responding as she had. Kissing him had been like a stiff drink on an empty stomach. It had gone straight to her head, and afterward left her feeling slightly dizzy and queasy.

What was wrong with her that she could react to him with such enthusiasm after he abandoned her? How could she be so weak? He insulted her, proved to her that he never believed in her—and she had clung to him like ivy to stone. Thank God she'd come to her senses and pushed him away before things could go further than a kiss.

And it would have gone further, of that she had no doubt. She would have taken him to her bed and kept him there until neither of them could move. It would have been amazing, and she would have hated herself for it come morning. Not just for succumbing to his kisses, but giving herself to a man who thought the worst of her.

As for Jack, he would probably have no qualms about sleeping with a woman who thought the worst of him. It was obvious that both of them blamed the other for the failing of their marriage. It was also obvious that neither of them was willing to accept that blame.

And why should she when she'd done nothing wrong?

A knock at her door thankfully kept her thoughts from venturing any further into unwanted territory. It was a beautiful morning and she would not allow thoughts of Jack to ruin it.

Indara slipped into the room, bright and summery in a bottle green day gown. "Finally, you are awake. Did you have a good evening?"

Sadie pushed herself upright, resting against the headboard. "I did." She noticed the letter in her friend's hand. "Is that for me?"

Immediately the slim package was offered to her. "It's from Ireland. I thought you would want it straightaway."

Her fingers trembled a little as Sadie took the letter and saw the familiar scrawl of Mr. Brown, the earl's secretary. The old man couldn't even write a letter on his own. "You were right. Thank you for bringing it up."

Indara nodded. She stood there a moment, watching with unveiled curiosity, obviously waiting for Sadie to open the missive and share its contents. As much as Sadie wanted to tear into it, she didn't want to share. Had no intention of sharing something that concerned such a private part of her past.

Her friend took the hint seemingly without offense. "I'll have breakfast sent up."

Sadie thanked her with a sincere smile, waiting until the door was closed once more to open the letter. It was short and to the point:

*Mrs. Moon: Thank you for your recent letter. The information was much appreciated and has been taken under consideration.*

Under consideration? What the hell did that mean? She balled the letter between her palms and tossed it in the bin beside her writing desk. What else could she expect? She'd done what she thought was the right thing by writing Jack's grandfather because the old man had been surprisingly kind to her at the time when she'd desperately needed kindness. But the Earl of Garret had never liked her much and approved of her even less.

She'd done what her conscience required, she allowed as she tossed back the covers and slipped out of bed. Whatever the earl did with it was up to him. She fulfilled her part of their arrangement and now she could wash her hands of the situation. She had more important things to occupy her thoughts and time, such as preparations for her shop. Now that she knew it was finally going to be hers, there was much work to be done.

She shrugged into a silky orange wrapper and sat down at her vanity. She hadn't braided her hair before bed and it was a tangled mess. She was still brushing the knots out when her breakfast tray arrived. She paused in her toilette long enough to eat her toast and drink a cup of coffee. She nursed a second cup as Petra helped her dress.

Just over an hour later she walked into her shop on Bond Street and began the task of making note of what needed to be done first. She'd made several similar lists in the past, but now that the papers were signed and the property was officially hers, she wanted to start fresh.

She had just finished jotting down how many teapots, cups, and saucers she would need and a note to buy a variety of china patterns, when the door opened. Her head jerked up at the intrusion, but any annoyance fast turned to pleasure as her gaze fell upon Mason's handsome face.

"I hope that smile's for my benefit," he said as the door closed behind him.

Sadie's lips curved even further as they moved toward one another. "I suppose it must be. I didn't expect to see you this afternoon."

"The surprise is a pleasant one, I hope?"

"Of course."

They met in the middle of the floor and Mason, mindful of the large window through which anyone might see them, settled for kissing her cheek rather than her mouth as Sadie hoped he would. Perhaps he could erase the lingering taste of Jack upon her lips.

She should feel more guilt for having kissed that bloody scoundrel with a man such as Mason paying court to her, but all she felt was annoyance.

"So," Mason arched a dark brow as he glanced around the open space, "is this large enough to host your legion of followers?"

Sadie rolled her eyes. "I would hardly refer to them as legion, but no. I rather hope that it's not large enough and that a table here is in constant demand. I want to turn ladies away in droves."

He smiled at her determined tone. "And you will. That far wall has no windows. A perfect canvas for a mural."

Sadie's heart skipped a beat. Mason's paintings were in demand among the elite, and he charged them a fortune for them. To have his work—an original—displayed on her wall would be a coup in itself, but to have him paint the *entire* wall . . .

"I cannot afford your fee," she said lightly, but it was true. She would never be able to afford him.

He slid her a sideways glance, full of amusement and something else—heat. "I'm sure we can work out some form of compensation."

She smiled, but a knot of unease tightened in her stomach. Was it lying not to tell him about Jack? Mason had never asked about her past, nor had he offered information about his. They were simply two adults who enjoyed each other's company, working toward something more intimate. Surely she didn't need to complicate that?

"The location is excellent," he commented, seemingly oblivious to her discomfort. Once again, his ebony gaze took in the entirety of the space. "I suspect you will do quite well here, luv. Quite well indeed."

She preened at his prophecy. "From your lips . . ." She didn't finish, because that's when his gaze dropped noticeably to linger on her mouth. He slipped one arm around her waist and pulled her toward the kitchen entrance, where they couldn't be seen by passersby.

"I'm going to kiss you now," he informed her with that rakish grin of his.

"I'm going to let you," she replied with a smile of her own. And then he did kiss her and for a moment he did erase all thought of that *other* kiss. Here was a man who enjoyed her. Respected her. Mason Blayne was the kind of man who didn't give himself lightly, because once committed he gave himself wholly. He would never run away from her to prove himself to a miserable old man. He would never call her a fraud.

So why didn't his kiss make her feel as though she was slowly melting inside?

Later, after they'd broken apart and talked some more about her plans, those thoughts continued to haunt Sadie, and she finally gave voice to them.

"Mason, you believe in what I do, don't you?"

He glanced over his shoulder at her from where he stood, measuring the wall he intended to use as his canvas. "I've seen you be right enough not to doubt your ability."

It wasn't quite the declaration she'd hoped for, but it was good enough.

"Although," he amended, bringing a slight slump to her spine as he jotted down the numbers on a small pad, "I believe our destinies are what we make them. Human nature is often changeable despite our predilection for the predictable."

Sadie silently sighed in frustration. Was the problem with her, and the kind of man she was drawn to, or was it merely that men in general had no imagination? No romance in their souls, nor hope that there might be a plan for every living being?

"I don't just make predictions for the future," she informed him. "Sometimes I discover a person's past without ever having any knowledge of it."

He slipped the pad and pencil inside his coat. "I'm sure you do." He didn't move, but she could almost hear a shrug in his words—the mark of a man who knew when to keep his opinions to himself, but wasn't quite talented enough to conceal them entirely. "I assume you will be reading at Madame La Rieux's soiree this evening?"

Bollocks. She'd almost forgotten. Sadie glanced at the watch brooch pinned to her lapel. If she left now she'd have enough time to visit the drapers and china shop before returning home to prepare for the evening.

"You forgot, didn't you?" Amusement lit Mason's fathomless eyes, erasing any displeasure she might have felt toward him.

Her smile was sheepish. "I did, yes. And now I must attend to some business before returning home. You will excuse me, won't you?"

He took one of her hands in his, gently massaging her fingers. His flesh was warm against hers, his touch soothing. A tiny spark of guilt blossomed in her gut for enjoying it. "On the proviso that you will allow me to accompany you to Saint's Row tonight."

A coy smile curved her lips as she vanquished any accusations of being an unfaithful wife from her mind. "Of course. I'll be ready at eight."

"Excellent. I understand the famous Jack Friday will be in attendance. I look forward to making his acquaintance."

All the moisture evaporated from Sadie's mouth. "Why?" She rasped, her heart pounding despite there being no way Mason could possibly know about her and Jack.

"He's expressed interest in my work. I'm in hopes that he'll commission something."

"I don't believe he plans to remain in London for long." And why hadn't she realized Jack would be at Vienne's that evening? She should have made an excuse not to attend. The idea of introducing Mason to him made her stomach clench most uncomfortably.

"Then perhaps he'll buy a painting I've completed. I do have a couple that you posed for. You said before that you wouldn't object to me selling them."

Sadie managed a stiff smile. "Of course not."

She hadn't the nerve to tell him not to get his hopes up. Jack Friday would no more buy a painting of her then he would have his tea leaves read.

Never.

When Jack walked into Saint's Row that evening, heads turned. During his short time in London he had caused something of a stir. It was completely unintentional, but he had something of a reputation as a man who knew how to make money, which made gentlemen seek his acquaintance. And he had been charming and flirtatious enough that the ladies sought him out as well. He took a certain pride in having attracted this much attention based on his own merit. If society knew who he really was, they would have kowtowed to him immediately, and where was the pleasure in that?

But there was one person who knew who he truly was and didn't give a rat's arse. He could be the king of bloody Persia, and Sadie would still look at him as though he was dog shite on her bootheels.

He could lie to himself and say that anticipation of

her presence at tonight's affair had nothing to do with his impeccable appearance, but why bother? Despite their history, there was part of her that was still attracted to him, just as he was to her, and he had no qualms in exploiting that. He wanted her despite knowing that it would be best for both of them to stay away.

There was no rational explanation for the thoughts squirming around in his head, so for at least tonight he was going to stop trying to explain.

He'd taken great care in getting ready. His black evening attire fit perfectly. A lot of hard work had given him this physique and he was proud of it, rather than ashamed as most noblemen would be. He carried himself straight, making the most of his good height. His jaw was smooth, his hair perfect.

And Sadie was nowhere to be seen as he entered the spacious, but still intimate salon. Soft lights glowed from polished brass sconces lining every wall, warming the creamy walls. Delicate plasterwork added an extra touch of distinction, along with rich, dark blue drapes and matching furniture. The carpet was plush beneath his feet, vines of the same blue, green, and a vibrant wine entwining on the pale background.

Groups of people clustered throughout the room, the men all clad in black, the odd touch of color in their cravat or waistcoat, while the ladies fluttered like exotic birds in every color conceivable. Surely there were hues there Jack couldn't even begin to name.

The air was scented with perfumes and colognes, some heavier than others, but a cool breeze from several open windows kept the room fresh, and kept the guests from wilting under the heat of so many bodies.

La Rieux greeted him—an odd mix of fire and ice with her bright hair and ivory skin. She wore a golden gown that bared her shoulders and nipped in her already small waist. For some reason she put him in mind of a phoenix, rising from the ashes.

"Monsieur Friday, how delightful to see you again."

He rather doubted that, but she sounded sincere, so he had to respect her as a liar. Jack smiled his most charming smile, and was rewarded with a surprised blink from the lady. She wasn't the only one who knew how to lie. "Madame La Rieux, the pleasure is all mine. Thank you for inviting me."

They chatted for a moment, business easing the tension between them. The lady was very excited about her plans to open a large shopping center geared toward aristocratic females where they could not only visit the finest clothiers, but purchase gloves, hats, and even some household items—all of the best quality.

"Shall I expect to see an effigy of you burned in the streets this Guy Fawkes night?" Jack inquired, only in slight jest. Last year on that date, shopkeepers in Bayswater had done just that to one William Whiteley, a linen draper who dared have the foresight to see the "Universal Provider" as the way of the future. Scared of this modern way of thinking, his competitors had protested against him all day, the charivari culminating in the burning of Whiteley's effigy in a bonfire on Portobello Road. Of course Jack hadn't been in the country to witness the event, but he'd certainly heard about it.

Trystan seemed to think the demonstration a sign that they were on the right track. Something that attracted that sort of attention *had* to be good business.

La Rieux smiled at him, her eyes bright as jewels. "I hope so, monsieur. I hope so!"

Damnation. She and Trystan might despise one another, but they were the same when it came to commerce. Perhaps hate wasn't what they felt for each other at all. Competition could be misconstrued as many things, after all. So could lust.

Another guest arrived, so Jack took his leave and went in search of a drink. A young footman was all too happy to pour two fingers of scotch into a tumbler for him, and he sipped the fine whiskey as his gaze lazily took in every detail around him.

"God must like me after all."

Jack turned at the familiar voice. Standing just to his left was Lady Gosling, a sultry vision in an oddly demure green gown that matched her eyes. She was smiling at him in that open manner women used to let a man know she was interested, but that she wasn't about to make a fool of herself for him.

"Must He?" Jack asked, brow rising with vaguely mocking interest. He couldn't see any signs of the "bite" Sadie accused him of inflicting, but that didn't mean it wasn't there.

The lady returned his amusement. "Yes, because He sent you here to keep me from dying of chronic monotony." She swept her champagne flute in a wide arc.

"Look at them. They're as interesting as pudding."

He took a drink of scotch. "Pudding can be interesting, if used properly."

She didn't blush, of course not. But she smiled in a manner that could only be described as *inviting*. "Clearly I've been deprived."

"Clearly." Flirtation dictated that he respond with an offer to advance her education on the subject, but he couldn't quite bring himself to do just that. She was beautiful, experienced, and obviously willing to shag him senseless—and yet something made him hold back.

The lady did not miss his lack of enthusiasm. "You are not yourself tonight, sir. I hope I've done nothing to offend?"

Why did women always assume a man's ill temper had to do with them? More often Jack's ire was directed at his own shortcomings rather than anyone else's. "What could *you* possibly do that would offend me?" He meant it to sound teasing, but it came out a little harsher than he intended, sounding more like an insult. She caught that as well, blinking in surprise and, yes, hurt. He saw a brief flicker of it before she covered it with an arch expression. "I could call you an insufferable boor, but I doubt the truth would offend you either."

She was quick, he'd give her that. Jack chuckled at the well-aimed barb. "Touché, my lady. Apologies for my loutish behavior. It has nothing to do with your charming self."

She seemed to relax a little then, and Jack realized just how much he enjoyed her company, sexual tension

aside. He simply didn't want to shag her. He didn't want
to shag anyone, except Sadie. So why not do just that?
Maybe that would fix him once and for all. Or maybe
it would make things worse. He didn't know and he
didn't care.

"Ah," Lady G spoke after a brief silence. "I see Madame
Moon and Mr. Blayne have arrived."

Jack affected his best bored expression as he turned
to look where she was staring. The first person he saw
was Blayne. The artist had an exotic look about him
that women tended to find appealing. Artists never had
any trouble garnering female attention; their reputation
for being wild and untamable appealing to a woman's
inner gamekeeper.

The notion of this man poaching on his wife made
Jack want to do a little hunting himself. He wondered
how Blayne would look with a bullet between his swarthy
brows.

But then his attention shifted to the woman on Blayne's
arm, and he forgot all about the artist. He forgot his
own name.

Sadie was talking to La Rieux, so she didn't notice his
appraisal, which was undoubtedly for the best. Wouldn't
be advantageous to be seen with one's eyes bulging and
tongue lolling like a thirsty hound.

She wore a gown of rich violet silk that gave her pale
skin a luminescent quality. Her shoulders were bare,
framed by tiny cap sleeves. The snug bodice lifted and
displayed her breasts in a seductive yet discreet manner
that made a man fantasize about holding those curves

in his palms. Only in his case it was a memory, not a fantasy. He could even remember the exact shade of her nipples, the way they hardened under his touch. He knew just how slight her waist was without the benefit of a corset, how lush her hips. He recalled the fullness of her bottom, the firm grip of her thighs. God help him, he remembered the first time between those long legs, trembling as he eased inside her, so desperate to plunge as far as he could but terrified of hurting her. Hurting the most beautiful girl he'd ever known. It had hurt her anyway, virgin that she was, and the guilt had damn near killed him.

So intense was that memory, and all the sensations that came with it, that Jack's breath caught as sudden pain gripped his chest, squeezing as though it sought to kill him then and there.

It was at that exact and precise moment that his gaze locked with Sadie's. He couldn't recover fast enough to keep the past from showing in his eyes—and hers widened in response. She saw everything, and all he could do was look away—too late.

Now she knew how much he had loved her. How much he had missed her. How empty he'd been without her. How bloody stupid could he be to reveal so much?

He didn't care how long Tryst wanted him to remain in England. He was going to write to his friend and partner in the morning and tell him he was leaving by the week's end. Unfinished business, be damned. Tryst could come home and take care of it himself.

"They make a striking couple, do they not?" Lady

Gosling inquired. "She's so pale and fey looking while he has the appearance of a heathen Gypsy."

He didn't have to ask to whom she referred. God was having a colossal laugh at his expense with this evening. "Yes," he growled. "Very striking." He'd like to strike Blayne until he bled from the ears.

She turned and glanced up at him, her smile draining away. "Good lord. Are you quite all right?"

"I'm fine." He tossed back the remainder of his drink. It wasn't nearly enough.

"You don't look *fine*."

Jack grimaced, the whiskey still burning. Madness seized his mind, driving out all sense or thought of decorum. "I'd like to shag you, Lady Gosling. What do you say to that?"

She actually shivered, like he was being sensual rather than crass. "I say, lead on, Mr. Friday."

Need, hot and vicious, rose within him. It wasn't for the woman standing in front of him, but it would have to do. If he didn't shag someone right now he'd never shag anyone again. His prick would simply wither and die, pining for Sadie Moon.

He could have tossed her over his shoulder and stomped off with her like a savage, but he still had some control over himself. He offered her his arm instead, which she took with an eager grip. He had taken but one step when they were stopped by none other than *Lord* Gosling.

"My dear," the older man drawled with a bitter glance at Jack. "They're about to start the auction. Come, so I might indulge your whim."

It might have been uttered to sound loving, but Jack heard the threat beneath the polite veneer, and he felt the tremor in Lady Gosling's hand just before she released his arm. "Of course, my lord. Mr. Friday, may I introduce my husband, Lord Gosling?"

Jack offered his hand and the baron looked at it as though it was smeared with feces. It was a cut of the most direct kind—the kind that drove Jack's temper into territory even more foul. The kind that made him want to reveal his true name, his true lineage, to this decrepit, crooked-toothed vampire and tell the baron to kiss his Irish arse.

He said nothing, of course. He merely dropped his hand and said, "A pleasure, *obviously*."

Baron Gosling sneered at him before seizing his wife by the arm and hauling her away. A few people watched the drama with interest. Most pretended not to notice.

Sadie noticed. Jack knew because he caught her staring for a split second before she jerked her gaze away. Jack set his glass on a passing footman's tray and took a full champagne flute in exchange. It wasn't as strong as what he needed, but it would do for now.

He hadn't known there was going to be an auction, but then he hadn't been formally invited; La Rieux had issued his invitation in person. At first he'd thought she'd done it out of some sense of duty, but now he realized she'd only wanted him there for his purse.

And now she was ringing a small bell to get everyone's attention.

"*Bon soir*, my friends," La Rieux said loudly, and the room quieted. "I want to thank you all for coming to my little gathering tonight to raise funds for The Saint Agnes House of the Magdalene for Wayward Girls and Women."

Jack raised his brows. La Rieux raising money for prostitutes and abused servants? His curiosity about her—formally null—rose a notch, as did his respect.

"First up for auction is a special treat. My dear friend, the talented Sadie Moon, has offered up a private *one hour* reading to the highest bidder. I'm sure you all know what an amazing opportunity this is. One hour to have all your questions answered, your path divined. Who will start the bidding at twenty pounds?"

Jack drained his champagne and grabbed another. Damn, but he'd spent much of his time in England either drunk or trying to get there. Of course Sadie would have to be up for auction. And of course the crowd would have to love it. And of course there would have to be a flurry of bidding.

People were stupid. If he told them he could piss on a plate and divine the future from it, they'd probably believe him.

Mason Blayne bid fifty pounds. Scowling, Jack looked at the man and saw the gleam in his eyes as he looked at Sadie. Jack knew that look and he knew what Blayne intended to do with that hour—and it wasn't get his leaves read.

Later, he'd blame it on the champagne and scotch not quite mixing properly, but that was when he felt something snap inside him.

No man was going to pay for the pleasure of shagging

*his* wife. If anyone was going to buy Sadie, it was going to be him.

"One hundred quid!" he shouted.

Heads turned at his outburst. A little cheer went up. He didn't know who looked more surprised, La Rieux or Sadie herself, but Jack didn't waste his time looking at them. He raised his glass at Blayne, who frowned.

"One hundred twenty," the artist called out.

"Two hundred!" Jack grinned at his own recklessness.

"Two hundred fifty," Blayne countered, a fierce glint in his eyes.

All eyes turned to him. "Will you bid, Mr. Friday?" La Rieux asked. Clearly she doubted his commitment.

Jack straightened his spine and stepped forward, putting himself at the front of the room with the other players in his little drama. His gaze locked with Sadie's. He saw bewilderment in her faerie eyes. Defiance too. Oh, and a tiny spark of anticipation. That tiny spark was all it took.

He grinned. "One thousand pounds."

Sadie looked as though she might faint. La Rieux seemed torn between her dislike of him and her joy at raising such a sum for her cause. Her head whipped toward Blayne, who shook his head. The artist's hands, Jack noticed, were balled into fists at his sides. Jack sympathized. He'd felt the same when he lost Sadie.

"One thousand pounds it is," La Rieux announced, looking a little shocked by the entire affair. "Once. Twice. Sold!"

The applause of the gathering was thunderous. Voices rose above the din, but Jack ignored it. His gaze was fastened on his prize. He strode purposefully toward her, forcing himself to look every inch the gentleman, while inside he let the savage crow in delight. She knew him well enough to be wary as he stopped before her.

He bowed to her, fixing his lips in a lopsided grin meant to present him as little more than a charming scoundrel. Only he knew the smile didn't reach his eyes and that Sadie saw his intention there.

She glanced at the book in his hand and licked her lips. "I'm afraid you overestimate my powers, Mr. Friday," she said somewhat hoarsely, "but your generosity is quite astounding."

"And you undervalue yourself, madame," he replied with surprising ease. Glancing over her shoulder he saw Blayne standing a few feet away, glaring at him. Jack acknowledged the other man with a slight nod before crossing to a small table obviously set out for patrons to write their drafts. He quickly filled out the cheque, his fingers trembling damnably as he wrote.

He must be out of his damn mind.

Once she gleefully had his draft in hand, La Rieux moved on to the next auction and the crowd no longer cared about Jack and Sadie, but Mason Blayne cared. That was obvious from the dark expression on the artist's face as Jack offered his arm to Sadie.

"How about it, Madame Moon?" he asked with his most charming smile. "Ready to read my leaves?"

# Chapter 9

The evening had quickly spiraled out of control. Sadie kept a smile fixed on her face as curious spectators watched them, craning their necks to hear their conversation.

"You are very generous indeed, Mr. Friday," she said with false tranquility. "But I would not dream of denying Madame La Rieux my assistance with the auction, nor these fine people of your company. Perhaps you would care to make an appointment?" It was the right thing to say, even though she wanted to yank him into a private room and tear into him for embarrassing her so!

"Of course," he replied, equally as calm and false. "At your earliest convenience."

Of course she saw that for the lie it was. Something had gotten him riled up and he wouldn't rest until he let it out; she'd known it the minute their eyes met—saw all the emotion in his gaze that tonight would not end gently. His feelings for her were just as jumbled as hers for him, and Jack had never been quite as proficient as keeping things bottled up as she.

A thousand pounds? How the devil could he afford such a sum? Had he truly become so wealthy that he could toss it away so easily? Or was this all about proving something to her? He should know she wasn't impressed by money—and never had been.

But she had to admit that part of her *was* impressed that he'd paid so much for her. Oh, he'd no doubt done it to embarrass Mason, but still. It warmed her more than it should have.

She'd have some explaining to do to Mason later, however. What the bloody hell would she tell him? She could no doubt lie in a manner he'd believe, but had the damage been done? A man had his pride, after all.

As if on cue, Mason chose that moment to approach them, giving Sadie no option but to introduce them and watch them posture.

Jack offered his hand first, along with a grin that was as mocking as it was charming. "Mr. Blayne, I'm a great admirer of your work. You will forgive my competitiveness, I hope? It is for charity, and all that."

Mason, gentleman that he was, accepted both hand and words with a graceful nod of his head. "Of course, Mr. Friday. The lovely Madame Moon has read my leaves in the past and I'm certain she'll have the opportunity to read them again. No need for me to be greedy. It is, as you say, for charity, after all."

They just stood there, taking each other's measure whilst trying to look disinterested. She could knock both their heads together for being so foolish.

"Oh, Mason, look!" she cried overenthusiastically.

"Vienne's about to start bidding for your painting. This should get people loosening their purse strings!"

That seemed to placate the artist somewhat, and he moved away from Jack to stand next to Sadie instead. Only then did Jack move to her other side, so that she was flanked by the two of them like cucumber between two slices of bread. She could just walk away from both of them, but she didn't.

Jack surprised her by bidding on Mason's painting. Mason was obviously surprised as well, casting a suspicious glance Jack's way. Ultimately the painting went to another buyer, which made Jack look all the better. He hadn't gone out of his way to win the painting as he had Sadie, but his bids made the other bidder climb higher, and the winning bid was indeed a large sum.

In fact, Jack bid on several items throughout the evening, helping Vienne's auction raise much more money. Sadie knew her husband well enough to know his sudden philanthropic behavior wasn't just out of the goodness of his heart. By bidding on other items, he diminished the fact that the only thing he'd actually won was her. It didn't change that he had humiliated her, but it softened it somewhat. Her reputation just might escape relatively unscathed.

Just when she thought him without conscience, he did this. Why? What was the motive behind it all?

As the evening wore on, the situation began to wear on her as well, until Sadie was certain she was going to drive herself mad with all these questions. She should just demand answers from Jack, but that would no doubt only make things worse. Besides, he was off being the social butterfly that he was, flitting from group to group, sometimes with Lady Gosling hanging off him, but more often without.

She shouldn't care who he was with, but she did. She cared about that even more than she cared that Mason had drifted away from her. He stayed with her after Jack wondered off, but shortly after that—once he was certain he'd vanquished the competition?—he went off to talk to some of his friends who were in attendance. In his defense, he had asked Sadie to join him, but she'd refused with the excuse that she had her own people to see, but that was a blatant lie. She didn't feel like talking to anyone. And now, sometime later, she felt even less like it with her mind on fire as it was. What she wanted—what she needed—was a little peace and quiet before she exploded.

She stopped a footman and asked him to have a pot of tea and a small plate of sandwiches sent to one of the small, more private salons. Once that was arranged, she sought out Vienne and told her where she would be.

"I just need a few moments alone," she replied when her friend expressed concern. "Half an hour at most, just to collect myself."

Vienne smiled knowingly. "I will keep the tomcats from sniffing after you."

Sadie winced slightly at the comparison, and squeezed Vienne's hand in thanks before making her exit. As she moved away from the heat and noise, she immediately began to feel some relief. Out of that stuffy room the air was cooler, the sound of chatter muffled. She rubbed the tender muscles of her neck as her footsteps fell softly on the floor.

The footman waited just outside the blue salon. As she approached, he bowed shallowly at the waist. "Tea and sandwiches, Madame Moon, just as you requested."

Sadie smiled at him. "Thank you. You may go."

Another bow and he took his leave. Sadie entered the small, opulent salon greeted by the fragrant steam of hot tea. It made her mouth water, as did the sight of the small plate heaped with a variety of soft, plump sandwiches. There was enough there for two people. Two cups as well. It made her feel alone.

She'd barely stripped off the first of her gloves before she heard the door close. Sadie whirled around, and her heart jumped into her throat at the sight of Jack sliding the bolt. The sound of it echoed through the room like a hammer striking a nail.

"Have you lost all your manners since you left, Jack Farrington?" she demanded, palm pressed to her chest. "What the hell are you thinking? If anyone saw you—"

"No one saw. Not even your watchdog La Rieux." Jack turned, and this time Sadie's heart didn't jump—it couldn't move at all. His face was a mask of anguish, his lips tight in that way that told her he was chewing the inside of his mouth. She hadn't seen that look on his face since the death of his mother.

"Do you . . ." His brows pulled together. "Do you remember the first time we made love?"

Immediately she was defensive. Did he think she could ever forget? Yet, he didn't seem to be looking for a fight. He couldn't even look her in the eye. No, it wasn't a fight he wanted.

"Yes," she replied in little more than a whisper. "I remember."

"Good." Now he looked at her, jaw tight. "Because I can't seem to think of anything else."

How was she to respond to that? "It's because we left so much unsaid. It makes sense that all those things would haunt us now."

"Haunt." He made a noise in the back of his throat—like a growl. "That's a good way to put it. You haunt me."

Sadie took a step toward him. "Jack—"

He held up his hand, scowling. "I can't sleep. I can't think. I can't even fuck." His harsh tone made the word all the more guttural. "You've totally unmanned me."

This should not make her as happy as it did, but she was so buoyed by his words her feet felt as though they might leave the ground. "You haven't . . . you haven't *been* with Lady Gosling?"

He glared at her. "No. I can't *be* with anyone because it feels like I'm being unfaithful. To *you*."

She had to dig her toes into the carpet lest she float away. "Do you think it's been any easier for me?" She pointed at the door. "Mason Blayne wants to court me and all I can think about is that he doesn't kiss like you. You and your bloody sweet kisses have ruined everything!"

Like a big cat, he lunged into the room. "You've ruined *me*."

They stared at each other for what seemed an age. Sadie's chest heaved with the force of each breath. She was so angry. So happy and sad at the same time. So restless. What did they do now?

She knew what she wanted to do. It was the wrong thing. It would only make things worse, and yet she wanted it more than anything she'd ever wanted in her entire life. Even more than she wanted her shop.

"Jack," she murmured, moving toward him with stiff, uncertain steps. "Jack o'the mornin'."

His frown eased at her thick Irish. "Sadiemoon, what are you about, lass?"

They were old words, often spoken long ago, but her heart remembered them oh-so sweetly.

Yes, she knew what she wanted. She didn't speak. She simply closed the distance between them and unfastened the buttons of his jacket. He stood still as a statue, watching her as she slid her hands inside.

His torso was solid beneath her palms. Warmth permeated the fine lawn of his shirt and brocade waistcoat. She could feel the muscle there as her hands moved up his ribs, stopping when they reached the right spot. Then, with just the right amount of pressure—something else she would never forget—she dug her fingers in and wiggled them.

His entire body jumped. Hands seized hers, but not before she got what she wanted—his smile. His laughter. So very ticklish was her husband.

Creases ran down his cheeks, fanning out from his eyes as they squeezed shut. Big, white teeth flashed in the tan of his face as laughter burst forth. Shamefully she had forgotten that sound and how much she loved it. Hearing it now was like opening a window on her soul and letting the sun in after too many dark nights.

It was like opening a dam inside her. Tears filled her eyes and spilled hotly down her cheeks. "I missed you," she rasped. "I missed you so damn much."

"God, Sadie." He cupped her face with his palms, resting his forehead against hers. "It's been so long."

Her hands clutched at his back as she nuzzled her nose against his. "But it doesn't feel it."

"Don't cry." He wiped her tears with his thumbs, lifting his head enough to gaze down at her. "I missed you too."

That only made the tears come faster. She wanted to tell him everything—why she hadn't been there when he came back. Wanted to share with him those dark days that had fallen upon her shortly after he left. But what good would it do? It wouldn't change anything. It would only bring those awful memories back, and make him feel worse than he already did.

They couldn't turn back time, no matter how badly both of them might wish it.

"I don't hate you," she confessed, recalling the awful words she'd said that night in the garden. "I wanted to, but I never could."

"Sshh. I know." His lips found her damp cheek, near her eye. "I know." His mouth was so soft and warm against her skin, tasting her tears. And when he claimed her lips with his, she could taste the salt there, along with champagne.

Sadie tightened her arms around Jack, pressed herself against him as she lost herself to his kiss. It was undoubtedly wrong, but it felt so very, very right. She opened her mouth to his tongue, meeting it with her own. His fingers tightened on the back of her head, as though he feared she might pull away. But she wasn't going anywhere.

He caught her lower lip between his teeth, sucking gently before kissing her deeply once more. Moaning softly, Sadie melted against him, like butter over hot bread. Every inch of her was alive and tingling—some more than others. Through her skirts she felt the hard length of his erection pressing against her. Oh, God. How she had missed the feel of him!

They moved as one, stumbling and swaying. Sadie had no idea where they were going until she felt the hard edge of something dig into her just below her bottom. The sofa, she thought.

Jack's hands left her face and came down to her hips. She lifted her own arms to his neck to give him better access. He gripped her firmly and lifted—as though she weighed next to nothing—so that she now sat on the back of the well-padded sofa.

Then he broke the kiss.

For a moment, she thought he meant to end things there, but he didn't move away. Didn't say a word. He just stood there, staring into her eyes as he lowered his hands to the fabric of skirts and started bunching it upward. She could stop him. She should stop him, but she didn't.

At her knee he slipped his hands beneath the froth of silk and slid fingers and palms up her legs, over her garters to the naked flesh above. If only she'd had the forethought not to wear drawers.

Her skirts were at the top of her thighs now, his hands buried beneath. Breath caught in Sadie's throat as one curious set of fingers slid between her legs to the damp cotton there. Still he didn't look away as he found the slit in the undergarments and eased his fingers inside.

Sadie shuddered, her eyes drifting closed for one excruciatingly delightful second as Jack touched her where she most wanted his touch. Light, like the brush of butterfly wings, he grazed his fingers through the moist curls, awakening her sensitive flesh.

"Open your eyes," he demanded, his voice little more than a whisper.

Sadie did as he commanded, lifting her gaze to his and holding it there as his wonderful fingers parted the lips of her sex to stroke and tease. She could feel how wet she was, knew she was bound to become wetter still and she didn't care. She was shameless at that moment, even going so far as to open her thighs further for his delicious exploration.

He found her magic spot—that little knot of flesh that stiffened and spasmed with delight at his touch. Gasping, she dug her fingers into his shoulders and arched her back, lifting her pelvis to his hand.

Jack's eyes brightened. His high cheekbones flushed

ever so slightly as his lips—those sinful lips—parted. With his thumb he strummed her, sliding one long finger down to easily slip inside.

"Oh!" How could she be quiet at such a moment? It was impossible.

His free hand slid behind to grasp her bottom, helping her keep her seat on the sofa, and also holding her exactly where he wanted as his finger stroked her deep inside, crooking upward, awakening all kinds of the most wonderful aches and sensations.

"Still responsive," he murmured, a smug but gentle smile tilting his mouth.

Sadie's head fell back as the pleasure between her thighs blossomed to something much richer. "Still talented," she gasped. "Oh, *Jack* . . ."

She came then. In a great, shuddering quake. Mouth open, eyes shut, holding on to him with all her strength as she lost all control of her body. It was glorious.

When she regained her senses, she lifted her head and opened her eyes to find him watching her still, that self-satisfied expression still on his face. Only he had unfastened his trousers while she recovered, and was stroking the hard, thick length of his cock as though he had all the time in the world.

Sadie licked her lips. "Is that for me?" It felt so good not to hide her eagerness. They had lost their virginity to one another, had learned and taught and shared. They had discovered all the beauty of each other's bodies without embarrassment or shame and they had delighted in it. To do any less now would be a lie.

And there had already been enough lies between them.

Chuckling, Jack removed his hand so that she could reach down and caress the silky heat of him. He groaned as she squeezed. "All yours," he replied, eyes sparkling.

Sadie grinned, tugging gently. He moved closer, until she felt the blunt head nudge against her still eager flesh. He shivered, broad shoulders twitching. And then he pushed, cleaving her wetness with one easy thrust, burying himself inside her as deep as she could take him.

For a second, time stopped as Sadie adjusted to being so filled. Her muscles flexed and danced around him, as though her entire body recognized him and welcomed him home. One of his hands pressed against her back as the other slid beneath her right thigh, lifting and holding her leg around him.

Sadie wrapped one arm around his shoulders, pushing his jacket aside so she could feel the heat of his skin through his shirt. Her other hand went to his cheek, where golden stubble on his strong jaw pricked her palm. Her thumb rested familiarly in the shallow cleft of his chin. Her gaze locked once more with his as slowly, teasingly, he began to move inside her.

"My fine and lovely Jack," she whispered.

He grimaced and she chuckled. He always winced when she called him "lovely" or "beautiful" even though secretly she thought he liked it.

"Sweet Sadie," he replied, withdrawing. "You still don't know when to stop talking."

She smiled, sighing as he filled her and withdrew once

more. "You always liked it when I talked, especially when I said things like, *harder, Jack. Faster.*"

He cut off her teasing with a blistering kiss that curled her toes so hard her slippers threatened to fall off. He pulled her chest against his, shoved his cock deep, to the hilt inside her, and began thrusting with a rhythm that had her panting against his mouth.

Sadie hooked her other leg around his and tangled her fingers in his short, thick hair. The taste of him filled her mouth, the smell of him filled her nostrils, and the length of him drove her to the very edge of reason as their bodies writhed. Beneath her the sofa moved on the rug, helpless against the force of their union. She churned her hips, adding to her own arousal as Jack's pounding thrusts brought her closer and closer to climax once more.

This time she came with mind-numbing intensity. As release tore through her, she cried out into Jack's mouth, clenching at him with her hands and body, squeezing him with the slick vise between her thighs.

He stiffened before the tremors of her own body began to subside. One last, hard thrust had him groaning, and she swallowed the wordless cry as he came inside her, holding her so tight she knew she'd have bruises in the morning, not that it mattered.

They stayed wrapped around each other for some time afterward. To be honest, Sadie was afraid he'd pull away and she'd lose him once more, even though she knew she would have to let him go eventually. They couldn't stay locked together forever. And yet, as she breathed the spicy scent of him deep into her lungs, she wished they could.

She couldn't even bring herself to regret this. How could she when it had felt so blissfully right? God, she hadn't known peace like this in years. It didn't matter that it only complicated things between them. Nothing else mattered, because she was with Jack.

He kissed her ear, stubble abrading her cheek. Warm hands lazily rubbed her back. "Are you all right?" he asked.

She could have cried right then, but she didn't. "I'm good."

Slowly, he eased away, pulling out of her. She felt his loss as acutely as she would her own limb. But he didn't go far, taking a handkerchief from his pocket and using it to wipe between her thighs. He'd always been attentive like this, even insisting that he sleep on the damp patch. It was sweet, really.

"You don't have to do that," she told him.

He glanced at her. "Yes, I do." Then he was done, stuffing the soiled linen into his pocket. He helped her down off the sofa, straightening her skirts.

Now it was awkward. Neither of them certain how to act. Like the first time, she realized. This was very similar, which made a sad kind of sense. They were different people now, despite their history. This was in a way, their first time together.

Was it also their last?

Unexpected tears burned her eyes and she made a great display of fixing her gown and hair. Jack, sensitive to her mood in a way that always touched and sometimes shamed her, fastened his trousers and moved to where the tea service sat.

"So, how do we do this?" He asked. "Do I pour or do you?"

He wasn't seriously going to go through with a reading was he? *Now?* "Jack, you don't have—"

"I know." He cut her off with a sharp glance. "I want to."

Oh God, now she truly was going to cry. All these years and he'd never wanted her to read for him before. Never cared to have any part of what she could do.

"All right." How embarrassing that she actually shook a little as she moved around the sofa to join him at the chairs. "I'll pour."

She wiped her palms on her knees as she sat down. She was aware of him taking the chair next to her as she lifted the still warm pot. She swished it around to stir up the leaves before tipping it over the flowered china cup and filling it with strong tea. Then, she plopped in two lumps of sugar and a little cream—just the way he liked it.

"You remembered," he remarked with a faint smile as he took the cup and saucer from her.

"I reckon there's not much that either of us has forgotten." She fixed a cup for herself and they sat there in relative silence, drinking.

It was odd to sit like this with him, but nice at the same time. There was awareness and a little awkwardness, but no tension. For the first time since his return they were able to be together and not fight. Who would have thought that all they needed to do to make things easier between them was have sex?

How could she face Mason after this? Should she tell him? No, there was no need just yet. Better to see how things progressed. She had no idea of Mason's intentions. He liked her, that was certain, but if he had more than an affair in mind he hadn't given her any indication. She didn't think she would even share this encounter with Vienne or Indara. Never mind decorum, she wanted to keep Jack to herself.

A faint smile curved her lips as she thought of Lady Gosling and what the woman's reaction would be to discover that *she* was the reason Jack hadn't succumbed to the baroness's charms.

"You look very satisfied."

She gazed at Jack over the rim of her cup. "So do you."

He only grinned in response and then drained his cup in one long swallow. He made a face as he replaced the cup on the saucer and wiped several leaves off his bottom lip with his thumb. "That's awful."

"You're supposed to strain them through your teeth," she explained. "Not swallow them."

"That would have been useful information five minutes ago." There was very little sting in his words, though. "Now what?"

She walked him through the process of turning the cup, making a wish and all that. When she finally took the cup from him and peered inside, she had a very odd lump in her stomach. What if she didn't see anything and he thought her a fake? What if she saw too much?

Tentatively, she studied the leaves. Some of the tension left her shoulders and the sick feeling in her belly lessened. Nothing had jumped up at her—and that was good.

"Your wish is very near the top of the cup, which means you'll get it soon."

"Good to know."

She glanced at him to find him watching her with a kind of heated amusement that both pleased and unsettled her. Was she part of his wish, or was he just humoring her? And how could he mock her and look like he wanted to eat her at the same time?

Cheeks warming, Sadie jerked her head down, turning her attention back to the cup. She saw the image and spoke without thinking, quickly processing the feelings that it evoked. "I see betrayal. Someone from your past will reenter your life."

"That's already happened."

A chill swirled at the base of Sadie's spine. It wasn't her, but she knew who it was. "Jack, there's something I need—"

But she was cut off—conveniently and damnably so—by a knock on the door. "Sadie?"

It was Vienne. She must have noticed that Jack was absent from the gathering as well.

Jack shot her a darkly amused glance, his thoughts obviously following hers. "Your protector has arrived to defend your virtue, I see. And it only took her twenty minutes." He rose to his feet and went to the door, unlocking. It opened to reveal the elegant French woman, key in her hand.

Jack smirked at her as he gestured toward Sadie. "*Bon soir, madam.* As you can see, she is still in one piece."

And thank the lord she was sitting demurely, teacup in hand. "Is something amiss, Vienne? Mr. Friday and I were just having tea." She should have been an actress. Somehow she managed to look her friend in the eye and not blush as she spoke. She almost convinced herself that nothing beyond a reading had transpired in that room.

Except that the taste of Jack lingered so sweetly on her tongue.


Where the devil was Jack Friday?

Certainly, it was the question on more than one set of lips. When Jack Friday made his amazing bid on the services of Madame Sadie Moon the crowd had turned positively beside itself to discuss, reflect on the gentleman's generosity, and turn what might have been an innocent occurrence into something ribald and risqué. That was, of course, until he bid on Mason Blayne's painting and several other items.

If he meant to call attention to himself it had worked. Everyone in that room respected the almighty pound, and the fact that Mr. Friday had one thousand—and more!—to simply toss aside made him slightly more virtuous. The fact that he considered Madame Moon's company worth that much made her a woman worthy of envy and jealousy.

While Theone, Lady Gosling, recognized jealousy as

a great motivator, she was not jealous of Jack Friday's generous purchase of Sadie Moon. Mason Blayne, on the other hand, was blatantly irked—never a good look for a man. Oh, he tried to conceal it, but there was a tightness around his mouth that belied his true feelings as he conversed with the Duke of Ryeton and his insipid little cow of a duchess.

Masculine pride was a fragile, delicate thing. And once bruised, a fellow tended to carry on as though a limb had been severed, though they thought they concealed it with great valor. Honestly, she could write an entire treatise on the subject. But Mason Blayne's feelings were the least of her concern at the moment.

She wondered once more where Jack was. And more importantly, where Sadie Moon was. Had no one else noticed that the two of them were absent? Apparently not.

If pressed, Theone would admit to a certain curiosity concerning the bizarre auction. It had been obvious to her from the beginning that lovely Mr. Friday had been in something of a state, even before he started bidding. It had also been obvious that he had been determined to win no matter what the cost—and that charity had been the last thing on his mind.

Sipping a glass of cool champagne, Theone allowed the tart bubbles to make love to her mouth as her mind mulled the suspicion forming there. Obviously there was something going on between Jack and Sadie Moon. Obviously the two of them were acquainted with one another—and not recently so. No two people could look at each other with so much tension after just a few days association.

No, there was a history there, yet Jack acted as though he had never met the woman before in his life.

Watching the two of them walk away had triggered something in her memory. What exactly, she couldn't quite put her finger on, though she knew the truth was there, just waiting to reveal itself. She had seen them together before—a long time ago, when all three of them were much younger, and in much different circumstances.

There was a secret between them, one that might prove very useful, if she could ferret out exactly what it was. She would have to be careful, however. If she remembered them, there was a very good chance one if not both of them might remember her. In fact, that might have already happened and they would have her at a decided disadvantage if she revealed herself too soon.

One thing was for certain. Jack Friday and Sadie Moon wanted to keep their secret. Once she uncovered that secret, all Theone had to do was ascertain how much her silence was worth.

# Chapter 10

**S**o he'd shagged Sadie. Now what?

This was the question Jack was still asking himself almost a full two hours later whilst standing on the back terrace of Saint's Row pretending to smoke a cigar.

Actually, he had every intention of smoking the damn thing, but he kept forgetting about it so it spent more time burning away between his fingers than between his lips.

After La Rieux's too-late rescue of Sadie, Jack had returned to the salon alone. Hardly anyone had noticed his absence and to those who did, he lied and said he'd had business to attend to.

He moved through the lingering crowd of people, nursing a glass of warm champagne and longing for something stronger that might overpower rather than complement the scent of Sadie lingering on him, the taste of her. He thought about the earnestness with which she gazed into his cup. She believed in the leaves. And now he knew his great folly. It didn't matter if there was truth in the bottom of a cup or not, Sadie believed there was and he had wounded her deeply with his mockery of it.

What had she said? He wondered as he stepped through the doors leading to the back terrace. A betrayal. Someone from his past. He knew better than to put any real belief in it, but Sadie's words stuck with him—almost as much as the haunted look in her big eyes. What was it that she had tried to tell him before her savior arrived?

And why did life seem so much brighter now? Was it just the sex? It had been incredible, despite his lack of finesse in the execution. He should have taken more time, but Sadie hadn't seemed to have any more patience than he. She had wanted him as much as he wanted her. At least he had that.

He stared out into the lantern-lit night. It had only been a few nights since he had looked over his shoulder at Sadie in almost this very spot and told her that he hated her too. And damned if he hadn't meant it at the time. Right now hate was the last thing he felt for her—and he felt a great jumble of things.

But the question still rang in his brain. Now what?

The French doors behind him opened, allowing the noise of the gathering to escape into the darkness. Two gentlemen, laughing, stepped outside.

"There he is!" a voice he recognized as Archer Kane's exclaimed. "Friday, old man. Everyone's been wondering where you dashed off to."

Jack grimaced as he turned. "Everyone?"

Archer's companion was none other than the Duke of Ryeton. The elder Kane brother flashed a sympathetic grin, made slightly sinister by the jagged scar on his left cheek. "Sorry, Friday. Having been the subject of many a conversation, you have my sympathy."

Archer laughed. "Only the stories 'bout you were *true*."

His brother scowled at him. "Not all, no."

Lean shoulders shrugged as Archer turned his attention back to Jack. "So, old boy, where did you get off to? You didn't happen to chase that pretty little fortune-teller to ground did you?"

Jack was generally an even-tempered man, but that question . . . that question made him want to belt Archer right between his ever-loving eyes. Some of that must have showed in his gaze because the grin melted off the other man's face.

"Forget I asked," he said, fishing a slim silver case from inside his jacket. "Cigar?"

The one in his hand had burned down to nothing, so Jack accepted the pleasantly scented tobacco and the offer of a light that followed. Soon, the three of them were smoking in relatively comfortable silence. So much for him not being much of a smoker.

"So," the duke began, a slow grin easing across his face. "*Did* you run that pretty little fortune-teller to ground?"

Archer burst out laughing, and Jack, seeing that Greyden was joking, soon joined in. It felt good to laugh, but it also hurt like hell, because neither of them knew that it was actually true. There was nothing clandestine about it. She was his wife, damn it.

And she always would be as far as he was concerned.

He knew that now. No amount of new names and years apart could change that. The reason tonight had felt so right was because it had been the two of them, together again.

La Rieux had whisked her away before he could ascertain if Sadie felt the same way. There was a very good chance that she did not. A very good chance that he could lose her again just as he was realizing he'd never stopped wanting her.

"Uh-oh," Archer intoned, nudging his brother with his elbow. "He's gone quiet. What do you suppose happened here this evening, Grey?"

The duke exhaled a stream of fragrant smoke. "I reckon it's none of our business, Arch." Then he cast a sideways glance at Jack. "Though I feel compelled to warn you, my friend, sometimes what happens at Saint's Row doesn't always stay here."

"Don't listen to him," Archer insisted. "He's just saying that because he thought he had an anonymous rendezvous here one night and he ended up married to her."

Jack's eyebrows rose as Grey shot his younger brother a murderous look. "Shut your mouth."

Archer merely made a face. "It's not like he's going to tell anyone. Besides, what difference does it make now that you're married?"

But Jack understood what Archer seemed oblivious to. It mattered because one never knew if scandal was going to elevate one's social status or destroy it. It was always about the woman's reputation, rarely the man's. And no man, especially someone trying to atone for his past as

Ryeton was, would want society gossiping about his wife giving up her virtue before the wedding night.

Then again, Jack had heard that was why they got married in the first place—they'd been caught in bed together. When his grandfather had discovered his affair with Sadie, he'd threatened to send him off to the continent and offered Sadie a great deal of money to go away. No special license for them.

They eloped two nights later. And Jack had been cut off without a penny, except what he managed to steal. The old man had thought he'd leave Sadie and come crawling back. Instead, he chose the girl he loved and tried to make a good life for them both. Then there had been that scrape with the law and Jack had jumped at the chance for a new life.

"Where are you from, Friday?" Ryeton asked, intruding upon his thoughts.

Jack's head jerked up. "County Kerry, in Ireland. Near Castlecove."

The duke nodded, but his pale eyes never left Jack's face. "Our father was acquainted with an earl up that way. Garrick or Garner . . ."

"Garret," Jack supplied, mouth incredibly dry.

The other man snapped his fingers. "That's right. Met the man once. Bit of a humorless bastard. Did you know him?"

He didn't want to lie, but what choice did he have? He was saved, however, by Archer's interjection, "You expect him to know some old fart of an earl just because they're from the same county?"

Ryeton rolled his eyes. "He might."

Archer scowled. "And he might not. What effing difference does it make?" He turned to Jack. "I'm off to the club. Want to join? Grey left his bollocks with the duchess and she wants him to go home with her."

Instead of being angry, the duke grinned. "You're just jealous because your bed will be cold and empty while mine is warm and cozy."

Archer, leaning back and turning his head to meet his brother's gaze, managed to look both amused and irked. "I reckon I'll have to find another bed, then." He directed that crystalline stare at Jack. "What do you say, Friday? Shall we sally forth?"

Surprisingly, Jack's first inclination was to decline his new friend's generous offer. But at that moment, he happened to glance at the lit interior of Saint's Row, visible through the French doors. Sadie was there, on the arm of Mason Blayne, and though she couldn't see him, he had a terribly good view of her as she smiled at the artist.

It was like a kick to the gut.

"Yes," he said to Archer, jaw tight. "Let's get the hell out of here."

Sadie didn't witness Jack's departure from the club, but she heard about it shortly after it happened. Vienne seemed to think it was news she would enjoy hearing.

"He won't be harassing you anymore this evening," the Frenchwoman announced with a kind of grim satisfaction that made Sadie wince.

"He didn't harass me." She pressed the back of her hand to her forehead where a dull ache was beginning to form just above her brow bone. "And even if he had, he paid for the privilege. A rather substantial amount."

Vienne sniffed. Obviously she had tried to forget Jack's donation. "That doesn't give him the right—"

"I gave him the right!" Sadie snapped. "I gave him the right when I allowed him to join me in the salon."

"As if you could have stopped him."

Sadie sighed. There was no swaying Vienne when she had her heels dug in. She was bound and determined to think ill of Jack and nothing Sadie could say would change that. How could she even attempt to change Vienne's mind when her own was in such a state of turmoil? She hardly knew her own feelings toward the man, they varied so much. One minute she despised him for walking out on her—and all that happened after—and the next she wanted to forget the past and beg him to give their marriage another try.

He'd left without saying good-bye. Rationally she knew that it was for the best, given the way bored aristocratic tongues liked to wag. Still, an acknowledgment of some kind would have been nice, seeing as how they'd shagged each other silly just a few hours ago.

"Forgive me," she said to Vienne after a brief silence. "I feel a headache coming on. I think I'll ask Mason to take me home."

Vienne smiled coyly. "A headache, but of course. Do go find Monsieur Blayne and have him attend to you."

Never in her life had Sadie ever felt the least bit slatternly, not even when in the presence of Jack's grandfather, but at that moment she felt tawdry and a little dirty. The idea of having any kind of intimate contact with Mason after being with Jack was wrong in so many ways. God, she couldn't imagine it.

"Will I see you for tea tomorrow?" Vienne asked, seemingly oblivious to Sadie's dismay.

"Of course. Same time as usual." Once a month they set aside a day for an afternoon of tea, cake with thick frosting, and gossip. It was time both of them took to forget about business and everything else in their lives and just be frivolous. Sadie cherished those days.

"Actually," her friend began, "would you mind if we met an hour later? I have a meeting earlier in the day with an investor."

"Of course not. An investor for your grand endeavor?" That was what Sadie called Vienne's plans to open a universal provider catering to the needs of the moneyed ladies of London.

Vienne nodded, her eyes bright. "I'm so very close to having all the money I need, *mon amie*. Trystan Kane's contribution put me within reach, and this meeting tomorrow could finally make my dream a reality."

Sadie was so very happy for her friend. She reached out and took both of Vienne's hands in her own. "Then we shall have to celebrate."

Her friend giggled—a decidedly girlish sound, odd coming out of that sophisticated face. "Fortune has smiled upon both of us as of late."

Sadie couldn't resist adding, "Yes, since Jack Friday came to town."

Vienne rolled her eyes, but she took the remark with the good humor it was intended. "Go home, you foolish woman. I grow weary of looking at you."

Chuckling, Sadie gave her a quick hug and went off in search of Mason. She hadn't seen him for quite some time. Earlier he'd come upon her before she could escape to the garden for some fresh air, and kept her by his side for a fair bit until someone whisked him away for a reason she couldn't remember. Usually he was in a hurry to escape such gatherings, claiming being around so many people overloaded his senses. Sadie suspected that had to do more with his artistic temperament than society, but who was she to judge? Half the time she couldn't wait to leave either. The social elite tended to grate on her nerves.

She found him in the salon talking to a small group of ladies and gentlemen, regaling them with a story about Rossetti. It was a tale she'd heard several times before, so she stood just outside the circle and waited. It didn't take long for him to finish, and when he was done, his rapt audience responded with a chorus of laughter. Even Sadie, as familiar with the story as she was, had to smile. Mason smiled too, though his faltered a little when he looked up and saw her there.

Guilt pinched Sadie deep inside. No understanding or arrangement existed between them, yet she felt as though she had betrayed him as keenly as if they had been lovers. He was a good man and he deserved better than she.

"You look tired," he commented as his audience dispersed, and she was able to close the distance between them.

"Headache," she supplied. "I thought we might take our leave, but if you would like to stay, I'm sure Vienne will lend me a carriage."

He made a small frown. "Don't be ridiculous. I'm more than ready to leave." He didn't offer his arm, but then he rarely did. Instead he walked with his hands clasped behind his back as was his habit, but he made sure to keep in step with Sadie, so he couldn't be too disappointed in her.

They called for Mason's carriage and collected their outerwear. The night was clear but a tad cool, and Sadie was glad to have her shawl about her shoulders as they stepped outside. They waited in mostly comfortable silence for the coach to appear, and when it did, a footman opened the door for them and assisted Sadie inside.

She took the forward-facing seat and moved to the far side, expecting Mason to sit beside her as he usually did. He surprised her, however, by sitting across from her instead. He looked at her as though she had disappointed him somehow.

He had no idea what happened between her and Jack. None. All he had were his own suspicions. The fact that he was so quick to believe the worst of her did much to alleviate her guilt—even though she deserved it.

He rapped on the roof and didn't say anything as the

carriage jerked into motion. Pimlico wasn't a short trip by any means. Did he plan to spend the whole of it in silence? Or was he waiting for her to confess her sins?

If one wanted to get nitpicky about it, she'd done nothing wrong. It wasn't a sin to shag one's own husband, was it?

Perhaps not, but when the devil had she begun thinking of Jack as her husband again? That wasn't the first time she'd used that title to describe him that evening. Had she used it before this night, or was this a result of said shagging? Because it didn't change anything. It only made the situation more complicated—for her anyway.

Despite that cynical thought, her mind couldn't help but drift back to what had taken place in the salon. She remembered every touch, every taste and sensation as though it were happening at that very moment. It had been far too long since she'd felt like that, and she had an awful sinking feeling that it would be a long time before she felt that way again.

Good thing she had a good memory.

They were probably halfway through the journey when Mason finally spoke, "You disappeared earlier. Were you all right?"

Thank the Lord for the carriage's dim lighting; he couldn't see her flush. "Yes. I just needed a little peace. Sometimes I find society so tedious."

"Of course. I'm sure it would be, with everyone going on about Mr. Friday and the astronomical amount he paid for you."

Perhaps it was just her guilty conscience, but that

sounded vaguely insulting. She tried to be flippant about it all: "It's the most anyone's ever paid for a reading."

Mason's gaze narrowed. "I don't think the reading was what he bid on." His tone wasn't accusatory, more sarcastic.

"Oh?" This was dangerous territory, but she couldn't help but push. "What do you reckon was his real aim?"

He made a scoffing sound, as though she couldn't possibly be so dense. "To spend time alone with you."

"He could have simply booked an appointment and had the same amount for a great deal less."

"Yes, but where's the grand gesture in that? Especially with no witnesses."

She wanted to tell him that he didn't know Jack at all, and that he was wrong, damn it, but she couldn't, because she wasn't supposed to know Jack Friday either. "It was for a fine cause," she replied, rather lamely at that.

"The only cause Friday's concerned with is his own."

"Why do you hate him so much? Because he bid on my reading, or because he embarrassed you by being able to bid more?" It might be a bit low on her part, but it was a legitimate question.

The light in the carriage might be dim, but it was bright enough for her to see the tightening of Mason's jaw. What was it about men? They could wage wars and build amazing monuments, but impugn their manhood or their pocketbooks and they came totally unhinged.

"I don't trust him," came the clenched reply. She

wasn't the only one full of lame comments it seemed.

Sadie didn't bother to ask if he trusted her. If he did she didn't deserve it and if he didn't he was wise not to. All and all, it was a no-win situation as far as she was concerned.

"It was for charity," she muttered.

A smirk curved Mason's well-formed lips. It was a most unbecoming expression for him. "You've never been naïve, Sadie. Don't start now. Charity was the last thing on Jack Friday's mind when he made that bid."

Sadie leaned forward, a feeling of menace twitching at the base of her spine. She was heartily fed up with everyone thinking the worst of Jack. Why didn't they think so ill of her? "What do you suppose was on my mind at the time, Mason? Do you think I agreed to read his leaves with the hope that he would ravish me? Or perhaps that I entertain hopes of seducing him?"

He drew back, obviously disconcerted by the question—and the vehemence with which it was asked. "Of course not."

"Of course not," she echoed bitterly, massaging her temples with her fingertips. Her head was pounding now. She sat back against the cushions and closed her eyes.

"But I do think you like the attention," Mason said in a quiet voice.

He was right, and Sadie couldn't find her voice to deny it, not even to spare his feelings.

Neither of them spoke again until the carriage rolled to a stop in front of her door.

They sat quiet for but a moment before a footman

opened the door and lowered the step. Mason walked her to the door, silent still.

"Would you like to come in?" she asked on the step. Not that she wanted him to come inside, but she felt as though it was rude of her not to offer.

"No." His gaze met hers but for a split second. "I'm leaving the city tomorrow and I want to get an early start."

"Leaving the city?" This was the first she'd heard of it. "Where are you going?"

"Yorkshire."

"When will you return?"

"I'm not certain."

Understanding dawned. Her wits were dulled by the headache, else she might have realized before this. What did it say about Mason's feelings for her if he left town rather than stay and fight for their fledgling romance? Either he gave up too easily or he saw a side of her character that wasn't very attractive.

"Well," she said, uncertain of what else to say, and too tired to be bothered to think of anything. "Safe journey."

A sharp, harsh burst of laughter broke from his lips. "Right." He looked down at his feet, at the door, everywhere it seemed but at her. "Good-bye, Sadie." Then he turned and walked back to the carriage, his shoulders rigid in that manner men employed when trying very hard not to slump.

It was too bad that it had to end like this between them, but Sadie couldn't bring herself to cry over it. She felt regret, but not loss. She opened the door, entered her house, and went straight to her room. She had just finished taking a headache powder when Indara knocked.

One look at her friend, who always understood no matter what she'd done, and Sadie's resolve finally broke.

"Oh, Indara," she sighed, her eyes filling with hot tears. "I've done the worst thing."

# Chapter 11

There was very little either nimble or quick about Jack after three hours of heavy drinking with the Kane brothers. The duchess had let Ryeton out to play, after all, and the three of them had carried on, going to a club Jack couldn't remember the name of, though he was certain his grandfather would be well acquainted with it, the person who founded it, its political leanings, and whether or not any of its members were worth half a damn. So long as the old man wasn't a member himself, Jack didn't give a damn what his grandfather's opinions were of his current surroundings. Still, in his drunken state, he pondered it regardless.

"You don't conduct yourself like most men of business, Friday," Ryeton remarked over the rim of his glass. The duke, Jack noticed, was decidedly less sauced than either he or Archer. Of course, His Grace had a beautiful wife to go home to and sobriety was always desirable when climbing into the marriage bed. Unless, of course, both were piss drunk. He remembered he and Sadie having more than a few very enjoyable romps after too much cheap wine.

"Obviously someone neglected to hand me a copy of the code when I signed on," Jack remarked with good-humored dryness. He felt very comfortable with these two, and he knew it showed. That perhaps was his first mistake.

Ryeton regarded him with a gaze that put Jack in mind of the threat of rain on a spring day—not quite blue and not quite gray. It wasn't an unfriendly gaze by any measure, but Jack found himself twitching under it regardless. Too late he realized that the Duke of Ryeton was one of those rare people who paid attention, always looking for what lay just below the surface.

"You should speak to my brother about that," came the duke's equally dry reply. "I believe he wrote the chapter on *gentlemen* who traffic in trade." The slight emphasis on "gentlemen" turned Jack's mouth arid.

"What the hell are you on about?" Archer demanded, words slightly slurred by too much scotch. "Of course Friday's a gen'lemen, despite having a day for a last name."

Neither Ryeton nor Jack glanced at the younger of the brothers. To be honest, Jack was afraid that if he tore his gaze away the duke might see it as a sign of weakness. Again, it was another mistake, because any man not born to the same world as the Kanes would have lowered his eyes by now.

"I know he's a gentleman." Ryeton's reply was smooth and deceptively light. And then: "What I want to know is why he pretends otherwise."

"Bollocks." Archer scowled at his brother, even as Jack's stomach took a dip. "Jack's top-notch. Cheats at cards, though." The unexpected and entirely untrue remark drew Jack's surprised stare. Archer didn't notice.

"Pay him no mind," Ryeton said with a dismissive wave of his hand. "He's always done that."

"Lie?" Jack asked, his gaze once again turning to the older man. Christ, now he knew how butterflies pinned to a board must feel—aside from dead.

Ryeton nodded, a slight smile tilting his harsh mouth. "He means it as a joke. He only does it to people he either really likes or thinks are simpletons."

Jack raised his brows. The movement seemed to cause his brain to tilt inside his skull. "Can't take offense to that then, can I?"

The duke's smile grew and Jack was reminded of Tryst. He'd been the victim of the youngest Kane's wit as well. Sadistic bastards, the lot of them. "My brother doesn't make friends easily."

"Astounding."

That drew a chuckle. At least the man appreciated when sarcasm was directed back at him. "I see now why both my brothers were quick to like you, Friday."

Jack watched him carefully. In the chair beside him Archer was singing a bawdy tune in a mumbled, off-key baritone. "But you are more cautious, aren't you, Your Grace?"

A dangerous glint brightened Ryeton's gaze—not threatening, but a little worrisome all the same. The Duke of Ryeton was on to him. And like a hungry dog, he wasn't about to give up that juicy bone now that he'd finally gotten his teeth in. Especially not when Jack was so close to his baby brother.

"I am," the duke replied. "Do you have any siblings?"

Jack shook his head. "I had an older brother. He died of scarlet fever as a child." Liam's death had made Jack's betrayal all the worse, walking away from that which hadn't been his birthright, but an honor bestowed upon him by a ten-year-old who left this world far too soon. He'd disgraced his brother's memory doing what he'd done, or so the old man had said.

All Jack had done was elope with the girl he loved, but whom his grandfather despised.

"My condolences," Ryeton said. Jack wasn't surprised to hear real feeling in the words. Obviously the duke could imagine the pain of losing a brother. "Were you close?"

Jack's throat tightened and an embarrassing burning sensation attacked the back of his eyes. "As two boys nine and ten often left to their own devices can be."

The duke nodded, understanding. "Did you not have other playmates?"

"Occasionally we were allowed to play with the village children." That was how he'd met his Sadie. "Grandfather did not encourage it."

Ryeton rested his chin on his hand, all innocent curiosity. "And who is your grandfather, Mr. Friday, that he should deem village children unfit companions for his precious grandsons?"

Caught.

Looking into those damn overcast eyes, Jack saw just how sober Ryeton was, and how readily he had fallen into the duke's trap. Nervous, he glanced at Archer, but his new friend was passed out cold in his chair and could offer no assistance.

Indignation rose within Jack's breast, along with a gluttonous portion of pissed-off defiance that destroyed the last of any pretense he might attempt to cling to.

Bracing one forearm on the table, he leaned closer. Ryeton didn't budge. In fact, the other man lowered his arm so that they mirrored each other, staring each other down like two pugilists eager to draw blood.

"My grandfather," Jack began in a low, controlled tone despite the furor inside him, "is the kind of man who would cast out his only heir for disobeying his wishes. And I, sir, am the kind of man who would rather be measured by my achievements than the misfortune of having been born to a class where men value wealth and blood more than decency and character."

For a second—perhaps two—the two of them stared each other down. Then Ryeton said, "Not all of us value wealth and blood above all else, Mr. Friday."

"No, but if someone said you must choose between your duty and your wife, what would you do?"

"I'd tell them to fuck off," the duke replied without pause.

Jack smiled tightly. "That's what I did."

"And so you were turned out without a penny."

"I was."

"Was she worth it?"

The question gave him pause, but the answer sprung immediately his lips. "Without a doubt."

"What happened?"

"I left with your brother to make a better life for us. She grew tired of waiting." It surprised him that he could say it without experiencing the flood of anger that usually came with thinking of that day when he'd walked into their flat and found it empty, Sadie long gone. In fact, saying it suddenly made him think of how it must have been for her without him there.

She'd been, what, seventeen? . . . alone in London. And he'd been so busy, he hardly had time to write as he wanted. Additionally, moving around so much, she was rarely able to find him. Sending home large amounts of money had seemed the perfect way to prove to her that he'd done the right thing, that he was working for their future.

He should have taken some of that money and brought her to him, but they'd done so much traveling and most of it rough. She would have hated it. Wouldn't she?

"I handled it badly," he added, ashamed. "I'd do anything to fix it if I could, but no amount of wealth can turn back time."

Ryeton blinked—not the quick surprised kind, but the slow, seeing-the-whole-picture kind. "The tea-leaf reader," he murmured, astonished. "Christ on a pony."

Stupid. Stupid. Stupid. He might have been safe if he hadn't mentioned money, but that coupled with his outrageous bid on Sadie that very evening revealed all.

He didn't deny it. He didn't confirm it either. What

he said didn't matter. It was what the duke planned to do with the information that was important.

"For the love of God, man," Ryeton snapped. "I'm not going to take an advertisement in the *Times*. Although it would be nice to have the gossips talk about something other than whether or not I've gotten Rose pregnant yet."

"Have you?" Jack asked dumbly, all too happy to discuss something that had nothing to do with him.

The duke smiled. "You don't ask me and I won't ask you, Friday. How's that sound?"

Jack found himself smiling as well. "That sounds fair."

Suddenly Archer bolted upright in his chair. "Damnation!"

Jack moved his chair a little to the left just in case his companion decided to eject the contents of his stomach.

"What did you forget?" Ryeton asked with a bored air. He glanced at Jack. "He's made a habit of this lately as well—getting sauced and forgetting a prior engagement. It's because of a woman."

"Iz-not," Archer muttered, swaying a little in his seat, " 's because of a heartless jezebel an' now Lady Martinique won't have me."

Jack wasn't quite sure what one had to do with the other, but he suspected Lady Martinique was the aforementioned missed engagement.

"I haf to go." Archer started to lurch to his feet, but his

brother rose quickly and managed to catch him before he could crash into the table.

"The only place you're going is home, you great awful mess." Ryeton smiled a bit as he spoke, turning the insult into an endearment. He glanced at Jack. "Drop you somewhere, Friday?"

Jack shook his head. "I appreciate the offer, but no."

Ryeton merely shrugged. "Suit yourself. Good night."

Jack watched them go. Archer mumbled something that he took as a farewell and allowed his brother to take him away. Jack waited until they were gone before making his own exit.

Home. It sounded good. He wanted to go home, and he was just drunk enough to punish himself by doing just that.

He took a hack to a decent but by no means affluent neighborhood in the theater district. A narrow little street with neat brick townhouses lined up like a child's blocks. He had a key for the front door of one and he walked up the stairs to the first floor flat.

It was exactly as she'd left it. Exactly as he had left it these long years. Only now it was musty, the remaining furniture covered by dust clothes.

He walked into the bedroom, to the narrow bed, and pulled the sheet from it, revealing a worn quilt beneath. He didn't even take off his shoes, he simply lay down on top of the quilt and stared up at the ceiling.

If he closed his eyes he could almost imagine Sadie

there beside him, curled against him as she always had, her fingers making lazy circles on his chest as they made their grand plans for the future. So many dreams they'd shared in this bed. Dreams, hopes, fears. And passion. A lot of love and passion.

Remembering it so clearly now, with dust and remorse clogging his throat, there was one thing Jack couldn't remember.

Why the hell he'd thought leaving Sadie was the right thing to do.

Every other Sunday Sadie visited a friend in the old neighborhood not far from Covent Garden. Helen Maguire was twenty years her senior, a retired courtesan and perhaps the most intelligent, interesting woman she had the pleasure of knowing—which was saying a lot considering her friendship with both Vienne and Indara.

Helen was her only remaining tie to this place—one she refused to give up. Unlike Jack, she wasn't hell-bent on obliterating the entirety of her past. If someone discovered her real identity, so be it. She had nothing to be ashamed of, but realistically she knew that it might not be good for her business.

And she certainly didn't want people to know she was married to Jack, though worse things could happen.

Regardless, it was highly unlikely that any of her clientele would be in Covent Garden on a Sunday morning, and even less likely that anyone would care should they see her there. She was beneath them, after all.

Sometimes, when Sadie drug up past bitterness at not

being considered good enough for Jack by his grandfather, she reminded herself that if the old man had accepted her she would never have met Helen. She wouldn't be friends with Indara, and probably wouldn't be friends with Vienne either, though she would no doubt be well acquainted with Saint's Row on a different level. It didn't take long for the bitterness to go away.

She enjoyed the life she had and adored the people who cared about her enough to be part of it. Though, now it seemed to be short one person with Mason's abrupt departure. That would no doubt affect the way his sister Ava greeted her when next they met. But there was nothing she could do about that. Mason's pride would heal soon enough. There were plenty of women who would eagerly take her place as his escort.

The fact that she thought that was proof of just how little she'd felt for him romantically. She missed his companionship more than anything else. True, she had been attracted to him, but no real attachment had been formed. She hadn't felt a real attachment since Jack.

What was it about him that had captivated her so? Back then Jack would look at her like she was the most amazing thing he'd ever seen, and that had been enough. He'd been willing to lose everything to be with her, but then . . . he'd decided he wanted it all back, only in a different way. That's why she hadn't been able to bring herself to stop Jack from leaving. She'd felt guilty for all he'd lost in marrying her.

He'd achieved everything he wanted, but he didn't seem happy—no more than she truly was. Had it been

worth abandoning their marriage—for either of them?
Probably not. Yet, she reckoned both of them would do
the same all over again.

Truth be told, she held some admiration for the man
Jack had become. He worked for what he had, no longer
expecting it to be handed to him on a silver salver. He was
successful without the old man's help, and that unsettled
her perhaps more than she wanted to admit, as did her
physical reaction to him. She'd been on him like sauce
on pudding, and she'd most likely do it again if given
the opportunity.

Perhaps the saddest and most humiliating thing was
that she could like him if he let her—if she let herself.
Hell, she could probably love him again. Not just because he was still her Jack in so many ways, but because
whenever he was near she felt whole again. And that was
something she would admit to no one but herself.

It was somewhere in the vicinity of ten o'clock in
the morning when she arrived at Helen's plain but cozy
townhome—early for a woman who still lived around
"town" hours and scheduled her life around her wealthy
lover, with whom she'd shared the last fifteen years,
content to be the one he came to when society and his
wife didn't take precedence.

"As the years go on we spend more and more of our
time together," Helen informed her with a bemused smile
as they shared a leisurely breakfast in front of the bow
window overlooking her sun-dappled garden. She wore
a dark blue morning gown that displayed her hourglass
figure to advantage and made her blond hair seem all the

more golden. "Publicly and privately. Old age thumbs its nose at propriety."

Good for old age. Sadie took a bite of a warm scone slathered with butter, delighting as the flavor embraced her tongue. As she chewed she wondered how her life might have been different if Jack had done what his grandfather wanted and had taken her as his mistress rather than his wife. Would they still be together? Or would he have abandoned her for a proper wife years ago? He wouldn't have felt the need to run off and prove himself if he hadn't been disowned. But perhaps he would have grown bored of her charms and moved on to someone else.

Perhaps her life wouldn't be much different than it was now, except that now she had her pride. She didn't judge any woman for making the necessary concessions to survive; there were worse fates than being a kept woman. She knew fine ladies with less honor and integrity than Helen had in her little finger, less grace than the older woman housed in her left foot.

How stupid she'd been as a girl to want to be part of that world! She'd fancied herself Cinderella and Jack her handsome prince. What would she have become if his grandfather had accepted her rather than revealing his disdain? Would she have become someone like Lady Gosling or the other ladies who seemed to hate everything and everyone around them because life had turned them bitter?

Or maybe she would have turned out like Duchess Ryeton, or her friend Eve Elliott, who was soon to be married. They seemed like decent, kind ladies. Certainly she'd never seen anything in their cups to suspect otherwise—except that Miss Elliot was marrying a man she didn't love.

"I thought I saw a ghost last night," Helen commented, interrupting Sadie's thoughts with the click of her spoon against china as she stirred a lump of sugar into her second cup of tea. "As his lordship and I returned home from our engagement." Helen never referred to her lover by name, though everyone knew who he was.

"Oh?" Sadie picked up a piece of crisp bacon and took a bite—heaven! She was thankful to her friend for interrupting her foolish thinking. "Who was that?"

"I could have sworn I saw Jack Farrington on Russell Street."

Sadie froze. Helen waited, watching her with curious and patient brown eyes. Helen was like Job in her patience. She'd sit there and wait for Sadie to respond until the sun set and never once press her.

"Jack Farrington?" she echoed. "Russell Street?" Since Jack's reappearance in her life, it seemed as though her cognitive abilities had plummeted to rival the lowliest simpleton's.

"Indeed," Helen replied meaningfully. "Of course, I might have been mistaken."

Sadie's head jerked up. She looked her friend directly in the eye. "I'm sure you must have been." The lie was bitter on her tongue, ruining the delicious taste of the bacon. She wanted to confide all in Helen, wanted her wise friend's counsel, but this wasn't Sadie's truth to tell. And if she was honest, it was different than confiding in Vienne and Indara, who didn't know him. They couldn't point out all the places where Sadie had been at fault. They wouldn't tell her things she didn't want to hear.

And so her old friend merely inclined her head, putting an end to the conversation. Like the skilled actress she was, she moved on to another topic as though nothing had happened. Sadie didn't make the transition quite so seamlessly, though she gave it her best. A cloud of awkwardness hung over the rest of her visit. It was still there a half hour later when she finally took her leave.

She'd wanted to leave as soon as Helen mentioned Jack. As soon as she stepped outside and into the waiting carriage, she instructed her driver to take her the short distance to Russell Street. She sat perched on the edge of the seat, staring out the window, her gaze sweeping the street for any sign of her husband.

*Former* husband.

The carriage came to a stop outside a red brick building as familiar as her own face. It was in much better repair now than it had been ten years ago when she and Jack had lived in the upstairs flat, still it had been nicer than she was used to. Jack had used the money he stole from his grandfather to secure it, and he'd sent money home when he was gone so that she could keep it.

Of course, she hadn't kept it. She'd made arrangements for the rent to be paid out of the money Jack sent—money she'd deposited into an account and never touched once she'd decided to leave. She'd needed more than his money then and he hadn't been there to provide it. She hadn't been able to bring herself to stay there after what happened.

As though drawn by an invisible tether, she climbed out of the carriage and stepped onto the walk. The driver asked if she wanted him to stand there and wait, and she told him yes, even though common sense told her to get back into the coach and drive away.

Her bootheels clicked lightly on the stone walkway, echoing the pounding of her heart as she approached the three-story building. What was she doing? There was nothing left here for her. Why, the door would be locked . . .

It wasn't. The knob moved easily under her fingers—fingers she hadn't even realized she'd wrapped around the cool brass. The door swung open, revealing the abandoned interior that smelled of old sunshine and dust.

She stepped inside. "Hello?"

No answer.

She should turn and go. Instead, she stepped inside. It looked different. It used to be that the door opened into a shared foyer with another entrance for the downstairs space and a staircase that led up to their flat. The staircase was still there, but the back wall of the foyer had been knocked out, removing the separation between the spaces.

Her feet moved of their own volition, even though her mind realized the folly of trespassing. Still, the door had been open.

What if someone was in there? It wasn't smart of her to venture into this place alone. There could be any kind of danger waiting, and yet she couldn't make herself turn around. She couldn't make her heart see this place as anything remotely dangerous, regardless of all the other emotions it evoked.

Up the stairs she climbed, gripping the dusty banister with her left hand, skirts with her right. There were scuff marks on the dark red runner. It muffled her footsteps as she climbed to the first floor, where she found the door to her old home standing slightly ajar. Someone else had been here recently. Coincidence? She didn't think so.

Fingers trembling, knees quivering, she pushed it open and hesitantly crossed the threshold. "Hello?"

Sadie paused just inside, her heart seized by a terrible revelation.

The place looked just the same as it had when she left. Of course there were dust clothes in place, but one had slipped off the old arm chair near the hearth. The rich green brocade was covered in a grayish film where the linen had slipped, but she recognized it immediately. She had upholstered the chair herself, with a great deal of bother and eventual pride.

She pulled at a sheet over another piece of furniture—the scarred tea table they'd found in a market one morning. Jack had carried it back to the flat on his shoulder and suffered for it later. That night they'd reclined in the bath together and she massaged his shoulder, chiding him for having to be "such a man."

Horrified, her gaze dropped to the floor. It was bare. The breath caught in her throat slowly slipped out. The rug was gone.

"Sadie?"

She whirled at the sound of his voice, head spinning dizzily as past and present seemed to collide. She had to tip her head up to see past the broad brim of her peacock-trimmed hat.

"Jack," she rasped.

He was still wearing his evening clothes, which were rumpled beyond decency. His hair was mussed, standing up in spikes of brown and gold. His jaw was covered with a day's growth of beard, and his eyes were heavy with sleep and hangover.

He looked good enough to eat.

He ran a hand over his eyes as though he couldn't believe them. "What are you doing here?"

"I was visiting Helen. She said she thought she saw Jack Farrington on the street last night."

"Shite." He winced and pressed two fingers to his forehead. "What did you tell her?"

"That she was mistaken, obviously."

"Obviously." He smiled grimly. "Thank you."

Straightening her shoulders, Sadie braved taking a step toward him. The memory of what they'd done the night before was still terribly fresh in her mind and on her skin. Every inch of her that had ever missed him begged to be touched by him again—not just for sex, but for comfort as well.

The rug . . . Thank God it was gone.

"What are *you* doing here, Jack?" Tilting her head again, she regarded him from beneath her hat. She could take it off, but she felt safer with it on. He hated her hats, and probably wouldn't try to kiss her while she wore it.

If she took it off and he didn't try to kiss her, she wouldn't be able to hide her disappointment.

He shrugged. "I own the place."

Sadie blinked. "Own it?" Yes, he'd made her a raging simpleton. All she could do was stupidly repeat what others said to her like some sort of parrot in a circus show.

Jack nodded. "I bought it when I came back." His gaze burned into hers. "It was going to be a present for you. I knew you loved this place."

She had loved this place. She still did, as awful as some of the memories were. Loved it more now that the damned rug was gone.

Nausea rose up in her gut as she looked around, imagining how he must have felt, returning there to find her gone. Had he wondered what had happened to the rug? Panic followed close on its heels, and she pushed past him into the room that had been their bedroom. She froze in the door.

It was still the same. All the same. And the bed had been slept in—or rather on. Their bed.

"You've kept it exactly as it was." As though she needed to say it.

"Almost," he replied from behind her. "The rug in the front room had a stain on it. I threw it out."

Sadie clutched the doorframe, head swimming as a hot sick sensation rushed over her. He didn't know. Couldn't know.

And she'd be damned if she'd remember it now with him standing there, blissful in his ignorance. She might have to kill him. Or perhaps fall at his feet bawling. One of the two.

She turned on him, so conflicted and shaken she didn't know which end was up, didn't know what she felt. Scarcely knew who she was.

He'd kept their home. Bought their home, for her. And he'd kept it even though she'd left him. Such a grand, romantic gesture and yet it seemed too little too late. Regret, rage, and guilt tore at her heart—at her very sanity. Was he trying to push her to the brink of madness?

He just stood there, behind her—where that damn rug once had been—watching her as though he wanted—*expected*—something from her.

Her hands curled into fists, nails digging into her palms. Only the pain kept her from slipping over that edge. "How dare you do all this. How dare you come back after breaking my heart and have kept this flat." Her voice shook. "You walk into my life like you have the right. You make love to me . . ."

"You didn't stop me."

"Of course I didn't!" She glared at him as he glared at her. "I wanted it as much as you did, that doesn't make it right."

"It was wrong, then, Sadiemoon?" he asked, his voice as strangely tender as it was rough.

She closed her eyes, dizzy from the wave of emotion that swept over her. "We've gone to great lengths to make new lives for ourselves, Jack."

"That doesn't answer my question."

"We're not good together."

"I disagree."

Her eyes opened. "Of course you do. You *always* do. Tell me, have I ever been right in your eyes?"

"You're not talking sense." The furrow between his brows eased. "This is because I called you a fraud, isn't it?"

Stupid, infuriating man! How could he know the answer so readily yet not understand why? "Yes, of course it is! You've never believed in what I can do. Never! You've always treated it like some great swindle."

"It's predicting the future through *tea*." If he rolled those green-gold eyes of his, she'd claw them straight out of his head. "What is it if not a swindle?"

"It's me." The flat of her hand struck hard against his chest. "It's what I'm good at, you great cruel arse! It's how I supported myself when you were off making your fortune."

"You didn't have to support yourself. I sent most of that goddamn fortune home to you!"

She ignored him, because what he had done wasn't the point. It was what he hadn't done, what he'd never done and probably never would be able to do. "I've made a name for myself and people from all over England come to have me read their leaves. I'm proud of what I can do and you treat it like a . . . a crime! I was never ashamed of myself for anything until I met you, Jack Farrington."

He recoiled, chiseled cheeks paling. "That's not my

fault. My grandfather was an arse, but I never thought you were beneath me. Never."

Tears clawed at her throat, made her feel like a stupid weakling. "You never believed in me."

He scowled as he stepped forward, taking her face in his long hands, forcing her to meet his gaze as he bent his neck a bit to stare long and hard into her eyes. "I might not believe in leaves but, Sadie, I've always believed in *you*."

# Chapter 12

"**Y**ou had a bloody awful way of showing it."
Sadie's big multi-hued eyes shone with unshed
tears as she looked up at him.

Jack managed a smile, even though there was a peculiar
pain in his chest. Listening to her had rubbed something
inside him raw. Such pain and suffering in her voice,
in her very demeanor, all laid upon him. How could he
ever fix that? "I was young and stupid. I thought I did
all right at the time."

Wide lips curved sadly. "Believing in me isn't exactly
the same as believing in what I can do, is it?"

"Beating a dead horse isn't exactly the same as riding
it either."

"That makes no sense."

"Exactly." At her droll look he tried again, "Look,
why does it matter so much to you that I don't believe
in tea leaves? I don't believe in tarot either, or palm
reading."

She shook her head, the plumes on her ridiculous hat

bobbing. "I can't explain it, but it matters. What if I didn't trust your judgment in business matters?"

"You'd be foolish. I can prove I know what I'm doing."

Triumph—and a little sorrow—lit her gaze. "So can I. Talk to anyone whose leaves I've read and they'll tell you that I've been right."

It was on the tip of his tongue to argue that they believed because they bent what she said to what they wanted to hear, but sense prevailed and he kept that opinion to himself. Instead, he said, "You never did finish that reading I paid a fortune for. Maybe we can try again?"

She eyed him suspiciously—an expression that hadn't changed much over the years. "How much of a gulpy do you think I am?"

She knew him too well to believe he'd give in that easily, but he was surprised to realize that he wanted to see her in action. Obviously she was doing something right to have all of London clamoring for her attention, and if reading his leaves pleased her, he would have her do it as often, and as eagerly, as she wanted.

"You," he replied honestly, "are the least gullible person I know."

She still didn't look convinced, but she didn't pursue it. "All right. I'll do another reading for you since you were foolish enough to pay so much for it."

"I'd pay more than that for an hour alone with you." And he meant it—even though it sounded far too smooth to be honest.

She actually flushed, the smooth ivory of her cheeks turning a sweet rosy color. "Scoundrel. You always were a charmer."

"You're the only one who's ever thought that."

A pointed glance. "Lady Gosling would agree with me."

Guilt gripped him hard. "Nothing happened with her."

Sadie shrugged, calling his attention to the snug fit of her peacock blue walking costume. She was like an hourglass on legs. Very long legs. "It doesn't matter. It's not as though we're legally married."

It wasn't the first time she'd said it, only this time it pissed him off. "I've always thought of you as my wife, Sadie. I always will."

A stricken expression claimed her features. "Oh, Jack—" Whatever else she'd been about to say was lost when he grabbed her by the shoulders, hauled her against him and kissed her. He had to duck beneath the brim of that ridiculous hat, but it was worth it. Her soft, warm mouth tasted of sweet tea and butter and he swept his tongue inside, eager to have as much of her as he could.

Her hands slid up his chest to twine around his neck. He brought his own down to circle her, pressing his palms against the long, supple arch of her back. A familiar tightening started at the base of his prick and it began to harden. He stepped forward, pushing her into the bedroom toward the bed.

Sadie pushed against him, her hands suddenly releasing

his neck. "No," she insisted, wrenching her lips away from his. "Not here."

Slightly dazed and extremely randy, Jack blinked. "Why not?"

She wriggled free of his arms. "I can't. Too many . . . memories."

Christ, were they that bad? he wanted to ask, but didn't have the balls. Honestly, he didn't think it was memories of the two of them that she found unsettling—it was her time spent alone in this place that haunted her.

For perhaps the dozenth time since his return, Jack felt like an arse. A *real* arse. He'd thought only of how much Sadie had hurt him by leaving, and never once about how much being alone must have hurt her.

She hadn't once asked him to stay all those years ago. She'd supported his decision, but looking back and remembering the look in her eyes, he knew now that she hadn't wanted him to go. And he remembered looking back the morning he left and seeing her, her back to the boat, her shoulders shaking as he drifted away.

He should have been a better husband, but he'd been too young, too desperate, and too determined to prove himself a man. Now, a decade later, he stood before this strange and beautiful woman and realized he wasn't much of a man at all.

And he wondered, if perhaps he could ever repair all the damage that had been done. There was still something between them. Was it enough?

"Tonight," he said. "At Saint's Row." He still had the key to the private accommodations La Rieux had offered him for the duration of his stay. He'd been surprised she hadn't asked for it back when she discovered who he truly was.

Sadie frowned slightly, her gaze drifting to his from a spot on the floor. "I can't meet you there. People will see us."

"No, they won't. Meet me in the garden. Nine o'clock."

For a moment, he thought she might refuse, but then she nodded. "All right."

Jack's heart swelled, forcing him to release the breath held deep in his lungs. "Good."

She nodded, obviously still quite distracted. "I have to go." Then, just as he thought she was going to run out on him, she placed her hand on his arm and raised her face to meet his gaze. "Nine o'clock."

And then she was gone.

Jack stood alone for a moment, in the middle of the little room that held so many happy memories for him and so many unhappy ones for Sadie. He'd bought this house for the two of them. It was a good house, appropriate for a man of business. The neighborhood was good, but not too fancy. Sadie would be comfortable here, more so than in a high-class neighborhood. She'd never felt at ease around his family or their friends—not that he blamed her.

Could he build something new for them in this house? Would she let him try to take away all the unhappy thoughts that lingered with her?

It seemed a world of possibilities had opened up before

him—a chance at happiness he thought lost forever. It was a chance he intended to take and fight for. Sadie was his. She was as much his as he was hers. No amount of years or alterations could change that.

So intent was Jack on his new mission when he left the house, he didn't notice the man in the carriage across the street watching him. The man who followed him at a discreet distance, all the way back to the Barrington before continuing on to his own home in Mayfair.

A man who was not at all pleased by this turn of events.

Sadie's head insisted that meeting Jack at Saint's Row that night was wrong, wrong, wrong. Her head, however, was absolutely no competition for her heart. That untrustworthy organ had her picking out just the right dress and obsessing for hours over how to wear her hair.

Honestly. She couldn't figure out how to wear her hair to meet a man who had seen her at both her best and her worst. Well, perhaps not her worst. That was another thing gnawing at the back of her mind. Her conscience wanted to tell Jack what had happened on the rug he tossed out, why she couldn't make love to him in that place with that memory kicking at her.

But what purpose would it serve to tell him that was where she'd miscarried his child? None. It would only hurt him. And if she confessed that, then she would also have to confess that she'd suspected the pregnancy before he left and hadn't told him. She hadn't wanted to make him stay, even though she had prayed every night that he would. But more than that, she didn't want to tell him that his grandfather had taken care of her after the miscarriage, that she had contacted the old man as soon as she began having problems because she was terrified that something was wrong with what she was certain was a son, and she knew the importance of an heir in that world.

The old man never came right out and blamed her, but she could see it in his eyes. Regardless, he'd seen to it that she had the best care, but even that hadn't been enough to save the baby. The Earl of Garret had stayed with her, and even escorted her to Ireland so that she could visit Granny—all that remained of her family.

Her grandmother had moved into her youngest daughter's house, too frail to be on her own. While Sadie liked her aunt Colleen, she didn't know the woman well enough to stay with her, nor did she want the woman to know her business. She stayed with the earl at his grand estate, in the room Jack had slept in as a boy. It was a kindness she never would have expected, as were the doctor and nurse he had monitor her. He did everything he could to help her recover from her loss. That's when he offered to help her start her new life. He only had two conditions; one that she never contact Jack, and two—that she notify him if his grandson should ever contact her.

At the time Sadie refused. She had believed Jack would return to her. But once her pain began to turn to bitterness, and the months turned into a year, then two, she contacted the old man. He helped her get started and she agreed to his terms readily, though she would only accept half the sum he offered. He suggested she invest it and let it grow, which she did.

She was still in Ireland when Granny died. Lord Garret helped pay for the funeral—anonymously. And then, since she was healthy and had nothing left to keep her in Ireland, he paid for her return to London.

On occasion she even fancied the old bastard liked her, but that was only in her more sentimental moments. He even consoled her when her letters to Jack went unanswered.

All of this would only make Jack feel guilty for leaving, which once upon a time she would have done with relish. But now . . . Now she just didn't have the taste for it. She didn't want to hurt him. Didn't want to be hurt by him. And yet, here she was, making herself pretty for him, bound and determined to run into his arms and say "damn the consequences" despite the mess that could result.

Finally, her hair was right—loosely piled on the back of her head in a style that would fall apart with the tug of one pin. Very good. Jack always liked her hair down. And her gown was a rich teal satin that bared a great deal of cleavage, made her waist look tiny, and drew attention to the sway of her hips. When she bought it, Vienne declared it a gown designed for seduction. At the time she'd thought to wear it for Mason, but it had sat in her wardrobe for months. Until tonight.

She arrived at Saint's Row at five minutes before nine. Her heart was already pounding in anticipation as she stepped down from the carriage. Her stomach quivered with a shivery feeling she hadn't felt in a long, long time. Most embarrassingly, she was already aroused—just by imagining what *might* happen with Jack tonight. No matter how confused she was regarding her feelings, her body wasn't confused at all.

Instead of entering the club through the main door, she slipped through the gate that surrounded the property. Vienne had given her a key to that and most of the rest of the club a long time ago. Before tonight she'd never had cause to use it. Lifting her skirts, Sadie ran across the lush grass, the cool night air welcoming her.

She slowed to a walk as she approached the back of the building where the gardens bloomed, fragrant and heady. Cautiously, she peeked around the stone steps of the terrace. It was early and the club had yet to fill up for the night—and it was a rare night when Saint's Row wasn't full. Vienne made sure she catered to any desire anyone could have. And tonight, Sadie was one of the catered.

A man stepped through the terrace doors, the snowy white of his evening dress bright in the darkening gloom. A smile curved Sadie's lips as she allowed herself to admire his loose-limbed grace and easy swagger as he came down the steps. Jack Farrington—er, Friday— walked like he was king of the world.

He paused at the bottom of the steps, on the gravel path. He turned his head away from her and then toward her. "Come out, Sadiemoon," he murmured. "I know you're there."

Immediately, she slipped from her hiding spot. "How

did you know?" she asked, glancing at the doors to make sure they weren't about to be found.

Jack grabbed one of her hands and guided her down the path, his smile turning to a broad grin. "I felt you watching me."

"No, you didn't."

"I did. I'd sense you anywhere."

Her heart tripped over the words like the toe of a slipper over a loose pebble. "Your Irish is showing," she informed him pertly. He said nothing, but his grin didn't change.

A few yards down the path, he veered away from the glow of the lanterns and pulled her into an alcove in the shrubbery. It was arranged so that it was indiscernible at a passing glance. Only if you knew the spot could you see how the hedgerow actually parted and overlapped, making a natural corridor that led to a small stone cottage concealed by flora and darkness.

Jack unlocked the door with his free hand and drew her over the threshold with him, into a softly lit interior that smelled of honey, cloves and . . . tea? Sure enough, there on a small table set for two, was a teapot, and several plates with cheese, meats, and scones. If she knew Jack, there were also strawberry preserves and clotted cream as well.

"I thought you had seduction in mind," she remarked, closing the door firmly behind her.

Jack turned to her, so close that she was caught between him and the heavy oak of the door. "I do. I thought perhaps the leaves might show you exactly what I intend to do to you this evening."

Awful, teasing man! Of course she shivered at the mere thought of what they might do—and at the idea of telling him what she wanted, disguised as a reading.

"Are you hungry?" he asked.

She was.

They sat at the table and enjoyed a leisurely meal. Neither of them ate much, but it wasn't long before they began feeding one another, as they used to years ago. They spoke of trivial things—revealing snippets of their lives apart while avoiding any subject that might cause too much pain for either of them. When Sadie began to feel that perhaps too much time had passed for them to ever find common ground again, Jack licked a dollop of cream off her finger and she felt an answering throb deep between her thighs. Something must have shown on her face because Jack smiled and nodded toward the pot of cream. "Save some of that for later."

Oh. Dear. God.

She never did get around to reading the leaves as he had teased. Once he'd made the suggestion with the cream, she'd looked at him and he at her and that was the end of the meal.

"I wanted to take my time at seducing you," he informed her, voice rough as he stood. "But I don't want to wait any longer."

Sadie rose as well. "You can take your time later. We have all night."

Jack's eyes seemed to light from within as he stared at her. "Turn around."

She did as he demanded and was rewarded with the feel of his long fingers loosening the buttons down the back of her gown. There were dozens of them, but he made short work of them. A gown made for seduction indeed. When the poufy little sleeves slouched down her arms, Jack helped them along, pushing the loose bodice down to her hips, and from there it drifted to the floor in a delicate pile.

Sadie stepped out of the gown. Jack surprised her by picking it up and draping it over a chair. That thoughtfulness did something peculiar to her chest—it pinched a little bit. She didn't have time to wonder at it, however, because now his fingers were working at her stays and within moments, he had her out of her corset and her shift and standing before him—her back still to him—in nothing but her stockings and shoes.

"Beautiful," he whispered against her ear. There was just enough of home in his voice to bring a slight dampness to her eyes. He sounded like the boy she fell in love with—deeper and older, of course, but enough that she loved him for it.

There was a slight tugging at her crown as he pulled the pins. Sure enough it only took one to tumble the entire coiffure. Her hair fell around her shoulders and down her back, cool against her skin. Jack dragged his fingers through it, combing it before bringing his hands around to cup her breasts. He lifted them, thumb and finger easily finding her nipples and squeezing gently. Sadie gasped, and her devil of a husband chuckled against her ear just before flicking his tongue along the lobe.

Closing her eyes, Sadie leaned back against the warm, solid wall of his chest. The light wool of his coat was slightly rough against her skin but she didn't care. She was totally focused on his mouth and his hands. His left hand stayed on her breast, the tip of which was as hard as granite and aching for his mouth. His right hand slid down her torso, over her stomach, and down to the apex of her thighs. One of his feet nudged hers, easing her legs open and widening her stance so that his questing fingers could continue their erotic journey.

Lightly—damnably so—he caressed the curve of her mound, traced a path along the damp cleft and then back, barely parting the swollen flesh. She pulsed there, tight with need but loving this sweet torture.

"Sweet Sadie," Jack murmured, his lips brushing her shoulder. "So eager."

She arched her hips in response, pushing herself against his hand. Another chuckle. His teeth grazed her shoulder and then his finger slipped between the lips of her cunny to stroke the knot of flesh that begged for his touch. She moaned and the fingers on her nipple pinched lightly, adding to the pleasure.

He played her ruthlessly for what seemed like forever, stroking and teasing, but never quite giving the release she craved. And then, when she thought she might have to kill him, his fingers left her altogether to grip her hips, and the lips that had kissed both her shoulders began a delicious humid descent down her spine. She felt his thighs brush her calves as he came to kneel behind her, tongue swirling little hot circles at the top of the cleft of her buttocks.

"Turn around."

Knees trembling, she yet again did as he commanded, knowing his intention and welcoming it eagerly. She looked down the length of her own body, flushed in the lamplight, to meet his bright gaze. He stared at her as his fingers slowly crept up her thigh, back to where she wanted them. Only this time, he didn't toy with her sweet spot, instead, he eased one finger inside her, parting her heated flesh, filling her. She sighed in delight, knowing he had more in store for her.

Reaching behind her shoulders, she gripped the mantel with both hands, arching her spine so that she offered herself up to his mouth brazenly. Jack smiled—the self-satisfied smile of a man reunited with a woman who burned for his touch and didn't care if he knew it.

"Do you know of how many nights I dreamed of eating you?" His voice stroked her just as effectively as any finger, tightening the tension within her. As he spoke, he moved his finger inside her. Her thighs clenched. "How many nights I tossed off to thoughts of you riding my tongue until you came?"

"How many?" her voice was a gasp as she writhed on his hand, aching for his mouth.

"Every fucking one," he growled and then pushed himself between her legs, his mouth and tongue easily finding the slick knot of nerves and licking mercilessly.

Sadie cried out—how could she not when he did this

so well? One hand let go of the mantel to clutch his head, pushing him deeper. His fingers tightened on her hips as he devoured her. She slung one leg over his shoulder, undulating against his tongue faster and harder until she came in a great rush of heat and joy. She sagged, knees turning to jelly. There was a nip of sharp teeth against the inside of her thigh and then Jack stood, lifting her into his arms.

He carried her to the bed, setting her on soft, clean sheets. Her shoes had come off during the journey but she hardly cared.

Jack stood beside the mattress, so tall and golden. Sadie watched as he shrugged out of his coat and tossed it aside, showing less regard for his own clothing than he'd had for hers. He wiped the back of his hand across his mouth before removing his waistcoat. She wondered if he'd liked how she tasted and the thought aroused her all over again. In one swift movement, she came up onto her knees on the mattress and pulled Jack's shirt free of his trousers.

"Let me help you," she said with a smile. And he did, until finally he stood before her, naked and too beautiful for his own good. She ran her hands over the taut flesh of his abdomen, up to his broad chest.

"I don't remember you being this hairy," she remarked, sliding her thumbs over his tight nipples.

"Did I have *any* chest hair when we first did this?" he asked with a grin as he joined her on the bed, drawing her against that wonderfully muscular—and hairy—chest.

"I don't think so. I like it."

"Good. I grew it just for you."

"And this?" She slid her hand down, over his flat belly to curve around his absolutely perfect cock. "Did you grow this for me as well?"

Jack regarded her from beneath heavy lids. "I think you grew that all on your own."

Grinning, Sadie slid down the length of him, but instead of touching him, she slipped off the bed and crossed the floor to the table.

"What are you doing?" he asked.

She turned with the pot of cream in her hands and a saucy grin on her lips. "I want dessert."

Jack lay back against the pillows and crossed his arms behind his head. His erection stood proudly in the lamplight. "Come and get it."

Back on the bed, Sadie set the pot of cream near his hip and braced herself on her elbow as she scooped out two fingers full of fluffy deliciousness. Lightly, she daubed the cream on the head of Jack's erection and then positioned herself over it. She raised her gaze to his, giving him a bold stare before lowering her head.

She took him deep into her mouth, running her tongue over the smooth skin, delighting in the salty taste of him mixing with the sweet cream. She'd missed this, the feel and taste of him, knowing how much pleasure he took from it. Already she could hear his groans, the light gasps every time she grazed a particular spot with her teeth. She glanced up. He was watching her, and she pushed back her hair, holding it so he could fully enjoy the view as well as the sensations. His hips lifted and she slid her hand down to grip the base of his shaft, stroking him with firm fingers as well as her mouth.

"Sweet God," he groaned. "I'm going to come if you don't stop."

Sadie didn't want to stop, but she didn't have the patience to wait even a few moments for him to get hard again, so she released him from her mouth and slid up the length of his body to straddle him. The damp tip of him brushed against her eager sex and that lovely chest hair tickled her nipples into exquisite tightness.

She brushed a lock of hair back from his forehead, fighting a rush of tenderness as she did so. "It's been a long time since I looked at you this way."

"You mean from this position, or as though I'm yours to do with what you will?"

Sadie smiled. "Both."

He smiled back. "So what are you going to do?"

Still holding his gaze, she reached down between them and guided his cock to the right spot. Then, she tilted her hips and pushed down, taking him inside. There was a second when both of them caught their breath. Every muscle in Sadie's body trembled as she slid down upon him, until the back of her thighs met his hips and they were as tightly joined as any man and woman could be.

Her inner muscles actually twitched, demanding one of them start moving, but Jack's hands had found their way to her hips and were holding her tightly, preventing her from lifting her own. She churned them instead.

The tendons in Jack's neck tightened as he arched his head back against the pillows. She was going to kill him. He was doing all he could to hang on to his control and not embarrass himself like some stupid virgin, and Sadie was doing her very damn best to unman him with that slick, hot vise between her legs.

Soft fingers pressed against his chest as her buttocks brushed his thighs. Her hips moved in a languid circle, slowly pushing him toward the edge of a precipice he wanted to throw himself over and avoid at the same time.

And then her motions quickened and her breathing changed. He could feel her body clutching at his and he knew that she was getting ready to come again. If he could just hold on long enough for her to spend first . . .

Sadie shuddered on top of him, her body dropping forward as the sweetest cry tore from her lips. That was all it took to destroy what was left of his resolve. Gripping her tightly, Jack arched up, digging his heels into the mattress so that he could drive himself deep within her. He came hard, with a ragged groan that seemed to go on forever inside his own head.

A few moments—or it might have been hours for all he knew—later, her warmth released him and she lay down at his side, curled against him like a cat. He wrapped one arm around her, pulling her close to his chest. God, she felt good—like security and hope and sex rolled into a sweet womanly package.

"I'm sorry," he muttered. "I wanted it to last longer."

She lifted her head to look at him, her dark hair a seductive tangle about her face. She looked at him as though he was daft—and she adored him for it. "All you've ever had to do is look at me and I'm screamin' like a *bean sidhe*. I'm not about to apologize for it, so you'd best not either."

Jack chuckled, lacing his fingers through the ones resting on his chest. She squeezed. "I've missed you, Sadiemoon."

Her gaze met his once more, and the things he saw there . . . they gave him such hope, he scarcely dare entertain it. And they scared him too, because there were secrets in the depths of Sadie's eyes, and the Sadie he knew never liked keeping secrets, not from him.

"I missed you too," she replied, and regardless of whatever he saw in her eyes, he heard the truth in her words. "More than you'll ever know."

"I'm sorry."

"For what?" Her voice was sharp in his ears. "For wanting to leave? Or for regretting it now that you're back?"

"Everything," he replied honestly, but he couldn't help reminding her, "I would have stayed if you asked."

"I know. You also would have resented me for it."

"That wouldn't have been any worse than how I felt when your letters stopped coming."

She frowned at him. "I didn't stop writing until long after you did. I didn't know where you were."

Jack returned the scowl. "Sadie, I wrote to you right up until just before my return. The letters were waiting for me unopened at our home."

The expression on her face was incredulous. "I received none."

"Neither did I."

He could tell that she found that hard to believe, but then something changed in her eyes. It was as though he could see the exact moment her mind made the right connection. When she looked at him again, it was with sorrow and regret, and just a hint of shame. "I think we both have been sorry long enough, especially for schemes not of our making."

"Meaning?"

Sadie sighed. "I think your grandfather intercepted our letters."

"What makes you think that?"

"I saw him after you left. He came to the flat."

He leaned back, putting some distance between them as her words sunk it, stinging ever so slightly. "You saw him and you're only mentioning it now?"

She nodded, cheeks flushing. "I didn't think it mattered before, but now I believe it does."

Anyone else and Jack would have thought it farfetched, but he believed it of his grandfather. It was the only way letters could have avoided both of them.

And there was nothing to be done about it now. It seemed that the realization weighed heavily on them both—and the awareness of just how much pain and anger they'd felt because of this interference. How much time had been wasted. Lost.

It was almost enough to make a man weep. "I'm hungry," Jack said, voice raw. "How about you?"

She glanced toward the table. "I think there's plenty of food left. Shall I get us a plate?"

He held her tight when she would have drawn away, and she turned back to him with a questioning gaze.

"What about that cream?" he asked with a slow smile. "Is there any left?"

Sadie's fae eyes brightened as one long leg drifted over his. "That's *exactly* the look I was talking about."

Jack grinned as her lips lowered to his. "Good thing these walls are thick."

# Chapter 13

Jack woke to find himself alone in bed. "Sadie?"

"I'm here."

He sat up against the soft pillows, blinking as his eyes adjusted to the lamplight. There were no windows in the little cottage—Saint's Row was all about discretion—and he had no idea if it was night or day.

Sadie was sitting at the table where they'd had their meal. She wore his shirt, which looked a damn sight more fetching on her than it ever had on him, and had a teacup in her hands. His teacup, judging from the look on her face.

Christ on a pony. They'd just had what he considered to be the singularly most glorious night ever, and while he could barely think, she was up and peering in the bottom of his cup for visions of the future?

Well, he knew better than to mock her for it. "Are you sure you want to look in there?" He inquired lightly. "Maybe I die tomorrow."

"Not you," she replied, frowning. When she looked

up from the cup she asked, "When was the last time you spoke to your grandfather?"

His jaw tightened. "When he told me I was as dead to him as my father and brother. Why?"

She glanced at the cup again. "I don't think he's well. I think it's his heart."

Jack snorted. "He doesn't have one." She didn't look amused, and he couldn't help but ask, "What do you see?"

Sadie turned and set the cup on the table. The movement caused the hem of his shirt to ride high up her long, round thighs. He wished he could claim his sudden erection was piss proud, but it was all because of a glimpse of leg.

"I see him dying," she answered bluntly. "In your arms."

He sat forward, looping his arms around his knees, over the sheet. "Never going to happen."

"Because I can't see the future in leaves." The bitter edge to her words raised his eyebrows. He really had struck a nerve with his skepticism. He made a mental note to keep his mouth shut in the future.

"Because I have no intention of seeing him before or after he drops dead."

"You have to eventually," she insisted. "You have an inheritance."

"Shag my inheritance."

"You don't mean that."

"You know I do," he insisted with good-natured force. "I'm Jack Friday now. Let the old man declare Jack Farrington legally dead and the title can pass on to my cousin Patrick."

A strange smile tilted her lips. "You'd really do that?"

He shrugged. "I'd be surprised if the old man hadn't done it already."

She seemed to ponder that—why, he had no idea—and found it to her liking. Slowly, she rose from the chair and came toward the bed. His shirt slid off her shoulders to drop gracefully to the carpet, leaving her gloriously naked.

She had a beautiful body—high breasts, small waist, flared hips. Her limbs were long and supple, strong too. And of course, she had a little bit of heaven between her legs. But while he found the wrapping beautiful, there was simply something magical about her that drew him to her. He had simply known the first time he laid eyes on her that she would always be part of his life, and when he married her—regardless of the legality of the ceremony—it was forever. He could admit that now. The question was, could she?

He didn't get a chance to ask her, and when she climbed into bed with him, enjoying the time they had together became more important than wondering how much more time they might have.

Just before dawn they managed to sneak out of their love nest and return to their respective domiciles without being seen. Before letting her out of the carriage, Jack gave her a kiss so sweet it brought tears to her eyes.

"When can I see you again?" he asked against her

lips, his thumb stroking her cheek as he cradled her head in his hands.

Was this really happening? It seemed too good to be true. Why hadn't they fought? They'd managed to discuss some parts of their time apart with ease, but there were other things they avoided. Jack never asked if she'd had lovers and she never asked him. It seemed both of them realized there would be things neither of them wanted to admit, or hear, and so silently agreed not to share them. She didn't care about things he'd done, she was only concerned with going forward and putting the past behind them. Maybe he was as well. Lord, she hoped so.

"Tonight," she replied. "I have to see Vienne and check in on the workmen at the shop, but tonight I'm free."

"I want to take you out. Let all of London know I'm courting you."

Sadie grinned. "It's a little late for courting, isn't it? You didn't even court me when we first met."

He brushed a light kiss across her forehead. "It would seem odd for us to suddenly be together, especially after the scandalous auction incident."

Sadie opened her mouth to respond, but he cut her off.

"Jack Friday would like very much to court Sadie Moon."

"All right," she conceded, flush with pleasure. "But don't think I'm going to tumble into your bed just because you buy me flowers."

Jack's eyes crinkled at the corners. How ridiculous was it that she wanted to kiss those fine creases? "You'll tumble into my bed because that's where you belong."

"Yes, *sir*," she replied breathlessly just before his lips came down on hers once more.

Moments later, when he'd broken the kiss, Jack gazed ruefully into her eyes. "You'd better go. The sun's coming up and I don't want to give your neighbors anything to gossip about."

Sadie could have done with another kiss, but she reluctantly admitted that he was right—again—and exited the carriage, with the suggestion that he meet her that evening for dinner at Saint's Row, and then in the club's garden later. He agreed with a heat to his gaze that kept Sadie warm long after she snuck into her house.

"Did you have a pleasant evening?" asked a familiar voice as she reached the top of the stairs, creeping toward her room.

Shoulders sagging, Sadie turned to face Indara, who was leaning out of her bedroom doorway. "As a matter of fact, I did."

Her housemate grinned, white teeth flashing. "Excellent. Would you like some help with your gown?"

Sadie rolled her eyes. She knew her friend would interrogate her mercilessly, but there was no way she could get out of this dress by herself and she didn't want to wake Petra and risk alerting the other servants to her late homecoming.

Indara didn't wait for her to acquiesce; she simply scampered across the hall in her nightgown and robe—both of which were bright crimson silk—and followed Sadie into her room.

Suddenly exhausted, Sadie tossed her belongs onto the bench in front of her vanity and kicked off her slippers. Then she stood in the middle of the carpet and allowed Indara to unfasten her gown.

"So," her friend began. "Where did you go?"

"Saint's Row. He had a key to one of the private cottages."

Her bodice tightened as Indara pulled it in excitement. "One of Vienne's love grottos? Whatever was it like?"

Chuckling at the term, Sadie didn't immediately reply. "Lovely, of course. Comfortable. Dark. Very conducive to seduction. I felt . . ." Well, now she just felt silly. "I felt like Jack and I were the only people in the world."

"That is how you should feel." Her friend's voice drifted over her shoulder and made Sadie pause. There was something wistful in Indara's soft tones. Regret? It occurred to Sadie that in all the years she'd known Indara, she'd never entertained the attentions of a man. Many had tried, but Indara rebuffed them all. She certainly had an appreciation for the male form, so why keep herself isolated and alone?

"You'll find someone someday," Sadie said, hoping she wasn't overstepping the bounds of their friendship.

Indara's nimble fingers paused halfway down Sadie's back. "I've already found him. He simply hasn't found me."

"Who—?"

Indara cut her off, resuming in her loosening of buttons. "It does not matter."

Sadie knew that voice. Her friend didn't use it often,

but it signified the end of that particular conversation. Still, Sadie couldn't help but remind her, "I'd tell you."

The exotic woman laughed. "Not if you didn't want to. You have your secrets, my friend. Let me have mine."

Sadie couldn't argue with that. The other night she had told Indara much about her history with Jack—including that she'd stayed with his grandfather for a short time. But she'd not said a word about the baby. That was her private pain and she wasn't going to share that with anyone. Instead, she'd told her friend that the old earl had lent his assistance to her during an illness. In the light of day she regretted sharing that much.

"Was it as good as you remembered?" Indara asked when the last button slid free.

Sadie turned to tilt a smile at her. "So much for secrets."

Indara only smiled, not the least bit contrite. "My people wrote the *Kama Sutra*. Physical pleasure is not the stuff of secrets. It is to be celebrated."

There were any number of Englishmen and women who would undoubtedly disagree, but who was Sadie to argue cultural differences. "Better," she replied. "It was better."

Her friend looked pleased. "That is a good sign, I think."

Sadie stepped out of her gown and turned so Indara could help with her corset. "I hope so."

"Did you tell him about his grandpapa?"

She knew revealing all to Indara would come back to bite her on the arse. "I couldn't."

*"Sadie."*

"He doesn't think the old man cares—and neither do I considering the last letter I received." She moved away, slipping out of the corset and setting it on the vanity bench as well. She braced one foot on the bench and attended to her stockings.

Indara, however, was not about to let her dismiss the topic. "But what if he does care? What if the earl comes to London and tells Jack that you were the one who summoned him?"

"I'll burn that bridge when I get to it."

Indara shook her head, dark tresses shimmering in the fledgling sunlight. "You know, I believe you truly hope Mr. Friday—or whatever his name is—never reconciles with his family, even if he wishes it."

"Of course I don't want that!" But she didn't sound quite sincere, not even to her own ears.

Indara looked at her, and it wasn't judgment Sadie saw in her friend's bright eyes; it was sympathy, maybe even pity. "You want him back, but only if he stays at his current social level. Heaven help him if he decides to do his duty and accept his inheritance. You won't want him then, will you?"

"He won't want me," Sadie retorted. "I'm not good enough for an earl."

"You were good enough for him once. You are good enough for him now. Your husband is not the snob, Sadie. You are."

"You're mad!"

"Perhaps, but I know you. And I know your dislike of

the aristocracy comes from fear, not repulsion. What did this grandfather earl say to you? That you were not good enough for his boy? That you would ruin his life? And then your husband runs off and you think the grandpapa was correct. You were not good enough to hold him. You ruined his life, and your own in the process. That is what you believe, is it not?"

She balled up her stockings and tossed them on the floor. "Definitely not!" But even as she spoke the words she had to wonder at their validity. She remembered how intimidated she'd been by Jack's family as a girl. How intimidated she sometimes was by the grand ladies who got her to read their leaves even now. She didn't have to be reminded of how she sometimes despised them for it.

Indara watched her, compassion etched in her striking features. Sadie could have slapped her for it. "Don't look at me like that, Dara. I know what I'm doing."

"Yes," her friend agreed. "That's what I am afraid of. I believe you truly understand just what kind of tragedy you are steering yourself toward."

Sadie snorted, but her rudeness was no deterrent to Indara's determination. "You've been given a second chance at true love. Few of us are rarely given even a first chance. If you ruin this, you will be a bigger fool than I could ever imagine. This time when he leaves you, it really will be your fault."

Sadie could only gape as her friend swept from the room with all the dismissive regality of a queen, while she stood there in her shift, rumpled, tender and sticky, looking every inch an urchin. Indara never allowed anyone to make her feel as though she was beneath them or somehow less. Indara looked everyone in the eye and kept her chin lifted at all times—as though she was the equal of any well-born man or woman. And though Sadie often thought her naïve, she admired her for that confidence.

Of course, Indara had never had to face the Earl of Garret. The man had wilted Sadie's confidence more than once. The entire time she'd stayed at his house he was very kind to her, but he never missed an opportunity to point out how ill suited she and Jack were. Now that she suspected—nay, was *convinced*—that he had intercepted letters between her and Jack, she wished to avoid him even more. Anyone else and she'd believe it too fantastic to be truth, but she wouldn't put any manner of underhandedness past the earl. If only she hadn't contacted him about Jack.

With that thought lingering longer than it should, Sadie unpinned her hair and crawled into bed. She was exhausted and wanted to get some extra sleep since Jack had kept her awake most of the night. She certainly wasn't about to complain, but if she was going to spend the coming evening with him as well, she needed to be rested for it. It wouldn't do to have society commenting on how tired she looked. No doubt those aristocratic harpies would have *something* to say if she showed her face with shadows under eyes.

The fact that she cared what they might say annoyed her, so she resolved not to give the matter another thought. Instead, she turned her mind to Jack and some of the particularly pleasant moments of their night together.

Yes, she reiterated with a satisfied smile as she burrowed into her pillow, it had been even better than she remembered. God help her if it continued to improve. She wouldn't survive it.

And yet, as she drifted off to sleep, sensual images drifting through her mind, she couldn't help but realize that there was something wrong with the whole situation, as though it was a play or a story she could partake in yet still not be a part of. It was as though she couldn't quite bring herself to view it as reality—her reality.

Perhaps because despite her hopes, she knew what she had seen in the bottom of Jack's cup. And she hadn't seen herself in any of it.

Jack was sitting at his favorite table at the Barrington, drinking a cup of strong coffee and reading business correspondence when a shadow fell across him. He glanced up, expecting to see a waiter offering more coffee, and was surprised to see Lady Gosling standing there instead.

He was instantly on guard, as a man should be when a woman dressed to impress sneaks up on him in the middle of the afternoon and smiles down at him like a shark bearing down upon wounded prey.

"What an unexpected pleasure," he said, forcing a smile. Odd, but just a few days ago he would have welcomed her company with twitching prick and open arms. Now he found himself decidedly uncomfortable.

She arched a finely plucked brow. "Pleasurable enough to ask me to sit, perhaps?"

No, this wasn't going to be good at all. "Of course." He gestured to the chair across from him. "Please sit."

She was very graceful, of course, but that canary-eating smile continued to hover about her carmine painted lips. It made him uneasy. Made him want to do something to wipe it right off her face. He didn't like feeling as though he was about to be attacked, or bullied. Since losing the comforts of his grandfather's world, it was a feeling he'd experienced more than he cared to admit, though he'd weathered every incident and generally came out the victor.

"Did we have an appointment?" he inquired, wanting her to get to the point and leave as quickly as possible. He'd be buggered six ways from Sunday if someone mentioned seeing him with her to Sadie.

The lady's smug smile deepened. "Aren't you going to offer me some kind of refreshment?"

He actually opened his mouth to tell her that he wasn't, no. But then the waiter appeared and asked if she would like anything and the damnable baggage asked for a cup of coffee as well.

"I do so enjoy coffee," she remarked brightly when the young man left. "It's such a rich, masculine drink. Don't you agree?"

Jack tilted his head. "I haven't given it much thought."

Lady Gosling tittered—a nerve-grating sound. "No, of course you haven't. You men always have so many things on your mind whilst we females are left to amuse ourselves."

He stared at her, forcing his eyes to stay still rather

than roll as they wanted. "A woman such as you must be terribly adept at amusing yourself."

Her gaze locked with his, and he saw not a trace of genuine warmth in it. "Indeed. I've been told I'm quite adept at amusement. Why, you wouldn't believe some of the things I do to keep myself amused."

"Do you often share these amusements?" In other words, speak your mind or shag off.

"Of course. It would be selfish of me to keep them all to myself, wouldn't it?"

"Generous as well. You're nigh on a saint aren't you?"

She shook her head. She wore a miniature top hat perched on her hair. One of Sadie's hats would eat such a poor excuse for headgear. "Oh no, Mr. Friday. Never that."

The waiter brought her coffee, keeping Jack from immediately responding. Usually he found matching wits and trading veiled conversation with a woman exciting. But after last night, and Sadie's more frank (and arousing) manner of speaking, he found himself bored.

He watched, jaw clenched as she stirred sugar and then cream into her cup. It was a drawn-out production, worthy of any actress at King's Theater. Then, she lifted the cup to her lips with both hands and took a ridiculously tiny sip. There was a slight reddish smear on the rim where her mouth had touched.

"Umm. Delicious."

"Would you like a top-up?" he asked, bone dry. "You practically drained it."

Another titter—this one more forced than the last. "Oh, Mr. Friday! How very droll you are."

This had gone on long enough. He was a busy man and he had a lot of work to get down before he could meet Sadie again that evening. He wasn't about to allow Lady Gosling and whatever game she played keep him from his wife.

"Actually, I'm very busy. I assume you came here for a reason other than the chef's excellent coffee?"

Dark green eyes narrowed, like a cat sizing up a mouse. "Rude as well."

"Rude is showing up without an appointment and expecting an audience. What I am, Lady Gosling, is out of fucking patience." Normally he wouldn't speak so to a lady, but who was he trying to kid? Lady Gosling wasn't a *lady* by any imagining. "Why don't you tell me what you want so I can say no?"

"You're not going to tell me no," she replied, an edge to her deceptively light tone.

"You're very sure of yourself." He was going to tell her no even if she gave him a goose that laid golden eggs.

"Oh, I am, Mr. Friday." She leaned her folded forearms on the table and leaned closer, that sharklike smile curving her lips once more. "Or should I say, Mr. Farrington?"

# Chapter 14

For a split second Jack's entire body seemed to shut down. He was careful not to let his shock show on his face. He was particularly careful not to reach across the table and grab the woman by the throat.

"I'm not familiar with that name," he replied smoothly. "You must have me confused with someone else."

Lady Gosling took another miniscule sip from her cup. "Jack Farrington was something of a confidence artist who lived on Russell Street with his wife *Sadie* who read tea leaves and conducted séances." Fluttering her lashes she flashed a patently false smile. "Does any of this sound familiar?"

"No, but it sounds like the stuff of novels. Go on."

From the tightening of her lips he guessed she was unimpressed by his glib tone. What had she expected? That she would toss this little bit of information at him and he'd immediately launch himself at her mercy? It was a little early for that, and he needed to find out just how much she knew. She knew his name, but did she know who he was?

"It seems there was a bit of trouble with someone claiming fraud over a reading Mrs. Farrington did, and shortly after that Jack disappeared leaving the poor little lady to fend for herself. Then she disappeared for a while as well. A few years later Sadie Moon arrived in London and set herself up as a tea-leaf reader. She's got a rather higher class of clientele, many of whom I doubt have ever heard of Jack and Sadie Farrington, but would no doubt find the story fascinating."

Jack rested his elbow on the table, tilting his head as he rested his temple against one finger. He smiled without amusement. "You know what I find interesting?"

"What?"

"That a *lady* such as yourself could make herself so familiar with the goings on of . . . Russell Street? That's near Covent Garden, isn't it?" It was something of a bluff, but it paid off when he saw her jerk the tiniest bit. "You didn't go down there yourself, did you?"

She didn't answer. She didn't have to. He could tell from the look on her face that was exactly what she had done, and now he knew something about her—that she wasn't all she pretended to be either.

"You come here accusing me of what, exactly? It seems the worst Madame Moon has done is change her name, if she truly is this Farrington woman." When Lady Gosling didn't reply, he continued, "Unless there's more to this sordid tale, my lady, I hope you'll excuse me. I have work to do."

She looked as though she'd like to strangle him. How could he ever have found her attractive? She was as cold and hard as a Hudson Bay winter—which he'd experienced firsthand. But there was a glimpse of desperation in her gaze that surprised him. "A woman matching Sadie Farrington's description was seen in Russell Street Sunday morning, near a house she and her husband once rented a flat in."

Jack shrugged. Again, he was careful to keep his features perfectly blank. "So?"

"I was very interested to learn that you own the building, Mr. Friday. And I believe you were there yesterday as well. Were you not?"

He was getting tired of this game. "Make your point, Lady Gosling, before I have you tossed out into the street."

For a moment, real alarm flashed across her face. "And risk having the whole of London learn your true identity?"

Jack leaned forward, feeling the balance of power tip a tiny bit in his direction. There were worse things that could happen than his identity becoming public knowledge, though he was surprised to realize that.

"What proof do you have of these allegations other than gossip and hearsay?" When she didn't respond, his smugness grew. "Just what I thought." He lifted one of the letters from his pile and turned his attention to it.

"I don't need to prove it," she snarled, leaning over the table. "All I have to do is whisper in the right ears that Sadie Moon was once investigated for fraud and the sweet little reputation she's made for herself turns to dust."

That was indeed worse than his identity becoming

public knowledge. Never in his life had Jack wanted to do violence to a woman like he did at that moment. Correction, he'd never wanted to do violence to *anyone* like he did at that moment. "What do you want?"

Lady Gosling smiled. "Ah-ha! Did the two of you reconcile the night of the charity auction? Is there a happy ending in store for our estranged lovers? That's when I knew there was something between the two of you, you know—when you paid a thousand pounds just for an hour of her time."

Seemed he had truly tipped his hand by that lapse in sense, but even now he couldn't bring himself to regret it because it had brought him and Sadie together again. "Name your price, woman or this meeting ends. *Now.*"

She pouted. "Rest easy, Mr. Friday. I'm not interested in ruining either you or Madame Moon. Personally, I believe she's the genuine article. All I want is your help."

"What sort of help?"

"One hundred thousand pounds and passage to New York City for two."

Jack's brows shot up. "You don't want much, do you?"

"I've looked into your finances. You can afford it."

He had no doubt she'd done just that, crafty bitch. "But do I want to pay it?"

"A small price to protect your secrets—and Sadie's."

She had him there. "What's to keep me from going to your husband and telling him what you're up to? From what I hear, he's the kind of man who might react negatively."

It wasn't his imagination; she paled. Thankfully the

dining area was relatively empty. If anyone was paying attention to their exchange they'd be mad with curiosity over the details.

"You're an honorable man," she replied, a faint strangled quality to her voice. "You wouldn't do that."

He almost laughed at that—at her audacity to say it and her naiveté to believe it. "You have no idea what I'd do."

"You'd protect someone you care about."

He scratched his chin. "You're not on that list."

"But Sadie Moon is." She leaned closer. He really could grab her by the throat if he wanted. "Give me what I want and I go away. No one ever learns your secret, or hers."

She had him by the balls and she knew it. She could say whatever she wanted about him and he'd weather it, but Sadie . . . He would rather face the old man than be the cause of her losing all she'd worked so hard to achieve. Never mind his own feelings on tea leaves and such, he would hate to see her lose her shop over such a stupid scandal. She loved her job and he refused to play any part in it being taken away from her.

He could go to the authorities, but that would bring unwanted attention as well. He hated being in this position, but it was his own fault he was there.

"I'll need a few days to get the money," he muttered, glancing down in disgust.

"Of course." She sounded giddy. "Shall we meet again on Thursday?"

Jack nodded. "Fine."

And then she did the damnedest thing. She reached

across the table and placed her hand on his arm and squeezed. "Thank you."

He trapped that hand with his own, preventing her from making the escape she'd obviously intended to make. She had begun to stand and had to sit again. Fear widened her eyes as he pinned her with a cold gaze. "I want you on a boat within the next day or you'll explain this not only to your husband, but Scotland Yard as well."

She swallowed hard, but didn't look away. "Agreed."

"Good, now get the hell out of my hotel."

He didn't have to tell her twice. The moment he released her she was on her feet and heading toward the exit. Jack turned back to his letters, just in case anyone was watching.

Three days to get one hundred thousand pounds. That wouldn't be a problem. It was more than enough time to get the money. What he hoped was that it would be enough time to find out why Lady Gosling was so very desperate to get out of London. And perhaps resort to a little coercion of his own.

"Only you could wear that color combination and make it fabulous."

Sadie turned at the sound of Vienne's voice. She'd had just walked through the door of Saint's Row. "Why, thank you, madame. You look lovely this evening."

Vienne was indeed a vision in a cream colored gown shot with gold threads that made her pale skin look as smooth and lustrous as pearl. Sadie, in sharp contrast to her friend's quiet elegance, wore a bruise-violet velvet gown with a tangerine underskirt. The dark purple worked well for her, however, and brought out the green in her eyes.

"I didn't expect to see you here tonight," Vienne remarked. "There's nothing special going on, just some dancing. Although Ryeton and his duchess are here, so that's good for business. And there's a rumor that Lillie Langtry plans to make an appearance, but I'll believe that when I see it."

The discordant mash of music and conversation drifted out of the grand ballroom as a guest slipped through the door. Sadie raised an impressed brow. "Sounds like a crush."

The Frenchwoman shrugged her slender shoulders. "It's late into Parliament's sitting and the people are bored. Many have already left town. Not so many balls and fetes to attend so they come here instead. Soon business will dwindle, but I don't mind. I will have other things to occupy my time."

She referred to her plans for a universal provider, of course. Sadie found the whole endeavor terribly exciting. She knew Jack was involved through his partner Trystan Kane, but she hadn't asked how much of an investor he was. Lord, she didn't even know how many businesses he was involved in or how many he owned himself. If they were truly going to reconcile, wasn't that something she should ask? Of course it was, and she would ask. Right around the same time he began to believe in her talent with tea leaves. Until then there didn't seem to be a point.

Perhaps that was unduly harsh and cold of her, but

it was the truth. She wanted Jack, was beginning to quite like the man he'd become, and was still infuriatingly in love with the boy he had been, but how could she ever have a future with a man who didn't believe in her—correction—in her abilities? She couldn't. She wouldn't.

She turned her mind away from such dismal thoughts and turned her head toward Vienne, only to find her friend watching her closely.

"I was going to ask what did bring you here this evening," the redhead remarked disapprovingly, "but I believe the answer to that just walked in."

Sadie followed the cool blue gaze to a sight that set her heart pounding. *Jack.* He was just about to enter the ballroom in the company of Archer Kane, and while Sadie knew there were women in London who preferred Lord Archer's dark hair and piercing blue eyes, her own eyes were only for her tanned, golden Jack. His shoulders looked so broad in his black jacket. The rich crimson of his waistcoat called attention to his strong chest and narrow waist, especially when he flipped his jacket open and set a fist to his hip as he explained something to his companion.

"For God's sake," came Vienne's exasperated voice, "put your eyes and tongue back in your head, woman. You look like a pug in need of water."

Sadie jerked, whirling indignantly on her friend. "I do not!"

Vienne simply shook her head and gave her a disgusted look. "He is glancing this way. Perhaps you should acknowledge him before he turns puggish himself."

Jack was indeed looking at her, Sadie discovered with a delighted flush. Remembering that they were supposed to begin their "courtship" tonight, she inclined her head at him. He bent in a small bow with a lopsided smile. That smile was enough to make her heart stutter against her ribs. But there was something not right—a tightness around his eyes, a stiffness to his jaw that raised concern.

*"Mon Dieu,"* came Vienne's exasperated whisper. "I cannot believe you!"

Jack and Archer stepped into the ballroom and Sadie turned once more to her friend. "What the hell is wrong with you?"

Vienne looked at her as though she were mad. Taking Sadie by the arm, she pulled her closer to the far wall, where there was presumably less chance of them being overheard. "Me? It is you who is the madwoman. Have you not learned your lesson where that man is concerned? Has he not hurt you enough?"

Strangely untouched by her friend's vehemence, she shrugged. "You could ask him the same question about me."

"No." Vienne shoved a finger at her. "Not quite, I do not think."

Sadie's head tilted over her right shoulder, not at all offended by Vienne's attitude. Her friend cared about her, that's all this anger meant. Reaching out, she took Vienne's long, cool hands in her own. "Has there never been that one man you'd risk having your heart torn to pieces for?

Who you'd give almost anything just to have a second chance with him?"

Vienne blinked, her face impassive. "No," she whispered. "Never."

Sadie shook her head and released her. She'd seen the truth in her eyes. "Liar."

Pale shoulders straightened, as though pulled by invisible strings. "Do not think I will help you pick up the pieces when he breaks your heart." Her voice held the tiniest tremor, a sign of weakness the Frenchwoman had never revealed before.

"Yes you will," Sadie replied with a warm, confident smile. "Because you're my friend and you always will be, no matter what happens. Just as I will be for you."

Vienne sniffed and looked away, but not before Sadie saw the shimmer of vulnerability in her eyes. "Go," she commanded. "Run to your ruin, and for God's sake, prove me wrong."

Sadie knew when she'd been dismissed, and wasn't the least bit offended. Vienne was not the kind of woman who liked to show emotion, especially not those she couldn't control. So, she left her friend and went in search of the beautiful man waiting for her inside the ballroom. Was he watching the door waiting for her to finally step inside? She'd wager he was.

Would he tell her what was the matter? A small part of her grew anxious. What if he'd found out she'd contacted his grandfather? Perhaps Indara was right. She should tell him, if for no other reason than she wouldn't have it hanging over her head for the rest of her days. Surely he'd forgive once he found out the old man had financed her shop. He knew what a bastard the earl could be—he'd understand that in her bitterness she'd betrayed him to achieve her own goal.

God, that made her sound awful, but that hadn't been a consideration when she'd sent the letter. She'd simply been fulfilling her end of a bargain. Even she could not have foreseen this outcome. If she were superstitious, she'd blame this on peeking into her own cup the night she saw Jack again.

Inside the ballroom ladies glittered and shone beneath the subtle chandeliers. The ballroom always put her in mind of a box of sweets—chocolate and cream with an elegant gold ribbon. She moved around the perimeter of the room, speaking warmly to the few friends she spied and greeting those of the upper ten thousand who deigned to acknowledge her. She was certain they looked down their aristocratic noses at her. Just once she'd like to walk up to one of them and say, *"Hello, I'm Viscountess Gerard. One day my husband will be the Earl of Garret."* They wouldn't be so quick to snub her then, would they?

Or perhaps they would. One never knew with this lot.

"Why, Madame Moon! Fancy seeing you here." It was Lady Gosling, looking just like a fat farm cat that had gotten into the milk pail.

"Lady Gosling." She didn't return the sentiment. This woman had chased after her Jack, and she didn't speak to people socially beneath her unless she had motive. Sadie had her pride, and would not act as though the woman had bestowed some great favor upon her.

The other woman raised a brow when it became obvious that Sadie wasn't going to offer any more conversation. "Like that, is it? I understand. Do say hello to Mr. Friday for me, will you, my dear?" Before she swept away, she shot Sadie a wink, as though they shared some secret. Odd woman, but that was the upper crust for you—too much intermarrying between first cousins. She shook off the encounter and continued on her quest.

She spotted Jack through the crowd, standing just a little further down the room with Lord Archer. She kept her gaze trained on him as she slowly moved forward—it wouldn't do to look too eager.

Finally, her dolt of a husband looked up and she caught his eye with a coy smile. He smiled back as she approached. Seeing his companion's shift in attention, Lord Archer turned. A dark brow climbed his brow, and Sadie could have sworn she saw him elbow Jack in the ribs.

"Madame Moon," Jack said smoothly, pressing a hand to his side where she thought she'd seen Lord Archer attack. "A pleasure to see you this evening. Do you know Lord Archer Kane?"

Sadie replied that she and Lord Archer had never been formally introduced and Jack performed the necessary formalities.

"Friday won't tell me what you saw in his tea leaves, Madame Moon, but you'll tell me all his darkest secrets, won't you?" Archer asked with a grin. He didn't look upon her with disdain at all, or in any other manner that might be offensive. He was simply being friendly.

Sadie smiled at the charming gentleman. "I never betray a confidence, my lord. But I will say that I saw great things in store for Mr. Friday."

"I don't doubt it." There was a roguish twinkle in his eye that made Sadie think Lord Archer was including her in those "great things." "Oh, lord. Here comes my brother."

When the Duke and Duchess of Ryeton joined them, Sadie stiffened and immediately wished she was elsewhere. Ryeton was the closest to royalty that she'd ever been. Oh, there were times she'd been at parties Prince Bertie attended, but she never saw him. She was always hired help at those events.

She was only slightly more comfortable with the duchess. She'd read Rose Danvers leaves before her marriage and had caught a glimpse of their passionate affair. She knew that the younger woman loved her husband very much, and sensed the emotion was returned.

This time Lord Archer made the introductions. The duke was cordial, bowed to her, and then immediately engaged the gentlemen in conversation after a quick glance from his wife. The duchess then turned to Sadie.

"Forgive me, Madame Moon, but I wonder if I might be able to secure a reading with you sometime in the near future?"

It wasn't the first time she'd been asked such a question in public, but Sadie was somewhat surprised all the same. After all, the duchess had wanted to make certain neither Jack nor Archer overheard her request. "Of course, Your Grace."

The duchess smiled—an expression that rounded her fair cheeks and brightened her dark eyes. She truly had the loveliest smile. "Thank you. I have something very particular upon which I wish to consult you."

Intuition made Sadie's gaze drop to the other woman's waist, incased in a gown of shimmery plum silk. The duchess blushed and Rose knew her guess had been correct. "I will do my best to answer your questions, but I feel I must warn you that sometimes the leaves are ornery and tell me very little."

"I have faith in you, and your leaves." Pretty dimples flashed. "After all, you were the one who told me that Grey and I would end up together, when even I had my doubts."

Sadie found herself smiling in return. "What a lovely thing to say. Thank you."

"Would tomorrow afternoon be convenient?"

Sadie replied that it would—even she had the sense not to refuse a duchess—and they talked for a few moments more before rejoining the gentlemen. The duke and duchess stayed with them for nearly another quarter hour before moving on.

Lord Archer sipped a glass of champagne and watched his brother walk away. "Poor Ryeton. Everyone keeps asking him when he's going to produce an heir. Not a problem you or I will ever have, is it, Friday, what?"

Jack and Sadie shared an uncomfortable glance. If Archer only knew.

"Ah, there's Lady Olivia Clark," Lord Archer remarked without waiting for a reply from Jack. "I must go flirt with her or the poor girl will be devastated. Excuse me."

Sadie stepped closer to Jack as the dark-haired man left to join a young woman with glossy hair and wide eyes who smiled at his approach. The girl's chaperone, however, didn't look nearly so impressed.

"He's something of a character," Sadie remarked, still watching the couple.

Jack turned to her. "I like him."

"You would." But there was no censure in her tone, only teasing.

He offered his arm. "Care to take a turn about the room with me, Madame Moon?"

"I would be honored, Mr. Friday." She set her hand upon his arm, delighting in the feel of the musculature beneath his coat and shirt. He was such a perfect specimen of manhood. No other was more glorious or perfect despite being humanly flawed.

As they walked, Sadie was aware of people occasionally watching them. No doubt they whispered about them as well. It hadn't been that long since the charity auction and gossips still speculated as to what had really happened during that hour in Vienne La Rieux's salon. However, this public appearance would at least paint Sadie as a pursued woman rather than a loose one—a fact she appreciated. Her business depended on her having a decent reputation. A little scandal could make a woman charming and terribly popular. Too much made her a pariah.

Jack led her to the terrace doors and a footman opened them so they might step out into the damp night air. Here they could talk in relative privacy, but still be seen.

"Did I see Lady Gosling pounce on you?" Jack asked once they stood facing each other. "What did she say?"

Sadie glanced up, frowning at his urgent tone. "Nothing. She wanted me to say hello to you." She rolled her eyes. "She seemed odd, though. More so than usual."

Jack made a scoffing sound. "I bet she did."

So she'd been right to be suspicious. Her heart twisted in the most awful fashion. She couldn't help it; her first thought was that he'd lied when he'd claimed nothing had happened between him and Lady Gosling. "Jack, what's going on?"

"Come with me." Hand on her arm he led her further away from the doors, toward the balustrade. They could still be seen by anyone else who stepped outside and looked, but weren't in plain sight and certainly not within earshot.

"I have to tell you something," he said in a tone that sent a shiver of dread down her spine.

She couldn't contain her fears. "Did you sleep with her?"

He looked horrified. "I told you before, God, no."

That gave her more satisfaction than she would have thought possible. "Then what?"

"She knows."

She stared at him blankly.

"Damn it, Sadie. She *knows*." He glanced up, obviously to make sure no one was about. Then he whispered,

"About that lovely Farrington couple from Russell Street. You know, the ones who got themselves into a wee bit of trouble? And she wants one hundred thousand and passage for two to New York to keep her silence."

Once, when she was young, one of Sadie's cousins had struck her in the chest with a bag of seed potatoes. The blow had sucked the air from her lungs, much like she felt right now.

One hundred thousand pounds? "Do you have that much?"

Jack made a face. "Yes, but I'm not eager to part with it."

Sadie turned her back to the terrace doors even though they were still very much alone. She caught Jack's arm. The reality of him kept her from imagining this was all a dream. Jack had one hundred thousand pounds? Presumably more than one hundred thousand. Dear God. And why was that what stuck in her mind when there was a larger drama unfolding? "How did she find out?"

"I don't know. She got suspicious the night of the charity auction and had me investigated." He looked disgusted—with both Lady Gosling and himself. "Had me followed, no doubt."

Followed? But why? Why would Lady Gosling care if she and Jack shared a history? The same could be said for many people, especially those of the upper class. Something about this didn't feel right. There had to be more. Was it just jealousy? Thinking Sadie was competition for Jack? That didn't ring true either, though it certainly made sense.

"But what made her suspicious? You wouldn't be the first man to offer up money for a pretty face."

"You're a damn sight more than pretty, ducks."

She smiled at his sincerity, but then turned back to the matter at hand. "How could she be suspicious of that unless she's seen us together before?"

"Maybe she overheard us talking here, that first night?"

"It's possible," Sadie allowed, but her mind kept reaching. "Maybe she knows us."

"How's that even possible?"

"I've always thought there was something familiar about her, as though I know her from somewhere else. Somewhere a long time ago." Bloody hell, why couldn't she remember? It was right there . . .

"If she knows us, maybe we know her." Jack's eyes brightened with a predatory gleam. "She was familiar with Covent Garden."

Covent Garden. That felt right. It fit with the notion that she'd had in the past of feeling there was something familiar about Lady Gosling. "I could ask Helen."

"Do that. I'll do some digging of my own, see if I can find out the identity of her traveling companion." He wrapped a strong, comforting hand around her upper arm. "I don't want to pay her, Sadie, but I will to keep her from making trouble for you all over London."

She could kiss him for being so sweet and protective. "Trouble for you too."

He shrugged. "So far she doesn't know who Jack

Farrington really is. Provided the old man doesn't find out I'm back, it doesn't matter."

Sadie swallowed. Now was the perfect time to confess. "Would it be so bad if he knew?"

A fierce scowl seized his brow. "Sometimes I wonder. There are days that I would love to flaunt what I've become in his face, and others where I like my life as uncomplicated as it is."

She couldn't help but smile. "I don't remember Jack Farrington being all that complicated." All joking aside, she knew it would be complicated if people discovered Jack's identity. He would be a peer of the realm and she would still be a tea-leaf reader.

He moved toward her, closing in like a slinky cat. "What about poor Mr. Friday? What do you think of him?"

Sadie smiled as his arm slipped around her. "I think he's a rogue and a scoundrel. And I've always had a soft spot for both."

His head lowered toward hers, and Sadie pressed a hand against his chest to stop him. "Someone might see."

Jack grinned. "I hope so."

All thoughts of confession disappeared as Jack's lips touched hers. Later, when they were alone and he could rage all he wanted, then she would tell him. When she could beg his forgiveness without all society hearing their business, she'd confide what she'd done.

"We should return," she said when their lips finally parted. She was breathless and giddy. "I wouldn't want you to do all your courting in private."

Jack offered her his arm and they headed back inside the warm ballroom. They'd just begun to approach Lord Archer when Vienne intercepted them. She had the oddest expression on her face, and she didn't even look at Sadie.

"Monsieur Friday, forgive me, but there is a gentleman here who would like to make your acquaintance."

"Of course," Jack replied. Then to Sadie, "Do you mind?"

She shook her head. "Of course not." She glanced at her friend who still would not meet her gaze. What the devil?

Vienne led them to a small group of gentlemen who were chatting animatedly. She placed her hand on the arm of a gray-haired man who had his back to them. "I found Mr. Friday for you, my lord."

Sadie's heart leaped into her throat. She knew who the man was even before he turned, but when his gold-green eyes locked with Jack's there could be no mistake. He was shorter and older, but blood always told true, and there was no denying those eyes or his nose or even the shape of his jaw.

Jack looked as though he'd been punched in the throat as he froze beside her. She tightened her grip on his arm as she too stared at a face she'd thought never to see again.

"Thank you, Madame La Rieux," the Earl of Garret said in a loud, clear voice, "for bringing me my grandson."

# Chapter 15

Jack was aware of conversation buzzing around him,
the increased volume and fervor of which could only
mean that others had heard what his grandfather said to
Vienne La Rieux.

And it felt, in a way, that everything he'd built on his
own was now ruined, forever tarnished by the public
knowledge that he was indeed a peer of the realm. He
knew this wasn't true, of course, because Tryst was the
son of a duke, but he felt it nevertheless.

He couldn't say anything, couldn't seem to think of
words at all. All he could do was stand there like an idiot
and stare at his grandfather, the Earl of Garret. He'd
known this day would come eventually, that was why he
hadn't returned to England since discovering Sadie had
left him. Odd, but he didn't feel nearly as angry as he
thought he would, and his grandfather didn't look nearly
as smug as he'd imagined. It was strangely relieving to
have the truth out.

The old man was of course older than he remembered. His thick hair, once the same color as Jack's was completely gray, but still thick and worn in a slightly outdated style that only made him more imposing. He was shorter now, but his spine was still straight as an arrow, and his eyes were still as cold and unyielding as they'd ever been.

At least he had the satisfaction of facing him as a man, and a successful one at that. He had his own fortune, one that he'd built with his own goddamn hands.

"I think," said Ryeton, coming to the rescue, "that this conversation should be played out in private. Madame La Rieux, I assume you can see to that?"

Jack barely glanced at the French woman who replied that she could indeed. He simply fell in line with the others as they left the ballroom. He couldn't quite focus on anything, but he saw every face that stared at him as he walked by. And then he felt warm fingers curl around his own. He turned his head to see Sadie by his side, tall and concerned. He smiled ruefully at her. She smiled back, but it didn't quite reach her eyes. He couldn't blame her. The old man had been a complete bastard to her before and after their marriage.

They ended up in La Rieux's office, a richly appointed room that managed to be imposing and stately and still feminine.

"Friday." Ryeton's deep voice cut through the haze that permeated Jack's brain. "Is this true? Is Garret your grandfather?"

The old man didn't look pleased at having his honor questioned. "His name is Farrington," the earl remarked coolly. "Friday is the foolish name he made up when he ran away ten years ago."

Jack was dimly aware of the others watching him, watching the old man. He fixed his gaze on Sadie. His grandfather hadn't mentioned her at all. Of course, he wouldn't. He never wanted the marriage, never acknowledged it. He certainly wouldn't bring it up now. Jack could, however. He could make his own announcement and ensure that Sadie stayed with him forever, but even in his fuzzy state, he knew that was not the right thing to do. He lifted his gaze to the duke's. "It's true." And then, just in case anyone thought he referred to his name change, "He is my grandfather."

Ryeton arched a brow. "Then I'm certain the two of you have much to discuss that does not warrant an audience. We will leave you to your privacy."

Jack's head jerked up and he turned his attention to Sadie. She untwined her fingers from his and stepped away. He wanted to keep her with him, but that wasn't the manly thing to do. And it wasn't fair to her. She looked so sad, though, as if this was good-bye for them. Forever. It hurt just to look at her.

The others hesitantly moved to do the duke's bidding. Sadie was the last one out of the room. She didn't turn to glance over her shoulder at him, and the click of the latch as the door closed behind her seemed to echo throughout the room like the tolling of a death knell.

It also snapped him out of the damned fog he was in.

"That was quite the entrance," he remarked, turning

to the man who had practically raised him. "I trust you accomplished what you set out to achieve?"

His grandfather opened his arms—not for an embrace, though, never that—and stood there in a Christ-like pose. "Can a man not journey to London to see his own grandson?"

"You didn't come to see me," he replied. "You came to teach me a lesson."

The earl didn't seem the least bit offended by his coldness, nor did he seem entirely smug. In fact, he looked as tired and relieved as Jack felt. "It's time for you to take your rightful place as my heir. It's time for you to do your duty to your family."

Of course it was. It was time because the old man decreed it such, and Jack had no say in it. He'd never had any say in anything—until he married Sadie. That act of defiance had been the most liberating thing he'd ever done.

And then he'd walked away from it because he still felt as though he had to prove himself worthy, both to her and the old man. Now, he had to admit that given the chance to do it all over again he wouldn't have given his grandfather that much power. He might still have gone, but he would have taken Sadie with him, or come back sooner. That he would have done differently.

"This doesn't change anything," he informed the older man. "I'm not giving up my life just because you showed your hand."

The old man shrugged. "I don't care what you do so long as you do what is expected of you. By tomorrow morning all of London will know you as my heir and this ridiculous game of yours will be over."

A game. That was how he looked at all Jack had achieved. He hadn't gone off to make his own way in the world, he had been playing a silly game.

Bastard. He couldn't even have the decency to be proud of what Jack had accomplished. He wasn't just a lazy, spoiled brat. He'd built something and his grandfather couldn't even bring himself to acknowledge it. But then, that shouldn't be a surprise.

But instead of lashing out, or arguing, he asked, "How did you know I was in England?"

"How do you think I found out you had returned?" A gaze much the same color and intensity of his own pinned him to the spot. "Who knows your true identity who would also know how to contact me?"

The answer struck hard and fast, leaving an awful taste in his mouth. "Sadie."

The old man smiled, that self-assured smug curving of his lips that Jack always despised. "Of course. You shouldn't be angry with her, though. It was part of our arrangement. I gave her a tidy sum to start a new life in return for her alerting me if you returned to England. Frankly, I'm surprised she lived up to her end."

"You're the reason she left me."

His grandfather shot him a pitying look. "She came to me after that. Her leaving was entirely your fault, boy-o."

Jack turned away, letting the truth seep through to his bones. Sadie had betrayed him, and he could scarcely fault her for it. She'd despised him enough to refuse the money he sent, but had no problem taking blunt from his grandfather. She must have hated him so much to do that. She must have been so hurt.

No, he didn't blame her for fulfilling her part of a business arrangement, or for thinking the worst of him. What he blamed her for was not telling him herself, for not confessing once their relationship had begun to heal.

He blamed her for not trusting him. For concealing a truth that affected them both so very, very much. If only she'd said *something* he might have been better prepared for this moment. He wouldn't feel like a stupid boy caught doing something naughty, waiting for his grandfather to get his cane.

"Wipe that look off your face," the old man demanded, all smugness gone from his stern face. "You act as though you're being led to slaughter rather than accepting your place amongst the aristocracy of Ireland and England."

"You were the one who said I didn't deserve that place."

"Whether or not you deserve it is immaterial. It is yours and you will accept it. You will assume your rightful place and by the end of next Season, you will have found a wife."

"I already have a wife."

His grandfather made a scoffing noise. "That's easily

remedied. I took care of it then, I can make it disappear now."

"You couldn't buy her off ten years ago. What makes you think you can buy her off today?"

"Because she's not some lovesick cow hanging off your every word now, my boy." A hint of smugness returned. "Because she's a practical woman. And because in her heart she knows the difference between what she wants and what's for the best—a difference you best be able to determine for yourself very soon."

Jack stiffened. "You have no control over me, old man. I might have to assume the title forced upon me, but beyond that, I don't answer to anyone but myself."

"Fight me all you want, boy. It doesn't matter. Sadie O'Rourke is a smart gel who knows her place, which is more than can be said for you. I wouldn't hope for anymore rendezvous in Russell Street were I you."

Rather than react with anger or petulance, Jack smiled mockingly. "Spying on me, grandfather? How very common."

The old man's eyes narrowed. "You only married her to spite me, or have the years made you forget?"

"I married her because I loved her."

"And left her because . . . ?" The old man arched a brow. "Because getting back at me meant more to you than she did. Don't kid yourself, boy. Do the poor gel a justice and let her go. You've done enough damage where she's concerned. Time to grow up and become a man."

Jack wanted to belt him. Honest to God, it was only a faint grasp on propriety that stopped his fist. "What do you mean, 'enough damage'?"

His grandfather shook his head. "I'm not going to argue any longer with you. I'm a tired old man. Should you decide you want to speak civilly, I'm staying at the family house in Berkeley Square. You remember how to find the place, don't you?"

Jack's glare deepened. "I do."

The old man sketched a bow. "Excellent. Good evening Lord Gerard."

"Fuck you."

But his grandfather didn't hear him, or pretended not to, either way it infuriated him.

He stood there fuming as the old man took his leave. He didn't know who he was more livid at—himself, Sadie, or the old man. No, wait. The old man.

"Are you all right?" came Sadie's soft voice.

He turned to face her. She stood in the open door, hands clasped in front of her. He reckoned the expression on her face was similar to the one Eve wore after Adam took hell from God for eating the apple.

"Been better," he replied honestly as she stepped inside. The sight of her drained most of the anger from him. She'd always had that affect—things always seemed better when she was there. "Why didn't you tell me you had contacted him?"

She shrugged, ivory shoulders smooth in the warm light. "I tried to a couple of times, but something always interrupted. I guess I hoped it would just go away. You said yourself that you didn't think he'd come for you even if he knew you were here."

"Bad gamble," he admonished lightly as that oddly relieved feeling crept back. He no longer had to lead a double life. No longer had anything to hide. But he wasn't going to use the name Farrington again. Old man, be damned.

She nodded. "It was. I'm sorry."

He watched for a moment, noticing the strain around her mouth, a certain sadness in her eyes. In a moment, he had a flash of insight—a sudden understanding that scared him more than anything else ever had.

"Are you a practical woman, Sadie?" he asked.

Her brow puckered. "I like to think so. Why?"

"My grandfather said you were a practical woman. He said you wouldn't stand in the way of me doing my duty." She wasn't stupid; he didn't have to fill in the rest. And now he knew why she'd looked so pleased when he talked of allowing the title to pass to his cousin.

Her smooth cheeks paled slightly. "He was right. I won't. And if you care for me at all, you won't ask me to."

"Sadie . . ." He moved toward her, but she took a step back.

"Two different worlds we come from, Jack. Ten years ago I was foolish enough to think it didn't matter, but I've had plenty of time to realize that it does and always has." She smiled sadly at him, but there was no regret or recrimination in her wide eyes. "You left me to prove something to your grandfather. You left because you just *had* to make a fortune. I don't blame you for that. How could I expect you to give up everything to be with me? I can't be a lady anymore than you can bring yourself to believe a person's fate can be revealed in a clump of leaves."

"I would give up everything to be with you." And by Christ he meant it!

Her hand on his chest stopped him from getting any closer. "No, you wouldn't. I wouldn't let you. I'll be your lover, Jack, and I'll always be your friend, but I won't be your countess. I can't."

"Damn it, Sadie. You're my wife."

"Only here." She tapped his chest, just over his heart. "There isn't a scrap of paper to prove it anywhere." His grandfather had seen to that.

He wrapped an arm around her, then the other, determined not to let her go. "I won't let you go."

Soft hands came up to cup his face. Her thumb brushed against his lips as she gazed up at him, her eyes also bright with unshed tears. "You can't always have what you want, Jack. You tried that once before and it didn't work. I'm not going to be the one who pays for it when you try again. It hurt too much last time."

"It's different now. *We're* different now."

"Are we? I'm still a girl who reads tea leaves and you still don't believe in them. You're still a boy trying to bend the world to your will. It was lovely trying to pretend otherwise, but the game is over. We have to go back to reality now."

"No," he insisted, trying to hold her close as she squirmed to get away. "There has to be a way."

"Please let me go."

It was the smallness of her voice that loosened his arms, and the sight of a tear trickling down her cheek that made him release her altogether. She didn't say anything else; she simply pivoted on her heel and ran from the room as though hell itself was chasing her.

Jack was still standing there, stunned and silent when Vienne La Rieux came in sometime later. One ginger brow arched at the sight of him. "I thought you'd left."

He smoothed a hand over the front of his jacket. "I probably should."

"Wait for a bit," she advised, closing the door and coming deeper into the room. "There are still enough people talking about you out there that you'll be mobbed if you show your face. You do not look as though you are up for that."

"No," he muttered on a strangled laugh. "I'm not."

"Sit then. I need a whiskey. Would you care to join me?"

He nodded and she went to the small mahogany sideboard on the far wall and poured two generous glasses. When she joined him, she gestured for him to sit in one of the wing-backed chairs in front of her desk. She seated herself in the other.

La Rieux fixed him with a not altogether unsympathetic gaze. "I want you to know that I was unaware of your relationship with the earl when I came to fetch you, my lord."

He winced at the slight deference in her tone. It had never been there before. "I appreciate that. Still, the association will be good for business, will it not?" He shot her a strained smile.

Her lips curved slightly in response. "*Oui*. I suppose you will want a cut of the profits, no?"

Laughter burst from his throat, strangled and raw but welcome all the same. To feel anything right now was a joy. "Of course." He rubbed his hand through his hair before taking a long swallow of whiskey. He grimaced, but didn't cough.

"Sadie ran away from you didn't she?" La Rieux asked after a few seconds silence.

Jack took another drink from his glass. It went down a little smoother this time, but just as warm. "She did. Happy?"

"Hardly. I do not like to see my friends in distress, my lord . . . Hmm, how very strange to call you that."

Jack tipped his head. "You're not joking. Strange to hear it as well." He took another drink.

"Let me tell you something about Sadie. She was hurt very badly when you left. I don't tell you this to hurt you, I tell you this because it's true. Something happened, something even I do not know. But she will not jump into your arms because you are titled again. *Mon Dieu*, in fact, she will run all the faster for it."

He nodded glumly. "She's always been that way."

"She doesn't see her own worth." La Rieux's tone was incredulous. "But, she cares for you. Why, I don't know. So, if you want her, you must make her see that worth.

You must make her trust you again. You must make her realize that the two of you, as much as it pains me to say, were made for one another."

How the hell would he do that? "Why are you telling me all of this?"

La Rieux raised her glass. "Because I feel sorry for you, you poor bastard."

Jack raised his glass as well. "That makes two of us."


The Duchess of Ryeton was indeed pregnant—at least that's what the leaves said. Intuition told Sadie that it was a boy, a fact that put a huge smile on the young duchess's face. A big hurrah for the all-important male heir, Sadie thought a little bitterly. Would the duchess have been this excited about a girl?

It was unfair of her, of course. Her Grace had never been anything but sweet to her, even friendly. She and her husband did all they could to put her at ease. It was Sadie who was making all kinds of judgments. Sadie who watched everything her hostess did and made some internal comment upon it. Really, she was quite ashamed of herself by the time the reading came to an end.

"Had you any idea that Mr. Friday was really Viscount Gerard?" The duchess asked, helping herself to a third cake.

Sadie was tempted—very much so—to reply that yes she had, and that she'd known for years as the two of them were man and wife. She wanted this woman—every woman in London for that matter—to know that Jack was hers.

But she shook her head instead. "No. I did not. We were not that intimately acquainted." The lie did not trip quite so easily off her tongue.

The duchess shot her a pointed, but teasing look. "I'm not sure I believe you, Madame Moon. But I don't blame you for keeping your own counsel. It's so difficult to know who one can trust in this town."

"I meant no offense, Your Grace."

Full pink lips curved into a wide grin. "None taken! My lord, you'll have to do better than that to offend me. But now that we're on the topic of the viscount and intimacy, I suppose he'll be looking for a wife."

Sadie's stomach twisted. "I suppose so."

"How would you feel about becoming a viscountess?"

Color filled Sadie's cheeks. "Your Grace, I have no ambition of the sort!"

"Well you should. I've seen how the man looks at you."

"A viscount could never marry a mere nobody."

"It's been my experience, my dear, that a duke, marquess, and, yes, even a viscount can do whatever the hell he wants. Pardon my language."

Sadie blinked. "I'm certain his lordship will succumb to his grandfather's wishes."

"Succumb." The duchess inclined her head ever so slightly. "What an interesting choice of words."

Much more of this and Sadie was going to start squirming. She felt as though the duchess was peering straight into her soul, seeing every lie and subterfuge. "Regardless, ma'am, I have not had an offer from the viscount, nor do I expect one." *Liar.*

"Oh? Did your leaves tell you that?"

"It's bad luck to read one's leaves."

"Really?" The younger woman held out her hand. "Then let me read yours."

Dumbfounded, Sadie stared at her. "Do you know how to read leaves?"

"No." Her Grace licked a spot of frosting from her thumb. "But surely you can tell me what the images mean?"

"It's more than just images, it's the feelings one gets from them."

The duchess shrugged. "I can interpret my own feelings. Indulge me, please. Once you depart, I will have nothing else to do but play with the dogs."

Certain it would be the height of bad manners, and possibly bad for business to refuse, Sadie agreed. Besides, once she returned the Earl of Garret's investment to him, she was going to have to work all the harder to come up with enough money to open her own shop.

There was no way she was going to keep the old man's money after the stunt he pulled the night before. Not even she had the stomach—the *practicality*—for that.

She had already finished her own tea, so she turned the cup upside down on the saucer and turned it three times widdershins while her mind dwelled on Jack and the look on his face when she'd left him last night. If she hadn't known better, she'd swear she'd broken his heart. No doubt her refusal hurt him, but he would rally again when eager mamas began shoving their daughters at him. She had to believe that. Had to.

She handed the cup to the duchess. "Tell me what you see."

The other woman peered into the almost translucent china. "I see a harp. With a circle around it."

Sadie stilled. "Are you certain it's a harp?"

"I may be new at this, but it looks like one to me." Lady Ryeton turned the cup so she could look inside. "See it?"

Indeed there it was, plain as day, a harp surrounded by an almost perfect ring of leaves near the top of the cup, which indicated it would happen soon.

"What does that mean?" Her Grace asked.

Sadie swallowed. "A harp signifies love while a circle means completion, or something coming full circle."

The duchess smiled again, lighting up her entire face. "So you'll experience completion through love, or a love coming full circle?"

"Something like that," Sadie murmured, heart pounding. Though how much belief could she put in the leaves when they were being read by someone with no experience, no gift for them?

But she'd seen it herself.

And who was she to say that the duchess hadn't the gift of sight? What kind of hypocrite would she be if suddenly she threw aside her belief in this ancient practice simply because she was terrified the leaves might be right?

"I see an hourglass."

Sadie nodded, pulling herself together enough to focus

on what the duchess said and remember the meaning. "The need to make a decision."

"And an . . . owl?"

"Gossip, more generally people talking."

"So, people are going to be talking about you? In London? *Quelle surprise!*"

Sadie tried to join in her light laughter, but her heart was stuck quite firmly in her throat, so much so that she thought she might choke on the lump there. People were going to talk. There was a decision she would need to make. A decision about Jack?

"There's a shoe in here as well. Does that mean you'll go shopping?"

Lips trembling, Sadie forced a smile. "Is it near the hourglass?"

"Yes! What does it signify?"

"That the decision I make will lead to a change for the better."

Dark eyes sparkled with pleasure as a bright smile curved full pink lips. Such a pretty woman, Her Grace was. "Ohhh. I'm quite good at this, aren't I?"

Sadie nodded. "You are indeed. Is that all you see?" Inside she prayed for that to be all.

The duchess held up her free hand. "Wait, there's something else. I see a . . . wedding!"

Frowning, Sadie reached out to take the cup. "That can't be right." No one ever just sees a wedding, especially not someone inexperienced with leaves and all their subtleties. But when she took the cup and looked inside, she saw—down near the bottom—what was clearly a man and a woman standing side by side and the woman was wearing what looked like a veil.

One look at the man and she knew in her heart it was Jack, but she couldn't get a clear feeling for the bride. Jack was going to marry, and as much as her heart swelled with hope, she knew the bride could not be her. Her decision was to let Jack go, and it was definitely best for everyone, so the woman in the cup was someone else.

"Very good," she praised Lady Ryeton as she set the cup on its saucer. Her shaking fingers made the two clatter loudly before she jerked her hand away and all was silent. "If I ever need a partner, I know who to enlist."

If anything, the duchess's grin broadened—something Sadie would have thought impossible. Honestly, the woman had so many teeth! And all of them very lovely. "Wouldn't that give the gossips something to go on about? The Duchess of Ryeton turns fortune-teller. You should not have put the idea in my head, Madame Moon, for now I'm tempted to do it!"

Her amusement was infectious. "I wish I had your spirit, Your Grace."

The duchess waved an airy hand. "Perhaps I should have spoke clearer earlier. Not only may a duke or viscount do as he wishes but, my friend, so might a duchess or a viscountess. Otherwise, what's the use of having money and a title? I believe it's my duty to give the papers gossip to print. I'm doing my part to create employment."

Sadie genuinely laughed at that, her estimation of the duchess rising higher and higher.

Unfortunately, it was time for her to take her leave,

so she congratulated the duchess once again on her pregnancy, and asked for her to confirm it as soon as she could. She also promised to keep the news to herself until it was made public. And then, armed with one of her journals, she set off to visit another house in Mayfair. This one much smaller than the Duke of Ryeton's, but still every bit as grand as the neighborhood demanded.

A stooped butler answered the door and took her card. Then he made her wait in a small but pretty sitting room as he went off to find his mistress. She didn't have to wait long.

"Madame Moon." Lady Gosling sounded surprised to see her. "Or should I say, Lady Gerard?"

Sadie watched the elegant woman as she glided into the room as though making an entrance on a stage. Although, she supposed that was appropriate. "Mrs. Moon will be fine, unless of course, you wish for me to refer to you as Theone Divine? That was your stage name, was it not? That's what it says on the playbill I found in an old trunk I have. A lovely likeness of you too."

Lady Gosling paused for a moment before seating herself next to Sadie on the sofa. "Well, well. Kitten has claws after all."

It took all of Sadie's willpower not to roll her eyes at the foolish comparison. "What I have, Lady Gosling, is a desire to keep my private life private, the same as you. I'm sure you wouldn't want society to find out that you're no more of a lady than I am."

Lady Gosling studied her, a peculiarly bemused expression on her face. "But you are technically a viscountess, are you not? If I think I am more of a lady than you, it is because I deserve this life. I want this life. You think you're better than me, better than anyone with a title because you claim you don't *want* it."

Sadie wrinkled her brow. "I don't think I'm better than anyone, but you're right—I don't want the kind of life you have."

"Not even if that means losing Jack?"

She said nothing, because she was afraid she might open her mouth and the wrong answer would come out.

Lady Gosling clucked her tongue. "Are you a snob or just afraid that you won't be able to live up to expectations?"

"Not all of us are such talented actresses, my lady. I don't pretend well."

Her companion rolled her eyes. "Please. You've pretended to be a widow for years. You pretended not to know your own husband, a feat I wish I could achieve. You could easily become part of this world if you desired. What I don't understand is why you don't want it."

Shaking her head, Sadie set her ledger on her lap. "That doesn't matter, and I'm certainly not going to discuss it with you. Promise me you'll leave Jack alone and I promise you the world will never hear of your secret from my lips."

"My dear woman, you needn't have gone to all this trouble to ensure my silence. It's not exactly good *ton* to blackmail a peer of the realm. In fact, it's frowned upon. Had I known his true identity in the beginning, I should have been wise enough to keep his lordship's—and your—secrets."

How could she treat this so lightly? "So you're not going to extort money from Jack?"

The lady sighed. "I suppose not, if you must know."

This was unexpected. Sadie regarded her narrowly. "I'm afraid I don't quite understand you, Lady Gosling."

Laughter rang out in the room, but it was tinged with bitterness. "That makes two of us. Though if Lord Gerard offers me money, I shan't refuse."

"What do you need money for anyway?" Sadie asked in a low voice, even though the door was shut. "And passage to New York? Are you running away with a lover?"

Her companion froze, then leaned forward to whisper, "It's none of your concern, Mrs. Moon. Suffice it to say, it's very important to me to leave London. To leave the one person keeping me in London. And, yes, there is someone who I will not leave behind."

The look in her eyes spoke volumes. Sadie thought about the marks she'd seen on Lady Gosling's upper torso, and some of the things she'd seen in the lady's cup. It began to make a frightening kind of sense now, especially when she remembered the few times she'd laid eyes on the baron. He never struck her as a kind man.

"You know," Sadie began, still holding the lady's gaze, "Lord Garret would probably pay a great deal to make certain the world never finds out about me and his son."

Dark brows shot up. "Mrs. Moon! How delightfully

wicked of you. But then, we're back to the 'extorting a peer' again and that's not a game with consequences I want to face."

No. Sadie could see why not. "There is something else I might have to offer you."

"Do tell. I'm your captive audience."

So cool and unruffled, she was. She was like the female equivalent of Lord Archer, only with more bite to her. Sadie opened the ledger on her lap to a page she'd marked. It was from a reading done a month ago. She showed it to Lady Gosling.

Dark green eyes read quickly, then read again before rising to lock with Sadie's. "Why didn't you tell me this at the time?"

"Because I thought it might upset you."

The lady laughed, somewhat harshly. "And now?"

"I wanted you to leave Jack alone, and after what you just said, I thought this news might be somewhat welcomed rather than frightening."

"It is welcomed," Lady Gosling replied. "Does that make you despise me?"

Sadie shrugged. "I'd despise you more for blackmail, but I think I understand your motives. No, I don't despise you at all. In fact . . ."

A long hand shot into the air, palm out. "Do *not* say you feel sorry for me."

Sadie smiled. "I don't. I do feel *for* you, however. And I hope this news changes things for you somewhat."

Her companion nodded. "It will if it proves true."

Slightly affronted, Sadie showed what little arrogance

she had. "Have you *ever* known me to be wrong?"

Amused, and obviously put in her place, Lady Gosling smiled. "No. I have not."

"And I'm not wrong now."

"How long before it happens, do you reckon?"

"Based on what I remember in relation to your cup and other events that have happened, I'd say a month at most."

Red lips settled into a grim, but satisfied line. "I can wait that long."

"You'll want to make sure affairs are aligned in your favor," Sadie suggested, slightly mortified at her own thoughts.

"Yes," Lady Gosling agreed. "I will. Thank you, Mrs. Moon. How can I ever repay you?"

"You know how."

The lady nodded. "Viscount Gerard is safe from me. And so are you. In fact, if there's anything I can ever do for you . . ."

Sadie shook her head. "That's not necessary." She stood. "I'll take my leave now. Good day, Lady Gosling."

A look passed between them, one of two women who knew exactly where they stood, who knew more about each other than either was comfortable with and yet had a strange respect for one another.

"My mother," Lady Gosling said in a soft, raspy voice. Sadie paused in the door with a questioning glance. "My mother is the person I won't leave behind."

Ah, that explained much as well. Often Sadie had seen what appeared to be someone elderly in the lady's cup, but when she'd bring it up, Lady Gosling pretended not to understand, or dismissed it. "You're not going to have to leave her," she promised. "I've never been more sure of anything."

The other woman nodded, and quickly averted her gaze. "Good day, Mrs. Moon."

Sadie left then, and she didn't even begin to question her judgment until she was in her carriage and on her way home. She'd saved Jack. She'd saved herself, and it had been as easy as telling Lady Gosling that her husband would be dead before the month was out.

# Chapter 16

Invitations began arriving the next day.

Jack had no idea who half the people were, but apparently they knew him. Or rather, they knew his grandfather and had now decided that Jack was worth inviting over for dinner or a party.

He refused them all, except for the one from the Duchess of Ryeton, who invited him to dinner to celebrate Trystan's homecoming. He could hardly refuse that one, even if he wanted to.

He hadn't seen Sadie since that fateful night at Saint's Row, though not for lack of trying. Twice he'd been by her house only to be told she wasn't at home. And once, he'd gone by her shop only to find it suspiciously empty. She was avoiding him, doing her best to shut him out of her life and force him into what she thought was best for him.

As if she had any idea what was best for him.

He wasn't about to let her go so easily, not after all these years, not when they'd been given a second chance. He didn't give a rat's arse what was expected of him.

He'd wasted too much time on stupidity and he was done with it. He wanted Sadie in his life, in his bed, and in his frigging house.

He wanted to know what the hell happened with Lady Gosling, who had sent round a note begging off their scheduled Thursday meeting. Seems that she'd suffered from a "change of heart" whatever the hell that meant. He was certain Sadie had played a part in it.

And he wanted to know what had driven Sadie to his grandfather, what secret the two of them shared. She wouldn't have needed much incentive to notify the old man of his return, but why had she gone to him in the first place?

More importantly, why had the old man given her the quid? He'd never made any secret of his feelings for Sadie. He thought her totally unsuitable to be Jack's countess and accused her of being after his fortune—hence Jack being cut off. He'd tried to pay her to go away and she refused it. What changed her mind?

It was curiosity that finally drove him to his grandfather's home in Berkeley Square late Friday afternoon.

He had been a young man of perhaps seventeen the last time he visited the large Palladian mansion with his family's crest above the door. He hated every moment of that Season in London because it kept him away from Sadie. He'd been certain she'd find another boy while he was gone. He wrote to her every day and bribed one of the footmen to post the letters for him.

It was raining as he stepped out of the carriage. Not a gentle summer rain, but a heavy deluge that splashed up from the gravel drive as he ran beneath the shelter of his umbrella toward the steps, soaking his boots and the hem of his great coat. He'd owe his coachman a hot toddy when they returned to the hotel.

He was met at the door by Alistair, the butler who had taken over the post from his father when Jack had been but seven years old. It was startling to see him with gray at his temples and lines on his face.

"Master Jack!" he cried, face splitting into a grin. "I mean, Lord Gerard. It's lovely to see you, sir."

The older man took the hand Jack offered, and was pulled into a quick embrace. "It's good to see you, Alistair. You may call me whatever you wish, don't you concern yourself."

"Thank you, my lord. Bless you, what a fine gentleman you've become! Allow me to take your coat and hat."

After being divested of his outerwear, Jack inquired as to the whereabouts of his grandfather.

"He's in his study, my lord," Alistair replied. "Shall I announce you?"

"That won't be necessary. I remember the way." He clapped the butler on the shoulder and crossed the threshold into the great hall. As he walked, his bootheels tapped on the marble tile, placed so that pale gray tiles surrounded a series of black ones arranged to make a multi-limbed star in the center of the floor. He paused on that star to glance up, up, up at the rotunda high above—a glass dome that on sunny days lit the hall with a splendid glow. Today he saw nothing but gray and wet through the thick glass.

Lowering his gaze, he looked around him at the high windows, the plaster work and statues that had graced this hall since long before his birth. As a child, before his parents' deaths, he'd played in this hall, pretending those statues were his friends, gazing out those windows to the world beyond. He'd been taught that the world within these walls was the most important of all, and at the time he'd believed it. The thought of someday making this house his home once again was a pleasant one. Especially if Sadie shared it with him.

That thought made him all the more determined to uncover the nature of this bizarre alliance she'd made with his grandfather, and to uncover why it was so important to the old man that Jack step up and take his rightful place *now*. It hadn't been important in the past or he would have heard. He might not have been in contact with the old man or his world, but Trystan stayed in regular contact not only with his brothers, but with his mother as well. The dowager duchess of Ryeton kept her son up to date on the comings and goings of society. If Earl Garret had come to London seeking out his prodigal grandson, Jack would have known.

He left the great hall and its memories through a door on the right. A matching one on the left led to the north wing, where his mother used to have her parlor and drawing rooms. The south wing was where the study and library were, as well as the dining room. And of course, upstairs on the first floor were rooms that could be opened up to form a much larger room where balls and musicales had been presented. How long had it been since this house had hosted a ball? Not since his mother's death.

The wall was lined with paintings—portraits of his ancestors. None of them were earls, however. Those portraits were confined to the library where they might be best displayed in all their pomp and ceremony. A proud, stuffy lot most of them had been. Jack always preferred these portraits, especially the one of the eighth . . . no, the ninth Lady Garrett. She had a right naughty look in her green eyes, and pretty red hair the color of a new penny. She looked like a woman with a rebellious streak, and Jack rather fancied he inherited his from her.

The earl's study was located in the front of the house, where the old man might sit at his desk and watch traffic go by, or observe those who came to call and decide accordingly whether or not to be at home to receive them. No doubt he'd watched Jack run through the rain, and no doubt he was wondering now what was taking that useless grandson of his so bloody long to come to him.

Swallowing a sigh of resolution, Jack raised his fist and knocked twice on the heavy door.

"Come in."

He winced at the haughty tone of his grandfather's command. That spiteful part of his nature made him wait almost a full count of ten before turning the knob and walking in.

Padrig Farrington stood with his back to the door, hands clasped behind his back as he gazed out the window at the street beyond. It was an imposing posture, one that had often intimidated Jack in his childhood.

He linked his own hands behind his back as he came to stand beside his grandfather, mimicking his exact stance, only standing a few inches taller. "You've been standing here like this ever since you saw me get out of my carriage, haven't you?" He couldn't keep the mockery from his voice.

The old man's head turned just enough so he could shoot Jack a black look. "You took so long I grew tired of sitting."

Jack shrugged. "I couldn't brush by Alastair without a proper hello."

His grandfather sniffed. "That's more than you've given me."

He kept his gaze locked on the street outside. "It's more than you deserve."

"Such bitterness. It warms me to see how much you still care."

"I don't care. Not about you."

There was just the slightest pause as the old man went still. Then he turned to almost fully face Jack. "Angry as I was, I never stopped caring about you, my boy."

What was that emotion that seized Jack by the throat? Was it love or rage? "You've always had an odd way of showing you care, Grandfather."

"Did you think I honestly wanted to cut you off? I thought you'd last a month at best and then come to your senses. How could I have known how stubborn you were?"

"I inherited my stubbornness from you."

His grandfather smiled a little at that. "Indeed you did. I've missed you, Jack my boy."

"I wish I could say the same." It was a lie. He had missed the old man on occasion.

A sigh punctuated the space between them. "Bitter till the end."

"You can force me to admit to being your heir, but you can't force me to like it. You cannot force me to like *you*."

"I only acted in your best interest. That's all I've ever done."

Jack's temper wore thin, rubbed raw by too many emotions. "What did you do to Sadie?"

His grandfather drew back, obviously affronted. "What are you insinuating?"

"She took your money. Why?"

"I assume because she wanted it. Beyond that you'll have to ask her." He turned away. "Now I believe we should make a public appearance together. The sooner the better. I want society to accept you as Viscount Gerard as soon as possible."

"What's the hurry? It's been more than a decade."

"The sooner they see you as Lord Gerard, the sooner they'll stop seeing you as Jack Friday. Preposterous name, by the way."

Jack merely shrugged. "And the sooner there will be a huge class difference between me and Sadie, right?"

"There always has been a huge class difference between the two of you. You're the only one who refused to see it."

"All I have to do is publicly reveal Sadie as my wife and you lose." Foolish to tip his hand, but he was angry and not thinking straight. He only wanted to needle his grandfather the way the old earl needled him.

"Does Miss O'Rourke even want to be your wife?" his grandfather asked, absently lifting a crystal paperweight from his desk and polishing it with his sleeve. "Last time I spoke to her, she wanted nothing to do with you."

"That's changed."

"Really? Has she told you she wants to be your wife?"

Jack fell silent. Bastard.

"I didn't think so," his grandfather responded, with a surprising lack of pleasure. "She's not one of us, son. As I said, you're the only one who refuses to accept that."

"And you could never accept that I loved her regardless."

"Then you left her." The paperweight was returned to the desk and the older man shot him a bored glance. "Not your shining moment."

"You don't get to judge me."

"No. That would be hypocritical of me, wouldn't it?" A faint smile played with the corners of the old man's mouth. "Although I must say, I'm impressed with the fortune you've amassed, even if it was in trade. Well done."

"I didn't do it for your approval." Maybe once, in the beginning, but sometime over the years his reasons had changed. Jack knew that now. He'd done all he'd done for himself, and partially in the hope that it would somehow make losing Sadie worth it. It never had. "And I didn't marry Sadie to spite you." No matter what she or the old man might think.

"There's not one shred of paper that says that gel's your wife, and until you can present proof, I refuse to acknowledge the daughter of a horse breeder as my granddaughter-in-law."

"It doesn't matter if you acknowledge her."

There was pity in his grandfather's gaze. And a healthy dose of triumph. "But it does matter if society accepts her, and they won't. You have to know that."

He couldn't stand it any longer. "I'm leaving. What you want or think plays no importance in *my life*." He wasn't aware that he'd raised his voice until his father's secretary, Mr. Brown, hurried into the room, a concerned expression on his middle-aged face.

"Are you all right, my lord?" the man asked, rushing to his employer's side.

"I'm fine, Brown," the earl replied with a kind smile. "You worry too much."

Jack scowled, but before he could demand to know what was going on, Brown fixed him with the same stern face Jack remembered from his youth.

"I'm afraid I need to insist this meeting end now, Lord Gerard. His lordship has had a very busy morning and I won't have him tiring himself by arguing with you."

As chastising went, it was very effective. "What's wrong with him?" Jack asked warily.

"Do not discuss me as though I'm not here!" His

grandfather pushed his hovering secretary away. "And there is nothing wrong with me. Go about your business, boy, we're done here. I will see you at Ryeton's fete later this week. We will make our first appearance together."

He could hardly argue, because he planned to be there regardless. He'd already told the duchess he'd attend, and it was for Tryst, so there was no backing out now, despite how much he might wish it.

He opened his mouth to respond, but when he glanced up his grandfather was already leaving the room. He caught a glimpse of his coat, then he was gone.

Grinding his teeth, Jack slapped his palm against his thigh. His plan to show his grandfather that he wouldn't be manipulated had been a colossal failure. He felt as though he was a boy cast out once more, and he was no closer to knowing the truth than he had been before leaving the hotel.

But there was one person who could tell him the truth. He just had to get it out of her.

One look out the window that morning and Sadie was tempted to go back to bed. Instead, she opened the curtains, sent for toast and chocolate for breakfast, and sat down at her desk to make a list for the day. She was going to go to the shop. The curtains had arrived, as had table linens, and she wanted to see how they looked now that the walls were finished.

The thought of the walls made her think briefly of

Mason. There would be no mural now, not by him at any rate. Sadly, she regretted that almost as much as she regretted how things had ended with them.

After breakfast, she grabbed her umbrella and took the carriage to Bond Street and set about hanging curtains, which had been freshly pressed and smelled ever so slightly of vanilla and oranges. The work should have kept her mind from wandering to thoughts of Jack, but not even sleep could do that. She'd dreamed about him most of the night. Dreamed that they'd made a life together rather than apart.

It was impossible. And even if it were possible, she'd be a fool to trust him with her heart again, wouldn't she? Regardless, Jack would soon have bigger issues to deal with and she would be the last thing on his mind.

It was all just talk. She knew that. It was just her mind's way of trying to protect her. If the old earl hadn't shown up, she'd be in Jack's bed right now, planning some great adventure. But now society was all abuzz with the news of his surprising revelation as a peer of the realm, and everything had changed. It would only be a matter of time before Jack changed as well. A person couldn't be part of that world and not have it affect them. Lady Gosling was tolerable proof of that. She'd gone from actress to baroness without regret and had the scars to prove it. Sadie supposed Jack had done her a favor by leaving when he had. She'd been too young and naïve to know how the aristocratic world worked. She'd believed their love could conquer anything.

Still, she had to wonder what it would be like to be part

of that world, just as she had wondered all those years ago. To be honest, back then she'd been nothing more than a girl with romantic fantasies of what it would be like to be a grand lady. Yes, she'd been disappointed when the earl had dashed those dreams by disinheriting Jack—something the old man would have since remedied—but a person can't mourn what was never theirs to lose.

As the old man himself had once said, he'd done her a favor by casting Jack out. Their world would have eaten her alive.

She'd just finished hanging the last of the sweetly fragrant chintz-patterned curtains when the door to the shop burst open.

Jack stood on the threshold, looking so fierce and beautiful with the rain behind him that all she could do was stare.

Was it foolish that her heart stammered at the sight of him? That she wanted to peel the wet clothes from his lovely body and warm the chill from his bones in her bed? He'd come crashing in just like the hero in a gothic romance and she was more than willing to succumb to his every carnal demand.

Yes, that was very foolish indeed, and very tempting.

"Lord Gerard," she said, slowly stepping down from the chair she'd been perched on. "This is unexpected."

He made a scoffing noise. "Is it?"

"You shouldn't be here," Sadie admonished as he closed the door behind him. "People will talk."

"It's not a crime for a man to visit his wife."

He was a dog worrying a bone, dear thing. "Society doesn't see me as your wife, Jack. They'll think I'm your mistress."

His eyes blazed gold with fury. "I don't give a fuck what they think."

Sadie swallowed. She wasn't afraid, but this side of him was one she'd rarely seen before. It was a little intimidating, and somewhat attractive at the same time. "I do. My livelihood depends upon these people hiring me to read their fortunes."

"Being my wife would solve all that."

"Being your wife would cause more trouble than it would solve, and you know it. Can we not discuss this right now? Why are you here?"

"I just came from my grandfather's."

Sadie straightened, remembering the awful image in Jack's teacup. "Is he all right?"

He scowled. "Your concern for the old bastard is touching. How much did he give you in exchange for your devotion?"

She frowned as well, and moved toward him so she could look him in the eye. "Don't be an arse. I offered him nothing but the promise that I'd alert him if you ever returned to London."

He watched her with narrowed eyes. "And?"

Damn it, he knew her too well. She'd known as soon as her tone changed ever so slightly on "London" that he would know it wasn't the entire truth. "Along with the proviso that should you return, I stay as far away from you as possible." There, she'd told him the complete truth—about that, at any rate.

"I'm surprised he didn't demand the blunt back after seeing us together at Saint's Row."

"It wasn't much. I doubt he misses it."

Jack laughed, harsh and sharp. "You sold yourself too cheap, then. No doubt he would have given you a small fortune."

"He tried. I wouldn't take it."

He eyed her strangely, as though he didn't quite recognize her. Sadie supposed she deserved it. The earl had tried to give her money years before in exchange for leaving Jack and she'd refused. No doubt he was disappointed in her now.

But instead of accusations, he simply asked, "Why didn't you tell me you'd written him?"

She could lie and make this so much easier, but truth sprang too readily to her lips. "Because I thought you'd run away again."

Jack winced. It was the slightest of expressions, but she caught it regardless. "You've made a sad habit out of meaning to tell me things long after I should know them."

"Well, you have a rather nasty habit of disappearing before I can tell you anything." *Careful, old girl. Getting a little too close there*. Her mind was full of that day he left and how she'd felt standing on that dock, wondering if she carried his child inside her. It wasn't his fault she'd kept silent.

"Fair enough," he allowed without rancor. "Now, tell me how you managed to rid me of Lady Gosling."

She waved her hand. "'Twas easy. I went through my ledgers and found notes from a reading I'd done for her some time ago. I'd neglected to impart information that directly affects her current situation. Once I told her what I knew, she was happy to take her claws out of you."

"What was the information?"

She wasn't so certain she should tell him. After all, it was Lady Gosling's privacy she was about to betray. But the woman had been trying to extort money from Jack. "I told her that her husband was going to die soon."

Silence hung between them, low and taut. Sadie watched as a multitude of emotions played over Jack's chiseled features. Finally, disbelief won out. "You told her that her husband was going to die?"

Sadie nodded. "I'm rarely ever wrong. Anyway, since she wanted the money to escape him, she decided that there was no longer a need for her to leave England. He'll be dead within the month."

She was aware of the weight of his stare, the sheer dumbfounded aspect of it. "I can't believe it. She didn't meet with me because you saw her husband's death? In tea leaves?"

"That's what I said." His inability to grasp the fact irked her. He still didn't believe in her—and he hadn't even thanked her!

"I'll be damned." He chuckled, and looked at her with eyes bright with laughter. "That's quite the gift you've got there, Sadiemoon." But he was teasing. He didn't mean it. He thought she'd pulled a right proper scheme.

"Yes, well . . ." She looked at the wall as she fought back a sudden urge to cry. "You don't have to worry about paying her off now."

"All because of you." He closed the distance between them. She didn't protest when he reached for her and pulled her against him, even though his hair was damp and a chill clung to his clothing. And when he kissed her, she allowed it because she didn't know when, or if, she'd ever get another chance to savor the taste of him or the feel of his lips against hers.

When his fingers moved to cup her breast, she caught them with her own, stopping him.

She pulled away. "We can't be together, Jack. Not now."

"Why not?" He honestly looked bewildered, as though he believed that if they shagged enough everything would be all right. It would fix itself. God, he was as infuriating as he was lovely.

"*Because*," she began with a deep breath, "you're a viscount and I'm a fortune-teller. Because I have no way of knowing if you'll run off and leave me again. Because we're not children anymore! Love is not enough."

"Do you love me?"

"I've loved you since the first moment I saw you." She slumped as though defeated. "But I won't be caught between you and your grandfather again, Jack. I won't be the weapon you use against him or the pawn he uses against you."

"You were never—"

"Yes, I was," she cut him off, her patience all but gone. "He blames me for the wedge between the both of you and you use me to keep it there. You had your problems long before I came along, and you can have them now. Just leave me out of it."

"Sadie, you can't just toss away what we have."

"I'm not. But you can't build a marriage on it either, Jack. We've changed over the years. We're not the same people anymore. I adore you. I love you, but I don't know you. Sometimes I don't think *you* know you."

"That's ridiculous."

"Maybe so. But I don't know if I can trust you, and you don't believe in me, and no relationship can last like that."

"It always comes back to those damn leaves, doesn't it?"

"No, Jack. It comes back to whether you can accept who I am. It comes back to whether or not you're done running from who *you* are. But even if you are done, we're from two different worlds."

"It worked once."

"No, it didn't." She couldn't keep the sorrow from her voice. "That's what I've been trying to tell you. It didn't work, or you wouldn't have left."

"I left for us."

"You left for you!" she shouted. "The only person you ever thought of was you!" She clapped a hand over her mouth, surprised at the force behind the words, and how much resentment had come with them.

Jack looked as though she'd just kicked his dog. He

backed away from her. "I'm sorry to have bothered you," he murmured hoarsely. "Good-bye, Sadie."

She wanted to stop him. Wanted to apologize and beg his forgiveness, but she didn't. She let him go, because she'd meant those awful words and she wouldn't take them back even if she could.

It was simply best for the both of them if they went off to their respective worlds and found the strength to not look back.

# Chapter 17

Not looking back was more difficult than Sadie thought it would be. Unfortunately, it seemed to be quite easy for Jack as he hadn't bothered with her again since leaving her shop two days ago.

To be honest, she was disappointed he gave up so easily. What sort of mess was she in that she pushed him away but wanted him to fight her on it? She'd expected—no, *hoped*—he would put up more of a fuss. Yet she'd told him she didn't want to be with him. That she couldn't trust him. Accused him of being selfish.

Was it any wonder he hadn't tried again?

She tried to justify it by reminding herself that he thought her talents a joke. He couldn't fathom that Lady Gosling would believe her prediction about her husband. But hadn't he asked her to read his leaves that night at Saint's Row? And asked again what she'd seen when they'd been sequestered away in Vienne's little cottage? He might not believe in the leaves, but he was interested in what she saw there.

Or perhaps that was merely wishful thinking on her part.

For now, she contented herself with the distractions Saint's Row offered. Tonight was a small gathering—a bit of cards and other games of chance in the card room and a lovely soprano with piano accompaniment in the music room. Right now Sadie was in the corner sipping a glass of wine. She found the roulette wheel almost mesmerizing.

"Where is your shadow?" asked a familiar voice.

Sadie jerked her attention away from the spinning wheel just as Vienne came to stand beside her. As always the Frenchwoman looked impeccable in a shimmering gold gown that made her appear to be the very embodiment of fire. "On the wall behind me," she replied drily.

Vienne smiled. "Ah, *bien*. I refer, of course, to Monsieur Friday, or Lord Gerard as he is now known."

Sadie took a swallow of crisp wine and rubbed at a tight muscle between her neck and shoulder. She'd leave an unsightly red mark on her bare flesh, but she didn't care. Her neck was killing her. "I do not know where he is."

Her friend's smile faded. "Has he hurt you? Bastard!" And then she began ranting in rapid French under her breath.

Sadie placed a hand on her friend's arm, torn between laughter and irrational tears. "Vienne, calm yourself. He didn't do anything. I did."

Vienne halted midstream and glanced up in surprise. "You ended it?"

She nodded. "I had to."

"What did he do?"

She laughed, couldn't help it. It was preferable to weeping. "You're always so quick to blame the man. Why is that?"

The redhead shrugged. "The man is usually the one at fault in my experience."

"Not this time. I told Jack it was over between us."

"Why? You seemed to forgive him so easily and rushed into his arms." Her face brightened just a little. "Was it all a ploy to make him love you, and then to toss him aside as he did to you?"

"No!" Sadie cried, aghast. "I'd never do such a thing."

Another shrug. "I would."

"I ended it because he's a viscount and I'm a fortune-teller. It will never work for us."

Vienne crossed one arm over her chest in a lazy fashion, her hand curling around the biceps of her other arm, which was raised, a glass of wine in her hand. "Is that not exactly what the two of you were when you married him? You had no *problème* with it then. What's changed?"

"We have," Sadie replied, sharper than she'd intended. "He has responsibilities now. And I . . . I've come to my senses. There's no place for me in that world."

The other woman considered that with a tilt of her head and slight purse of her lips. "So, sometime during the last week or so you've become older and wiser, is that it?"

"Yes." If she said it with enough determination perhaps she would eventually make it so.

"I find the heart does not always subscribe to that belief." Vienne's shoulders lifted in a prefect Gallic shrug. "It tends to be once a fool, always a fool."

"How fortunate then that I am not governed by my heart."

Vienne's gaze was quick. "My dear friend, I've never met anyone more ruled by her emotions than you. Lie to yourself if you must, but do not lie to me."

Sadie bristled at the chastising tone. "I'm not lying. And really, Vienne, I hardly think you are the correct person to comment on whether or not a person thinks with their heart."

Arched eyebrows rose. "Because I do not have one?"

Sadie gave her a *don't be foolish* look. "Because you never allow your heart to enter any decision."

The other woman laughed—a mockery of joy. "*That*, my friend, is where you are wrong. My heart tries to influence me all the time. I've simply learned to do the opposite of whatever it suggests."

"You are all the better for it, are you not?"

A faraway glint entered her cool gaze. "I'm not certain. I . . . *Dieu doux!* What is *he* doing here?"

At first, when Sadie followed her friend's gaze, she though Vienne's shock was because of Jack, who had just entered the room looking lovelier than a man had the right to. But as her heart skipped a traitorous beat, she realized that Vienne wasn't looking at Jack. Her wide gaze and flushed cheeks were caused by the man at Jack's side.

He was perhaps the same height as Jack, no more than

an inch or two shorter. His build was leaner, but he had the straight spine of a man of power. And the easy grin of a charmer. And his eyes . . .

It was his eyes that ignited Sadie's recognition. Of course, it had been years since she'd seen the gentleman, but even if she'd never seen him before, the resemblance to his brothers would have betrayed his identity. Trystan Kane had a bright gaze very much like his brother Archer, only a darker blue. And his nose and jaw were very similar to the Duke of Ryeton's. His hair fell somewhere between the two—just a shade shy of sable, with glints of auburn when the light hit it.

He was a handsome man, not as handsome as Jack, though. But Sadie was surprised at the resentment that rose within her as she watched the two of them. This was the man who had taken Jack away from her. The one person who knew the man Jack had become better than she did.

Who knew him better than she probably ever would.

She hated Trystan Kane.

They were engrossed in conversation with an older gentleman, some lord Sadie didn't know but had seen often enough here at the club. She thought perhaps he might have been a friend—a special friend—of Vienne's once upon a time.

Beside her, Vienne was stiff, a far cry from her normal, in-control self. Pale save for dark splotches of crimson on her cheeks, she stared at Trystan Kane with even more intensity than Sadie had. But now, Sadie's attention had drifted to Jack, and her feelings, while different, were no less consuming.

He laughed at something one of the men said. She could hear his laughter from where she stood, a rich, unabashed sound that wrapped around her heart and squeezed tight enough to restrict circulation. Her neck bent as her head tilted in contemplation, and she ignored the pain as her stiff muscles protested. She was too busy studying the creases in his cheeks, the lines around his eyes—the genuine happiness in his face as he shared in some secret joke. She used to make him laugh like that, with her silliness. For that matter, he used to make her laugh until she thought she might pee. God, she missed that. She hadn't realized how much until this very moment. And she felt that loss almost every bit as keenly as she'd felt the absence of their child so many years ago.

Damn, it hurt. So, very, very much that her throat closed and her eyes stung though no tears came. It was too painful for tears.

Jack's head turned and she unintentionally caught his gaze. The laughter seemed to fall from his expression, replaced by surprised aghast. That's when Sadie knew that everything she felt was reflected in her own expression, and she jerked herself upright at the same moment she tore her gaze from his.

Stupid of her to reveal so much.

She turned to Vienne, who was still watching Trystan Kane. Her elegant friend actually jumped a little when Kane turned to glance in their direction.

*"Merde,"* Vienne muttered a few seconds later. "They're coming over, aren't they?"

Sadie sighed, giving in to the inevitable. "Yes."

Vienne whispered a few more swear words before quickly drawing herself upright. At once, the cool mask was back in place and even Sadie, who had witnessed it, thought perhaps she had imagined her friend's emotional reaction.

"Madame La Rieux," Kane said in voice like honey over gravel. "Good evening."

Was it Sadie's imagination or was there something of a challenge in the man's address and the sparkle in his amazing eyes? There was certainly something in how he offered his hand—something gentlemen only did with each other, never with a lady. He was either being very rude, or treating Vienne in the same manner he would any business associate.

Vienne seemed to shove her own hand into his. Sadie imagined the two of them squeezing at each other's fingers until blood ceased to flow, but neither being smart enough to let go.

"Lord Trystan." Vienne's jaw was clenched. "When did you arrive in town?"

The tension between the two was so palatable, Sadie's heart rate sped up. She raised a questioning gaze to Jack, who looked as amazed as she. He shrugged.

And then he smiled, and it was like the sun coming out from behind a cloud. She smiled back.

"Jack," said Kane, breaking the spell. "Who is this delightful lady?"

It took a second for Sadie to realize he was referring to her; she'd been distracted by Jack's sudden frown.

"Sadie Moon, allow me to introduce Lord Trystan Kane, my friend and business partner."

Out of habit, Sadie offered her hand. "How do you do, Lord Trystan?"

Trystan Kane's eyes brightened so that they appeared flawless gems in the tan of his face. "The famous Madame Moon! Delighted to make your acquaintance." He took her hand in his—he'd let go of Vienne, or vice versa—and bent his head to brush a light kiss across the top of her gloved knuckles. "The women of my family sing your praises, madam, and with good reason, I hear. But I'm afraid in their enthusiasm for your abilities they neglected to inform me just how lovely you are."

Dear Heavens! The man was positively magnetic. Sadie blinked under the onslaught of his charm. In fact, she was rather mortified to think that it might have been more of a fluttering of eyelashes rather than a simple, stoic blink. "Thank you, Lord Trystan. It's a pleasure to finally meet you."

"Finally?" He flashed her a grin that could only be described as flirtatious. "Have you been waiting to meet me?"

She had to admire him as a flirt and a charmer. She didn't take him seriously for a second, suspecting that he was acting this way to annoy Vienne more than anything else. However, she noticed that Jack didn't seem to like the exchange either, and even though she'd been the one to push Jack away, she couldn't help but enjoy knowing he was jealous of her. For too long she believed he'd walked away because he didn't care; so, discovering that he was possessive of her, filled her with a wonderful warm feeling.

"I have," she replied coyly. "I've heard such *scandalous* things about you, how could I not?"

Surprise flickered in the depths of those incredible eyes, understanding as well. "Indeed? I promise to endeavor to live up to your expectations."

Suddenly, they'd gone from potential foes to partners in coquetry. He grinned, an expression that made him look very boyish and approachable.

Jack, on the other hand didn't look amused at all. He was standing there with his chin tipped down, watching the pair of them from beneath lowered brows. Vienne as well looked as though she'd like to knock their heads together.

"I don't wish to keep you, Lord Trystan," Vienne ground out. "I'm sure you have other people you wish to speak to."

*"You're* not keeping me at all, Madame La Rieux," he replied smoothly, and Sadie saw Vienne stiffen at the thinly veiled insult. "But you are right, there are a few gentlemen here whom I should say hello. Madame Moon, will you excuse me?"

"Of course, my lord. Enjoy the rest of the evening." She dared glance up at Jack. "Lord Gerard." How false and strange that title felt on her tongue!

It obviously seemed strange to Jack as well, because

his brow furrowed even deeper, just for a second, before going perfectly smooth once more. "Mrs. Moon. Madame La Rieux."

The gentlemen bowed and took their leave. The second they were out of earshot, Vienne turned on her. "What in the name of God was that about?" she demanded in a strangled whisper. "You practically threw yourself at him. In front of your own husband!"

Astounded to hear such accusations from her of all people, Sadie turned to her friend. "Me? I didn't know whether to pin his arms behind his back so you could take a swing, or send you to one of the private rooms."

"The former," Vienne replied, her normally smooth tones sounding surprisingly hoarse as much of the tension dissolved from her face. "I've no desire to repeat the latter."

It took that a moment to sink in. *"What?"* Then Sadie lowered her voice: "You slept with Trystan Kane?"

Her friend nodded stiffly. "One of the biggest mistakes of my life, and one of the few times I allowed my emotions to rule my actions. I've regretted it ever since."

"Was . . ." How best to ask this delicate question? She needed to know the sort of man with whom Jack had aligned himself. "Was he unpleasant?" She meant his temperament, of course.

Vienne met her gaze with a frank and somewhat rueful one. *"Non.* He was the *most* pleasant I've ever experienced. That, my dear friend, is why I regret it." And then she drifted away, off to play hostess with the rest of her clientele. Her exit left Sadie alone once more, standing in her corner feeling lost and slightly off balance. Just as she had begun the evening.

Later that evening, Jack had a few words for Trystan, his friend and business partner. They shared a carriage to the hotel they co-owned, and staggered into the lift together to make the climb to the top floor. He was half pissed, or else he would have kept his mouth shut. As it was, he left Tryst outside his suite at the Barrington with what he called his own bit of "fortune-telling."

"Flirt with Sadie again and I'll break your effing nose."

And then he toddled off to bed—and for the first night in several, slept like a babe.

The Duchess of Ryeton's "intimate" dinner for her brother-in-law was no less than thirty people, of which Jack and his grandfather were two. Jack had no idea how his grandfather managed an invitation given that he had no prior acquaintance with the duke or the duchess. He could only surmise that the duchess had invited the old man because he was Jack's family, and Jack was so close to Trystan. That in itself was slightly embarrassing and made all the more so by the fact that it was obvious his grandfather looked down his nose at the whole proceeding.

Oh, his grandfather gave rank all the courtesy it demanded and was pleasant enough to Ryeton's face, but Jack saw how he looked at the scarred duke and his pretty bride. He had to know the rumors that their marriage had been brought about by the two of them being caught making the beast with two backs. Ryeton had a horrible reputation in his younger days and the scandal clung to him still.

The old man despised scandal, though he'd had no trouble stirring the pot by descending upon London and announcing Jack to be his grandson.

Regardless, the earl sat at the table and made a tolerable attempt at being a gracious guest, though he rarely spoke unless spoken to and only looked pleasant if someone glanced in his direction.

He was only there so he and Jack could be seen together. And to make Jack miserable.

"Too bad the duke's sister is already married," the earl remarked later in the drawing room, when the gentlemen joined the ladies. "Despite her unfortunate connections, she'd make an excellent viscountess."

Jack cringed, though they were far enough away from the others to avoid being overheard. Ryeton's sister Bronte was indeed lovely. "She's already a viscountess," he replied. "She married Lord Kemp last month and will someday be Countess Branton."

The old man batted at the air as though brushing away a fly. "It was just an observation."

Speaking of observations, Jack observed that something wasn't quite right with his grandfather. He'd had good appetite at dinner, but afterward, when the cigars and port came out, he'd gotten a little flushed. And now he was slightly damp around the hairline and seemed to be somewhat breathless.

"Are you all right?" Jack asked.

"Fine," came the gruff reply. "I just need a little air. It's deuced hot in here."

"Step out onto the terrace." Jack gestured toward the doors. "I'll get you a glass of water."

It spoke volumes that his grandfather didn't argue with him. Frowning, Jack stopped a passing footman and asked him to fetch a glass of water. Then he turned his attention to the terrace doors in time to see the old man step outside.

"I know that look," Trystan remarked as he walked up to him. He had a snifter of brandy in his hand. "What's going on?"

Jack shook his head. "I'm not sure." He had apologized for threatening to break his friend's nose the morning after the altercation. Trystan accepted his apology, ribbed him a few times during the day and that was it. They hadn't spoken of it again, and Jack was thankful. He spent so much of his time thinking about Sadie that not having to discuss her with Tryst was a welcome respite.

"Do you want me to call for the earl's carriage?"

Another shake, as he craned his neck for a glimpse outside. "No. I'm sure it's just a little dyspepsia. He'll be fine."

"All right. Listen, about that property on Bond Street, you were correct, the rent is paid in full for this quarter."

Jack turned away from the window, directing his attention solely on his partner. "Excellent. And you'll alert the tenant that the rent will be paid for the remainder of the year?"

A knowing smile tilted Tryst's lips. "Why don't you tell the lady yourself?"

"Because she won't accept it from me."

"She's going to know you settled the account regardless of who tells her."

Jack shrugged one shoulder. "It will be better coming from you, trust me." If he went to Sadie, she'd think he was trying to buy her, especially when he thought of it as more of a peace offering. Regardless of how he felt about fate and tea leaves, it was obvious that she was good at what she did and that people believed in her. Hell, people *swore* by her. Since his arrival in London he'd heard so many people rhapsodize about how many times she'd correctly predicted things that he felt an odd kind of pride. It didn't matter what he thought, he'd rather see Sadie happy doing something he didn't understand than see her miserable, unable to realize her dream. So, he'd paid her rent for three quarters of a year's lease to give her a leg up.

"Fair enough," Trystan allowed, raising his drink. "I have to go talk to some people I haven't seen in twenty years. Breakfast tomorrow?"

"Nine o'clock," Jack replied. "I'll let you sleep in, you lazy arse."

The two of them shared a grin and Trystan left to join a small group conversing nearby. Jack tried once again to catch a glimpse of his grandfather.

"Your water, my lord." Somehow the footman had appeared without him noticing.

Jack took the heavy crystal glass from the tray. "Thank you."

He made his way across the room and slipped out onto the terrace. It took a moment for his eyes to adjust to the diminished light, but torches flickered along the balustrade and he was soon able to locate his grandfather standing just off to his right, near the stone railing.

"Drink this," he instructed when he reached the other man.

His grandfather glanced up as though surprised to see him. He had been rubbing his left arm, but ceased to take the glass and raised it to his lips. Jack thought the water sloshed a bit.

"That Olivia Clark, the Earl of Angelwood's granddaughter, she'd make you a fine wife. Good teeth."

"She's too young, and I already have a wife." Why did he bother? It would make things so much easier if he just agreed with the old man. It didn't mean he had to actually marry the chit.

"A proper wife. One who knows our world and can give you sons."

"My current wife is familiar with 'our world' and she can give me sons."

His grandfather choked on a mouthful of water. Jack noticed that he wiped his mouth with the hand holding the glass, as though his left one didn't work. "Miss O'Rourke's a lovely girl, boy, but she'll never give you a son."

"How do you know that? The sex of a child isn't determined by the social standing of its mother."

"I know because I was there when the doctor told her she'd likely never carry a child to term."

Everything stopped. In that one split second it felt as

if the entire world had been sucked into a vacuum, held there and then spat back out again. His chest seized and he gasped for breath. "What the hell are you talking about?"

The old man shook his head. "Not my place to tell."

"You started it," Jack rasped. "Explain. Now."

A pained sigh drifted off into the night before his grandfather took another sip of water. In the torchlight it seemed his face was even more damp than before, but Jack didn't care if the old man sweated a bit.

"Shortly after you left for America, I received a letter from Sadie"—Jack didn't miss the use of his wife's Christian name—"saying that she was pregnant and afraid that something was wrong. I didn't doubt the child was yours, and so I immediately left for London. By the time I found her she had already miscarried. Poor thing. It had happened on the rug. She was scrubbing at the stain, crying that it wouldn't come out. I bundled her up, had a doctor look at her, and as soon as she was fit for travel I took her back to Ireland to recover. A girl needs to be near her family in such cases. I did what I could for her, given that the child would have been my blood."

Jack stared at him. It was as though he was listening to the old man speak down a long tunnel. "Miscarried?" Was all he could manage to say. The rug. He'd seen that rug and never once imagined what had caused that mark on it. *Oh, Christ.*

"A girl," his grandfather replied. "That's what she said. Not an heir, but still, I felt the loss."

"*You* felt the loss?" Jack snarled. Were the man not over seventy he would have smashed his fist into his stupid face right then and there. "What about Sadie? What about me?"

"Sadie was fine. I bought her the best care in the world, and I took care of her. I did your job because you were too busy thumbing your nose at me. You can't blame this on me, boy-o."

He was right, but that didn't make Jack any less angry, or the pain any less raw. If he'd only been there.

Sadie had been pregnant when he left. Had she known then that she carried his child and let him go regardless? Why hadn't she demanded that he stay? He would have stayed. Dear God, he would have stayed.

"Why didn't you try to find me?" he demanded. "I sent letters home detailing where I was. You had the resources, you could have found me!"

The old man's gaze pinned him to the spot, remorseless in the torchlight. "It was better this way." He'd always thought himself absolutely right in everything, excusing his coldness with claims that it was for the best.

Rage and anguish tore at Jack's heart. He choked on the lump in his throat. "Better for whom?"

"For you." There was no shame in those eyes so like his own. It wasn't cruelty that drove the old man, it was unswerving conviction of how things should be. The man fancied himself God. "I hoped you would go on and make a new life for yourself. And when Sadie asked me for my help, I offered it so she could do the same."

Just so he could keep them apart. He'd denied Jack

the right to grieve for his child just so he could keep him from Sadie. He wondered if that's what had happened to the letters neither he nor Sadie ever received. "You soulless bastard," he ground out. "I may have to be your heir, but we're finished. As of tonight I want nothing more to do with you."

"Jack, don't do this." His grandfather reached for him, but Jack backed away, shaking his head in an effort to keep his hatred and sorrow at bay.

"I've wasted enough of my life trying to prove myself to you," Jack informed him, his voice tight with so many emotions. "If I have to spend the rest of it making it up to Sadie, then I will. If she won't be my countess then I won't have any. Hang your precious bloodline."

The old man grimaced and then the glass fell from his hand and smashed on the stone floor. His hand came up and clutched at his left arm again, then at his chest. This time when he reached for his grandson, Jack caught him.

"What's wrong with you?" Jack demanded. Faced with such obvious suffering, thoughts of himself and any wrongdoing fled.

"Jack . . ." his grandfather gasped, and collapsed.

Bearing the old man's full weight, Jack slowly lowered him to the stone floor. "Help!" He shouted toward the terrace door. "Please help!"

Aged but strong fingers grasped at his lapel, pulling him down so he had no choice but to meet his grandfather's cloudy gaze. "Boy . . ."

Then the old man fell silent and his eyes seemed

to change. The terrace doors opened and a man and young woman walked out. It was Olivia Clark, the young woman his grandfather thought would make an excellent viscountess. Jack might have appreciated the irony were he not so scared.

"Get a doctor," he cried. The young woman gasped, pressing fair hands against her bosom. The gentleman did his best to shield her from the sight as he assured Jack he would get help, and then he quickly drew the girl back inside.

Within seconds the doors opened again and Ryeton was there, on his knees beside him; Trystan and Archer as well. Ryeton barked orders and Archer vaulted down the stone steps, running to the stables to get a horse so he could fetch a doctor. All the while, Jack knelt on the stone, his grandfather cradled in his arms, clutching at his chest. He would have stopped Archer, had he been able to think clearly. He knew a doctor would be of no use.

He knew the exact moment the old man died, felt it in his gut. He reached up and closed his grandfather's eyes, but he didn't let him go, not just yet. He stayed where he was, with Ryeton and Tryst beside him, holding in his arms the man he'd spent so much of his life being angry at. Ryeton and Tryst spoke to him, and he replied, but he had no idea what he said. When the doctor finally arrived, Archer hot on his heels, he made Jack lower the body to the stone so he could examine it. Jack stood up and watched dumbly as the doctor poked and prodded at his grandfather before finally declaring him dead.

"My condolences, Lord Garret," the doctor said with

a sympathetic hand on his shoulder. "His heart couldn't take the strain."

Jack nodded, unable to say anything.

Ryeton arranged for the body to be taken back to Berkeley Square, and Archer volunteered to accompany Jack back to his grandfather's . . . No, it was his house now. Archer accompanied him home, where he poured them both a stiff drink, and sat in silence with Jack in the library until Jack was ready to talk.

And Jack did talk. Later he wouldn't remember half of it, but he talked a lot. Archer just sat there and listened, and when a solitary tear rolled down Jack's cheek, Archer pretended not to see it.

Sometime late into the wee hours of the morning, Jack woke. Reason and feeling began to return, lifting his mind from the heavy fog that had descended upon it. Archer was asleep on the library sofa and he was in one of the wing-backed chairs, a knit blanket over him. Archer must have covered him up when he passed out. He sat for a moment, the details of the night before crawling through his memory like visages from a bad dream. And when reality finally descended upon him, it left him cold and shaken.

His grandfather was dead. It was his heart, and he'd died in Jack's arms.

Just as Sadie had predicted.

# Chapter 18

Sadie heard the news immediately upon waking. Indara, knowing their history, came at once to inform her that his lordship's grandfather had died on the Duke of Ryeton's terrace the night before.

Sitting on the edge of her bed, nightgown twisted around her knees, Sadie's heart hurt for Jack. Despite the animosity between him and his grandfather, he must be mourning right now—mourning all those things that might and should have been.

Neither reason nor common sense played a part in her decision to dress and make her way to Berkeley Square. There, she was greeted by a kindly faced butler with graying hair and sad eyes.

"I'm Sadie Moon," she told the man, for the first time so terribly aware of all the times Jack had called her that with a loving tone. It was no accident that she'd chosen that for her new name. She'd wanted him to be able to find her should he try. It had hurt so much when he hadn't. "A friend of his lordship."

The butler, so overwhelmed by his own grief, didn't question her relationship or the propriety of allowing her inside. He simply nodded and stepped back from the entry so she might come inside.

"Lord Gerard . . . pardon me, Lord Garret is in the library." He gestured through the door on the right.

Sadie honestly felt for the man and she touched his shoulder before leaving him. "I'm so very sorry for your loss." She meant it. The late Earl of Garret had been a proud, almost tyrannical bastard, but he had been good to her once and she knew that if only she'd had the fortune to be born a lady he would have welcomed her as his granddaughter-in-law.

Her footfalls echoed as she walked across the marble floor. She didn't look around at her surroundings for fear of lamenting their loss. By rights she was mistress of this house, though it was a duty she would never fulfill. Someday another would guide and govern this grand place, but never her.

*Why not?* a voice in her head—her own voice—whispered. The old man was dead. Why couldn't she say shag it all and take her rightful place at Jack's side? Was it simply cowardice that kept her impotent?

Shaking her head, she tossed these thoughts aside. None of that mattered right now. All that mattered was Jack.

She found the library easily as the door was open and she could see the floor-to-ceiling shelves filled with volume after volume. She knocked once on the heavy wood—she had no idea what sort it was—and stepped inside. Four pairs of eyes turned at her entrance, but it was the pair that remained fixed on the carpet that concerned her.

She went straight to him, not caring that the Duke and Duchess of Ryeton bore witness, nor the duke's two brothers. She nodded at them by way of greeting, but did not pause.

Down on her knees she went, as gracefully as her narrow skirts would allow, between Jack's feet. She grasped both his hands in hers, alarmed by how cold his were. He looked like hell, his gold-green eyes red rimmed. His strong jaw was covered with golden-flecked stubble, and there were grooves around his mouth and eyes that she'd never seen before. He was still wearing evening clothes.

*"Mo chroi,"* she whispered—*"My heart."* When he didn't immediately respond, she continued whispering to him in Gaelic, telling him that it was going to be all right, that his friends were there for him. That she was there for him.

He didn't say a word, but she knew he heard her because he squeezed her hands. That was when he finally lifted his gaze to hers. It took all her strength to look into those lost eyes. To be honest, she was surprised the death of his grandfather had hit him this hard.

Then he murmured, "I know about the rug."

Sadie recoiled. She would have jumped to her feet had he not had such a firm hold on her hands. She couldn't tear her gaze away from his as she realized he wasn't just mourning his grandfather, he was mourning their child as well. The old man had told him, no doubt to prove to him that she was unsuitable as a wife. After all, she probably couldn't bear children.

Bowing her head, she pressed her lips to his knuckles. "I'm so sorry," she said, and she was. For everything.

She became aware of the other people in the room, and she slowly rose to her feet, tugging her hands free of Jack's.

"Has he eaten?" she asked Lord Archer, the only person here who was also dressed in evening clothes and looked almost as bad as Jack. None of them seemed the least bit surprised to see her, or shocked at her obvious intimacy with Jack.

He shook his head, a lock of sable hair falling over his forehead. "He says he's not hungry."

"Are you hungry, Lord Archer?"

He seemed surprised by the question. "I could eat, yes."

Sadie went to the bellpull and gave it a hard tug. A few moments later a young maid appeared. The poor thing looked lost and pale. Obviously the whole house felt the same way. It should have been the housekeeper who came to see to them.

"Yes, missus?" the girl inquired.

Her accent was so heavy it practically formed a shamrock in the air. Sadie couldn't help but warm to the sound of it. The old earl had been something of a snob himself, hiring as many Irish staff as he could. She asked the girl to bring a pot of strong coffee, enough cups for everyone, some bread, butter, and jam—strawberry,

Jack's favorite. Then in her dusty Gaelic, she asked if the maid understood.

The girl smiled at her, brightening a little, not so afraid, and nodded. Sadie thanked her, asked her to hurry, and sent her on her way. Then she turned to Lord Trystan: "Could you arrange to have some of Jack's clothing sent over from the hotel?"

Lord Trystan nodded and rose to his feet. He didn't seem the least bit surprised by her use of Jack's Christian name. "I'll see to it. I have the need to feel useful." He clapped Lord Archer on the shoulder. "I'll collect something for you as well."

Archer set his own hand over his brother's and thanked him. Sadie envied their closeness, and was glad that Jack had such friends to rally around him.

When Trystan left, Ryeton came forward. "What can we do?"

Sadie glanced at him in surprise. Somehow she'd stepped into the role of lady of the house without meaning to. It felt right to her, as though it was where she belonged—at Jack's side. "Do you know what arrangements have been made?"

The duke ran a hand through his short thick hair. "The late earl is resting comfortably." He cast a quick glance at Jack, obviously not wanting to say something that might upset him. "And I sent word round to his solicitor. I expect he'll arrive soon to discuss the earl's wishes."

"Ireland," Jack said, startling them all.

Sadie turned. He was still on the sofa, but he seemed

to have snapped out of his fog. "I'll take him back to Ireland. To the family plot."

Ireland. Home. Sadie could see feelings similar to hers in his eyes. She hadn't been back since her trip after losing the baby. It was too painful—too little family left and too many memories, both happy and sad. Yet she'd recovered there and grew strong again. Still, would Jack be able to look around that village, around his estate, without remembering something the two of them had shared there as friends and eventually lovers?

Part of her longed to return with him, but there was nothing either of them could do to bring back those happier days.

Perhaps she ought to stop dwelling so much on the past and what she'd lost and think about the future and all the tremulous hope it offered.

Shortly the maid returned with food and Sadie fixed Jack a cup of coffee the way he liked it, along with two thick slices of bread slathered with butter and jam—also the way he liked it. "Eat it," she commanded gently. "All of it."

He took the meager meal without fuss. "Thank you."

And then, because she couldn't help herself, she ran her fingers through the cropped silk of his hair. What she would give to take some of this away from him. She'd take it all if she could.

She turned to find the duke watching her closely. Arching a questioning brow, she crossed the floor to stand before him. "Your Grace?"

"You'd make a good wife," he commented kindly, his gaze far too knowing.

Sadie swallowed, throat dry. "Thank you." She glanced at the duchess, who sat near the window. She looked tired, a sight that put fear in Sadie's heart, even though she knew it wasn't rational. "If I might be so bold, Your Grace, I suggest you take Her Grace home. She shouldn't be overtired in her condition."

The duke looked startled, but then he seemed to remember who he was talking to. He took the advice to heart, drained the remainder of his coffee with one long swallow, and took care of his beautiful bride. They made their farewells to Jack, and made him promise to let them know if there was anything he needed. Anything at all.

Trystan returned sometime later, to find the three of them sitting in silence in the library. Sadie nibbled on a piece of jam slathered, butter-heavy bread and made a list of things that needed to be done while Archer sat with Jack, making meaningless small talk designed to distract.

Sadie once again went into action. Now that Trystan had brought fresh clothing, she summoned the maid and told her to have baths prepared—one for Jack and one for Archer. The elder of the two remaining Kane brothers protested, but neither Sadie nor Jack would hear it. In fact, Sadie told the girl to prepare a room for Archer, so that he might take a nap after his bath. After all, he'd spent most of the night sitting up with Jack.

As luck would have it, two of the guest rooms were

kept open when the earl was in residence, so the maid asked Lord Archer to follow her and she'd show him to one with its own private bath.

Trystan squatted beside Jack and spoke to him in a low voice. Sadie couldn't hear their conversation, not that she was trying to eavesdrop. Jack nodded, and a few moments later Trystan stood once more. He turned and walked over to Sadie. "My apologies, Madame Moon, but I have to take my leave. Jack had an appointment this morning that I'm going to attend in his stead."

"That's very good of you, Lord Trystan."

He smiled, but there was little joy in it. "He's my partner, and my best friend."

Sadie's heart pinched, and she felt guilty for blaming this man for Jack leaving her. "He's lucky to have you."

Intriguing blue eyes sparkled at her, as though they shared a secret. "I think, my lady, that he is also quite fortunate to have you." He lightly squeezed her upper arm and turned to leave, but something gave him pause and he looked at her once again and said in a low voice, "This might not be the best time to bring this up, but I'm to tell you that your rent on the shop in Bond Street has been paid for a full year."

Sadie's eyes widened. "I beg your pardon?"

Lord Trystan cast a quick glance over his shoulder to Jack. "Perhaps he's not the only lucky one." He winked at her and strode from the room, leaving her to ponder this amazing announcement.

Within a few moments, Sadie's attention turned to

Jack. Wonderful, heavy-handed, generous man. He'd eaten the bread she'd given him and was sitting on the sofa watching her.

"Why didn't you tell me?" he demanded, but there was no emotion in his tone. It wouldn't have sounded half so dreadful if he'd been angry.

She'd only insult them both—and their unborn child— by pretending ignorance. "I did. Or rather, I wrote to you. I think we both know what happened to our letters." Was it shameful to place blame on a dead man's shoulders?

"Not then," he amended. "Now. You told me so much about your life without me, but you left that part out. Why?"

She shrugged. "I didn't know how to say it without it seeming as though I was trying to punish you."

He said nothing, just nodded and looked away. He was going to punish himself, it seemed.

Sadie gathered up the clothing Trystan had placed on the back of a chair, draped them over her arm and went to Jack. She held out her hand. "Come."

He slipped his hand in hers and stood, following her out the door, down the corridor, and up the large staircase. At the top they ran into the maid, who directed them to Jack's chamber.

It was the earl's chamber, Sadie realized with horror as they stepped inside. The huge tester bed was freshly made up and the room was spotless, but there was a pair of the late earl's shoes near the wardrobe, and his personal items on the dresser. Of course the maid would bring Jack here, where he could use his grandfather's shaving soap. It was his room now.

She hung Jack's clothes on a hook just inside the bathing room and left him long enough to turn on the taps to fill the tub. Then she turned to him and lifted her hands to his already loosened collar.

Jack caught her fingers in his. "I can do it," he said gruffly.

"All right." She couldn't quite meet his gaze. She would have moved away, but he held her still.

"Why are you here, Sadiemoon?"

Now she lifted her eyes to his. Did he really have to ask? Perhaps after the way she'd been lately, he did. "Jack." She gave her head a gentle shake. "Did you really think I wouldn't come?"

"He never accepted you. You never liked him. *I* never liked him."

She smiled softly at him, lifting her hand from his to brush her fingers across his rough jaw. "But we both loved you."

*Loved.* Past tense. As in, *I once loved you, you stupid twat, but then you walked out on me, and I lost our child and now I can't look at you without thinking about it.* Or perhaps she spoke of love in past tense simply because his grandfather was dead. Maybe all wasn't entirely lost.

But it felt lost. He'd made a boat load of money this last decade—particularly the last five or six years. And to what end? He'd just inherited that much and probably more. So in the end, had he achieved anything that made leaving Sadie worth it?

He couldn't bring himself to drop to his knees and beg forgiveness. He couldn't seem to allow his eyes to fill with tears and find release in bawling and snotting like an infant, but he needed *something* to rid him of this numbness and the threat of simmering helplessness that seemed so hell bent on permeating it.

He kissed her instead, greedily and without finesse, with desperation eating at his soul. She kissed him back, seeming to know exactly what he needed, and as his tongue invaded the sweet recesses of her mouth, his fingers dropped to the buttons up the front of her day costume. He wanted to rip them open, but he didn't. He tortured himself by unfastening each and every one. Once again, Sadie's hands went to his cravat.

They undressed each other quickly, without the tease of slow seduction. Neither of them was interested in taking things slow. They kissed and tore at stubborn garments, tossing and kicking them around the room until finally both of them were naked and practically vibrating with the depth of their mutual need.

Somehow, Sadie remembered to turn off the flow of water into the tub just before it climbed too high. The bath could wait. Having her couldn't. As soon as she straightened from the tub, Jack grabbed her about the waist and pushed her back against the wall. He could have taken her as she bent over the tub, but he wanted to see her face—needed to see her face.

As tall as she was, she was willowy, and when he

cupped the backs of her thighs, she wrapped her arms around his neck and lifted her feet, bringing them up so that she wrapped those long legs around his waist.

This new shift in height put her breasts on level with his mouth and he sucked on her nipples as he guided his hard, aching cock to the already damp notch between her thighs. Above him, Sadie arched and he held her about the waist with his other arm as he found the correct angle and shoved himself inside her.

She was wrapped around him like ivy, meeting every fraught thrust with hot, wet acceptance. Jack knew, without asking, that she understood what he felt, and that she would take whatever he gave. They never had the chance to grieve together, and this frantic coupling was the only way he could think to connect with her.

Neither of them lasted long. Emotional need whisked their arousal to new heights and they ground and thrust against one another with the kind of abandon that was sure to leave them both bruised and tender later.

When climax struck, it took with it all the pain and numbness of the last twelve hours—of the last ten years— and destroyed it, at least temporarily. He came with great, racking spasms that threatened to buckle his knees, but he managed to remain upright, Sadie still clinging to him as her own cries rang in his ears.

Finally, he slipped from inside her and she lowered her feet to the floor. Much of the emptiness returned, filling him again with guilt's numb embrace. Sadie took his hand and led him to the tub. She climbed in with him, lowering them both into the still hot water.

"Lie back" she instructed, wetting a cloth. "Close your eyes." He did as she commanded, and she placed the cloth over his face, pressing it against his jaw. Jack sighed. The heat felt good.

A few moments later, when the cloth had cooled, Sadie removed it and brushed shaving soap over his beard. She shaved him slowly and carefully, but with the skill of a valet, wiping the removed whiskers and soap onto the cloth so they didn't pollute their bath. He remembered how, years ago, she had loved to shave him, as though it were a treat for her whenever he agreed to it. Now, having finished the task, she took another cloth and rinsed away the soap residue. Then she soaped the cloth and began to bathe him.

"Sadie," he murmured, "you don't have to do this."

"I know." She ran the cloth over his chest. "I want to. Let me."

He did. And when she had him clean and smelling of sandalwood and bay rum, he also let her touch him. Lying back against the warmed porcelain, he allowed her long, gentle fingers to caress him into a state of mind that was almost peaceful, almost void of turmoil. Then her hand reached down beneath the water and wrapped around his cock, already half-mast from her touch.

"Sadie . . ." What was he going to say? What could he possibly say? No? That would be a lie. That he didn't want her to feel like she had to do this again? That would be a lie as well. He wanted her, and while he didn't want her to feel like it was her duty or something equally as foolish, he wanted to be inside her again. The rapid swelling of his prick was proof of that.

She straddled him and lowered herself onto him, inch by delicious inch. All the while she kept her gaze locked with his. There was such tenderness and caring in her faerie eyes, mixed with desire and want, and a multitude of other things he was scared to even try to decipher.

She sighed softly as he filled her completely; sat for a moment on his thighs before beginning to move. Water sloshed gently against the sides of the tub, threatening to spill over, but not quite.

Sadie's hands slid up his chest, up his neck to cup his face and stroke his hair. She planted little kisses on his face as she slowly rode him, rubbed his scalp, and caressed the lobe and ridge of his ear. "Let me take it all away," she whispered, a pleading edge he'd never heard in her voice before.

Jack's hands slid over her thighs and hips, up to splay across her back, holding her close. He didn't try to steal the rhythm of their bodies, but rather allowed her to lead, feeling her warmth seep into him with every stroke. He needed to make her feel good. He needed to hear her come again. Maybe he'd find the forgiveness he sought in her climax.

There was no quickening of pace, no frantic thrusting this time. Just the slow, gentle lapping of water as they moved together, gazing into each other's eyes when they weren't kissing a section of the other's exposed skin.

He felt the tremors in her thighs and knew she was

going to come soon, heard her increasing sighs and moans. He was barely holding on, waiting for her.

"Sweet Jack," she murmured, brushing her lips across his forehead. "I never should have let you go." She shuddered then, and made a low keening noise as she came.

Jack didn't have time to respond, didn't have time to be shocked. Her words and climax sent his own release rushing over him and he couldn't do anything but groan out loud as orgasm claimed him. It was so strong, so emotionally raw it robbed him of breath as well as reason, and when sense began to return, he was ashamed to realize that tears were beginning spill down his cheeks. His only consolation was the fact that Sadie was weeping as well.

He wrapped his arms around her, holding her as though she was all that was left of his sanity. She held him as well, burying her face in his shoulder.

They stayed like that for quite some time. The tears ebbed and gave way to sniffs and little kisses, as well as to the occasional embarrassed apology—which both of them tried to make but was sushed by the other. Then they stopped talking and kissed some more, holding each other until the water became too cool to stay in any longer. Only then did they climb out of the tub and dry off.

"It happened just like you predicted," Jack said later as they lay together on the bed, Sadie draped over him, her head on his shoulder. It seemed he had reached absolution through sex, as just a few minutes earlier they'd worshiped each other with their mouths and he was now lying peaceful and quiet with his arms around her.

She raised her face. "I know."

Wrapping his arms around her, he held her as tight as he dared. "I'm so sorry, Sadie. More than you'll ever know."

She smiled, so very sweetly, blinking back tears. "I *do* know. Now stop torturing yourself and get some sleep."

He was so very tired—bone tired. Maybe now he could finally rest. "Don't leave."

"I won't."

But even as his eyes drifted shut, he knew she was lying.

# Chapter 19

Sadie didn't go far. While Jack slept she dressed and crept downstairs to deal with servants and anyone who might come to call.

She found the late earl's secretary, Mr. Brown, red-eyed and lost-looking, in the old man's study. He sat in front of the desk, hands hanging between his knees as he stared at the carpet.

"Hello," Sadie said. "Mr. Brown, correct?"

The man looked up, frowning slightly. "Do I know you?"

She smiled. "We met years ago. I'm a friend of the new earl. Mrs. Moon."

He nodded, accepting the information with the disinterestedness of grief. "Do you know if Mr. Walters has been here yet?" When she tilted her head in question, he added, "His lordship's solicitor."

"Lord Garret hasn't seen him." He went back to staring at the carpet. Poor thing looked as lost as a child. "Can I get you anything? A cup of tea, perhaps?"

Mr. Brown nodded. "That would be lovely, thank you."

She turned to leave. "I'll have the housekeeper send it up directly."

"Oh," Mr. Brown said, "please don't bother her."

Bemused, Sadie faced him once more. "I'm sure she won't mind." Of course she couldn't be sure of that at all, but the household still had to run, despite the tragedy.

The man looked uncomfortable. "She's taking the news very badly. Very badly indeed."

Obviously the old man's servants thought better of him than his own family, because not even Jack was so overcome that he couldn't function. In fact, if it weren't for him finding out about the baby, he probably would have gone to that meeting Lord Trystan attended in his stead.

She had wanted to dig a hole and bury herself in it when he told her he knew about the carpet. And when he cried with her . . . well, it was like someone opened a door and showed her everything she'd missed out on by allowing him to leave her ten years ago. Astoundingly, Jack forgave her for it. They forgave each other.

"I appreciate that the woman is overwrought, but there is a household to be run, nevertheless."

Mr. Brown flushed a deep rose. "Her relationship with the master was more . . . *intimate* than most, my lady."

Sadie was too shocked to correct his form of address. Intimate? The old man and his *housekeeper*?

Why that hypocritical old bastard! Telling Jack that she wasn't good enough for him when all the while the earl was sleeping with the hired help!

"Had she been with the earl long?" Sadie inquired with just enough innuendo that Mr. Brown could not mistake her meaning.

The man's flush deepened, which Sadie took as a keen embarrassment over having to discuss such matters with a woman. Mr. Brown was a proper gentleman. "More than twenty-five years."

That jerked her brows up. Almost all of Jack's life. That was longer than most married couples were given together. Certainly the old man had been a widower at that point. Twenty-five years. He'd undoubtedly been loved by the woman if she was that undone by his death.

And he'd never come down off that high horse of his to make an honest woman of her. But perhaps the old man hadn't been such a hypocrite after all. Recently he'd maintained only that Jack and Sadie shouldn't be married, not that they couldn't be lovers.

"I won't bother her, then." Sadie curled her lips slightly. "I'll see to your tea, Mr. Brown."

She left the study and began searching out the entrance to the kitchen, which she found in a corridor off the great hall, behind the staircase. The maid who had waited on them earlier approached at the same time to tell her that Lord Archer appreciated the hospitality but had taken his leave just a quarter hour earlier. Sadie thanked her, and then asked if she would see to having tea and sandwiches prepared for Mr. Brown.

"Oh—" She stopped the maid with a hand on her arm as another thought occurred to her. "Could you see that a tray is prepared for the housekeeper as well?"

The maid looked surprised—and somewhat touched—by the request. "I will indeed, my lady."

"I'm not—" But the girl was already descending toward the kitchen and there didn't seem to be a point to protesting after her that Sadie wasn't a lady, not in the sense she meant it.

But she could be. All she had to do was take a gamble.

She stood there a moment, beside the grand staircase and looked around at the empty hall. What was there for her to do now? Jack was resting, the servants were looked after. The solicitor had yet to arrive, so there was nothing left for her to do.

A muffled knock on the front door sounded, as though Fate had been listening to her thoughts.

The butler, whose name she'd discovered was Alistair, didn't seem to be around, so Sadie crossed the marble floor to answer the knock. Perhaps it was the solicitor. Who else would come calling when there was a black wreath upon the door and the earl's body on ice in the cold room?

She pulled open the door and got her answer. It wasn't the solicitor.

It was Lady Gosling.

"You don't have an ounce of shame do you?" The words slipped out before she could stop them. "This house is in mourning."

The lady—beautiful and hard in a rich green walking costume that matched her eyes—arched a fine brow. There was a flicker of something in her eye, however, that shamed Sadie just a tiny bit. It looked like hurt.

"I wanted to pay my respects to Mr. Fri— To Lord Garret."

"He's indisposed."

"Perhaps, then, I might pay my respects to you?"

The question was a bit of a shocker, truth be told. Sadie shrugged and stood back from the doorway so the woman might enter. What did it say about her that she'd prefer the company of a woman she didn't much like to being alone?

"The household is in a bit of a fuddle," she informed her guest as she swept inside in a jasmine-scented breeze. "I cannot promise you any kind of refreshment."

"The former earl was Irish, was he not?"

Sadie frowned, unsure of what that had to do with anything. "As is the new earl."

Lady Gosling smiled. "Don't get your knickers in a twist, it wasn't meant to be an insult. Am I correct in assuming that therefore there must be whiskey in the house?"

"Of course."

"That will do. Lead on, my good woman."

Sadie did just that, forced to realize that while she didn't want to like Lady Gosling, she sort of did. She didn't trust her any further than she could throw her, but she had a certain charm and strength Sadie had to admire. The woman truly didn't seem to care what other people thought, *seem* being the operative word.

Sadie took her to the library, where she knew for certain there were strong spirits in the cupboard. She busied herself pouring a glass for each of them and tried to ignore Lady Gosling gazing around the library like a clerk from Christie's doing an appraisal.

"Here," she said, shoving one of the sturdy glasses at the other woman as she moved to seat herself in one of the chairs.

"My thanks." The lady took the whiskey and dropped onto the sofa in a very 'un' lady-like heap. She made a face. "I bloody hate corsets sometimes, don't you? Difficult to get comfortable with a length of whalebone digging into your side."

Sadie's eyebrows rose as her eyes widened. Here was a peek not at Lady Gosling, but at Theone Fielding, a.k.a Theone Divine, actress. "Yes, it is." The woman seemed to be trying her damnedest to get comfortable, however.

Lady Gosling glanced around the room once again. "It's a lovely house. Have you taken over as lady of it yet?"

"No, and I've no intention." Why did she sound so affronted? It was a reasonable question given what the woman knew of her connection to Jack. Yet, it seemed so gauche to be thinking of taking over when the household had just lost its lord and master.

Obviously Lady Gosling didn't share her thinking. "Why ever not? The old earl's dead. No family to protest. Good lord, girl! You could be a countess!" And since that trumped a baroness, the lady was suitably stumped.

"Until a few weeks ago I hadn't seen my . . . Lord Garret in more than ten years. It wouldn't be wise for either of us to put ourselves in a situation from which there is little escape."

"I beg to differ. You'd be a *countess*. Just in case you're not aware of how the whole peerage game works, that would be a good thing."

Sadie scowled at her. "I'm aware of how the peerage works. Marrying into it has done you a world of good, hasn't it?"

Lady Gosling paused as she lifted her glass. She gave Sadie a droll smile. "Nicely played, my dear. But while I plot to change my current predicament, I wouldn't give it up if my only option was a return to Covent Garden."

"That's your choice, but I'm not about to do anything that might adversely affect not only me, but Lord Garret as well." God, it was bizarre referring to Jack by that title! "I'd rather continue on as I have been these past years."

Was that a sneer? "For a woman possessed of such remarkable insight you are perhaps the most stupid female I've ever known."

"I don't recall asking for your opinion, Lady Gosling."

"Of course not. Forgive me, *my lady*. I cannot imagine being given the chance to love once let alone twice. Obviously I know not of what I speak."

Mockery aside, the woman had a point.

"It's not that simple," she protested.

Lady Gosling's smile actually turned sympathetic. "How often we say that when it really is that simple." She drained the rest of her whiskey. "So, I've appeased my conscience with a visit and now I must be on my way."

Being in the woman's company was like being in the middle of some sort of maelstrom, ducking flying debris. Sadie felt constantly off balance. "All right. Thank you for stopping by."

The lady flashed her teeth and winked. "You should really work on your false sincerity. I could teach you, if you like."

Sadie refused—politely—and rose to see the lady out. She didn't trust her not to stuff a vase or painting under her skirts.

"Give my regards to his lordship, will you?" Lady Gosling requested at the door.

Sadie nodded. "Of course. Thank you for coming by."

The woman brightened. "Very good! I almost believed that. Now, don't roll your eyes, that ruins it."

"Good day, Lady Gosling." Sadie reached around her to open the door. "I'll tell Lord Garret you called."

Suddenly, a firm hand came down upon Sadie's arm, and she lifted her gaze to see Lady Gosling watching her most intently.

"Madam, you've given me plenty of good advice in our short acquaintance and your predictions always do right by me, so allow me to give you a prediction of my own. I once told you that all actions have a cost, we simply must decide if they are worth paying. If you do not act in the best interest of your own happiness you will regret—and pay for it—for the rest of your life."

Sadie opened her mouth to utter what she was certain

would be a witty retort, but the lady cut her off with, "You don't want to end up like me, do you?"

Sadie shut her mouth, and Lady Gosling smiled tightly. "I didn't think so. Good day, Lady Garret. I hope the next time we meet I'm the one with the black wreath upon my door."

And then she was gone. In your face one moment and then whisked away like the scandal she was.

Sadie closed the door behind her and returned to the library. She needed another glass of whiskey.

It was late afternoon when Sadie woke Jack to tell him that the family solicitor was downstairs in the drawing room.

Groggily, Jack threw back the quilt and swung his legs over the side of the bed. Thank God Trystan had brought him fresh clothes.

"I'll have Cook make coffee and a plate of biscuits," Sadie informed him as she handed him his clothes. "Do you . . . do you want me to meet him with you?"

"Yes. Please." It wouldn't look right and the servants would talk, but he didn't give a flying frig what the servants or the solicitor thought. He was lord of this house now and Sadie was his wife, whether she wanted to admit it or not. His only comfort was despite her vocal abhorrence to the role, she played it very well.

She watched him closely for a moment, then nodded. "All right."

When she was gone, Jack changed into the dark gray suit. He finished knotting his cravat as he made his way

down the hall to the drawing room. Sadie hadn't speci-
fied which one, so he assumed it was the first one—the
green drawing room.

He was greeted by a tall, lanky man in a brown suit
with a thick head of ginger hair and a nose that was
impressive even by English standards. "Lord Garret?
I'm George Walters. I'm sorry we had to meet under
such sad circumstances."

Jack accepted the man's handshake and sincerity with
a mumbled reply. Then he gestured for the man to be
seated. "I hope you're a coffee man, Mr. Walters because
I've sent for a pot."

The solicitor smiled, revealing a slightly crooked tooth.
"I am indeed, my lord. Thank you." He then set about
digging through the leather case on the sofa beside him,
retrieving a stack of papers and a reading-glass case.

A knock on the door announced Sadie's arrival with
the coffee. In fact it was the housekeeper, Mrs. O'Reily,
who carried the tray. The poor woman's gray hair had
started to come loose from its normal tight bun and
her bright blue eyes were rimmed with red as though
she'd been sobbing long and hard. Sadie followed close
behind, eyeing the poor woman with a mix of curiosity
and sympathy.

Jack introduced both of them to Mr. Walters, uncertain as to whether that was proper procedure or not. It
had been a long time since he'd thought of himself as
social superior to anyone, or inferior for that matter,
and his knowledge of such foolishness had diminished
accordingly.

"I thought it a good idea to have Mrs. O'Reily join us," Sadie informed him, casting him a meaningful glance, which, unfortunately, meant nothing to him. Then she turned to Mr. Walters. "I think you'll find that she's mentioned in the will?"

Mr. Walters gaped at her. "I . . . I cannot say. Normally the will is not read so soon."

She arched a brow at him. "You have it with you, do you not?"

"Why, yes."

Sadie busied herself fixing cups of coffee. Jack noticed she made one for Mrs. O'Reily as well. "Well, then surely you can tell us what it says?"

The thin man turned to Jack. "My lord, this is highly irregular."

Jack shrugged. "Mr. Walters, *nothing* about this situation is regular. Why don't you share the will with us as Mrs. Moon suggests? I promise you, I have no plans to contest anything within it."

The solicitor was uncomfortable, but seemed to relax a little when Sadie gave him coffee and a plate of delicious smelling sugar biscuits.

"If it makes you more comfortable, sir," Jack suggested, "you can speak only of matters pertaining to people in this room."

The reedy solicitor relaxed further. "As you wish, my lord."

What followed was both surprising and, then again, not. For example, Jack wasn't the least bit surprised to hear that everything entitled came to him—that was simple law. He was a bit surprised, however, to hear that almost all of his grandfather's personal wealth and possessions were his as well. The servants were left generous gifts, especially Alistair, Mr. Brown, and even more especially, Mrs. O'Reily. The woman was bequeathed a generous pension and a small house in Chelsea.

Even more surprising than this, was how Sadie held the woman as she sobbed. She shot Jack a glance that told him everything he needed to know and much he wished he didn't. Mrs. O'Reily and his grandfather had been lovers.

Was that why she wanted the woman there? Why she wanted Jack to hear this now? Because she was willing to be his lover but not his wife? That better not be the reason, because he wasn't going to play that sort of game. He wasn't going to hide his feelings for Sadie and marry some poor, unsuspecting girl just because that was how things were done. Sadie was going to be his wife or nothing at all, and he had his heart set on the former.

"There's something for you as well, Mrs. Moon," Mr. Walters said, cheeks flushing.

This could not be good, Jack thought, watching the birdlike man shift on the sofa. Sadie felt it as well, he could tell from her sudden stillness. She patted Mrs. O'Reily on the back and then gently set the woman to the side, so she could compose herself. "What of me, Mr. Walters?"

He cleared his throat. "It says, 'To Sadie Moon née O'Rourke, I leave the sum of fifty thousand pounds so that she might continue with her business pursuits and provide a comfortable living for herself. I bequeath this to Mrs. Moon on the proviso that she agree to have no future contact with my grandson and heir, Jack Farrington. Should Mrs. Moon violate or disagree to this clause, then the sum will be kept in trust and settled upon my grandson's bride, provided she be of good birth and social standing.'"

Perhaps it wasn't appropriate, but Jack burst out laughing. He glanced at Sadie, who's mouth had fallen open. As soon as her lips closed, she too began to chuckle, and soon Mr. Walters and Mrs. O'Reily were left watching in confusion as the two of them cackled like Bedlamites.

"Is that all, Mr. Walters?" Jack asked, voice cracking as he settled himself to rights a few moments later.

The man looked at him as though he thought him completely mad. "He goes on to say that if neither provision is met the funds are to be put in trusts for your future heirs. That's the end of it, my lord."

"Very well. What of my grandfather's wishes pertaining to his burial?"

Mr. Walter's consulted another sheet of paper. "He wanted to be interred in the family crypt on his estate in County Kerry."

Jack nodded. "Of course. If you would be so good as to leave that information with me, or share it with my grandfather's secretary, Mr. Brown, so he can send word ahead of me, I would appreciate it. I'll leave for Ireland tomorrow."

Sadie's head jerked up. She was no longer laughing either. "So soon?"

It filled him with perverse warmth to see such alarm in her expression. She didn't want him to go. But was that because she wished him to stay with her, or because she was afraid he might not come back?

Foolish girl. She had no idea that she was honestly stuck with him for the rest of their lives.

He nodded sharply. "I have to get him home and properly taken care of." Really, there was no need to go into all the things that could happen to a body, and happen all the faster because it was July.

"I would be more than happy to discuss the arrangements with the late earl's secretary," Mr. Walters said, placing his papers back in his case. "Mr. Brown and I have known each other a great many years."

"I'm sure you have." Jack rose to his feet and the solicitor followed suit. "If you will come with me, I'll see if I can find him."

"Try the study," Sadie suggested. "I think you'll find him there."

She knew more about his household than he did. What else had he missed while asleep? "Thank you," he said, bowing slightly in her direction. "Follow me, Mr. Walters."

The thin man followed him from the room, across

the great hall, and down the corridor toward the study. Sure enough, Mr. Brown was exactly where Sadie predicted he'd be. She did seem to have a knack for these things.

He shook the solicitor's hand, took his card, and thanked him for his assistance. He also assured him that while he had his own counsel for business transactions, he would retain Mr. Walters's firm for all things related to the earldom, as the company had taken care of such matters for almost fifty years. It was a similar situation to what he planned to do with Mr. Brown. He already had a man who assisted him with business matters, but Brown knew the family, and the title, not to mention all the servants in all the households. Jack had no intention of letting the man go.

Mr. Walters seemed relieved to hear that news, and was smiling as he entered the study. Perhaps he didn't think Jack a total madman after all.

When he returned to the drawing room, he half expected to find it empty, figuring his lovely little bird of a wife had decided to take flight. Instead, he found her waiting for him, and Mrs. O'Reily was nowhere to be found.

"How's the grieving widow?" he inquired, with more sarcasm than was polite. He meant no disrespect; it had merely been a surprise.

"Grieving, of course," came her lilting reply. "I think she'll be all right. How are you?"

He shrugged. "Been better. I'd be worse if you hadn't been here to help me. Thanks."

She shook her head. "You'd be fine, but you're welcome."

Awkward silence fell then, leaving them both standing there, staring at each other. All that intimacy between them earlier seemed strange now—something that made each of them feel vulnerable and unsure. He entertained bringing up the absurd clause in the old man's will, but thought better of it. They'd had a laugh over it, but he didn't want to put it in her mind as a valid choice.

"So," she said, licking her lips. "You're off to Kerry tomorrow?"

He nodded. "You could come with me." He didn't have to be a tea-leaf reader to know what she was going to say.

"You know I cannot do that. I have much to do in regards to my shop. Besides, people would talk."

It was on the tip of his tongue to say to hell with what people said, but it wasn't his reputation that would suffer, it was hers. He didn't want to do anything to cause her grief, not when he felt he'd already done so much. So much that he desperately wanted to spend the rest of his life making up to her.

"Sadie, *we* need to talk. Either we do it now or we do it when I get back, but we need to discuss our future. Together."

"Do we have a future, do you think, Jack?" she asked, her voice tight with genuine curiosity.

"Sadie, you're my wife."

She took a step toward him, hand fisted anxiously in front of her. "I know what I've been and what I am. What

I need to know is if you want me to be your wife. After all, there's no proof of our marriage. You could have someone else, someone better suited to the role."

"All the proof I need is right here." He placed his hand over his heart. "In my heart, you will always be my wife. There's no one better suited for me than you. And even if there were, I would always think of myself as *your* husband. Do you understand?"

She nodded, mute. He knew he'd gotten through to her when he saw her lower lip tremble.

He moved toward her, hands out in supplication. "So, don't we owe it to ourselves—to each other—to try again?"

"What if it doesn't work?"

Did he kiss her or shake her? What would it take to make her see reason? To make her brave enough to give him—give them—a second chance. "What if it does?"

She paced a small expanse of the carpet. He could practically see the war waging in her head between the part of her that wanted to believe and the part of her that was terrified. "Perhaps I should take the money and do what the old man wanted—leave your life forever."

He scowled at her. She wasn't that foolish, was she? "This isn't a melodrama, Sadie. This is our life! What we should do is what will make us both happy."

"At the risk of both of us being ostracized from society?"

"That's a bit of an exaggeration, don't you think?"

"Your grandfather loved Mrs. O'Reily and he couldn't bring himself to marry her. For twenty-five years that poor woman was his closest companion and she can't even mourn him the way she ought, because that's how this world operates."

"I don't care. You're my wife. I lost you once, I won't lose you again."

"You may not have a choice."

"Are you going to walk away from me, Sadie? Take your revenge for my stupidity ten years ago?"

"Of course not."

"Good, because it won't wash. There's always a choice, Sadie. Ten years ago, if you'd asked me not to go, if you'd told me about the baby I wouldn't have gone."

"And you would have resented me for it."

He stared at her. "Is that what you think? Christ, Sadie how could I resent you for wanting me here with you and our child? I would have crawled back to my grandfather on my hands and knees and begged him to look after you before I'd turn my back on you."

Tears spilled from her wide eyes. "I thought you wanted to go. You had to prove yourself to your grandfather."

"Yes, I did. But had I known the truth, had I known the consequences, not even my pride would have been worth losing you. Ten years, Sadie! We can't get that back, and I don't want to lose any more."

When she didn't say anything, he added, "I know you're afraid, but if we don't let go of the past, then you're right—we don't have a future. We can't have one.

I want a future with you, and I don't care about the cost, because I've already paid more than any man should have to. So have you."

She wiped at her eyes with the backs of her hands, sniffed and squared her shoulders. Her watery gaze locked with his, her jaw trembling. "Take your grandfather home, Jack Farrington. When you come back to me, we'll talk."

# Chapter 20

Sadie had plenty of time to think about the things Jack said while he was in Ireland taking care of his grandfather's funeral and other estate-related issues. She was still thinking about him when her shop, The Tea Leaf, opened to a very successful first day.

She missed him. She wanted him here with her to see how well her business—and his investment—was paying off. She wanted to share this pride and happiness with him.

And secretly, part of her had to admit that every day he was gone was another that she wondered if he was ever going to come back. Oh, she trusted him and believed in him, but it was difficult to shuck off that old fear entirely. She was trying, though, and determined to rid herself of all doubt if it was the last thing she did.

Jack would come back to her. He always did, even if the last time he'd been rather late. There was no one left to conspire against them. The future was theirs, wide open to be anything they wanted. All Sadie had to do was conquer her prejudices and fears. All she had to do was not give a damn what anyone said or thought. She had to accept that she would become part of that rung of society she often mocked and regarded with derision.

She had just finished a reading in the back room when the Duchess of Ryeton entered the shop with her husband, mama-in-law, friend Eve Elliott, and Lords Archer and Trystan in tow. The three gentlemen looked decidedly uncomfortable to be the only men in an establishment they no doubt had decided was strictly feminine territory.

Fortunately there was a table for them. Sadie didn't know what she would have done if there hadn't been room. It wasn't good *ton* to keep a duchess waiting. But more than that, she thought fondly of Her Grace and would hate not to be able to oblige her.

These people, the Kane brothers and Her Grace especially, had been good to her—friends to her. That was humbling in the worst way, and made her see how wrong she'd been in her judgment of the aristocracy. They were not all like Jack's grandfather—who had only been a product of his own pride. They were good people, people she considered herself fortunate to know.

And if she married Jack—again—she would be in a position to know them better.

The duchess's face lit up when she spotted Sadie. "What a crush!" She gushed, as she took Sadie's hands in hers. "My dear friend, this is simply astounding! How proud you must be."

Proud? No, that was an emotion she was going to temper for the time being. "I am very pleased," Sadie allowed truthfully. Then she showed them to the one empty table, and since she didn't have anyone waiting for a reading, she joined them at their request.

"Any news from Ireland?" Archer asked sometime later as he lifted a scone loaded with clotted cream and strawberry preserves to his mouth.

Sadie flushed the tiniest bit, a little embarrassed to discuss Jack in front of Miss Elliott and the dowager duchess, but neither of them seemed concerned. They watched her with the same polite curiosity as the rest of the table.

"Yesterday," she replied. "Lord Garret hopes to return to London before the end of next week."

"Excellent," Trystan remarked, with obvious release. "I need him."

The duchess slid her brother-in-law an amused glance. "I'm sure you are his primary consideration in all Lord Garret's actions, Trystan."

He grinned, not the least bit chastised. "I expect not, my dear sister. Perhaps secondary." He winked at Sadie. Her cheeks warmed even further as she lifted her cup to her lips. How odd it felt to sit with them this way, to be so accepted by them. As though she'd been born to their ranks.

She liked it. And while she knew not everyone would be so accepting of her, she knew there would be those who let her in. And even if no one did, she didn't really care. She already had enough friends—friends that made her life so very full.

"I wonder, Your Grace," she said, turning to the

duchess, "if you would care to see the private reading room?"

The duchess looked slightly surprised. "Why, yes, I would, but only if you call me Rose as I've requested."

Sadie smiled at the teasing chastisement. "Of course, Rose."

Begging pardon from the others, the two of them rose to their feet, and carrying her cup and saucer, Sadie led the way to the small but comfortable room set aside for readings. It was decorated much like her tent at Saint's Row, in muted shades of purple and orange that called to mind the exotic east. The air smelled faintly of tea and cloves—incense that Indara had given her as a gift. Even the lighting was soft and muted, but bright enough for Sadie to work by.

"It's beautiful," Rose proclaimed with an air of approval. "But, no offense, my dear. I don't really have a need for you to read my leaves."

"None taken," Sadie replied with a smile as she sat down at the table and flipped her cup over on her saucer. She turned it three times counterclockwise before righting it and sliding it across the spotless cloth toward her friend. "I want you to read mine."

Jack Farrington, former useless bastard and new Earl of Garret returned to London on a gray and drizzly day. He hadn't written to tell Sadie of his arrival because he wanted to surprise her.

And because he hadn't wanted to give her a chance to run off or come up with a stupid excuse as to why she couldn't be his wife—because, really, at this point any excuse was going to be a stupid one in his estimation.

Unfortunately, because he hadn't told her he was coming, he also didn't know where to find her. He checked both her shop and her house before finally having the coachman take him to Saint's Row, where he found her having tea with Vienne La Rieux.

Damn, she looked good. The cut was the only thing prim and proper about her magenta day gown with black piping. Perhaps it was his imagination, but he suspected the touch of black was a sign of mourning for the old man, not that he deserved it.

She was a little pale, but that was undoubtedly his fault for surprising her like this.

La Rieux looked from him to Sadie and back again, like a cat watching a bouncing ball. Then, she set her cup and saucer on the low table before her and rose gracefully to her feet. "Dear me, I just remembered something I must attend to. *Excusez-moi.*"

As she passed Jack she stopped briefly. "I'm glad you're back, now she will stop fretting about you. Also, your partner is an ass."

Jack drew back from the vehemence in her tone when she mentioned Trystan. "I'm aware of that."

She nodded then and carried on out the door, leaving Jack staring after her. What the hell had he missed? He turned to Sadie. "Should I even ask?"

She stood. "I don't know, but she's been raving about having Lord Trystan's head, and other parts of his anatomy on a platter for the last week."

Jack didn't bother to hide his amusement. "And so it begins." He could feel his gaze soften as it lingered on her. "Damn, it's good to see you." It felt like an eternity rather than just a few weeks since that night when he first entered this club and discovered her in that dark little room.

She flashed a bit of cheeky smile and said, "You came back."

He smiled similarly in return. "Didn't the leaves tell you I'd be back?"

"It's bad luck to read your own leaves."

"So you've been waiting with bated breath?" He asked it teasingly, not truly believing for a moment that she had doubted him. He'd written to her every day and knew that this time, she'd received his letters.

Her smile turned sheepish. "I got Rose—Duchess Ryeton—to read the leaves for me. She told me you'd be back soon."

He laughed as he closed the distance between them. He laughed so much with her, and God willing it would never stop.

She met him halfway, allowing him to pull her to him in midstep, lifting her off her feet and into his embrace. He kissed her, her mouth eagerly clutching his. She tasted of tea and sugar, and of home and hope. So damn good he could weep.

No more running. No more debating and no more worrying about what society might think or if their past might come back to haunt them.

"Thank God you had the duchess to counsel you," he

joked when he lifted his lips from hers sometime later. "Did she see anything in there about Trystan and La Rieux taking each other's eyes out?"

She smiled. "No."

"Archer getting called out for flapping his smart mouth at the wrong person?"

A giggle this time. "No."

"How about the two of us living under the same roof sometime in the near future?"

She sobered enough that Jack's heart plummeted. "About that . . ."

He could remind her that they were already married, but he didn't because he wanted to hear what she had to say. "Go on."

She eased out of his embrace, but didn't go far. Jack sensed she needed the space and so he let her go. "I think . . . that is, Rose—and I—saw what we both believe to be a pregnancy in my cup."

This was not what Jack had expected. *This* left him a little light-headed. "You? Us?"

She nodded, face strangely serious despite this wonderful news. "Jack, you should know that there's a very good chance I cannot carry a child to full term. I would spare us both the heartache of another loss."

Then he saw the fear and sorrow in her eyes. Christ, how he wished he could take that dark time away from her so she'd never have to feel it again. It made him feel the weight of what he was about to ask her all the more.

"But would you also deny us both the joy, if this time it's different?"

She looked surprised, as though she hadn't allowed herself to consider that. "Would you take that risk?"

He nodded. "I would if you think you might be willing." Really, it was her decision. She was the one who would change physically, and would subsequently physically feel the loss if things went badly.

Sadie looked away for a moment, her hand pressed against her mouth, then she turned back to him, a glimmer of hope in her beguiling eyes. "I suppose if there's a chance I might lose the child, there's also a chance I might not, isn't there?"

A smile pressed the corners of his mouth upward. "There is at that." Then from his pocket he withdrew a small velvet box, and flipped it open with his thumb. "Everything's going to be different this time."

Her eyes lit up when she saw the delicate marquis emerald inside—so green and fine, no Irishman—or Irishwoman—could possibly find fault. A tiny mote of tears brimmed along her bottom lashes as she lifted her gaze to his.

"What do you say, Sadiemoon, will you marry me? Again?"

She stood there, a smile as bright as the sun on her face as tears trickled down her cheeks. "I think I might have to say yes."

This time Jack's heart felt as though it had been tossed into the air and given wings. He picked her up with an arm around her waist and swung her around in sheer joy.

"I love you. Always have, always will. Did your leaves tell you that?"

"No," she replied, a tear slipping down her cheek. "They didn't."

"So perhaps they don't know everything?" He was teasing, of course. He'd managed to come to terms with Sadie's talent for fortune-telling, and comfortably shelved it amongst the things he couldn't define but, regardless, believed in—like God and love and second chances.

"Perhaps not. I suppose that's why I have you." Her tone was equally light, and perhaps a touch sarcastic? "I love you, Jack Friday."

He grinned, cheeky bastard that he was. "I know." And then he kissed her.

*At Avon Books, we know your passion for romance—once you finish one of our novels, you find yourself wanting more.*

May we tempt you with . . .

- **Excerpts** from our upcoming releases.

- Entertaining **extras**, including authors' personal photo albums and book lists.

- Behind-the-scenes **scoop** on your favorite characters and series.

- **Sweepstakes** for the chance to win free books, romantic getaways, and other fun prizes.

- Writing **tips** from our authors and editors.

- **Blog** with our authors and find out why they love to write romance.

- **Exclusive content** that's not contained within the pages of our novels.

Join us at
**www.avonbooks.com**

**AVON**

*An Imprint of* HarperCollins*Publishers*
www.avonromance.com

Available wherever books are sold or please call 1-800-331-3761 to order.

FTH 0708